KEY NORTH

By

J.E. McBee

ALSO BY J.E. McBEE

Fugitive Dust

For Linda, who makes everything possible.

1

1972

There were five of us that August night: Mouse, Jocko, Fisheyes, Guinea and me. Eli Michaels had driven us to the parking lot at Devil's Hole State Park in his father's pickup truck with our inner tubes and life preservers. He stayed just long enough to drop us off and help us haul our gear to the top of the staircase that descended down the sheer gorge face to the edge of the river before returning to his truck. As he prepared to pull away he leaned through the open driver's side window, shaking his head. "I hope you guys know what you're doing. I think you're fuckin' nuts."

Mouse's smile was broad and easily seen in the moonlight. "Don't worry about us. We've been planning this for months." He indicated the full moon above and the cloudless, star-strewn sky. "The gods are with us."

Tubing down the Niagara River at night had been Mouse's idea. It had been percolating in his mind since the beginning of summer, when he started checking weather reports and water conditions and rounding up inner tubes large enough and sturdy enough for the journey. Most of his efforts involved recruiting volunteers. Anyone could float down the Niagara River between Riverton and Delifin in the light of day – it was a favorite pastime of local youth. But convincing his friends to try it at night? That was a different story.

Mouse had pulled out all the stops. He cajoled and pleaded for weeks with anyone who would listen until he had convinced four of us to join him. He promised that it would be no more dangerous than a trip during the day – a promise I found a bit hollow. But he was relentless in his argument, persuasive as a silver-tongued preacher wringing the last dollar from the wallet of a dirt-poor parishioner. By the night of the full moon in August, four of us were standing with him at the trailhead leading down into the gorge, slipping on our life jackets so one of our hands would be free to use flashlights to illuminate the treacherous path while in the other hand we carried our inner tubes, listening to last-minute instructions.

At first glance, Mouse hardly seemed like a leader. Barely five eight, he was the shortest of the five of us by several inches, but the sheer force of his personality had resulted in this expedition. Once he'd settled on a plan he felt had merit, he wouldn't take no for an answer. When he saw the faintest flicker of doubt or hesitation on a candidate's face, he upped the pressure, unwilling to back down until the deal was sealed, on occasion managing to make the objects of his pressure feel wracked with guilt for having held out so long.

Mouse gazed around the tight circle, brimming with confidence. "First: take your time on the way down. There's no hurry - these steps have irregular spaces between them all the way down and we don't want anyone to fall. We'll go down single file. Leave plenty of space between you and the guy in front of you. And use your flashlights." He glanced around the group. "Any questions?"

We shook our heads. Mouse continued. "Good. Second: don't lose your grip on your tube. We don't want anyone crawling around on the rocks off the path, even with a flashlight. We have to stay on the path."

Fisheyes piped up. "What's the water temperature?"

"Seventy-four off the sand docks yesterday. It might be a degree or two cooler here, but it should be fine." Mouse looked around the group once more. "Any more questions?" Silence. "Okay, follow me. Nice and easy. Plenty of space between us."

Devil's Hole State Park was part of a master plan developed by landscape architects Frederick Law Olmsted and Calvin Vaux in 1887. It was opened to the public in 1927 and featured a pathway hewn from dolomitic limestone that descended three hundred feet to the edge of the Niagara River. Throughout the years the pathway had deteriorated due to rock falls, erosion and an ill-fated construction project, so footing was unreliable. It was a popular day hike area, but closed after sunset. According to the law, we were, at the moment, guilty of trespassing.

Mouse was in the lead, followed by Jocko, Fisheyes and Guinea. I was in the rear, flashlight aimed downward onto the twisting path, concentrating on one step at a time, careful not to crowd Guinea, who walked warily ten feet ahead. No one spoke. Instead, we listened to the sounds of the gorge as we descended: the bleat of a gull startled by rare nocturnal interlopers, the occasional rustling of brush adjacent to the path as we passed. As we descended the steep pathway, the sound of the river racing across boulders smoothed by thousands of years of flow increased from a gentle hum until it resembled the roar of a jet engine in the distance.

Forty-five minutes after we began our descent we reached the river's edge. By the time I was able to find an open flat spot to drop my tube Mouse had already produced a dark gym bag and was instructing the rest of the group to lighten their loads. "Flashlights, shoes, watches, wallets, keys. Anything you have that you might consider valuable, put it in here. I'm coming back first thing in the morning, at first light. Nobody will be down here again before me."

Fisheyes was puzzled. "Why would anyone bring keys? That's why Eli drove us. So no one would need keys until we got back to the Riverside."

Mouse nodded. "Exactly. But you never know."

Jocko pointed to his feet. "I'm keeping these on, at least until I get out of the rocks and into the current. Once I'm headed downstream I'll decide whether or not to let them go."

Mouse shrugged his shoulders. "Suit yourself. Whatever it takes to get you guys into the river."

I sat on my tube, removed my shoes and dropped them into the bag. As Mouse had requested earlier in the evening, I'd left everything else in my father's Ford parked back at the Riverside Inn in Riverton, our destination.

Mouse held the bag up. "Last call." No response. He zipped the bag and, following the beam from his flashlight, walked carefully in his bare feet to a large boulder fifteen feet off the path and slightly up the bank, where he dropped the bag and covered it with some recently uprooted brush. He retraced his steps and addressed us. "Here we go. The best ride of your life. Just hang on tight and don't tip over. Stay between the American shore and the middle of the river if you can – there are fewer whirlpools there. Don't forget that the power plants expel water instead of take it in, so you'll get a push toward the middle as we go by. Once we're by the power plants it's an easy float to the sand docks. Aim for the boat launch, on the north end of the docks by the silo. There should be plenty of light once we go under the bridge." He looked at each of us. "Any questions?"

Shaking heads all around. "Okay, boys. Follow me. Leave about thirty seconds apart, as soon as the guy ahead of you is in the current." One last smile. "See you at the Riverside for last call."

Walking carefully over the slick, submerged rocks, Mouse maneuvered his tube to the edge of the still pool and propelled it into the current, hopping on top and emitting a war whoop as he was swept northward, toward Riverton.

Jocko was second. He waited thirty seconds before pushing his tube into the current and hopping in, gripping the sides with all his strength. Fisheyes was next, not bothering to wait, pushing off less than ten seconds after Jocko. Guinea followed and I was next, chosen by Mouse as the second-most reliable member of the team, the man pulling up the rear, the one with all the other tubers ahead of him.

I was surprised by the turbulence of the water and the noise it created, even though we'd checked it out several times in the last two weeks as part of our preparation for tonight. Watching in the light of day from the shore was one thing. Being in the midst of the current that only recently had gone over Niagara Falls, with darkness limiting our perceptive abilities, was something completely different. Later, when asked to recall the ride, I told the police that the sound of the water reminded me of a freight train behind schedule, straining to catch up.

I concentrated on Guinea in front of me. Of the five of us, he was the only one who wasn't heading into his junior year of college. Instead, he'd joined his father's construction company as a laborer after high school, with the idea he would learn the business from the bottom up before assuming the helm once his father felt it was time for him to step aside. He was a strong swimmer, with impressive biceps and calves shaped on local construction sites, a good man to be following tonight. I didn't have to worry about Guinea. He could take care of himself.

Of the five, I was probably the weakest swimmer. Mouse and Fisheyes had been on the school swim team, Guinea was just as good in the water as those two, and Jocko was one of the best all-around high school athletes in the area. Which is why my anchor position on this trip had caused me some anxiety during the past week. Would I be up to the challenge? Able to keep an eye on things from the rear in case something went wrong? Most of us knew the journey wasn't going to be easy. We hoped that we might get lucky, me especially.

12

Using my legs, I managed to keep my tube pointed downstream as I picked up speed immediately. The current of the river between Riverton and Delifin, our normal tubing route, was seven knots. On our daylight scouting trips, we estimated the current at Devil's Hole to be twenty knots, maybe more. A wild ride requiring enormous concentration during the day. At night? It was time to find out.

I resisted the temptation to use my arms to steer, relying instead on my legs so I could grip the tube tightly. Losing the tube was my worst nightmare. Even with a life jacket, I feared being in the water here. I wasn't sure I had the strength to avoid being dragged down into the larger eddies and whirlpools, several of which had to be navigated before we reached the gentler waters beyond the bridge.

The river began to froth as we rounded the first bend to the left and approached the American power plant. I hung tightly to the tube as I crested one wave, dropped several feet down into a trough, and then was spit out on the far side, toward the tailrace on the American side. The outflow nudged me back into the middle of the river, its level elevated suddenly by the constriction in the channel. There was a definite sensation of speed increasing as the channel narrowed, heightened by the sounds of the turbulence and the spray as we sped by the power plant, toward the international bridge.

Moonlight on the calmer areas near the shore produced a gunmetal hue on the water as I looked ahead for Guinea. After several moments I found him thirty feet ahead of me, in the middle of the channel, heading toward Canadian waters. It looked like his hands were off his tube, grappling with his life jacket, but I couldn't be sure given the reduced light and distance between us. He was approaching the last stretch of dangerous water before the river calmed north of GorgePark and the Riverside Inn beyond it.

I was leaning forward, squinting against the spray, watching as Guinea slid his arms out of the life jacket and tossed it toward a vortex to his left which sucked it noiselessly beneath the surface. Guinea was next, rolling off the tube into the whirlpool, sliding beneath the surface not far from where the life jacket had disappeared.

I was frozen on my tube, immobilized for a moment by what I had just witnessed. I held on as tightly as I could while I kicked my legs vigorously to keep away from the area where Guinea had disappeared.

Had he taken his life jacket off deliberately? That's what it had looked like from my vantage point behind him.

I was numb. I tried to yell to the others ahead but my voice failed me, emitting a fractured croak as I continued to grip the tube with all my strength. Once I was past the last whirlpool, the one that had claimed Guinea, I kicked my legs furiously to turn my gaze back upstream, to see if there was any sign of my friend resurfacing.

I continued to float north, staring back into the darkness beneath the bridge, looking for any sign of life. When I was adjacent to the fishing dock at GorgePark I used my legs to orient myself downstream again. I saw Guinea's tube ahead, drifting toward the middle of the river in the direction of the docks in Queenston. Beyond that, to the right, I could see a lone figure who had to be Fisheyes heading diagonally toward the sand docks and the boat launch on the northern end, our designated rendezvous location.

I followed, using my arms as well as my legs to propel me toward shore now that I was in the calmer waters by the ski club building. I could hear music drifting down from the patio bar at the Riverside Inn. We'd made it in time for last call. Mouse was probably already at the bar, working on a Blue by now.

There were several security lights illuminating the dock. I aimed for them, my arms suddenly heavy, like lead, completely exhausted but determined to make it to shore to let my friends know what I'd witnessed, my mind racing, wondering if we had to call the cops, hoping Mouse would know what to do. This midnight ride had turned into much, much more than we'd bargained for. As the enormity of the situation began to sink in, I knew the four of us had to come up with some sort of story, something plausible to satisfy the barrage of inquiries sure to follow.

I hauled myself out of the river and walked up the ramp with my tube. As I headed up the hill to join the others at the bar I looked back toward the bridge, hoping for a miracle, but saw only black water.

2

THE PRESENT

Sal Ducati was up before dawn on Sunday morning. He'd been unable to sleep much last night, his mind flooded by images associated with John Corelli that had kept him awake, unable to surrender to the physical exhaustion brought on by one of the longest days he'd endured since becoming mayor of Riverton, New York. Tomorrow morning Corelli's trial, referred to by both the local and national media as the "Trial of the Century" in Riverton, was scheduled to resume after a series of postponements engineered by Corelli's savvy defense attorney, Max Grossinger.

Corelli, a history teacher at Riverton Middle School and former town councilman in Riverton who'd lost his bid for re-election last November after being charged with two counts of statutory rape involving two of his female students the previous summer, would be making his first public appearance in months. Although the postponements had eroded much of the initial national interest in the trial – Grossinger's express intent – crews from CNN and Fox News had arrived yesterday and were billeted at the new luxury hotel by the waterfront, the Riverton House.

At first light Ducati, fueled by two cups of coffee, was out of the house, trash bag in hand and a spare in his back pocket, heading for Main Street to pick up litter. He was a familiar figure to residents, stooped over as he roamed the streets each morning, determined to rid Riverton of unsightly debris. It was May and the last snow had finally melted, leaving the detritus of winter where snowplows had piled it during the previous months. With camera crews in town, he wanted his village to look as pristine as possible, especially with tourist season looming.

The Corelli situation had been a nightmare for Ducati. He and John Corelli had been friends for years, part of the same Saturday morning foursome at the Riverton Country Club. Their wives were close, and they had even vacationed together twice on trips to Italy and Hawaii. The mayor had known nothing about Corelli's attraction to his young female students until Riverton Chief of Police Rod Wakefield had laid out the evidence against Corelli last June, the day before he was arrested at his home. Wakefield knew the two were close and wanted to let Ducati know before it became public knowledge that his friend and political ally was about to be charged with two counts of statutory rape.

He left his house on North Third Street and walked past the red brick schoolhouse that now housed the village municipal offices and police force toward Main Street. He counted five police vehicles in the lot, the entire village motor pool. Early morning commuters, familiar with the mayor's idiosyncratic dawn patrol, honked as they drove by. Ducati never looked up, his eyes constantly on the move, looking for anything that didn't belong.

He felt a slight twinge in his lower back as he reached for a Styrofoam coffee cup. Time to see Doc Brennan again, maybe have him poke around a bit. He'd been doing the exercises suggested by his physical therapist after his last spinal surgery, but on occasion he still felt discomfort whenever he made a sudden move without thinking. It was something his surgeon had warned him about: he was no longer a spring chicken, and with advancing age came the inevitable erosion of his health, from his failing memory to his ailing body.

He straightened up slowly and dropped the cup into the trash bag. He looked both ways before crossing Fourth Street on his way to Main, his gait shuffling, pace slow. He hoped the media types, the national guys from out of town, were like the ones he'd encountered last summer when the story first broke: eager consumers with generous expense accounts. Village restaurants and bars should get a healthy bump from these thirsty journalists to kick off the summer tourist season

For the first time since he'd sold his Ford dealership ten years earlier, just before the economy cratered, he wished he was back in the car game again. Selling sedans and mini-vans would be a breeze compared to addressing the media and testifying as a witness for the defense during Corelli's trial. No wonder he was having trouble sleeping.

He'd been approached by both Max Grossinger and Liz Corelli to testify as a witness for the defense. Grossinger had sent a registered letter and Liz had called several times, leaving pleading messages on his phone that he had yet to answer. Just the idea of being in the courtroom made him anxious. The thought of having to testify made him nauseous. He hadn't signed on for anything like this. Being the mayor of Riverton was supposed to be more like a hobby, something to occupy his time after he sold his dealership, not an ordeal that interrupted his sleep and made his stomach churn.

16

He stopped at the light on Fourth and Main. Despite there being no cars in sight, he waited dutifully for the light to change and trigger the crosswalk sign before proceeding. On the other side he walked by the charming white gazebo and green space where the Riverstock Festival was held each July. On an overcast Sunday, just past dawn, there were several vehicles parked in front of Borelli's Bakery.

Just one donut. Or maybe a muffin. Ducati pushed through the door, curious to see who the early morning customers were. As he scanned the narrow waiting area he heard a voice to his left. "Mr. Mayor! Good to see you!"

Ducati turned toward the voice. Seated at one of the small tables near the end was Rich Stebbins. He was gesturing. "Join me," he said, indicating a vacant chair.

Ducati smiled. He liked Stebbins, the second-generation owner of the only full-service station in the village a block east of the bakery on Main. He walked over and sat down gratefully. "Thanks, Rich. My back was starting to act up. I could use a break."

"Coffee?"

Ducati nodded. "Black."

Stebbins caught the eye of one of the young women behind the counter, pointed at the mayor and made the universal needs-a-cup-of-coffee signal. She smiled and nodded, understanding. He turned back to the mayor. "Ready for tomorrow?"

"The trial? Ready as I'll ever be, I guess."

Stebbins was in his late sixties, six feet with thinning hair and a slender frame that had fleshed out some around his waistline during the last several years. He'd begun to ease himself out of the business last summer, preparing to pass it on to his son Raymond so he could spend more time at his cottage in Ontario on the Muskoka River, rocking on the expansive front porch, watching the river flow by, or wandering down to the shore, rod in hand, to try his luck. Running a service station had become an increasingly difficult enterprise, especially since gas stations exempt from New York taxation began to spring up on the Tuscarora Reservation on the eastern border of the village. He kept his pumps open but fuel sales plummeted. In order to compensate for lost revenue, he'd put together what many in the village, including Ducati, thought to be the

17

best group of mechanics in the area. Money lost at the pumps gradually had been recouped through vehicle repairs.

Stebbins wasted no time getting to the point. "You going to testify?"

The mayor shrugged. "I don't know. Maybe. If I get called."

"For the defense?"

Ducati nodded. "Max Grossinger was the first to ask."

Stebbins was intrigued. He leaned forward. "Who else asked?"

"Liz Corelli. She left me a couple of messages. I haven't talked to her yet."

Stebbins tried to sound sympathetic. "That has to be a rough one. You didn't know about any of this, did you?"

Ducati shook his head. His voice was faint. "Rod Wakefield told me about it the day before they arrested him. He wanted to give me a heads-up. He tried to show me some of the stuff they found on his computer and phone, but I said no. I couldn't believe it." Pause. "Still can't."

"Nobody knew, according to what I've heard. It caught everyone by surprise, especially Liz. And the kids." Stebbins tried to lighten the mood. "How about all this media? Pretty good for the bars and restaurants. The Riverton House, too. Ray told me they've filled the second floor just with people from CNN and Fox."

"Anne told me that she hadn't talked to any of the other networks." Anne Moretti was the mayor's executive assistant. "I'm surprised that MSNBC isn't coming back. They had the biggest group here when the story broke last summer."

Stebbins shrugged. "Politics is all MSNBC cares about in an election year. I wouldn't be surprised if they didn't show."

The young woman emerged from behind the counter and brought the mayor his coffee. She waited expectantly, pad and pen ready, as he finally gave in. "An orange pecan muffin. Just one."

18

"Coming right up, Mayor." She spun on her heel and returned in under a minute with his muffin on a small plate and a napkin. Just as quickly she spun again and was on her way back to her post.

Ducati took a tiny, bird-like nibble from the top. He dabbed at the corner of his mouth with the napkin, then took a sip of coffee. "Should be good for your business."

Stebbins' face remained neutral. "As long as they don't hear about the stations on the reservation, we might make a few bucks."

"You've got your brochure down at the hotel, right?" Ducati asked.

"Lots of them. Ray spoke to the manager."

The mayor grinned. The youngest of Rich Stebbins' three boys, Raymond Stebbins was the only one to show any interest in auto mechanics. His oldest brother Ronnie was an artist in San Luis Obispo, while middle son Rob made custom furniture in Greenwich, Connecticut. Both had left years ago and rarely returned to Riverton. Raymond was the default choice to become the third-generation boss. Rich had taught him well – Ray was an excellent mechanic with a knack for figures and an awareness of the importance of marketing.

Traffic inside the bakery was brisk, customers stopping in to buy fresh pastry and bread before heading to church, some, like the mayor out for a morning stroll, stopping to chat with old friends. Most of them recognized Ducati and Stebbins and acknowledged them with a wave or brief greeting.

By the time the mayor finished his muffin and coffee, the sun had risen above the tree line, bathing Main Street in ethereal morning light. He rose, motioning for Stebbins to stay seated. "It was nice chatting with you, Rich. Always good to see old friends."

"Hang in there, Sal. Maybe it'll be a short trial. Maybe you won't even have to testify."

The mayor dropped his trash into a nearby container. He looked back at Stebbins, a small smile playing on his lips. "Wouldn't that be nice?"

3

Rod Wakefield looked forward to Sundays. It was his day off, the only day he was allowed the luxury of sleeping in, and he took advantage of it. His wife Sally would slip out of bed, make a pot of coffee and retrieve the paper from the end of the driveway. She enjoyed the solitude, being able to read the paper and enjoy her morning coffee in the sunroom which looked out on their backyard while her husband slept. Especially on a sparkling spring morning like this.

She was glad to let Rod sleep. In his position as Chief of Police in Riverton she knew he had a lot on his mind with opening statements of the trial scheduled for tomorrow. He'd been putting in extra hours with the district attorney's office the past three weeks, making sure that all chain of custody protocols had been followed regarding the evidence, especially the explosive material found on Corelli's school and home computers. He was determined that there would be nothing for Max Grossinger to use, no loose ends, to discredit the prosecution's case.

He'd also been consumed with courtroom security since efforts to move the trial to the more spacious county courthouse in Lockport had failed. Instead, the trial would be held in the Riverton Town Hall, in the same space where traffic court was held each Tuesday and Friday evening. The combination of providing adequate space for the national media and developing a system of admittance for the local population, who'd been captivated by the case since the day of Corelli's arrest, kept Rod up past midnight for most of the last month.

Sally read the front-page headline in the Sunday *Niagara Gazette*: **Corelli Trial Set To Begin**. She sipped her coffee as she scanned the article, looking for any mention of her husband, relieved when she found none. Outside, two blue jays squawked optimistically as they flocked to a freshly filled bird feeder hanging from one of the lower branches of a mature red maple. On the ground below, two mourning doves waited patiently for any seed dislodged by the frenzy above, heads bobbing and weaving like shifty pugilists.

Sally had seen Liz Corelli several times since the news broke last year. Each time it had been at Spot Market, and each time she'd looked ashen, her face haunted as she shuffled through the aisles. It wasn't an image that encouraged conversation, so she'd kept her distance. She really didn't know Liz other than through her husband's occasional dealings with Rod as a former member of the Town Council. She knew the Corelli's had two children, a boy and a girl, each of whom had been whisked off to stay with relatives in Iowa instead of returning to Riverton High School last fall after their father had been arrested. She felt especially bad for them.

She heard some movement behind her. Rod was standing by the door to the sunroom, clad in pajama bottoms only, running his fingers through his hair. She looked at the clock on the wall: 10:11. She smiled. "I was beginning to think I'd have to call the EMTs."

"That has to be a new record," Rod said. "I don't ever remember sleeping this late." He pointed toward Sally's cup. "Is there more?"

She nodded. "In the pot."

He returned with a cup and sat on the loveseat opposite his wife. They'd been married the week before Rod had joined the Marines thirty years ago, when his first assignment after basic training had been in the mountains outside Matagalpa in Nicaragua as part of an elite group supporting the Contras during President Reagan's second term. Most of the things he'd witnessed there had remained unshared with Sally, too horrible for her to digest. For one of the few times since then, he was keeping certain details of John Corelli's obsession with young girls, photographic evidence extracted from his computers' hard drives, from Sally. Once the trial began, however, he knew the sordid details would be revealed by the district attorney.

He gestured toward the paper. "Anything good this morning?"

"You mean anything other than the trial?"

"Yeah."

She grabbed one of the sections from the table between them. "How about the comics?"

"Perfect."

They read in silence. Occasionally Sally would glance at Rod and wonder what was going through his head. He'd been his usual stoic self in the run-up to the trial, rarely offering anything new in conversation. Only when she prodded him, which wasn't often, did he

21

offer any news or opinions. She knew her husband well, knew when to hold back and let him come to her. If it was important, he'd tell her. Otherwise, she'd let him decide what he thought was important enough to share. After thirty years, she felt she knew a bit about how the military mind processed things. If he wanted to tell her anything, he'd do it at his own pace.

He chuckled, placing the comics on the table and replacing it with the sports section. His beloved New York Yankees were in the midst of a six-game losing streak, having lost on the road in Tampa the night before. He glanced at the standings. Toronto, who'd had the best start of any team in either league, had lost as well – at least they hadn't stretched their lead.

Sally interrupted his thoughts. "How about some breakfast?"

He looked up in anticipation. "What do you have in mind?"

"Bacon and eggs, toast, maybe a grapefruit."

"Sounds good to me."

She rose and went into the kitchen. Soon the smell of bacon frying wafted out to the sunroom, bringing a smile to his lips. Nothing like bacon to start the day off right, he thought. Like many families, they didn't eat as much bacon as they used to, so when it was offered, it was to be savored. He'd finished with the sports, glanced at the classifieds – he was playing with the idea of a new fishing boat – and had just finished the front-page headline story on the trial when Sally called out. "Time to eat."

Before he sat down he asked, "Do I need a shirt?"

She looked him up and down and smiled. "No shirt, no shoes, no service in some places. Not here, though. I like looking at you nearly naked. It won't disrupt my appetite a bit."

He smiled as he settled into a chair. "Good. What's on your plate today?" he asked as she poured them both some orange juice.

"I'd like to get out in the vegetable garden and turn the soil over a bit. It looks like we'll be planting soon."

"You've got a good day for it," he said. "Need any help?

22

"If I do, I'll let you know."

They ate without conversation. He was pleased that she still liked to see him with his shirt off, even though the six-pack abs he'd had as a young Marine had evolved into a twelve-pack, verging on a case. To him it seemed she'd hardly gained a pound during the last thirty years, but whenever he mentioned it she would smile and shake her head. "You'd be surprised." She was petite, five one, and her hair remained the same color it had always been, although he couldn't be sure that she hadn't helped it retain its sandy brown hue through artificial means.

When he was finished he stood and carried his plate and silverware to the sink. He rinsed them and placed them in the dishwasher before returning to the table and doing the same with Sally's dishes. She looked up in mock surprise. "Why, thank you. Should I get used to this kind of service?"

"Better late than never." He smiled. "I think I'm going to hop in the shower."

She leaned closer and sniffed. "Good idea. I'll be out back digging in the dirt if you need me."

As the pulsing hot water pelted his skin, he thought ahead to tomorrow. He'd made sure everyone on the force would be on duty for the start of the trial. If there were no incidents, maybe he could cut back on personnel, at least on the day shift, as the trial progressed. The Town Council had given him the green light to authorize overtime at their monthly meeting in April on a week-by-week basis, plus the New York State Police had promised to assign a pair of troopers to assist with site security for the duration of the trial. He'd take it one week at a time, hoping for the best but remaining prepared to deal with the worst.

One of the hardest decisions he'd had to make was how to limit access to the courtroom itself for the local press. Normally that wouldn't be a problem, even in the compact court area at Town Hall, but he had to balance their numbers to accommodate the presence of the cable networks in town. He'd called Sal Ducati last week to see if he'd heard anything else from MSNBC and was told that the network was concentrating on the upcoming political conventions instead and wouldn't be sending a crew to Riverton to cover the trial. Their absence allowed him to approve more journalists for admittance to the courtroom, enough to mollify the local dailies, weeklies, bloggers and network affiliates from Buffalo, which gave him one less thing to have to worry about.

He dried off and dressed quickly, donning a long-sleeved T-shirt, a pair of well-worn jeans and sneakers. The thermometer outside their kitchen window read 70. Scattered clouds at the highest levels were the only mar against the blue spring skies. After a breakfast like that, a walk down to GorgePark and a circuit or two on the hiking trails there would be an excellent chance for him to get a little exercise and clear his head.

When he was ready to leave he opened the back door and called out to his wife. She was on her knees in the garden, busily at work turning the soil, removing weeds and tossing them into a plastic tub by her side. "I'm going to take a walk down to the river. I should be back in an hour or so. Do we need anything in the village?"

She shifted to a sitting position, removed her gloves and dabbed at the perspiration glistening on her forehead. "Not that I can think of."

Rod patted his back pocket. "I have my cell with me. Call me if you think of something."

"I will."

"See you in a little while."

4

Two minutes after traffic ground to a halt, Gillian Hudecki grabbed her cell phone and began to try to find out what had happened. She had been on her way home from her office in Amherst and had just passed the Elmwood/Delaware exit on the 290, heading for Riverton, when she reached the impasse and could move no further. Horns honked intermittently and several drivers, impatient at the delay, exited their vehicles, peering ahead to see if they could determine why they were stalled at the height of the afternoon rush hour.

Using her phone, she was able to find the answer quickly on the website of a local news affiliate in Buffalo. Fresh video shot from their traffic copter showed the aftermath of a collision between a Mercedes and a commercial truck in the northbound lanes of the South Grand Island Bridge. It would be hours before the bridge could be cleared and normal traffic flow could resume.

She glanced at the clock on the dashboard: 5:23. Great, she thought. She was stuck, the last exit before the bridge three hundred yards behind her. She cursed to herself before scrolling through the contacts on her phone and punching in a number.

Scott Jamison answered on the third ring. His voice was bright, cheerful. "Hi, babe. What's up?"

"Nothing good. I'm stuck in traffic on the 290. It looks like I'm going to be here for a while. There's an accident on the bridge, a semi blocking both lanes."

"Where exactly are you?"

"Just past the Delaware Avenue exit, in the right lane. It's like a parking lot here. There's no place for me to go."

"So you'll be late for dinner." Disappointment oozed from his voice.

"Unless someone comes and gets me in a helicopter."

Silence. The two of them had planned a romantic dinner together tonight to mark the anniversary of their first date ten years earlier. Their reservation at the Café Martinique on Main Street in Riverton was for

6:30. Since the restaurant's opening two years before, it had become their favorite, a bit pricier than the other restaurants in the village but ideal for special occasions. Like an anniversary.

Gillian broke the silence. "Maybe you should call the restaurant."

"To cancel? Or try to move it back?"

Another horn blasted, this one two cars behind her. "It's Tuesday. Maybe they won't be so busy. How late do they serve?"

Scott thought for a moment. "Ten, I think. It's not tourist season yet."

"Call them and see what they say. Then call me back."

"Okay."

Three minutes later Gillian's phone rang. "They serve until ten. The woman I spoke with said it shouldn't be a problem. Their last reservation now is at 8:30."

Gillian's voice was laced with doubt. "I'll try, but it doesn't look good. Turn on the TV, see what they say. It should be all over the six o'clock news."

Scott glanced at his watch. "I think I'll hop in the shower now. I'll call you back when the news comes on." Pause. "Are you okay?"

"Yeah. Just frustrated. It's our anniversary."

His tone was reassuring. "I know, babe. Don't worry. We can always reschedule."

"I know. But after yesterday, I was really looking forward to this."

The day before had been the first day of the John Corelli trial. Because of her connection to Max Grossinger, Corelli's attorney, she'd managed to get on the very short list of those in the general population who were allowed a seat in the tiny space at Riverton Town Hall. As one of the principals at Amherst Orthodontic Associates, Gillian had supplied braces to both of Grossinger's teen-aged children from his second marriage. When she'd reached out to him several weeks earlier about attending the trial for opening statements, he'd assured her there'd be no problem. The next day he'd sent her a text, telling her she was in. All she had to do was call Town Hall and pick up a pass.

She called in a favor, arranging for another of her associates to cover for her. Mondays were typically slow in the office, so Gillian had no problem convincing Therese Short to see her patients. Gillian had done the same for Therese four years ago during Therese's two-week honeymoon in Barbados; she could hardly turn Gillian down for one day.

Gillian had asked Scott to drop her off at Town Hall on his way to work to avoid having a car anywhere near the site of the trial. He was a commercial painter, finishing up a project in Riverton at Village Pizza, which had been partially destroyed by a grease fire in the kitchen in December. He'd landed the contract because Brian Kennedy, the owner of the restaurant, had been one of his teammates in a slo-pitch softball league twenty years earlier. He'd completed final interior touch-up work on Monday, his last day on the job before the building inspector was scheduled to come through on Wednesday to confirm that the pizzeria would be code-compliant and able to re-open by the weekend. He'd also received his last check, including a performance bonus for finishing ahead of schedule.

So their dinner tonight at Café Martinique had a dual purpose, to celebrate their anniversary as well as a big payday for Scott. He tried to sound upbeat. "Don't worry. Just get home as soon as you can. How's the charge on your cell?"

She looked at her phone. "Sixty-two percent. I'll stay off it until I hear from you."

"Good," Scott said. "Hang in there. I love you."

"I love you, too."

Scott showered and dressed and was toweling off his thinning brown hair when the local news came on. He sat down in his favorite chair with some tortilla chips and salsa. Not too many, he told himself. They were going out to dinner later.

The crash on the bridge led off the news, bumping the latest from the Corelli trial. Video from the station's traffic copter revealed the extent of the backup. The snarl of westbound traffic on the 290 extended beyond the Main Street exits in Williamsville, where state troopers were in place, re-directing traffic to the Kensington Expressway. The reporter on the scene used to be one of the anchors of this very newscast but had been re-assigned as part of a corporate reorganization several years earlier. It seemed incongruous to have such a well-known local news figure dispatched to the scene of a fender bender, but he seemed to be handling it like a professional, dispassionately relaying the facts as he knew them to the audience. There appeared to be no injuries, but because of the size of the truck and its location blocking both lanes just below the apex of the bridge, a Thruway Authority spokeswoman conceded that it would likely be hours before normal traffic flow would resume.

Great, thought Scott. Unless Gillian could somehow maneuver her car out of the bumper-to-bumper gridlock and get back to Delaware Avenue, their celebration, at least for tonight, was off. Judging from the video supplied by the copter, she would be lucky if she managed to make it home before midnight.

He dialed Gillian. She picked up immediately. "What does it look like?"

"Not good. Traffic is backed up to the Thruway split. The cops are set up there, sending traffic to the Kensington and toward Rochester."

"Did they say if anyone was hurt?" Gillian asked.

"No injuries, according to Channel Two. But the semi is wedged between both guardrails, completely blocking both lanes. Unless you can turn around somehow and avoid the island, you're going to be there for a while. Hours, probably."

Gillian couldn't keep the dejection out of her voice. "Great. Then dinner is off."

"Not off," he corrected. "Just postponed."

"We can't do it tomorrow night," she said. "I have the scholarship dinner at the Saturn Club."

"Then we'll do it Thursday. I might even buy some new clothes for the occasion."

"Did you cash your check?"

"I did. I'm probably as flush as I've been since we met."

Which isn't saying much, she thought. Instead she said, "That's great. I better hang up, save some juice. You might as well get yourself something to eat. One of us should have dinner."

"Do you have water with you?" he asked.

"Yes. I filled my traveler at the office before I left."

"Okay. I'll call you later."

She clicked off the call and tossed her phone onto the passenger seat beside her. The honking had ceased as weary travelers, no doubt informed by their smart phones as to the details of their situation, settled in to wait for the truck to be removed from the bridge.

Gillian usually carried a book with her, but had left it at home today, convinced that the paperwork awaiting her after her day in court would leave little time for leisure reading. She had the Kindle app on her phone and could read one of the books stored there, but that would drain the phone's battery quickly. Who knew how long she'd be stuck here?

As six o'clock came and went, she began to feel warm inside her car. She turned the engine on long enough to lower the two front windows halfway and was rewarded with enough breeze to ease the temperature inside the vehicle. Most of the other drivers had turned their engines off as well, resigned to a long wait. Might as well conserve fuel, especially if they were going to be here for several hours. With the windows down she did notice the faint aroma of hydrocarbons being burned, but it smelled more like oil than gasoline or diesel, like it was coming from the small refinery just south of the twin bridges.

Her mind kept returning to the bizarre circus of the courtroom yesterday. It was only the second time during her forty-five years that she'd been inside a courtroom. Four years ago she'd been selected as a member of a Niagara County jury pool and had reported dutifully to the county courthouse in Lockport, the same place that had been rejected as a change of venue for the Corelli trial. Against all odds, her number had been drawn out of a hat as one of the potential jurors. She'd counted over two hundred people in the vast waiting hall, people who'd received the same letter on county stationery, requesting their presence as a candidate to perform a basic civic duty.

After all the numbers were selected she'd proceeded to the jury box with the other eleven selected – she was Juror 2 – where she and the others were questioned one by one by both of the attorneys in the case. The charge in question was an alleged rape, and each of the attorneys was asking specific questions designed to either categorize the jurors as sympathetic to the prosecution or the defense.

When the Assistant District Attorney prosecuting the case came to Gillian, she began by asking her if she or any members of her family had ever been involved in a case of rape; she replied that they hadn't. What did she do for a living? When she told the prosecutor she was an orthodontist, the prosecutor smiled and said no more questions. After some perfunctory questions from the judge, the defense attorney declined to ask a single question. After a meaningful glance between the two attorneys, the prosecutor spoke, exercising her first peremptory challenge, excusing Gillian from the proceedings. Weeks later, when she'd mentioned the abrupt end to her career as a juror to an attorney over cocktails at a fundraiser, he broke into laughter and explained. "You're a trial attorney's worst nightmare – someone with an advanced degree who's been raised and educated to be a critical thinker. That's the *last* thing a prosecutor wants on their jury. Too easy for someone like that to find reasonable doubt."

Inside the packed Riverton courtroom, she'd recognized one of the jurors in the Corelli trial, a woman who worked behind the deli counter at Spot Market in Riverton. The woman avoided eye contact with everyone, keeping her eyes focused on the back of the chair of the juror seated in front of her, looking as uncomfortable as a person could without becoming physically ill. The rear of the courtroom was occupied by camera crews from CNN and Fox News, as well as representatives from three local television affiliates from Buffalo. The rest of the seats were occupied by family members of the victims on one side, and of the defendant on the other.

Gillian was seated on the end of the last row on the Corelli side of the aisle. Ahead, in the front row behind the defense table, Liz Corelli sat up defiantly, eyes lasered straight ahead, standing by her man, dressed in a conservative gray suit over a cream-colored blouse with a single strand of pearls around her neck. She wore sensible shoes, flats. Gillian thought that might be in case she wanted to escape the media quickly when the inevitable barrage of questions began at the end of the day's testimony.

But there was no testimony from any witnesses on the first day of the trial, only the opening statements of each of the attorneys. The prosecution began laying out their case methodically, from the moment each of the girls first walked into John Corelli's classroom until the discovery of the pictures and videos on Corelli's computers and his subsequent arrest. Gillian listened raptly as Niagara County District Attorney Charles Moreland calmly and matter-of-factly related a tale of horror and revulsion and abuse of power that culminated, he assured the jury, in unspeakable criminal acts with not one but two underage females.

After Moreland's two-hour opening statement, the judge surprised the majority of the crowd by announcing the lunch break after conferring with both attorneys at the bench. Justice Harold Marquis used his gavel to quiet the murmur in the room after the two attorneys had returned to their respective tables. He announced the recess, stating he wanted to give Max Grossinger an uninterrupted period of time for his opening statement. The courtroom emptied.

Precisely at 1:00 the judge brought the court to order. "Mr. Grossinger, you may proceed with your opening statement."

There was an undercurrent of anticipation as the dapper Grossinger rose to his feet. Today he was resplendently attired in a charcoal Armani suit, with Galet loafers and a colorful silk tie purchased on a recent vacation in Tuscany. By now most of those following the Corelli trial were familiar with Grossinger's astonishing record as a defense attorney. It was rumored he'd been approached by O.J. Simpson's defense team when the former Buffalo Bills' running back had been arrested for the murders of Nicole Simpson and Ron Goldman twenty years earlier but had declined, claiming an unyielding docket. The real reason was that he'd rightfully anticipated how long that trial might last and did not want to give up a year of his professional life, especially in Los Angeles. He had a reputation as a tenacious advocate for his clients earned over forty years of trial experience and was considered a nightmare opponent by prosecutors, regardless of the amount and quality of evidence against the clients he defended.

His opening statement stretched for two and a half hours. He kept moving all that time, maintaining eye contact with the jury, silently evaluating their body language as he told the tale of John Corelli, born to immigrant parents who'd traveled from Napoli to settle near other family members in Niagara Falls and raised four children, of which John Corelli was the youngest. He'd graduated from Niagara Falls High School and had continued his education at Niagara University, where he graduated

31

cum laude with a B.S. in Adolescence Education. Later, while working as a teacher, he'd earned a Masters' Degree in Education at Buffalo State College.

He'd married his high school sweetheart as soon as he graduated from Niagara University and had been a teacher at Riverton Middle School for twenty-two years. Never in those twenty-two years had he received as much as a parking ticket, until now. He and his wife Liz had two children, a boy and a girl, both of whom had been students at Riverton High School before their father's arrest.

Gillian had to admit the man was mesmerizing. For two and a half hours there wasn't a noise other than an occasional cough in the courtroom as Grossinger made the case for Corelli's acquittal. Don't pre-judge, he warned, until all the evidence has been heard. Assuming guilt, he told the jurors, was the worst mistake they could make. Just listen to the evidence and their decision would be clear; John Corelli was an innocent man.

The phone on the seat next to her rang, jarring her from her reverie. Scott's voice sounded optimistic. "How's it going? Any movement yet?"

"Nothing," she replied glumly, looking at the cars near her. Several people had moved outside their vehicles to enjoy the last light of the day. "I haven't moved an inch since we last talked. What did they say on the news?"

"According to Channel Two, they've sent a crew from Grand Island. They should be there by now." What he didn't tell her was that they were still trying to find a tow truck in Niagara Falls substantial enough to remove the disabled truck from the bridge. "Are you hungry?" As soon as the words escaped his lips, he regretted them.

"Starving. Thanks for asking." She sounded exhausted.

"Sorry. I wasn't thinking."

"I guess we can forget about dinner tonight. Make a reservation for Thursday instead."

"I'll call them as soon as I hang up with you."

32

"Thanks. I'll try not to be too late." She glanced at her phone. "I don't have much power left. I'll call you again when we start to move, if it's not too late."

"Don't worry about the time," he said. "All I want is you back home again."

"You and me both."

5

As soon as Gillian hung up, Scott returned his attention to the new fish finder that had arrived via FedEx delivery yesterday afternoon. He went over the instructions one more time to confirm that everything had been assembled correctly, not satisfied merely by the fact that there were no components left in the box in which it had been shipped. He was looking forward to using the new device this upcoming weekend in Lake Erie, off Dunkirk, when he planned to trailer his sixteen-foot skiff south along the Thruway in search of some walleye.

After he'd cleaned up the shipping materials that had been scattered throughout the family room and tossed them into the trash, he loaded the fish finder into the rear of his van and returned to the house. He was hungry; he'd skipped lunch today, saving himself for the anniversary dinner. He looked in the refrigerator but it was nearly barren, the only offerings an aging container of milk, two apples and some raspberry preserves. He checked his watch. It wasn't too late. Maybe he could make it to the club before they stopped serving food.

The Riverton Rod and Gun Club was located east of Riverton on one hundred acres of mixed hardwoods and meadow that provided a buffer between the few neighboring houses on Norman Road. It was Scott's home away from home; if he wasn't working, fishing or hunting, you could usually find him at the bar of the club, regaling anyone within earshot with one of his stories, most of them accounts of previous fishing and hunting trips. He was a natural raconteur, and the bar at the Riverton Rod and Gun Club was his pulpit.

He dialed the club and waited patiently for someone to answer. Caroline Cooke was working alone behind the bar tonight and it was happy hour. She picked up on the sixth ring. "Riverton Rod and Gun Club, Caroline speaking."

"Hey, Caroline. It's Scott Jamison. How long are you serving dinner tonight?"

"Till eight, I think. Let me check." She covered the phone and shouted something unintelligible toward the kitchen. In a moment she was back. "Eight o'clock. Would you like to order something?"

"Beef on weck, with fries and cole slaw. I'm leaving the house right now."

"I'll save your seat at the bar."

"Is it busy?"

"It's Tuesday, first night of the trap shoot league. But I think we can squeeze you in."

"You're the best, Caroline. See you in a few."

As he brushed his teeth he looked into the mirror, trying to shake the lingering guilt he felt about going out to eat while Gillian was stranded on the 290. She wouldn't mind, he told himself. A man has to eat. He rinsed out his mouth, dabbed at some toothpaste stubbornly clinging to the corner of his mouth with a hand towel, combed his hair and headed for the door.

*****

Ten miles to the north, Kelly Porter was having her usual Tuesday night fare at The Galley, grilled Swiss on rye, before returning to the Delifin Athletic Club for the Tuesday night cribbage tournament. It had been a slow day for her behind the bar, notable only for who wasn't there. For the first time in two weeks, the mysterious stranger was missing from his usual seat at the end of the bar by the men's room.

The man had shown up for lunch two weeks earlier, ordering a cheeseburger with two pickles, no fries, and unsweetened iced tea with lemon. He'd eaten his lunch alone, paid his bill in cash with a generous tip and walked out the door. Kelly had tried to engage him in conversation but the man was taciturn. With the exception of requesting a receipt for his lunch, his only words during his visit were noncommittal monosyllabic responses to Kelly's questions, which were designed to draw him out, to shed some light on who he was and where he'd come from. He'd been in every day since, ordering the same items from the same seat at the bar, then strolling out the door when he was finished.

Until today. He hadn't shown up today and Kelly had missed his presence. Because of the timing of his arrival in Delifin, Kelly thought he might be one of the national media guys staying in the area to cover the Corelli trial. But he'd been at the bar yesterday, the first day of the trial, and had ordered his usual lunch. If he was in town for the trial he would've been at Riverton Town Hall instead of the end of the bar at the Delifin AC, munching silently on his burger.

She'd asked several of her regulars if they knew who he was, but no one had anything to offer. Even John Herrington, who last week had returned from wintering in the Caribbean and was once again living on his thirty-six-foot sloop *Soleil* moored in the river below just off the Delifin Yacht Club, had nothing to say when Kelly asked if he knew anything about the man. Herrington responded to her queries with arched eyebrows. "Does Patrick know you're obsessed with this guy?" Meaning Patrick Porter, Kelly's husband.

Physically, the man was unimposing, average. She guessed he was in his late forties or early fifties, an inch or two under six feet, with an average build, no facial hair, visible tattoos or other distinguishing marks. He dressed casually, usually in jeans and a long-sleeved shirt, and had dark brown hair swept straight back along with thick, bushy eyebrows that looked like they needed to be trimmed regularly. His fingernails were clean and neatly clipped, and there was no wedding ring on his left hand.

She knew she was spending too much time thinking about him, but she couldn't help herself. It was her nature to be inquisitive – it was one of the traits that made her such a good bartender. The more she knew about her clients, the better her tips tended to be, so she was able to convince herself that trying to ferret out the stranger's story was economical rather than intrusive. She'd even found herself peering into the man's wallet on several occasions when he was paying his bill, trying for any scrap of information, a picture or credit card, anything that might be a clue to his identity, but so far she'd failed to come up with anything connected to the man's identity. She wasn't even sure he had a cell phone; unlike most of her customers who kept their phones in sight, within reach at all times, she hadn't seen him with a phone. In a bar where everyone knew everyone else, the identity of this mysterious stranger was driving her crazy.

If he came in tomorrow she'd ask him flat out: what brings you to Delifin? He'd established a pattern at the AC – he'd have to expect some curiosity surrounding his sudden appearance in their small village at the juncture of the Niagara River and Lake Ontario. It was only human nature.

She finished her sandwich, took one last swig of her tea and signaled to the waitress to bring her check. She'd spent enough time speculating about the stranger at the end of the bar. It was time to play some cribbage.

*****

By the time Rod Wakefield pulled into his driveway Tuesday evening it was nearly nine, already dark. He was exhausted – he couldn't wait to get that first ice-cold beer in his hands. When he walked through the door he heard Sally's voice call out from the kitchen. "Are you hungry? I made a meatloaf."

Rod sat down to take off his shoes. "I hope you didn't wait for me."

She poked her head through the doorway. She was smiling. "Who else would I be having dinner with?"

"I don't know. I don't want you to have to wait for me every night." He walked over and gave his wife a hug and brief kiss before settling into his chair at the table, where a cold beer awaited him, already opened. He took a long swallow. "Thanks. I needed that."

"Tough day?" she asked as she sat down opposite him. Alongside the meatloaf was a bowl of mashed potatoes and some green beans slathered in butter.

"Not really. Just long. There was a minor fender bender when one of the guys from CNN pulled out of the parking lot without looking, but no one was hurt."

"Did you get to see any of the trial?"

He shook his head as he took another swallow of his beer. "Not much. A little bit in the morning, hardly anything during the afternoon session. I let Randy DiPietro handle security inside today. I stayed outside mostly."

"Who testified today?" she asked between bites of meatloaf.

"Fred Malinowski, the private investigator. He was the only witness, according to Randy. Moreland concentrated on asking him about the images on Corelli's computers and the software he'd used to get inside his hard drive. The camera guy said a lot of it was pretty technical stuff."

"Did they show any of the pictures or videos?" she asked.

"No. Randy said he thought Moreland was setting the stage to do that tomorrow."

The videos were the smoking gun, the key evidence in the prosecution's case. Rod had seen the unnerving pictures and the lurid videos last summer after Malinowski, under contract to the Riverton Police Department, fresh search warrant in his possession, had extricated them from encrypted folders on both of Corelli's computers. Once had been enough, even for a veteran lawman, a Marine who'd witnessed firsthand all manner of atrocities years ago in Nicaragua. He didn't want to see these pictures and videos again.

"Will you have to testify tomorrow?"

"Moreland didn't say, and he told me he'd tell me the day before I had to get on the stand. So I guess I'm good until Thursday, at least." He indicated the meatloaf with his fork. "This is really good. It's different from your usual meatloaf, really juicy."

Sally smiled, pleased that he'd noticed. "I tried a new recipe I found online. You like it?"

He nodded as he took another forkful. "It's a keeper."

After they were finished Rod helped Sally clear the table and load the dishes into the dishwasher. He offered to wash the pots and pans, but she waved him off, shooing him instead toward the family room of their tidy ranch-style home. "I'll clean up in here. Why don't you relax? There must be a ball game on."

"You sure?"

Sally could tell from his tone that he was only asking to be polite. "Positive. I can handle this."

"Thanks." He grabbed a second beer and headed for the family room, where he settled into his favorite chair and checked the channel guide to see if the Yankees were playing. They were, hosting the Twins tonight at Yankee Stadium, trying to end a seven-game losing streak. He hoped the game hadn't ended yet as he punched in the channel on the remote and sank back in his chair, which was contoured to his body after years of service. He wondered if there were any peanuts or Crackerjack in the house.

6

It was nearly midnight when Gillian swung into the driveway of the house she shared with Scott Jamison in the village of Riverton. By the time the disabled truck had been removed from the bridge and traffic finally began to flow again, her stomach was growling nonstop. She pulled off at the first exit on Grand Island and went to one of the nearby fast food places, where she bought two cheeseburgers and a chocolate shake from the drive-thru window that she devoured on the drive home.

The house was dark inside when she pulled into the driveway next to Scott's van. A single light above the front entrance illuminated the door and allowed her to let herself into the house. Scott had left a light on above the stove in the kitchen that enabled her to make her way noiselessly to the bathroom, where she quickly brushed her teeth before heading to their bedroom. Scott was asleep, snoring audibly as she slipped out of her clothes and slid naked between the covers next to him.

She was exhausted, yet her mind refused to let her sleep, dwelling instead on what she had scheduled tomorrow morning at the clinic and what she planned to wear to the fundraiser tomorrow evening. Next to her Scott's breathing was rhythmic as she tried to get her mind to slow down enough for her to drift off. He'd always been able to sleep regardless of the conditions, even while sitting up on a noisy plane. She'd occasionally resented him for it, but tonight she was more perturbed than usual. Tomorrow would be a busy day and she was already two hours beyond her regular bedtime, while Scott, who had finished a job on Monday, could sleep in.

She wondered how disappointed he'd been when she'd told him earlier that they'd be unable to celebrate their anniversary tonight. Scott wasn't what she considered overly romantic, but they'd both been looking forward to an evening out together. Ten years was a real milestone, the longest either of them had been in a relationship, and that deserved a proper celebration. Many of her friends had doubted from the start that the relationship would last, given the age difference between the two. Scott would turn sixty-four in August, a year away from collecting Social Security, while she had turned forty-five in February. To her the age difference was meaningless; what mattered was that they both loved the outdoors. They loved to fish and hunt, and they both loved guns.

Gillian Hudecki had been born and raised in Celoron, New York, the same village on the shores of Lake Chautauqua in the southern tier of New York just west of Jamestown where Lucille Ball had been born. After graduating from Jamestown High School, she'd attended the University of Buffalo, where she'd earned both her Bachelor of Science and DDS degrees. From the beginning she knew that she wanted to concentrate on orthodontics, having suffered through adolescence and early adulthood with misshapen teeth. Her father worked as a carpenter at one of the furniture factories in the Jamestown area, and with five older siblings, she'd known there wasn't enough money in the family budget for her to have her teeth fixed.

She'd accepted a position with a small practice in Depew immediately after graduation. She found a house for rent in Lancaster with a friend from college that was a five-minute drive from the office. Life was good. She was young and she was working, doing exactly what she'd dreamed of doing since she was a teenager, making more money in her first year after dental school than her father had made during his last five years working at the furniture factory. Who else among her friends could say that?

She dated occasionally but nothing serious developed. Her focus was her career, which left little time for any sort of meaningful relationship. Unlike some of her friends from high school and college, she felt no biological urge to start a family. The work was enough for her; it was what she lived for, what motivated her. Correcting misaligned teeth, shaping them into inviting smiles, was rewarding. She was improving the quality of the lives of her patients, even if they were, for the most part, too young to realize it yet.

Her long-term goal from the beginning had been to open her own practice. Seven years earlier she left the office in Depew where she'd been employed since graduating from dental school and established Amherst Orthodontic Associates with one of her former colleagues, Therese Short, in a newly constructed medical park on Sheridan Drive. The business had grown exponentially – even though the economy remained sluggish in the aftermath of Wall Street's collapse, there was no shortage of parents in the more comfortable eastern suburbs of Buffalo willing to plunk down a few grand in exchange for symmetrical bridgework for their sons and daughters.

Scott had been supportive of her plans to establish her own practice from the start. They had been together for three years when,

41

after six months of discussion and preliminary planning, she and Therese approached one of the local banks for a loan. Once they had secured funding and signed a lease for space in the new medical office park, he painted the inside of their suite for free and helped the two women find an architect to design the space and a reliable contractor to install the sophisticated equipment. He'd been invaluable during the process and she found herself even more in love with him because of it. He'd sacrificed time on the water and in the woods, time most precious to him, in order to help her realize her dream.

He began to snore next to her, a low, rhythmic wheeze. She reached over and nudged him gently, enough to make him shift positions slightly. The snoring stopped. Not a care in the world, she thought with a wistful smile, as she turned her back to him, closed her eyes and tried to will herself to sleep.

*****

On Wednesday John Herrington motored his dinghy to shore from *Soleil* and secured it in the transient docking area of the Delifin Yacht Club before heading up the hill to the AC for lunch. His was one of the few boats already in the water. Most of the others were still on their storage cradles at the northern end of the yacht club property, awaiting their turn with the crane. Memorial Day, the unofficial start to the boating season in Delifin, was in two weeks and he knew the waterfront area would be a blur of activity as anxious owners worked diligently to make sure their boats would be polished, rigged and seaworthy by the time their turn to launch rolled around.

Kelly Porter was behind the bar, slicing lemons and limes, when he clattered through the door by the parking lot. He walked to the end of the bar that overlooked the lake and the river below and took a seat opposite her. Kelly looked up and smiled. "Good morning."

Herrington glanced at his watch. "Technically, it's afternoon."

She flashed him a sardonic smile as she continued to slice fruit and store it in containers beneath the bar. "Some of us have been working this morning and lost track of the time."

He indicated the bar area with a sweeping gesture. "You only have one other customer. How hard could you have been working?" He peered toward the man sitting at the opposite end of the bar by the door to the men's room. "Who's that?"

42

She put her knife down and leaned across the bar, lowering her voice conspiratorially. "That's the guy."

"The mysterious stranger in town?"

She nodded. "Comes in, sits at the end of the bar, orders the same thing every day, pays his tab in cash and walks out."

"You still don't know his name?"

"Nope."

Herrington viewed the man with renewed interest. Kelly had mentioned the newcomer to him the last time he'd been in the bar, but this was the first time Herrington had seen him. He was dressed casually in a flannel shirt and jeans, with a full head of brown hair and dark eyes. Nothing distinguishing about the guy, he thought.

"He didn't show up yesterday," Kelly said. "First day he's missed in two weeks. I wasn't sure he was coming back."

Herrington reached for today's copy of the *Niagara Gazette* on the bar and scanned it, looking for the weather page. "Then there's your opening."

"What do you mean?"

"To ask questions."

Kelly frowned. "I've tried that. Nothing."

"Don't tell me you're losing your touch," he teased. "Maybe you should loosen a button or two on your shirt and lean forward a bit the next time he needs something."

She shook her head in mock disgust. "Typical Herrington. Your solution to every problem in the world involves more cleavage."

It was Herrington's turn to smile. "Not every problem. But most of them? Yeah."

"You're a pig."

John Herrington gave her one of his dazzling, flawless smiles. Because he lived on his boat and didn't own a car, he was a frequent

43

customer at the Delifin AC, traveling the short distance to shore for lunch and to read the *Gazette* most weekdays. Each fall he placed his boat in storage and headed for Miami, where he rented another boat and sailed it single-handedly to the Caribbean for the winter and most of the spring, flying back to western New York only when the ice was out of the Niagara River and *Soleil*, his thirty-six-foot sloop, was ready to be launched.

His follow-the-sun lifestyle was the result of two events in his past, one tragic, the other fortuitous. His parents had died in a plane crash years earlier while he was a student at Niagara University, and as their only child, he had inherited a significant estate. He'd sold the family home in Riverton Heights and moved to a small apartment in the village of Riverton while continuing his studies at Niagara. It was while living there that he first heard of an interesting start-up on the west coast from his father's broker, who managed to get him in on the ground floor. That start-up was Microsoft, and by the time he was ready to sell some of his stock after several splits and an astonishing run-up in price, he was set for life. He put his diploma into storage, bought a boat and embarked on a nautical life free from financial worries that was the envy of many. Including, he felt, Kelly Porter.

"You seem irritable today. You must not have done well in the cribbage tournament last night."

Kelly was nonplussed by the obvious attempt to get her goat. More typical Herrington. "That has nothing to do with anything and you know it."

"Wow," he said. "You must've *really* done bad."

Kelly was about to snap back when she saw the stranger at the other end of the bar raise his hand in an attempt to get her attention. "I'll be right back," she hissed as she headed to the other end of the bar.

"Don't forget to ask him his name," he said *sotto voce*, just loud enough to carry the length of the bar.

The man's wallet was on the bar next to his cell phone as Kelly asked, "Can I get you anything else?"

The man shook his head. "Just the check. And a receipt, please."

44

She reached into a pocket of her apron, withdrew his check and quickly jotted down the final amount. After two weeks of ordering the identical lunch, she knew the total by heart. He extracted some bills from his wallet, counted them, and placed them on top of the check. "Keep the change."

She handed him a receipt. "Thanks again. See you tomorrow?"

The man stood. "Probably." Without another word he headed into the men's room and Kelly returned to an expectant Herrington at the other end of the bar. "Well?"

"I didn't ask him."

"Figures." He indicated the television above the cash register. "Would you mind switching to The Weather Channel? Tonight is the first Wednesday night race at the yacht club. I was listening to the marine forecast on the boat before I came over and they were talking about the possibility of a late-afternoon storm today."

She found the remote by the cash register and changed the channel. "Are you planning to race tonight?" Normally Herrington wasn't a participant in the Wednesday evening series.

"Not on my boat. But one of Hal Paulson's regular crew has the flu and he asked me to fill in."

That got her interest. She smiled. "So you're going to be taking orders from Hal tonight?"

"Not if this storm kicks up," he said, indicating the television. "I'm a fair-weather sailor."

"But if it doesn't?"

"Then I guess I will."

7

The man exited from the men's room at the Delifin Athletic Club and walked out the door. As soon as he was gone Kelly leaned forward, animated. "Why don't you follow him, see where he goes? He has to be staying somewhere close in the village. Besides, you don't have anything better to do."

Herrington was unfazed, still watching for the local weather on the television. "You want a private eye, call Fred Malinowski. And what makes you think I have nothing better to do?"

It was Kelly's turn to smile. "Years of experience."

*****

The man walked out of the AC parking lot and headed north along Main Street, toward Fort Ontario. A stiff breeze was blowing from the north, and he ducked his head into it as he continued toward the small apartment he'd rented on Stonewall Street. The sky was overcast, threatening a storm, but to the east it looked mostly clear.

He smiled to himself. The inquisitive bartender had tried again to figure out who he was and what he was doing in Delifin. Once again he'd deflected her attempts by ignoring her questions, following the same pattern he'd established on his first day in town: ordering his lunch, eating it, paying his bill and then leaving. No idle chitchat; he had work to do.

He'd recognized the Delifin AC as the hub of the small village on his second day there. Only two streets, Main and Lockport, sported businesses, and then for only a block each. The rest of the village contained a wide range of housing, including 19th century farmhouses, post-war ranch homes, small apartment complexes, and recently constructed housing developments. Although he didn't speak to anyone while he ate his lunch at the bar, he kept his ears open and he overheard enough to get a pretty good handle on the village and its inhabitants, enough to convince him that the research he'd done prior to selecting Delifin for his latest project was solid. He'd made the right choice.

He enjoyed the bartender's attempt to figure out who he was and what he was doing in town. The AC was the sort of place where everyone knew your name, like the bar in that television show he'd watched when he was young. Being the mystery man, stimulating the local gossip hounds into speculation and conjecture, was a role he hadn't anticipated for himself, but it was something he'd embraced during the previous two weeks. He knew it wouldn't last much longer – the nature of his project required contact with the local population. But it sure was fun while it lasted.

When he reached the small gray duplex with the purple shutters he reached into his pocket for the key. As he inserted it into the lock, he glanced at the thickening clouds overhead. It looked like rain.

*****

The alarm startled Gillian. She'd slept poorly and wanted more than anything to stay in bed a little while longer, but that was out of the question. She had a full day of patients scheduled, including several that had rescheduled from Monday when she was at the Corelli trial. After her work day, she was attending a dinner at the Saturn Club in Buffalo, a fundraiser for scholarships awarded to high-achieving local girls planning to pursue a post-secondary education in science and technology. Wednesday promised to be her second late night in a row.

She turned over. Scott was gone. From the kitchen she heard the radio playing something with a salsa beat. The unmistakable aroma of bacon drifted down the hall. She smiled. She liked it when Scott had a rare respite in his work schedule. It meant they ate bacon for breakfast.

By the time she finished showering and was dressed, the aroma was tantalizing. She applied her makeup effortlessly – she didn't wear much – and headed for the kitchen. Scott was standing by the table, wearing the apron Gillian had given him for Christmas several years earlier, smiling from ear to ear. "Breakfast is served."

She sat down. "This looks fabulous." Besides several slices of bacon, there were scrambled eggs with peppers, onions and some sharp grated cheddar, whole wheat toast and orange marmalade. A pot of freshly brewed coffee rested next to a container of orange juice in the center of the table.

Scott removed his apron and folded it carefully before sitting opposite her at the table. "After last night I figured you deserved a Sunday-style breakfast this morning."

Gillian poured herself a cup of coffee and smiled. "You didn't have to do this."

"Of course I did. You didn't expect me to sleep in, did you?"

She shook her head as she sipped the steaming coffee. "I figured you'd be gone already this morning, trying out your new fish finder."

He reached for a slice of toast and passed the dish to her. "I decided to do that this afternoon instead."

"Where are you going?" she asked as she slid some eggs onto her plate.

"The state park in Wilson. I want to make sure the thing works at depth before taking it to Dunkirk this weekend."

"Couldn't you do that in the river?"

He dribbled hot sauce over his eggs. "Probably. But I want to stop and get some of Michele's nuts and specialty popcorn. We're almost out."

"Good idea."

The conversation halted as they ate with gusto, Gillian mentally going over her patient list for the day, Scott marveling yet again at the amount of money in his checking account after he'd cashed the big check from Village Pizza yesterday. He was enjoying the feeling of having a bit of a cushion for a change.

Gillian wished she could linger a bit, maybe thank Scott in a special way for the wonderful breakfast, but it was getting late. On a good day it took her almost forty minutes to get from Riverton to her office on Sheridan Drive in Amherst and her first appointment was at 9:00. She gulped down the rest of her coffee, gave Scott a quick peck on the cheek and headed for the door. She called over her shoulder. "Don't forget. No dinner for me again tonight. At least not here."

He was at the sink, washing the dishes. "Any idea what time you might be home?"

"Not a clue. I'll leave as early as I can."

*****

48

By the time Lenny Campbell was ready to leave for Wilson to check on his boat, it was past noon. The day before he'd called the marina where he and his brother Red stored their Sea Ray during the winter and told the man who'd answered that he would be there first thing in the morning to confirm what the marina had been telling him on the phone – that the craft was ready to launch.

But his mother had called just as he was about to leave and asked him to take her to Riverton to do some grocery shopping. By the time he dropped her off at her house and helped store the items she'd purchased, the morning had slipped away. He debated calling the marina to let them know he'd be a little late, but decided against it. The boat wasn't going anywhere.

Traffic was light as he headed east on Lake Road, past the cottages and mansions that boasted panoramic views of Lake Ontario. Overhead, there were increasing patches of blue where the clouds began to separate and break up. The wind was from the north and gentle breakers rolled onto the rocky shoreline. It looked like it might be sunny by the time he reached Wilson.

It had been Red's idea to store the boat in Wilson after two consecutive years of poor service at the marina in Delifin where he rented a slip during the boating season. Both he and Lenny had expected the boat to be winterized and then prepared for launch by the time the ice was out of the river, but the Delifin marina staff had dropped the ball, moving the Sea Ray into their partially heated storage barn but then doing nothing to protect the hydraulic systems against the ravages an upstate New York winter.

They were hoping for better luck in Wilson. One of the other boaters in Delifin had recommended the DiCarlo Boat Yard, next to the Sunset Grille in the inner harbor. Today would be the litmus test on that recommendation. As he pulled into the lengthy driveway that led to the boat yard, he hoped that friend knew what he was talking about, especially after the difficulties they'd encountered the last two years.

He parked his Cadillac next to the side entrance of the building. Down by the gas pumps, there was a 40-foot Beneteau on the hydraulic lift, with a mechanic examining it from the ground, poised to hop aboard. He saw Lenny approaching and called out "You Campbell?"

"That's me. I'm here to check on---"

"Your Sea Ray," he finished. "Be with you in a sec." He walked over to the outdoor basin and scrubbed his hands, wiping them on the least oily rag within reach. He turned back to Lenny. "What can I do for you?'

"I just want to make sure she's ready to launch next week," Lenny said.

"Are you on the list?"

Lenny shook his head. "I was hoping to do that today."

"No problem. Let me get the launch log from the office." He returned momentarily with a large three-ring binder. "What day were you thinking about?" he asked, pen poised over paper.

"How does next Wednesday look?" His brother Red was coming in from Vail on Tuesday to help him motor down to Delifin and set up their summer berth at the marina there.

The mechanic scanned his log. "We could do it in the afternoon, say two o'clock. How does that sound?"

"Perfect," Lenny replied. "Is she ready to roll?"

"Completely. I went through the mechanical punch list on your boat on Monday. All we need to do is polish the hull."

"You fixed the problem with the lower unit?" The boat had been plagued with a mysterious leak in the lower unit that had caused all sorts of downtime last summer.

"I think so. Of course, we won't know for sure until it goes into the water."

You better hope it's fixed, Lenny thought. Instead he said, "How about a quick look?"

"No problem. Follow me."

The mechanic led him to a large metal barn attached to the rear of the marina office. The *Scottish Rogue* was on a cradle on the lower level, near the end of the first row. Lenny walked up and gave it a quick inspection, rubbing his hand along the gleaming white hull. He thought it already looked polished, but it wouldn't hurt to do it again since they

50

were paying for it. The most prominent maintenance task during the season was cleaning the hull below the waterline, which was done when the boat was afloat. Lenny figured the water temperature was still in the low fifties. He was in no hurry for a swim until it warmed up considerably, and he was sure his brother was on the same page.

"Looks good to me," Lenny said. "Do I need to sign anything today?"

"Nope. Just bring your checkbook next week." The mechanic's smile revealed a missing incisor.

"How about cash?" His brother was a firm believer that, if you don't have the money in your pocket, you can't afford to buy whatever it is you're trying to buy.

"Even better." He and Lenny shook hands. "I've got to get back to work. I'll see you next Wednesday."

Lenny pointed to the gas pumps. "How much is marina gas this year?"

"Three bucks," the mechanic said. "Your tanks will be full next week. Your bill will reflect the purchase."

Three dollars a gallon was less than they'd paid in the last few years. "Let's hope it stays that low."

The gap-toothed mechanic grinned again. "I guess that's up to the Saudis."

8

Gillian was on her way to the coffee machine after finishing with a patient when she saw Maria Canova and her mother in the waiting area, along with Charley Bukowski, her 3:00 appointment. She knew the Canova's weren't on the list for today and looked quizzically at Kimberley Montague behind the reception desk, who motioned her over. As Gillian bent over the desk, Kimberley explained in a low voice. "Maria broke her retainer. Her mother wants to know if we can squeeze her in today."

"Who do we have at 4:00?"

Kimberley checked the book. "Carla Cromwell, for an adjustment."

She glanced at the clock above the desk. "I shouldn't be too long with Charley. Tell them I'll see them before Carla. If they can't wait, ask them to leave it overnight and we'll do it first thing in the morning."

"Okay."

What she thought would be a busy Wednesday had thus far exceeded her estimate. They had been going non-stop since 8:30 and Gillian had already seen one other walk-in, sacrificing her lunch hour in a moment of weakness. Later, when the lunch time patient had left, Therese poked her head into Gillian's office, shaking her head. "You are the softest touch I know. Can I borrow a hundred until Tuesday?"

"Go to hell," Gillian responded cheerfully. "You would've done the same thing if it had been your patient."

"Maybe, maybe not. Depends on whether I had lunch plans." She smiled before turning and walking away.

Making room for the Canova's meant that her day ran a little longer than normal. By the time she was finished with Carla Cromwell and had changed into the clothes she'd brought with her, it was nearly 6:00. Gillian was fretting about being late for the 6:30 dinner at the Saturn Club as she walked to her car in the parking lot. It would be tight; getting from Sheridan Drive to Delaware Avenue meant a trip on the

Kensington Expressway at the height of the afternoon rush hour. She doubted she'd be there by the time everyone sat down to dinner.

For a moment she entertained the thought of blowing the dinner off and heading home instead, but just as quickly rejected the idea. She'd promised Angela Oliverio, chairperson of the event, that she'd say a few words about opportunities for women in the dental health field. Reluctantly, she waited for a gap in the traffic on Sheridan Drive, then turned right toward the 290 and its connection to the Kensington.

*****

On Wednesday morning District Attorney Charles Moreland called Rod Wakefield to the stand as his first witness. A day earlier, private investigator Fred Malinowski had been the prosecution's only witness. The experienced Moreland's questions to Malinowski had been simple and direct, easy for the jury to follow as Malinowski explained how he had discovered incriminating text messages and photos exchanged between Corelli and his two victims on both his home computer and the laptop supplied to him by the school district.

Wakefield had originally been told by Moreland he would testify later in the trial, but the district attorney had shifted his strategy late Tuesday evening, after the completion of Fred Malinowski's testimony. Moreland's late phone call caught Wakefield just before he turned in. "What can I do for you, Counselor?"

Moreland's tone was apologetic but straight to the point. "Sorry for the late call. I know I told you that you would be testifying next week, but I've changed my mind. You're going to be my first witness in the morning."

Wakefield paused before replying. "What changed your mind?"

"Malinowski's testimony. I think the jury needs to hear about how the warrant was developed after you received the complaint from the parents of the first victim now instead of later. I thought I saw some uncertainty in a couple of the jurors today as Malinowski explained how he opened the encrypted files. Ever since Edward Snowden and Wiki leaks, people have been wary of Big Brother spying on them electronically. I want you to remove any doubt from their minds right up front that any of our evidence was obtained in a tainted manner. You telling them how the warrant was secured through old fashioned, diligent police work can nip that speculation in the bud."

53

Wakefield digested Moreland's words before he replied. "Will you be asking the same questions you did when we prepped a few weeks ago?"

"Exactly the same. The only thing that changes is that I want to ask them tomorrow. Will you have any problem with your duty roster if you have to testify tomorrow?"

"Nothing major," Wakefield said. "I should be able to handle it in the morning. Full dress uniform?"

"Of course," Moreland replied. "Nothing impresses a jury like a man in a uniform, especially one they all know."

"What time do you need me there?"

"Judge Marquis likes to start promptly at 9:00. Be there by 8:30 if you can."

"No problem. See you then."

Wakefield pulled into the parking lot at town hall just after 8:00 Wednesday morning and huddled with Moreland for five minutes before entering the courtroom. When Judge Marquis struck his gavel precisely at 9:00 to quiet the murmuring in the courtroom and called the session to order, Moreland wasted no time. "The prosecution would like to call Riverton Chief of Police Rod Wakefield."

Wakefield had been standing in the rear of the courtroom and strode forward confidently to the witness stand as soon as Moreland mentioned his name. The bailiff raised his arm and addressed the chief. "Do you promise to tell the truth, the whole truth, and nothing but the truth, so help you God?"

"I do."

"State your name for the record."

"Rodney Wakefield."

"You may be seated."

Wakefield sat down and crossed his arms in his lap. He resisted the temptation to scan the courtroom and instead concentrated on Charles Moreland as he approached the bench. Moreland gave him a quick wink that no one else in the courtroom caught before he began. For the next two hours Moreland's questions gave the jury a clear understanding of how the accumulation of witness statements led to the issuing of a series of search warrants pertaining to John Corelli's computers, which yielded information that resulted in additional warrants pertaining to Corelli's cell phone, home and vehicles.

Max Grossinger jotted down an occasional note as Moreland questioned Wakefield but otherwise sat silent. As he had planned, Moreland wrapped up his questioning fifteen minutes before the lunch break. Satisfied, he turned to the judge. "No more questions for the witness at this time, Your Honor."

"Thank you, Mr. Moreland." The judge looked toward the defense table. "Your witness, Mr. Grossinger."

Grossinger stood and spoke clearly. "No questions at this time, Your Honor."

"Very well." He turned to Wakefield. "You may be excused, Chief."

Wakefield rose and returned to the rear of the courtroom, which was shoulder-to-shoulder with spectators. He pushed gently but insistently through them and out the door. Overhead the sky was clogged with clouds, a pastiche of gray. That wasn't so bad, he thought, breathing deeply as he reflexively scanned the parking lot. Moreland had stuck to the script they'd rehearsed, keeping everything simple. No big words, no surprises. Except for Grossinger's decision not to cross-examine him. He hadn't expected that.

He glanced at his watch. Almost lunch time. He doubted that Judge Marquis would entertain another witness before the afternoon session. The judge was a man of routine, and he liked to eat his lunch no later than noon. When the doors opened a few minutes later and the spectators, led by the news crews, began to pour out, he was at his post at the entrance to the parking lot, prepared to direct traffic.

*****

It was 11:15 when Gillian swung into the driveway at home after the scholarship dinner. There were no lights on in the house and Scott's van was missing. After a momentary twinge of uncertainty at his absence, she remembered it was Wednesday night, the night when the

55

men's slo-pitch softball league played at Blakeslee Park in Riverton. Even though he no longer played, he sometimes watched the games, and when he did he often went to the bar with the players for beers and chicken wings.

As she exited the van clutching the gym bag that contained her clothes from work, she noticed several puddles in low-lying areas of her asphalt driveway. Looks like it rained pretty good, she thought as she stepped around the water, fumbling in her purse for the front door key. The dinner had run long, as these affairs often did, and she was weary, ready for bed.

Inside, she turned on the porch light for Scott and tossed the gym bag into the laundry room before heading for the bathroom to release an insistent bladder and to brush her teeth. As she brushed she thought the night had gone reasonably well. Her speech had lasted ten minutes, about what she had figured it would, and there were no questions to field when she wrapped it up. The turnout had been tremendous, with lots of talented young women from high schools all over western New York in attendance. Angela had done another outstanding job organizing the event. It was her third year at the helm and she'd managed to raise a significant amount of money for the scholarship fund in each of the previous two. From the looks of things, she'd hit another one out of the park tonight.

In the bedroom she shrugged out of her clothes, leaving them tangled on the floor, and slid gratefully beneath the covers. Within minutes she drifted off into a sound and dreamless sleep.

9

The alarm jarred Gillian awake at 6:45. Groggily she reached over without opening her eyes to hit the snooze button, hoping for five more minutes. She hadn't stirred all night, yet still felt tired, the cumulative effect of her two previous late nights. Five more minutes.

She felt no more refreshed the second time it rang, but knew it was time to get up. No Scott; he must already be up, making coffee or perhaps a light breakfast before she left for work. He was considerate that way, one of the most thoughtful and kind men she'd ever met. It was one of the main reasons she fell in love with him.

She showered and dressed, mentally going over her appointments for the day in her head. She needed to do some grocery shopping today and was hoping to get out of the office on time. Most of the patients scheduled for today were adults, part of the surprisingly large demographic of older patients opting to have their teeth straightened, men and women whose parents were either unwilling or unable to afford the work when they were children.

As she sat on the edge of the bed to put on her shoes, she realized that there was no coffee aroma in the air. That was strange. Scott was usually the first one up and always made coffee – it was part of their morning ritual.

She walked into the kitchen. Everything looked in its place. There was no sign of Scott, no dishes in the sink to indicate he'd been here and left, no note. She walked into the living room and peered out the front window. No van in the driveway.

She checked the rest of the house, a tiny alarm going off in her head. There were no dirty clothes in the bedroom or laundry room to indicate that Scott had returned to the house last night. A feeling of dread was starting to build as she went from room to room, looking for signs Scott had been there since yesterday morning and finding none.

She dug her phone out of her purse and punched in his number. Her call went straight to his voicemail. After the beep she tried to keep her voice calm. "Call me as soon as you get this." She waited a few minutes, then tried again. Same thing. This time she didn't leave a message. She told herself that the battery on his phone must've died, something that happened fairly regularly with Scott, who was old school, reluctant to fully embrace the technology offered by today's cell phones.

She put on a pot of coffee and headed to the spare bedroom they'd converted to a sort of office for the two of them. She flipped open her laptop and tried to remember the names of his old softball teammates as she searched for the league's website. After several minutes she found it and quickly navigated to the results of last night's games. Her heart sank. Last night's games had been postponed because of weather. He hadn't gone out with the guys for wings and beer. She shuddered as the cold realization of his unexplained absence sank in.

Fighting to remain calm, she went outside to look for his boat trailer. He usually parked it on the narrow strip of lawn next to the garage when it wasn't in use. She dodged several puddles carefully in the driveway as she turned the corner. The trailer was gone. Had he taken it for an early morning fishing trip? Had it been there when she returned to the house late last night? She tried to remember, but she had been exhausted. It could've been there, she told herself, and she just hadn't seen it.

But if he was fishing on the river or the lake, why did his phone go directly to voicemail? He *always* made sure his phone was fully charged before he went out on the water. His sixteen-foot skiff had no marine radio. He needed the phone with him, fully operational, in case anything went wrong.

She went inside the house and checked the office again, looking for his address book. He was one of the last people Gillian knew who still kept a hard-copy address book instead of storing that information on his phone or computer. As she shuffled through a pile of papers that belonged to him, looking for the slim blue notebook, she wondered who to call. Scott didn't have a lot of friends. Plenty of acquaintances but not many friends. The few friends he had were members at the Riverton Rod and Gun Club, people known to both of them.

She glanced at her watch. It was too early to call the club to see if he had been there last night. The address book wasn't on the desk. She went through the drawers but came up empty there as well. She began to feel full-blown panic. Where was Scott?

She poured herself a cup of coffee to steady her frayed nerves and tried to think. Who could she call? She went through a list of his friends in her head, but she didn't know any of their phone numbers. The only person she could think of was his mother.

Dolores Jamison lived alone in a small basement apartment on Tuscarora Street in Riverton, adjacent to GorgePark. She was a widow – her husband Karl had been killed by a drunk driver when Scott, their only child, was eleven. Dolores had never remarried. Instead, she dove into a bottle, eventually turning the home the two of them shared into a battle ground, a place Scott grew to despise and dread. As soon as he turned eighteen he moved out. Other than an occasional birthday card, Scott had had little contact with his mother since.

Gillian knew it was a long shot, but hers was a phone number she did know. With trembling fingers, she punched it in. Just when she thought it was going to voice mail, Dolores answered in a slurred voice. "Who ish this?"

Eight o'clock and already hitting the booze. She tried to keep her voice from cracking. "Hello, Dolores. It's Gillian, Scott's girlfriend."

"I know who you are. I'm not an idiot." Pause. "What time ish it?"

"Almost eight."

"In the morning?"

"Yes. I was wondering if you'd seen Scott."

"Why would I see him? He lives with you, doesn't he?" The contempt in her voice was unmistakable.

"He does, but he didn't come home last night. I was wondering if you've seen him at all in the last few days."

Gillian heard the sound of a lighter and a quick intake of breath on the other end of the phone before Dolores responded with a sneer. "Maybe he finally found someone elsh. Another woman."

"Is that a no?"

"Whadda you think?"

Gillian tried to remain patient. "I don't know what to think, Dolores. That's why I'm asking for your help. Have you seen him?"

59

Long pause. "I haven't seen that bastard for a year. Maybe more, I don't know." Her voice trailed off.

"Will you do me a favor?"

"Depends."

"If you hear from him, would you call me?" Gillian tried not to sound like she was pleading. "It's very important."

"Maybe he found a new chippie to replace you," she said. She laughed. "About time."

"Just call if you hear from him. It's important."

Gillian hung up without saying goodbye, her eyes moist. Despite promising herself not to let Dolores get to her, the woman's bitter words had stung. Was Scott with another woman? Was that even possible? As soon as the thought formed, she knew it was. He was a man, after all. Men meet new women all the time.

She decided to call Therese, who answered on the second ring. "Gillian. What's up?"

"Do you think you could cover for me this morning?"

Therese detected the waver in Gillian's voice. "What's wrong?" she asked, concerned.

"It may be nothing, but Scott didn't come home last night and I can't reach him. His phone goes straight to voicemail."

"Have you called the police?"

"Not yet. I tried his mother, but she wasn't any help."

"How about friends?"

"I thought of that, but I couldn't find his address book. I don't know any of their numbers."

Therese knew Scott well enough to know this behavior was highly unusual. "I think you should call the police, Gillian. Don't worry about the office. I'll have Kimberley reschedule your appointments."

"But I already missed one day this week. I can't----"

60

"Yes, you can," said Therese firmly. "Let me handle things at the office. You find out what happened to Scott. Call me when you know anything."

"Are you sure?"

"Positive. Call the police. Let me know what's going on later. I'll handle things here."

"Thanks, Therese."

*****

By the time Anne Moretti informed Rod Wakefield that the coffee was ready, he was halfway through the logs of overnight calls. It had been a quiet night in Riverton. A report of a barking dog, a vandalized road sign on River Road, a domestic call concerning one of the department regulars, a Vietnam veteran whose bottled-up resentment and anger occasionally resulted in cuts and bruises for his long-suffering wife. Standard stuff for Riverton from the night shift.

It was his turn to hold down the fort at the village municipal offices today. With the Corelli trial demanding the attention of most of his officers, he'd been operating with only a single officer and Anne at the red brick station house all week. After testifying yesterday, it was his turn today to file reports and handle anything that might occur in his jurisdiction unrelated to the trial. For the first time in a long while he was looking forward to catching up on his paperwork.

Anne was at her desk, on her laptop, when he arrived at 7:45. She looked up and smiled as he walked in. "Good morning, Chief. How did it go yesterday?"

He placed his hat on the corner of his desk and turned back. "Piece of cake, easier than I thought it would be."

"You and Moreland rehearsed, right?"

He nodded. "Chuck stuck to the script. Simple questions, one or two-word answers. Nothing to confuse the jury." He looked around. "How have things been in the office?"

"Quiet," she said. "Only a few calls overnight." She held up the logbook. "Do you want to go over them now?"

"Sure. Coffee?"

"It's brewing now. I'll bring you a cup when it's ready."

"Thanks, Anne. What would I do without you?" He thought for a moment, then added. "Don't answer that."

Anne couldn't resist. "I often wonder that myself. Should I shut the door on my way out?"

"You can leave it open. Is Sal in?"

"Not yet," she replied. "He's probably on trash patrol. I think he's worried someone from the national press is going to find some litter to film."

"Let me know when he comes in."

"Will do, Chief."

He busied himself with the reports. In a few minutes Anne returned with a cup of coffee, which she placed on the corner of his desk. She turned and left without a word. He took a grateful sip and returned his attention to the logbook. A quiet night, he thought to himself. The kind of night he liked in Riverton.

Ten minutes later the phone rang in the office. Anne answered it. A minute later a red light flashed on his direct line to Anne. He picked up. "What is it?"

"I have someone on the line who wants to report a missing person."

"A missing person? Who's calling?"

"Gillian Hudecki. Says her boyfriend didn't come home last night."

10

The name was unfamiliar to Wakefield. "Is she still on the line?"

"I have her on hold."

"Put her through."

Anne switched the call. "Ms. Hudecki, I'm Chief Wakefield. What can I do for you?"

Her voice was low, barely audible. "My boyfriend didn't come home last night."

"Pardon me for asking, but is this unusual behavior? Has he ever done anything like this before?"

"Never."

He wanted to look Gillian Hudecki in the eye while he was questioning her. "Would it be possible for you to come in and give us a statement?"

She paused a moment before responding. "I'd have to call work and tell them."

"Why don't you do that and then come into the office. You know where it is?"

"In the old school building. I'll be there as soon as I can."

Anne had a fresh pot of coffee brewed by the time Gillian arrived twenty minutes later. She buzzed Wakefield. "Gillian Hudecki is here, Chief."

"Send her in."

He stood as Gillian entered the room. She was wearing a pair of jeans, a sweatshirt and sneakers, with no makeup. She looked like she had thrown on the first things she could find. He extended his hand, which she grasped limply. "I'm Chief Wakefield." He indicated the guest chair opposite his desk. "Please take a seat."

She sat down as Wakefield eyed her casually yet critically. She was a brunette, average height with a slim build. Wakefield thought she was in her forties. Her eyes were red as if she'd been crying. He indicated a note pad on his desk as he began. "Why don't you tell me what happened?"

Wakefield jotted down notes as Gillian, in a voice that quavered occasionally, told him that Scott wasn't home when she returned to the house they shared late Wednesday night after the scholarship dinner. She hadn't thought much of that at the time; she figured he was out with some of his friends after their softball game, having a few drinks. But when he still wasn't home in the morning, she'd tried his cell phone several times. Each time it went directly to voicemail. She left two messages, but he hadn't called her back. That's when she called the police.

As he listened to her story, Wakefield had his doubts. A late night out, a couple of beers. It wouldn't be the first time a man met a fresh young face in a bar and hadn't made it home. He asked her for the names of his drinking companions and the bars they liked to frequent. He jotted down two names she could remember and a couple of local bars. But when she mentioned Scott's plan to test out his new fish finder and the fact that his boat and trailer were also missing, he pressed her for more details. "There's no sign of the boat or trailer?"

She shook her head. "That's what got me worried. The boat and trailer should've been back next to the garage, especially if he went out drinking. He would never drive around with the boat and trailer attached to the van – he'd drop it off at home first, then go out."

"Do you know where he planned to go to test the fish finder?"

She nodded. "He told me he was going to Wilson."

There were several ramps in Wilson. "Do you know where?"

Her voice cracked as she answered. "He usually goes to the state park, next to the harbor."

"Have you called anyone down there?"

"No. I called you first."

Wakefield jotted a final note. He looked across the desk at Gillian. "I think that's enough for a start. If you leave your contact information with Anne, we'll call you as soon as we find out anything." He stood and walked around the desk, offering her a hand up. "Don't worry. There's probably an innocent explanation. There usually is."

The bleak look on her face told him she thought otherwise. "I hope you're right. He's never done anything like this before."

"I'll call you as soon as I know anything." He watched as she walked slowly to Anne's desk, pulled out one of her business cards and wrote her cell number on the back. When she was out the door, Anne turned toward the chief. "What do you think?"

"Call the sheriff's department and see if they can send someone out to Wilson to check out the boat ramp."

"What time did he go out boating?" Anne asked. "There was a wild storm that blew through yesterday afternoon."

He shuffled through his notes. "She's not sure, but she thought it might've been sometime in the afternoon."

Twice-divorced Anne was skeptical. "How do we know he didn't find some overnight comfort away from his own home?"

"I was thinking the same thing. Which is why we need to check out the boat ramp first. I'm going to run down some of his friends, see if he went out with them last night. No calls until you hear back from the sheriff's department." He walked back into his office and closed the door behind him.

He spent the next hour on his computer and on the phone, finding out what he could about Scott Jamison. He searched the law enforcement databases first. There wasn't anything there – no arrests, not even a traffic ticket. But there was something familiar about his name; Wakefield was certain that he'd heard it before somewhere. Next he tried Google and found several references to local fishing tournaments, but nothing more. No indication of why he might be missing.

No luck with the names Gillian had supplied, either. He reached them both and their stories were identical: there had been no softball games the previous evening. They'd been cancelled after the late-afternoon storm left the fields unplayable. And there had been no plans to

65

meet Scott at the Bloody Bucket, the dive bar down by the river where they usually congregated after games. Neither of them had seen Scott in weeks.

Anne knocked once and then poked her head into his office. "The sheriff's office called back. They found Scott Jamison's van in Wilson, at the boat ramp in the state park."

He closed his laptop and stood, grabbing his hat from the coat rack. "Call them and tell them I'm on my way."

There were three cruisers in the lot thirty minutes later when Wakefield pulled in. Several deputies hovered around the battered dark green Ford van. All of them wore latex gloves.

Wakefield slipped on a pair of gloves as he exited his vehicle and approached the van. He nodded to Frank Militello, the ranking officer on the scene. "What do we have, Frank?"

"Pretty much what you see, Chief. The van's locked and there's no sign of the boat."

Wakefield leaned forward and peered through the driver's window. There was a cell phone and wallet neatly arranged on the front passenger seat. No sign of any keys. Not good, he thought.

"Who called it in?" Militello asked.

Wakefield stepped back from the van and turned toward the deputy. "The girlfriend. He didn't come home last night."

"Do you think she has another key to the van? We've tried all the usual hiding places and came up empty."

"She might," Wakefield said. "but I'm not sure I want to notify her just yet. No need to upset her any more than she already is, at least until we know a little more." He looked at the other two deputies, then back to Militello. "Any of your guys have a coat hanger?"

"You think we have probable cause?"

"Don't you? I'd say a man leaving his cell phone and his wallet in the car while he takes his boat out on Lake Ontario meets the threshold."

The van was neatly parked between the lines in the trailers-only section of the lot. The trailer behind it was empty, and there was an extension ladder attached to the rack on the roof of the van. There were several dents and rust spots on the van, indicating long-time use. Inside, they could see drop cloths, paint and brushes through the rear window of the van.

Militello turned and addressed his men. "Either of you have a coat hanger?"

The younger of the two flashed a grin. "In my trunk." He popped the trunk of his cruiser and returned to the van with a metal coat hanger in his hand. It was already bent into the proper shape to jimmy the lock.

"Can you use it?"

"Does a bear shit in the woods?" Careful not to lean against the van, the deputy slid the improvised tool down the gap between the door frame and window on the passenger's side until he found the latch. With a practiced twist, he lifted the hanger up and the lock popped open. In less than thirty seconds.

Wakefield looked at Militello and smiled. "Glad he's on our side."

Militello instructed the deputy. "Just the cell phone and the wallet. Don't touch anything else."

The deputy reached in and gingerly grasped the cell phone first and then the wallet and dropped them into evidence bags Militello was holding open. He sealed the bags and placed them in his vehicle.

"Shouldn't we check the cell phone now, see who he might've called?" the deputy asked.

Militello shook his head. "We'll do it back at the house. By the book."

"Have you called the Coast Guard?" Wakefield asked.

"Not yet," Militello replied, pointing across a small inlet toward the boatyard on the other side. "I'd like to talk to someone at the marina, see who was working yesterday. Maybe they saw something."

"I wouldn't wait too long," Wakefield advised. "Especially if he was out in that storm." He'd worked with Militello before and knew that his rise in the ranks of the sheriff's department had little to do with his ability as an officer. It was well known in the local law enforcement community that, several years earlier, Militello had responded to a daytime call of a possible rabid raccoon in the backyard of a Riverton home. Instead of calling the animal control officer in the town and trapping the raccoon, Militello had pulled out his service revolver and fired three shots from the hip, killing the animal while the family inside the house ten feet away, including two young children, had watched in horror. The next day a new nickname resonated in the halls of the sheriff's department: Rocky Raccoon.

Militello stared across the inlet, weighing Wakefield's words and their implications. "Maybe you're right." He turned back to the young deputy who'd jimmied the lock. "Go over to the marina, see if anyone saw anything unusual yesterday." As the deputy walked to his car, Militello pulled out his cell phone and punched in the number of the Coast Guard station in Delifin. In a clear, strong voice he identified himself to the dispatcher and continued. "I'd like to report a possible missing boater on Lake Ontario, off Wilson. Departed sometime yesterday from the Tuscarora State Park boat ramp in a sixteen-foot outboard, painted in camouflage colors. The subject's name is Scott Jamison, age 63, from Riverton, New York."

Once the Coast Guard became aware of a boater missing on the lake, the search operation began to move swiftly. Boats were dispatched immediately from the Delifin and Rochester Coast Guard stations and were joined by a vessel from the Niagara County Sheriff's Department. The Canadians responded with a boat from the Port Weller Coast Guard station and air support provided by a C-130 and a Griffon helicopter sent from the Joint Rescue Coordination Centre in Trenton, Ontario. Lake Ontario was a daunting area to cover, and aircraft were critical in any search-and-rescue mission.

As soon as the Sheriff's Department boat arrived, Militello brusquely joined the crew, brushing aside the protests of the officer in charge, pulling rank. As they departed the harbor in Wilson, Wakefield returned to his car and drove back to Riverton, chuckling to himself at Militello's grandstand play. If they found Scott Jamison, Frank Militello was going to be on the boat, prepared for interviews and photos, willing to take whatever credit he could for the success of the mission.

Let Militello search the lake. He was going to concentrate on Gillian, see if he could nail down Jamison's movements over the last few days. He called Anne from the car. "Is Gillian Hudecki still around?"

"No," Anne said. "She left for work right after you took off for Wilson."

"Call her, see when she can come back in."

"Did you find Jamison's van?"

"It was in the parking lot at the state park, near the boat ramp. No sign of the boat or Jamison."

"So he did go out on the lake?"

"It looks that way."

It was almost one by the time Wakefield returned to his office. There was a sandwich on his desk when he arrived. Anne poked her head in. "I figured you'd be hungry. It's a beef on weck."

"You're a lifesaver, Anne. Remind me to think about giving you a raise." He took a big bite. When he'd finished chewing he wiped his mouth with a napkin and looked at Anne. "Where are we with Gillian?"

"She's trying to re-arrange her schedule. I told her we're going to need to talk to her as soon as possible. She thinks she can make it here by three."

"Let me know when she gets here. Until then, no calls. And close the door."

He ran Jamison's name through all the local and federal legal databases and came up empty. Nothing. He Googled Scott Jamison and was overwhelmed by the number of responses. He tried to narrow the search using keywords to eliminate the other Scott Jamisons, but he still had several thousand hits. It was the kind of legwork he'd hand off to a junior officer in a heartbeat, but most of his officers were assigned to the Corelli trial. He sighed and began to systematically wade through the list, trying to find any clue that might shed some light on what had happened to Scott Jamison.

He'd eliminated several hundred entries but found nothing about the Scott Jamison he was interested in, the one from Riverton, when Anne buzzed his phone and told him Gillian Hudecki was back. "Send her in."

Gillian's eyes were red, as if she'd been crying. Wakefield indicated his guest chair and wordlessly nudged a box of tissues toward her as she sat down. "Thanks for coming back in."

"Did you find him?" Her voice was filled desperation, her tone pleading.

"Not yet. We did find his van, but there was no sign of Scott."

She sat upright with hope. "Where was the van?"

"In the parking lot of the state park in Wilson."

Gillian tried to fight off tears but failed. Her voice was barely audible when she finally responded. "So he's missing." A statement, not a question.

"Yes," Wakefield said gently. "But we have every resource at our disposal looking for him as we speak. If he's on the lake, we'll find him." He cleared his throat. "I'd like to ask you a few questions, get some background information, maybe tie down his movements on the day before he went missing. Would that be all right?"

Gillian nodded, reaching for a tissue. "Okay."

"Would you like anything before we get started? Coffee? Water?"

"Maybe some water."

"I'll get it for you," Wakefield said, rising to his feet. "I'll be right back."

He returned with the water, which she sipped gratefully. For the next two hours he probed her as gently as he could, cognizant of her precarious mental condition but at the same time determined to unearth anything that might resemble a clue as to Jamison's whereabouts. She told Wakefield that she and Scott had been together for ten years. He was self-employed as a commercial painter and had been as long as she'd known him. She told him about how Scott had just finished a big job at Village Pizza after last year's fire and had received his final check on Tuesday. She insisted that he was about as happy as she'd ever seen him when he'd proudly showed her the check. "We were going to celebrate Tuesday night, go out to dinner, but I got caught in the gridlock of that accident on the Grand Island Bridge and didn't get home until midnight."

As Wakefield jotted down notes, he watched Gillian's face closely. Everything she'd said and done up to this point seemed genuine to Wakefield. He believed her when she said she loved him, and the devastation she displayed when he told her Scott was missing felt real to Wakefield. She insisted there was nothing wrong with their relationship, that either of them were unhappy. When he asked about the possibility that Scott might have another girlfriend, prefacing the question with an apology, she actually smiled a little. "Absolutely not. His mistress is the outdoors. He spends all his free time hunting and fishing, or at the Rod and Gun Club. There's no time for another woman."

He filed that away to confirm later. Next she gave him a list of Scott's friends and acquaintances. He wrote down the names, verifying the spelling on a couple of them, before he shifted the focus of his questioning to her movements on Tuesday and Wednesday. She repeated again how she'd been delayed by the auto accident on Tuesday and how she had gone directly from work to the Saturn Club on Wednesday for the scholarship dinner and had returned home late.

"How late?" he asked. "Try to remember. It's important."

Her face was pinched as she tried to recall. "I walked in the door at quarter after eleven, brushed my teeth and went straight to bed."

"And there was no sign of him."

"No."

"Was that unusual?"

She shook her head. "It was Wednesday night. Sometimes he goes out with some of his buddies who play softball for beers and wings after the game. That's where I thought he was."

Wakefield glanced at his notes. "But you didn't know the games were rained out that night?"

"No. I was at the dinner in Buffalo until 10:30. When I went outside there were no puddles on the ground. It looked like it hadn't rained there."

He continued for ten more minutes, trying to draw something, anything, that might be helpful from the distraught woman. Finally, he looked up. "I think that's all for today. We'll call you if we hear anything."

"Should I go to work tomorrow?"

He nodded. "By all means. If we need anything else, we'll be in touch."

Gillian rose shakily to her feet and extended her hand. Wakefield grasped it and tried to reassure her. "We have a lot of people out looking for Scott. We're going to find him."

She looked at him uncertainly, her face flooded with doubt. "I hope you're right." She turned and walked out of the office.

*****

72

Kelly Porter looked up from washing glasses as she heard the door open. In the dim light of the bar's interior she could make out John Herrington as he approached. "I didn't think I'd see you today." She indicated the clock above the cash register. "You're late."

Herrington plopped himself down on a stool opposite Kelly. "I had a long night last night," he said, grinning lasciviously. "A really long night."

Kelly's face twisted in disgust. "I don't want to hear about it." In the next moment she contradicted herself. "With Rachel, I hope. Gin and tonic?"

"Please." He reached for the newspaper. "Of course it was Rachel. I'm a one-woman man these days."

"So you're not seeing the porn star anymore?" The previous summer Herrington had become peripherally involved with Jessica Callaway while helping his best friend Tom Martin out of a jam. He'd visited with Callaway on Captiva, Florida, in November and the two of them had continued a casual conversation via emails and text messages while he'd wintered in the Caribbean.

"Not since November."

It was 2:15, Thursday afternoon at the Delifin AC. The lunch crowd had departed; they were the only two in the place. Kelly finished washing the glasses and set them in a rack to dry before making Herrington's drink and sliding it across the bar. Herrington's attention was absorbed by the obituaries as Kelly withdrew a business card and placed it on the bar in front of him, next to his drink. "What's this?"

Kelly smiled. "The mystery man gave it to me today, unsolicited."

He examined the card slowly. "Parnell Gomez. What kind of name is that?" He turned the card over; there was no other information on the card. No phone number, no email, no occupation. He looked at Kelly expectantly. "So?"

She hesitated. Having him beg her to spill the beans on the mysterious stranger would be nice, but Herrington wasn't biting. After another long moment she finally responded. "He's a writer."

"He told you that?"

"Not exactly," she said. "He slipped the card to me today with the money for his bill. After he left I Googled his name. Seems he's written a couple of books."

"What kind of books?"

"Fiction. There are two novels of his listed at Amazon. I ordered them both."

He looked at the card again. "Parnell Gomez," he repeated. "Pretty unusual name. I think I would've remembered it if I'd read any of his books. Do you know the titles?"

Kelly nodded. "*Escape From Vagina Ridge* and *Highway 41 Revisited.* I've never heard of them, or him."

"*Escape From Vagina Ridge?*" Herrington smiled. "Sounds like my kind of book."

"What a stunner," she muttered, her response dripping with contempt.

No rebuttal from Herrington. Instead, he took a sip of his drink. "You'll have to let me read it when you're finished with it."

"Yeah, sure."

He finished with the front section of the paper, placing it on the bar and grabbing the second section. "Lots of activity on the water today."

"What do you mean?" she asked.

"I was up, having a cup of coffee this morning on deck, when all three Coast Guard boats screamed out of the station, headed for the lake. A little while later, the sheriff's boat sped by and headed for the lake as well. Something must be up."

"Did you try the marine band?" Herrington was a radio aficionado and kept track of both the police and marine channels regularly aboard *Soleil*, berthed in the river below between the Delifin Yacht Club and the Niagara-on-the-Lake Sailing Club on the opposite shore in Ontario.

"Nope. I figured if it was big, we'd hear about it. I was more interested in waking up." He thumbed through the paper quickly and tossed it back on the bar with disdain. "Nothing in here worth reading about except the trial. This paper gets thinner every year."

"I'll tell Glenn you said that the next time he comes in." Glenn Donaldson was a longtime columnist for the *Niagara Gazette* who lived in Delifin and occasionally frequented the bar. Herrington knew him by sight but was not friendly with him.

"He's one of the few guys still employed there. Most of what they print these days comes from Gannett or the wire services. If it wasn't for the obits and the comics, I wouldn't read it at all."

"Have you seen Tom lately?"

Herrington shook his head. "It's been awhile. Now that he's back to work and has a girlfriend, his time is at a premium."

"Me either," said Kelly. "It's probably been three months since I've seen him in the bar. I hope he's doing okay."

"He says he's been traveling a lot."

"Some things don't change." He drained his glass and placed a ten next to it on the bar before getting up.

"Leaving so soon?"

"I need a nap. Rachel wore me out last night. And this morning." He smiled expectantly, waiting for her to respond.

Kelly refused to bite. "Why don't you ever bring her here when she spends the night?"

"It's her upbringing. She thinks a bar is an undignified place for a woman to spend her time during the day." He smiled broadly. "But she said to say hi to you."

12

The list of Scott Jamison's friends that Gillian provided to Chief Wakefield was a short one. She'd explained to him, almost apologetically, that the two of them didn't socialize much. If Scott wasn't working on a job, she said, he was usually fishing or hunting, depending on the season. Other than an occasional get-together during the summer with some of his old softball buddies, his social life revolved around the Riverton Rod and Gun Club.

Wakefield began contacting names on the list as soon as his meeting with Gillian ended. His first call was to Caroline Cooke, who was tending bar at the Rod and Gun Club Tuesday night when Scott arrived for dinner and drinks. She picked up immediately when Wakefield called. "Yes?"

"Caroline Cooke?"

Suspicious. "Who's this?"

"Rod Wakefield, Chief of Police in Riverton. Do you have a few minutes to answer some questions?"

More suspicion. "About what?"

"Were you working at the bar at the Rod and Gun Club on Tuesday night?"

"Yes."

He could sense her terse answers were a defensive mechanism, meant to buy time while she tried to figure out why the chief of police would want to ask her some questions. He tried to allay her suspicions. "Do you remember seeing Scott Jamison at the club Tuesday evening?"

"I do. He came in for dinner and stayed for a few drinks at the bar afterwards. Why do you ask?"

"Scott's missing. I'm trying---"

She interrupted. "What do you mean, missing?"

"Apparently, he took his boat out on Lake Ontario sometime Wednesday and didn't return. We found his van near the boat ramp in Wilson, locked, with no sign of the boat or of Scott. I'm trying to retrace his steps the day before he went missing."

"Missing," she managed in stunned disbelief. "Are you sure?"

"It appears that way. Can you remember when he arrived at the club Tuesday night?"

It took a few moments for Caroline to respond. When she did, her tone was softer as she recalled the evening. "He called first, asked how late we were serving dinner. I told him eight o'clock. He said he was on his way over."

"Do you know what time he arrived?"

"I think it was about 7:30."

"Was he alone?"

"Yes. I saved him a seat at the bar 'cause we were kinda busy Tuesday. It was the first night of our spring trap league and the place was packed."

"Did he eat?"

"Beef on weck with some fries."

"Any drinks?"

"A few," she said. "One with dinner and several after."

"Was that unusual?"

"Not at all. He's one of our regulars and he knows how much he can drink before he has to drive home. He's very careful about drinking too much."

"Does he ever take a cab? Or does he usually drive himself?"

"He always drives himself. He likes to brag about knowing all about his body mass and blood alcohol levels."

"Would you say he was intoxicated Tuesday night?"

"No, I don't think so."

"How late did he stay?"

She thought for a moment, trying to recall. "We closed at ten, and he left just before last call. Maybe 9:45."

"By himself?"

"Yes."

"Is that unusual?"

"Leaving by himself? No. Sometimes he comes in with his girlfriend, but most of the time he comes in alone and leaves alone."

"So there was nothing out of the ordinary."

She shook her head. "I didn't say that."

Wakefield was interested. "What do you mean?"

"After dinner, he bought a round of drinks for the bar. Said he'd just finished a big job and that he was celebrating."

"Was that something he did a lot?"

"No," she said emphatically. "It's the first time I ever saw him do that and I've been working at the club for nine years. Cost him a couple hundred dollars because we were so busy. He didn't seem to mind, though. I think he kinda liked the way people came up to him, thanking him."

"Did he talk with anyone in particular that you can remember that night?"

She tried to recall. "We were really busy, especially after the trap shooting ended. I think he talked a little with Lenny Campbell. Charlie Jaeger, too."

"Do you have phone numbers for them?"

"Lenny lives in Delifin. He's in the book, one of the last guys I know who still has a landline. Charlie, I don't know. I think he lives someplace in Riverton. He's retired from the park police."

Wakefield jotted the names down at the other end. "How did he seem to you that night?"

"Pretty happy, I'd say. Whenever I stopped by he was telling one of his stories, smiling from ear to ear."

"Not depressed at all?"

"Not at all. He was having a good time."

Wakefield jotted down another note before responding. "Thanks, Ms. Cooke. You've been a big help."

"Call me Caroline. Are we done?"

"For now. I may have some follow up questions."

"Any time," she said in a somber voice. "I like Scotty. I can't believe he's missing. Not on the lake – it doesn't make any sense. He knows more about Lake Ontario than any other person I know. He's the last person I'd expect to be lost, especially there."

"Thanks again for your help, Caroline. I'll be in touch."

*****

Scott Jamison's disappearance received top billing in Friday morning's *Gazette*, displacing the Corelli trial, which had been the lead story since last Sunday. Details were sketchy because there was little to go on. The Sheriff's Department, who'd assumed the lead in the investigation, had agreed with Wakefield's suggestion that certain things, such as Jamison's cell phone being found in the car, be withheld from the public. Both agencies involved realized that the implications of that act, had it been deliberate, were ominous.

"Do you know this guy?" John Herrington was sitting at the bar at the Delifin AC, eating a bowl of potato soup while reading the account of Jamison's plight on the front page.

Kelly shook her head. "Nope. But he must've been what all the commotion was about yesterday at the Coast Guard station. It says they're searching for him, along with the Canadian Coast Guard."

Herrington shook his head. "That's a big lake to search. They're going to need all the help they can get." He finished the last of his soup and pushed the empty bowl across the bar for Kelly to take.

"They're using boats, planes and helicopters," Kelly observed.

"Yeah, but according to this he was missing for almost a day before anyone knew it. And that storm on Wednesday was nasty – if he was out in that, there's no telling where he might be now. Other than the bottom of the lake."

"Mr. Optimistic, as always."

"Come on. You don't think he's alive, do you?"

Kelly shrugged. "Who knows? Maybe he planned to disappear, start over somewhere with a clean slate."

"You watch too much television," Herrington said.

"Maybe yes, maybe no." She knew Herrington hated watching television. He was a radio man, a throwback to a different era. "John Corelli's probably happy. Anything to take the heat off him."

Herrington shifted his attention to the Corelli article. "He's still on the front page, just not the lead. Says here the IT guy at the school testified yesterday. I wonder how much longer the trial will last."

"I guess it depends on whether or not the girls will testify."

"That has to be a tough call for the district attorney. These are underage girls. Haven't they been through enough already?"

Kelly looked at him quizzically. Empathy and compassion were not trademarks of John Herrington's personality. "They say there are pictures and video. Maybe the girls won't have to testify. Maybe the prosecution has enough without them."

"Maybe. But the thing that's bugged me from the start is why did they do it? Corelli's bald and he must weigh close to three hundred. Why on earth would teenage girls want to sleep with a guy like him?"

"It's not about sex, it's about power. He's an authority figure, with tremendous influence over their future in the form of grades."

Herrington didn't see it that way. Never married, with no verified children, when it came to sex it was all about physical attraction and little else. Like many men, Herrington failed to grasp the differences between the genders when it came to the dynamics of power, as clueless as a blind man during a blackout. "So they sleep with the guy?"

Her reply was swift, her voice harsh. "Don't try to put this on the girls. They're the victims here. Somehow this asshole made them feel like they had to sleep with him, so they did."

Herrington held up his hands in mock defense. "Whoa. Hold on. I'm not blaming the girls."

Her voice retained an edge. "Sure sounds like it to me."

"That wasn't my intention." He suddenly felt the need to change the topic. He looked pointedly toward the opposite end of the bar, then back at Kelly. "Where's the writer today? Gomez."

She pointed to the clock above the cash register. "It's too early for him. Remember, you were waiting for me when I opened the doors this morning. It's not even noon yet."

"So you're expecting him." A statement rather than a question. "Are you going to tell him you know about his books?"

"I haven't thought about it," she replied after a moment.

"Bullshit. You probably stayed up late last night, thinking of questions to pepper him with."

She smiled beatifically "Wrong again, Sherlock. I was in bed by ten."

He continued. "Did you get his books yet?" His tone indicated he didn't believe her.

Men, she thought. "I just ordered them yesterday afternoon. When they arrive, I'll let you know. You could always try The Book Corner, you know. They might have some in stock if you're that interested."

"You mean buy my own copies? Why would I do that when I can borrow yours when you're finished with them?"

81

Despite having enough wealth to support himself comfortably for the rest of his life, Herrington was a notorious skinflint, the last to reach for the check under most circumstances. He made daily trips to the mainland from *Soleil* to read the newspaper at the AC instead of subscribing himself. Kelly wouldn't be surprised if the majority of his wardrobe came from thrift shops. "They should be here by Monday. Would you like to read one while I read the other?"

Herrington pondered the offer for a moment before replying. "Sure. Can I read the one about the vagina?"

"Why am I not surprised?"

13

By late Friday the search teams had covered more than 3700 square miles of the lake, aided by reinforcements that continued to arrive throughout the day. In addition to the crews working on Thursday, an Ocean Sentry aircraft was dispatched from the Coast Guard Air Station in Cape Cod to continue the search overnight, while a Canadian Hercules airplane and an MH-65 Dolphin helicopter from the Coast Guard Air Station in Detroit arrived Friday morning.

Because the clouds that had threatened rain all day Thursday had lifted by Friday morning, optimism among the members of the search and rescue mission was as high as could be expected, given the search was approaching the critical 48-hour milestone. The water temperature was in the low fifties, and if Jamison was in the water, they knew that hypothermia was his worst enemy. If they still hadn't found Jamison by nightfall, his prognosis would be grim.

When the search effort resumed Friday morning, Wakefield was busy tracking down leads. On Thursday evening he'd reached Lenny Campbell, who agreed to come in Friday morning to give a statement. There was a fresh pot of coffee in the break area when Anne buzzed him to tell him Campbell had arrived.

Wakefield stood and extended his hand as Campbell entered his office. "Thanks for coming in on such short notice, Mr. Campbell. Can I get you anything?"

"Coffee would be nice."

Lenny Campbell was in his fifties, balding, with a paunch whose origins lay in beer and fried foods. He walked with a slight limp as he seated himself in Wakefield's guest chair. Wakefield glanced at his notes briefly before returning his gaze to Campbell. "Do you mind if I call you Lenny?"

"Be my guest."

Wakefield's cop sense detected what he perceived to be wariness in Campbell's body language. "I'd like to talk to you about Tuesday night. According to Caroline Cooke, you were at the Riverton Rod and Gun Club that night. Is that correct?"

Campbell's eyes were neutral. "Yes."

"Can you recall what time you arrived?"

"About five thirty. It was the first night of the spring trap league."

"What did you do next?"

"We shot skeet till a little after seven, then went back to the bar."

"Did you see Scott Jamison at the bar?"

Campbell shook his head. "Not at first. He came in a little while after we'd finished shooting."

"Can you recall what time that was?"

"About 7:30, I guess. I was on my second drink."

Wakefield wrote in his notebook. "Did you talk with him?"

"Not right away. He was hungry, so he had some dinner first. Wolfed it down."

"At the bar?" Wakefield asked.

"Yeah. He likes to sit at the bar, especially when he's alone."

"He was alone on Tuesday?"

"Yeah."

"What happened after he finished his dinner?"

"He ordered a drink for himself, I think, before he ordered a round for the bar."

"Was that unusual?"

Campbell snorted. "You could say that. I've never seen him buy a round for the bar before. Usually he's tighter than the skin on a wiener."

"Was there anything else you noticed about him that night that was different?"

Campbell thought back, trying to remember. "Not really. He was the usual Scotty, except for when he bought the round."

"Did you talk with him at all that night?"

"For a few minutes. He told me he was going fishing in Dunkirk this weekend. He had a new fish finder that he was anxious to try out."

"Did he say anything to you about testing the fish finder first in Wilson?"

Campbell shook his head. "No. Not a word."

"What time did you leave the club?"

"About nine, I guess."

"And Scott was still there?"

He nodded. "Sitting at the bar."

"Have you been in contact with Scott since that night?"

He shook his head vigorously. "No."

Wakefield jotted down some final notes before he stood. "Thanks for coming in, Lenny. You've been a big help."

"That it?"

"You're free to go."

Campbell stood and shook hands with Wakefield briefly. Before turning to leave the room he looked back at Wakefield. "Have they found anything on the lake yet?"

"Not yet."

"That's strange. They should've found the boat by now, at least. It's impossible to sink those Starcraft boats unless you put a mortar through them."

When Lenny was gone Wakefield summoned Anne to his office and handed her his notes. "Type these up and add them to the file."

"Will do, Chief. Get anything good?"

85

"Nothing new. He was there, he talked with Jamison, he left before Jamison did. Pretty much the same as the bartender said."

Anne handed him a couple of pink telephone record slips. "Gillian Hudecki called twice. Once last night, once this morning. Wants to know where we are."

"How did she sound?"

"Desperate."

*****

At 12:15 Parnell Gomez walked through the side door of the Delifin AC and sat in his usual seat by the men's room door. Herrington noticed him first. "There's your boy," he whispered to Kelly across the bar. "Go make him comfortable."

She shot Herrington a withering glance before walking to the other end of the bar. "Mr. Gomez, I presume. The usual?"

He nodded. "Unsweetened ice tea with lemon,--"

"And a cheeseburger with two pickles, no fries." She finished the order for him.

Gomez smiled. "You remembered."

It was Kelly's turn to smile, a megawatt dazzler. "How could I forget?" She poured him a glass of tea and added a slice of lemon before placing it on a coaster in front of him. "I'll put your order in right away."

"Thanks."

The bar was filling up. Friday was usually the busiest day for lunch at the AC, especially when there was a hint of summer in the air. At the yacht club below, boats were being worked on industriously as the boating season loomed. Once the ice boom at the juncture of Lake Erie and the Niagara River is removed, it's a mad scramble to get pleasure boats ready for operation, and the marina staff was working from dawn to dusk in order to assuage the demand. The bright orange mooring balls had been in the river for two weeks, but Herrington's sloop was one of only three boats already berthed in the river. With the start of the season less than two weeks away, there was still plenty of work to be done.

86

"So," Herrington said when Kelly returned from the kitchen. "what did he say?"

She looked at Herrington with a practiced look of disdain. "He told me his lunch order."

"Nothing else?"

"He didn't ask about you, if that's what you're getting at."

Before Herrington could form his reply Kelly was off again, summoned by a waving hand holding an empty glass. She filled several orders with the efficiency of a seasoned pro, the smile never leaving her face until she returned to Herrington. "You want another drink?"

He placed his hand over the top of his glass. "That's it for me."

She grabbed his bill from next to the cash register and placed it next to his empty glass. He paid in cash and stood to leave. "Have a good weekend. Say hi to Patrick for me."

"Do you need change?" Kelly asked.

Herrington smiled and shook his head. "Keep it."

"Thanks."

He passed two of the local charter captains coming in the door as he was leaving, their day's work done, their thirst at its peak. He said hello but kept walking; he wanted to get back to his boat to listen to his marine band radio to find out the latest on the search for Scott Jamison. Most people would think that listening to Coast Guard chatter as they searched Lake Ontario for a missing boater was odd, if not aberrant. But to Herrington, a man who lived on a boat year round and understood the dangers inherent in the live-aboard lifestyle, it was intoxicating stuff, better than anything on television.

Peter Malecki, the owner of the Delifin Athletic Club as well as its lunchtime cook, came into the bar area with a plate containing a cheeseburger and two pickles, looking to Kelly inquiringly for guidance. She reacted swiftly, grabbing the plate and placing it before Gomez. "Would you like anything else?" she asked, eying his empty glass. "More tea?"

"Please," he said, pushing the glass across the bar. He looked around the crowded bar area. "Is it always this busy in here on Friday?"

"Not like this," Kelly replied as she refilled his glass. "It's the beginning of the Canadian holiday weekend, Victoria Day. It looks like we have a few of them in for lunch today."

"How can you tell?" Gomez asked, scanning the room.

"The accent. If you've lived around here long enough, you can't miss it."

"Ah," Gomez said, nodding. "Local knowledge. Very important."

Kelly gathered her courage. "Are you writing another book?"

He smiled. "You looked me up."

A bit of scarlet crept into her cheeks. "I did," she admitted sheepishly. "I Googled you after you gave me your business card."

"What did you find?"

"That you've written two books, *Escape From Vagina Ridge* and *Highway 41 Revisited*."

"Anything else?"

"Not really. You don't have a website like a lot of other authors. I couldn't even find out where you're from."

Gomez ignored her clumsy probe. "That's by design. I'm not big on fame. Fortune? No problem. I like money as much as the next guy. But I like my life the way it is. Too much publicity, too much attention, and the next thing you know you can't go out to dinner without some nitwit coming up to your table, interrupting your meal to ask for an autograph."

Kelly was confused. "I didn't realize you were famous."

"I'm not. And that's the way I like it." He took a bite of his cheeseburger.

Kelly got the hint. "I'll let you eat your lunch. If you need anything else, just holler."

"Thanks."

The lunch crowd didn't disperse until after three. Kelly was busy the entire time, filling food and drink orders at the bar as well as on the porch overlooking the river. While she worked, she pondered one thought wouldn't go away.

Why was Parnell Gomez in Delifin?

14

When she woke Friday morning it was the first time in ages that Liz Corelli wasn't filled with dread at the prospect of facing the day. She had played the part of the faithful, dutiful wife to perfection for months, expertly hiding the revulsion she felt for her husband as she appeared by his side in public and, earlier this week, in the front row of the courtroom, behind the defendant's table.

But today she'd been granted a reprieve. The Corelli dog, Rex, a mixed breed rescue dog the family had adopted from the SPCA several years earlier, had an appointment with the veterinarian this morning to try to determine why he'd become lethargic in the last week. It was surreal the way the dog's condition had begun to deteriorate at the precise moment John Corelli's trial began. It had to be a coincidence – didn't it?

She put on a pair of jeans and a sweatshirt and had a cup of coffee before she went to the drawn curtains in the living room and parted them just enough to check if there were any members of the press camped out front. In the week after the announcement that the oft-delayed trial would resume on Monday, crews from both CNN and Fox had parked on the street in front of the Corelli house, hoping to get a shot of the defendant's wife suitable for the evening segment on the case. Thus far she'd managed to dodge them; now that the trial had resumed they seemed to have lost interest.

Perfect, she thought. Now all she had to do was run the gauntlet at the courthouse, coming and going, for as long as the trial lasted. Despite the best efforts of seasoned pros trying to provoke a reaction from the aggrieved wife, Liz had kept her mouth shut so far, refusing to fall prey to words which, on more than one occasion, had her blood boiling.

She grabbed the leash from a hook by the back door. "Rex! Rexy! Come here, boy."

In a few moments the dog ambled in from wherever his latest napping spot was. Normally the sight of the leash meant they were going for a walk, which elicited much excitement from Rex. Not today. He eyed the leash with indifference and allowed Liz to slip it over his neck without any of his usual exuberance.

With Rex in the back seat, window cracked so the scents of their surroundings were available to him, Liz backed out of the garage and headed toward the vet's office. When they'd first adopted Rex they'd taken him to Dr. William Maddox, who operated his practice from a historically significant house in the Village of Riverton at the corner of Fourth and Main. But Maddox had retired several years earlier to spend more time with his daughter's family in Santa Fe and had sold the practice to Shannon Martin. Rather than search for a new vet, they decided to stay with Shannon.

It had been a wise move. Shannon Martin had taken Maddox's practice and brought it into the 21st century, updating equipment, expanding the client base and hiring more staff to accommodate the increase in business. Plus, there was something about doing business with a woman that Liz preferred. Bill Maddox had been pleasant and competent, but he had several old school values concerning a woman's place in the world that had rubbed Liz Corelli the wrong way.

Morning traffic was light in the village as she cruised down Main. Borelli's Bakery was busy as usual, with several tables of customers seated outside. The aroma of fresh pastries caught Rex's attention as they were stopped at the light at the corner of Main and Fourth. Liz turned away, hoping no one in the bakery would recognize her despite the fact that her driver's side window was tinted.

When the light changed she crossed Fourth and turned right into the parking area behind the office. Only two cars there, which raised her spirits. She wanted to be in and out as quickly as possible. She didn't know when she might have another day to herself, at least not until the trial ended, so she wanted to make the most of it.

Renee, a veterinary technician working behind the counter, greeted Liz and Rex with a big smile. "This must be Rex."

Rex's ears perked up when he heard his name, but he lost interest quickly when no food was proffered. He slumped down on the floor in front of the counter, a glum expression on his face. Renee continued after checking her notes. "He's been lethargic lately? No energy?"

"Yes," Liz replied. "It started about a week ago."

"Any changes to his diet recently?"

Liz shook her head. "We've been feeding him the same food for years."

"How about his appetite?"

Liz thought for a moment. "I guess he's been eating a little less, but not much. He seems to have lost enthusiasm. Almost as if he's depressed."

"We'll figure it out. Have a seat. Dr. Martin will be with you shortly." She smiled again and disappeared into the examination area momentarily before returning to the front desk. "It'll just be a few minutes.

True to her word, Shannon Martin appeared from the examination room in five minutes, a broad smile on her face. "You can bring him back now, Mrs. Corelli. Let's see what's bothering Rex."

Liz and Rex followed Dr. Martin through the door and into a gleaming, immaculate examination room. Renee followed. When Liz was seated, Renee and the doctor lifted Rex up onto the examination table and began to poke and probe. Rex was implacable, bored with the whole thing. All he wanted to do was to go back to sleep.

Liz watched closely as Dr. Martin checked Rex's teeth and ears. She'd heard from a friend of a friend that the doctor was divorced and that her ex-husband had lost his job the previous summer under murky circumstances. She wondered what indiscretion, what misdeed had precipitated their divorce. Surely it was something he had done, she thought. Wasn't it usually the man's fault in a marriage when things went wrong?

While she examined Rex, Shannon could sense Liz's eyes on her, watching her closely. She knew all about the Corelli's and their problems. Her son Devin, a senior at Riverton High School, had had Mr. Corelli for a teacher when he was in middle school. There had been no problems – Devin received an A in the class and there had been nothing out of the ordinary that she had been aware of while Devin was in Corelli's class. Last year her daughter Christine, an eighth-grader, had another teacher for the same class. When the news broke about the charges of statutory rape, Shannon had been thankful that Christine hadn't been exposed to whatever he'd been offering.

When the news of Corelli's trouble broke, Shannon felt strongly at first that Liz must've known something. How could a secret that horrific remain hidden from a man's wife? But the more she thought about it, the more she considered how her husband Tom had been caught completely unaware several years ago when she told him she wanted a divorce. He'd had no idea that his behavior had contributed to her desire to ultimately go her own way. It wasn't a stretch to imagine that Liz Corelli, a stay-at-home mom with two teenagers to care for, possessed the same level of ignorance as to what was going on in her spouse's life.

The examination lasted twenty minutes and concluded with Renee taking a sample of Rex's blood. Rex remained his laconic self throughout the procedure, barely managing to remain conscious as the vet and her assistant drew his blood sample. Dr. Martin handled the sample to Renee, who placed it in a refrigeration unit, and turned to Liz. "That's it for today. We'll run some tests on Rex's blood. It'll probably take a week to get the results. Until then, you might want to try some senior food for Rex. Anything different to see if his appetite improves. And see if you can collect a stool sample."

"That should be easy enough," Liz said. "They're all over the backyard."

A light went off in Shannon's head. "Is your yard fenced in?"

"No," Liz replied. "We usually put him on a leash when he's in the backyard. Is that okay?"

"Of course," Shannon said, removing her latex gloves and tossing them into a stainless steel trash container. "Renee will show you out."

After Liz and Rex had gone, Renee returned to the examination room to inform Shannon that her next patient, a tabby named Cleopatra, was waiting. Before she returned to the reception area Renee said, "Why did you ask if they had a fence in their backyard?"

"A hunch. Rex has been lethargic, out of sorts, but there's been no real change in his routine, unless she was hiding something from us." She paused before continuing. "This stays in this room. Agreed?" Renee nodded. Shannon went on. "Right now the Corelli's are Riverton's least loved family. I think that's pretty obvious. It wouldn't be too much of a stretch to think that someone might want to poison their dog."

93

"Poison," Renee echoed, nodding her head slowly in agreement. "That could be it."

"The blood sample should tell us."

*****

After paying his lunch bill, Parnell Gomez nodded to Kelly as he walked out the door. The sun was trying to peek through the cloud cover as he walked north along the sidewalk toward his rented home on Stonewall Street. Instead of turning right to go home, however, he continued north until he was in Fort Ontario State Park.

He veered off the pavement and headed toward the edge of the bluff overlooking the river. He sat in a bench and gazed across the river to Canada. He'd visited Toronto once with his parents when he was little, staying in a shabby motel on Lakeshore Boulevard while the family attended the Canadian National Exhibition. What he remembered most about the trip was that the motel had no pool, despite his father insisting that it did in the car on the way there. His father's lie had spoiled the entire trip for Parnell, who'd been excited at the chance to go swimming in an exotic foreign land. Not even the allure of cotton candy, carnival rides and greasy French fries could overcome his disappointment. Because his father had lied about the pool, Parnell began to question everything he said from that moment on. It was the beginning of the end of the charade that had dominated the daily existence of the Gomez family. Trust which had once been unquestioned was now gone.

He'd wanted to go to Canada again on this trip once he determined how close he would be to the border, but in the confusion of packing for an extended stay in Delifin, he had somehow forgotten to pack his passport. He hadn't realized at the time that, since 9/11, Canada Customs required a passport for any visitor entering the country. So all he could do was stare wistfully across the river at Niagara-on-the-Lake, the gorgeous village opposite Delifin along the Canadian shore that he'd read about online while planning his trip. Next time, he thought.

He watched the activity around the waterfront for twenty minutes before he rose to depart. His usual pattern since arriving in Delifin had been to work in the morning, take a break for lunch at the Delifin AC, return to his rented house for a nap, then work again until he was ready for bed. Pretty boring stuff, but effective as far as the work went.

94

The book was beginning to take shape, the logical next incarnation after the meticulous outline he'd spent the last year developing. As he exited the park and turned toward home, he smiled, recalling his encounter with Kelly at lunch today. She knew who he was now, had already looked him up on the Internet. It wouldn't be long before the word spread about the mysterious stranger in town who was writing a book – there's no better source for generating gossip than a small-town bartender.

15

Several of Scott's friends from the club, using their own boats, joined the search effort Friday morning. Despite the gentle insistence of officials from both the Coast Guard and the Sheriff's Department that their presence on the search grid would be a hindrance rather than a help, they declined to take that advice. Instead, their position was summed up succinctly by one of Scott's fishing buddies from the club, Brad Thompson: "We're fuckin' goin'."

A group of Scott's friends had gathered spontaneously at the club the night before after finding out that one of theirs was missing at sea. In the discussion that followed, several controversial subjects were broached, including the one everyone remembered clearly – Scott's unprecedented generosity in buying the bar a round of drinks on the night before he disappeared on a lake he knew better than most people know their own homes.

Most of the courage displayed that night in broaching delicate subjects could be directly linked to another unusual move, the decision of management of the Riverton Rod and Gun Club to provide an open bar for the group's discussion. It was their contribution to the cause, for one of their own, and there was little argument that the liquor had loosened some tongues.

One of the loosest belonged to Charlie Jaeger. The retired police officer, still trim at 70, with white hair and exotic grey eyes that in the right light made him seem more ghostlike than human, had been able to get through to Frank Militello earlier in the day. He was animated as he related the conversation to the group gathered at the bar. "They've found zip. Nothing. Not even the heat imaging equipment has turned up anything like a body. It's like he vanished off the face of the earth."

"They let Rocky Raccoon join the search party? They *must* be desperate." The sarcastic voice from the edge of the crowd belonged to Robbie Burnett, a union ironworker and frequent guest at Jamison's hunting cabin in the Southern Tier who'd been a year behind Scott at Riverton High. "I'd say they need our help."

Six of them showed up at the boat ramp in Wilson at dawn Friday morning. Because Charlie Jaeger was a retired cop and his boat was equipped with a marine radio, no one objected when he took charge of the operation. When all of them had arrived, he addressed the group. "Stay within sight of one another. I checked the recent current patterns. They indicate that, if he's still out there, he's probably drifted toward Rochester. We'll go out three miles, then rotate to the east. If you don't have a radio on your boat, stay close to someone who does. Any questions?" Heads shaking. "Then let's go."

Jaeger's cop instincts told him that their mission was futile, that Jamison had been missing for too long for there to be a happy ending to their expedition, but after last night's emotional meeting, he knew they had to do something to try to locate their friend, even if the odds weren't good. None of the guys who showed up this morning trailering their boats wanted to sit this one out. For their own peace of mind, they needed to know that they had tried, that they had done something to help find their friend.

They stayed on the lake until dark, cruising slowly eastward in a loose pattern, but other than a couple of empty plastic water bottles, they saw nothing that might have been associated with Scott Jamison or his boat. Finally, at 9:00, Jaeger signaled the rest of the group that they were going to call it a night. The dark waters were difficult to search during the day – at night they were impossible.

When they were back on shore, boats out of the water, Jaeger suggested they get something to eat at the Sunset Grille before heading home. One by one the others shook their heads; they were tired. It had been an exhausting, disappointing day, and their communal bond had eroded as the day passed with no encouraging results. All they wanted to do now was go home and go to bed.

As he watched taillights disappear in the gathering darkness as members of the search party headed for home, Jaeger checked his marine band radio one last time to see if the Coast Guard had found anything. They hadn't. They had suspended their search for the night as well. As he reluctantly got into his pickup to drive back to Riverton, he wondered how much longer the Coasties would continue to search. He knew discussions to suspend the search were probably underway already, the debate lively. The forecast for Saturday was for more wind and rain, less than ideal conditions for finding a needle in an aquatic haystack. If they *did* continue the search through Saturday, it would almost certainly be the last day.

*****

After Lenny Campbell departed, Rod Wakefield spent the rest of Friday trying to run down known associates of Scott Jamison. Gillian had given him a list of Scott's closest friends, and Caroline Cooke had provided a separate list of club members present Tuesday evening when Scott had surprised the crowd with his largesse. Wakefield cross-referenced the two lists, creating a third, more focused group. Wakefield decided to start with the names on the third list and expand the questioning from there.

He ran into problems immediately. He discovered that the five names on his focused list were all part of an impromptu search party that had been organized the night before at the club when he managed to reach Charlie Jaeger late that afternoon. Jaeger told him that he and the other men on Wakefield's list were searching for Jamison on the lake and would be unavailable until tomorrow at the earliest. He promised to call Wakefield back as soon as he could and said he would pass on his request for interviews to the other four once they were back on shore.

He picked up a picture of Scott Jamison from the file that Gillian had provided on her last visit. It was a head shot, and in it he looked defiant, unsmiling. It was exactly the sort of photo taken at the time of an arrest, but Jamison had no record – he'd checked all the local, state and federal databases. Although he was certain he'd never met Jamison, there was something familiar about him, something lurking just beyond the reach of his memory.

*****

After he left the Riverton municipal building, Lenny went to Spot Market to pick up a few things for his mother. She'd turned ninety in March and rarely drove any more, although she'd managed to retain her driver's license. Lenny did most of her grocery shopping for her.

He noticed more Ontario plates in the market lot than usual as he searched for a place to park. He wondered why until he remembered it was the start of the Canadian holiday weekend. Despite the fact the Canadian dollar currently was worth considerably less than its American counterpart, that hadn't stopped the steady stream of cars coming across the bridge to buy gas at one of the gas stations on the reservation. Even with the unfavorable exchange rate, gas on the rez was cheaper than it was in Ontario, and it wasn't unusual to see extra red gas containers lined up next to cars, waiting to be filled, before the visitors returned home.

As he wandered through the produce aisle, he wondered how the search party was going. Charlie Jaeger had called him from the club late last night, wondering if his boat was in the water yet. Did he want to join the search party? Lenny was relieved that he didn't have to lie to Charlie as he declined, telling him the *Scottish Rogue* wasn't due to launch until his brother Red arrived from Colorado next week. Charlie sounded drunk on the phone, and it wasn't a stretch to think the other members of the search party were similarly intoxicated and would be hung over at dawn. Besides, what could those guys do that the Coast Guard wasn't already doing, with much more sophisticated equipment?

He crossed items off the list as he picked them up: tomatoes, garlic, pasta, lettuce, green peppers, onions, cucumbers, bottled water, tea, chocolate chip cookies. He counted the items in his basket and headed for one of the express lines, where he stood behind a gray-haired woman with scoliosis who had a full cart despite the sign above the cash register reserving the line for shoppers with twenty items or less. He fumed but said nothing while he waited. He expected deficient math skills and indifferent attitudes toward authority from younger shoppers, not from someone old enough to be his parent.

Rather than take the parkway, his usual route home from Spot Market, he opted for River Road. As he drove by the red brick municipal building he wondered if the search party would find anything. Wakefield had mentioned the Coast Guard had been utilizing aircraft equipped with heat imaging technology but had turned up nothing so far. Not for the first time since he'd been reported missing, Lenny wondered if Scott was on the lake at all. The last reported sighting of his sixteen-foot Starcraft had been at 3:30 Wednesday afternoon, forty-five minutes before an unusually strong thunderstorm had swept through the area, plenty of time for him to have come ashore somewhere. What if it hadn't been an accident at all, but instead a plot for Scott to disappear? Was buying a round for everyone at the club Tuesday night Scott's way of saying goodbye?

As he drove past the stately homes on River Road, heading toward Delifin, his phone chirped. He looked at the phone; it was the call he'd been expecting. "What's up?"

"How did your meeting with Wakefield go?"

"Pretty well, I think. He mostly wanted to know about Tuesday night."

99

"What did you tell him?"

"Just what we discussed: that I saw him at the club that night after I finished shooting."

"Nothing else?"

"Nothing else. That seemed to be enough for him."

"What if he wants to look at my phone?"

Lenny's tone was reassuring. "He won't. You have an airtight alibi – you were at work Wednesday. He's probably already checked it out. There's no need for him to want to look at your phone."

"You know that's not true."

"You deleted the texts, right?"

"Yes."

"Then relax. You have nothing to worry about."

"Are you kidding? I watch the cop shows. They have ways of finding stuff on your phone after it's been deleted."

"I told you to get a burner, but you wouldn't listen."

"I know, I know. I should've listened to you."

"Don't worry about that now. You're going to be okay."

"Have you told your brother yet?"

Lenny hesitated before replying. "Not yet. I'll tell him when the time is right. Maybe when he's in town next week." He paused a moment before continuing. "I've got to go. I'm almost at my mother's house."

"Will you call me later?"

"I'll call you tonight when I get home."

"Don't forget."

16

It was the nature of a cop's wife to expect the phone to ring at all hours and Sally Wakefield was no exception. So when the phone rang on Friday at dinner time she sensed whatever news she might receive from her husband on the other end would probably not be uplifting. "You're going to be late," she offered.

Rod sounded tired. "You know me well. I hope you didn't go to any trouble with dinner."

"Not really. I had a feeling you might be working late tonight, so I made a tuna casserole. The microwave will revive it whenever you make it home."

"I shouldn't be too much longer," Rod said. "I'm just wrapping up some phone calls on the Jamison case."

"Any news?"

"Nothing yet. It's not looking too good. I talked to Militello a half hour ago. He thinks the Sheriff's Department will pull the plug this weekend if nothing is found by Sunday."

"How about the Coast Guard?" she asked.

"The same, I think. Providing air support is pretty expensive, and the Canadian guys will have their hands full on the holiday weekend."

"That poor man. What a horrible way to die, all alone. How awful for his family."

Rod knew better than to try to sugarcoat police business when speaking with his wife. Missing person cases were rarely solved to anyone's satisfaction; she was aware that after two days, the chances of finding Scott Jamison alive in fifty-degree water were close to nonexistent. "The best we can hope for now is some closure for his mother, his girlfriend and his friends."

She could relate to the emotions Jamison's family was going through, the uncertainty. It was a place she'd been several times as the wife of a cop. "Try not to be too late."

"I'll do my best."

After she hung up she turned on the television and watched the local news. Veteran District Attorney Charles Moreland, cognizant that testimony on a Friday leaves a lasting impression over the weekend, brought out one of his big guns today, adolescent psychologist Tamara Russell. The clip showed Dr. Russell testifying that the victims of John Corelli were permanently damaged goods, robbed of their childhood by the uncontrollable urges of a vicious sexual predator. Using a PowerPoint presentation filled with compelling statistics, Dr. Russell explained in language the transfixed jury could understand how traumatic the experience would continue to be for the two victims as they grew into adulthood, of how their sense of trust and self would never be whole again.

Sally knew John Corelli peripherally through Rod, who as police chief had to deal with Corelli in his former role as town councilman from time to time. They had attended several political functions together over the years but were not close. After one such event four years ago, the dedication of a new recreational complex in Riverton, Sally had confided to Rod that she felt sorry for his wife Liz, a woman who in Sally's mind had simply fallen in love with the wrong man, an all-too-common affliction in some women. If he was as guilty as the evidence indicated, she hoped that justice would be swift and unerring. Not for Liz Corelli, whose world was as decimated as those of the victims and could likely never be salvaged, but for Rod. He'd been a different person since he'd made the initial arrest last June, on edge and unpredictably irritable instead of his usual calm and easy going self. She wanted the old Rod Wakefield back.

When the news ended she watched the weekend weather forecast before she turned off the television, dismayed by the offerings. What was it that Bruce Springsteen wrote years ago? Fifty-seven channels and nothing on, she thought as she went into the kitchen and started to wash the dinner dishes.

*****

By the time Robbie Burnett arrived at his apartment in Riverton Friday night, he was bone tired. They'd been on the water searching for Scott Jamison until it was too dark to see anymore. On the way home, his fishing boat on a trailer behind his pickup, he resisted the urge to stop at the club for a nightcap. It was Friday and he knew the bar would be open

102

late, but he wasn't in the mood to discuss the lack of results produced by their efforts on the lake today. All he wanted was some sleep.

He pulled into the recently paved parking lot of the six-unit apartment building on Tuscarora Street and backed the trailer onto the lawn before unhitching it from his truck. He lived in the unit on the end, closest to the river on the ground floor, and his landlord, Warren Bancroft, generously allowed him to park his trailer on the grass. The rear of the property was adjacent to GorgePark, the riverside park dedicated to the performing arts that had been built on the pile of rubble excavated during the construction of the hydroelectric generating station less than a mile upstream.

Burnett, a lifelong bachelor, lived alone in the small two-bedroom apartment, which resembled a college dorm room, with clothes scattered haphazardly throughout on chairs and various areas of the floor. He let himself in the back door and stepped around his collection of work boots and sneakers and headed straight for the kitchen and the refrigerator. He grabbed a beer, popped the cap and sank into his most comfortable chair in his tiny living room before draining half the bottle on his first swallow.

He hadn't bothered to check his phone while they'd been on the lake – he'd been too busy working the grid that Charlie Jaeger set up. He fished it out of his pocket and was surprised to see he had two messages from the same unknown number, one just before noon and one just past 6:00.

He listened to the messages. They were from Rod Wakefield, who identified himself as Riverton's Chief of Police, asking if Burnett could call back and set up a meeting at the municipal building to discuss Scott Jamison's disappearance. Probably wanted to ask him about Tuesday night at the club, he thought. About how Scott had bought the bar a round. Charlie had told him earlier that evening as they removed their boats from the lake that Wakefield had left him a message, wanting to talk about Scott Jamison. "I wouldn't be surprised if he called all of us," Charlie declared in the parking lot before the group headed their separate ways. "We were the last people to see him alive, except for Gillian."

Burnett was especially troubled by Scott's behavior Tuesday night. He'd known Scott Jamison since they were students at Riverton High School. They'd bonded over their mutual love of baseball. A year behind Scott, Burnett had made the varsity as a junior and won the starting position at second base during pre-season practices that spring. Scott was the team's star, a fireballing right-hander who'd pitched two no-hitters the year before as a junior and three more as a senior, leading Riverton to an undefeated season and the sectional title in their classification.

With a fastball measured by a scout with a radar gun that topped off at 90 mph, Jamison had been heavily recruited, finally deciding to accept a full ride to the University of South Carolina after rejecting offers from Southern Cal and Texas. But the week before he was to leave for Columbia and freshman orientation, he called the coach and told him he'd changed his mind. He wouldn't be attending South Carolina at all. Instead, he passed on college altogether, opting instead to stay at home in Riverton.

For several years he worked menial jobs in the area before convincing one of the local banks to loan him money to start a commercial painting business. Most people who didn't know Scott well were stunned by his decision to forego a full college scholarship and the chance to make it to the major leagues. Burnett, however, was not surprised at all. He knew Scott's true love was the outdoors: hunting and fishing. He'd been an average student at best, uninterested in academic achievement. Although he loved baseball, he loved the natural world more.

Which made his disappearance so troubling. Two things stood out to Burnett: the uncharacteristic generosity in buying everyone in the bar a drink Tuesday evening, something which his friends all agreed had never happened before, and the fact that he would allow himself to be caught unawares by a storm on the lake. He was simply too miserly with his money to buy the bar a round and he was too knowledgeable a waterman to be surprised by any change in the weather while on his boat.

When he'd first heard that Scott was missing on Thursday, he immediately thought back to Tuesday night. Had he been saying goodbye to his friends at the club that night when he bought them all a drink? And when he found out from Charlie that the sheriff's department had discovered Scott's cell phone and wallet left behind in his van in plain sight on the passenger's front seat, he tried to think back to Tuesday evening to see if he could recall something to buttress his growing suspicion that Scott may have decided to check out for good.

But it didn't make sense. Scott was crazy about Gillian. In the ten years they'd been together he'd never seen his friend happier. Like Burnett, Scott had been single by choice until he met Gillian Hudecki, who'd changed his world dramatically. Although they hadn't married, they were as tight as any married couple he knew. Scott often joked about it. "Why get married and ruin everything? Look at the marriages of our friends." As far as Burnett knew, Scott hadn't strayed since they'd been together. He hadn't even *looked* at another woman with intent. Which made suicide, if that's what they were looking at here, too baffling to comprehend.

As hard as it was to accept that his friend had been that troubled and no one had noticed, he was even more mystified by the other obvious conclusion: that Scott had been unable to make it back to shore after the storm rolled in. No one knew Lake Ontario better than Scott Jamison – he'd been fishing there for over fifty years. The Scott Jamison he knew would never have allowed himself to be overcome by a storm on his home turf.

He'd echoed these sentiments to Charlie Jaeger in the parking lot, who'd been thinking the same thing. "The only way Scott wouldn't be able to get back to shore would be if something had happened to him on the water, a stroke or maybe a heart attack."

What that didn't explain, thought Burnett as he finished his beer and grabbed another, was why he'd left his cell phone behind. He could understand the wallet's presence in the truck – with a full tank of gas, he'd have no need for cash on the water, especially if it was just a short run to check out the calibration of his fish finder. He'd done that himself many times. But he knew Jamison's sixteen-foot Starcraft had not been equipped with a marine radio. Leaving his cell phone behind deliberately, as it appears he did, made no sense at all. Unless he hadn't planned to return to shore all along.

17

It began to rain several hours before dawn on Saturday. By first light it was a steady downpour, with a strong wind gusting to twenty knots from the north producing whitecaps on the lake surface. The Niagara County Sheriff's Department was the first to pull the plug on the search for Scott Jamison when Frank Militello noted the monochromatic battleship gray horizon that made the surface of the lake indistinguishable from the overcast sky and the pounding rain. You can't find what you can't see.

The Canadian Coast Guard was next. They informed the command at the Delifin Coast Guard station that they would not be sending any aircraft today because of limited visibility. An air search rescue mission was costly under ideal conditions. Since it was a holiday weekend in Ontario, they felt it was prudent to keep their aircraft on the ground until the weather eased.

Militello made a courtesy call to the Riverton Police Department, informing the weekend dispatcher that Niagara County had suspended their search operation "until further notice." Which in police jargon meant forever. The dispatcher waited until 8:30 before phoning Rod Wakefield at home to pass on the news.

The chief wasn't surprised. He listened without comment as the weekend dispatcher, a summer intern from the Niagara University Criminal Justice program, told him that the search had been suspended. When the young man had finished, Wakefield spoke. "Any call backs on the Jamison case?"

"Not yet."

Wakefield thanked him before hanging up and returning to this morning's soggy *Niagara Gazette*. The front page lead had shifted again to the Corelli trial and yesterday's testimony from prosecution witness Dr. Tamara Russell.

Sally came out of the bathroom with slightly damp hands. "Who was that on the phone?"

Rod looked up from the paper. "The station. They've suspended the search for Jamison." He gestured outside. "The rain made it an easy call."

"Completely?"

"Militello called this morning and told Kevin that the county and the Canadians were out. I haven't heard from the Coast Guard in Delifin yet, but I imagine they're thinking the same thing."

She poured herself a cup of coffee and joined him at the table. "What about you?"

He knew where she was headed but played dumb anyway. "Me? What about me?"

She held his gaze. "Are you going to keep working on the case or shift back to the trial?"

"I think Randy has a handle on the courthouse. Seems like a waste of time to have the chief of police directing traffic in the town hall parking lot. So yeah, I'll stick with the Jamison case a little longer, interview a few more witnesses. I think there's more to this than we know."

She placed her hand over his and gave it a gentle squeeze of affection. "If anyone can get to the bottom of things, it's you."

He smiled. "Thanks for the vote of confidence."

Her eyes danced. "It's part of the marriage contract, isn't it?" She took a sip of her coffee. "The search isn't the only thing affected by the weather. So much for going to the nursery today."

Rod nodded. "I guess the backyard garden will have to wait another week. Too soggy to plant anything today."

"What about some breakfast instead?" she asked.

"What do you have in mind?"

"How about some oatmeal and half a grapefruit?"

"Sounds good to me." He went back to reading about the Corelli trial as Sally got up and retrieved the dried oats from the pantry, measured them and some water according to instructions on the box and heated it in a pan on the stove. While the oatmeal cooked she sliced a grapefruit and placed each half in a small bowl and placed them on the table. As she returned to the stove to stir the mixture, her face lit up. "Why don't we visit your uncle today instead of working in the garden? It's perfect weather for a visit. Plus, we haven't seen him for almost a month."

Rod was silent for a moment. As soon as he saw the rain when he woke up he knew the nursery trip would be doubtful. Instead, he thought he might go into the office and make a few calls. Militello hadn't said anything, but Rod was confident that the volunteer search team from the rod and gun club probably wouldn't be searching today. He wouldn't have a better time to talk to them - the more time that passed, the quicker memories faded. If he'd been on duty today, that's what he'd be doing. But Sally was right – they were overdue for a visit.

Cal Roberts was approaching his 80th birthday in July. For the last three years he'd been a resident at Scherber Manor, an assisted living facility located in the north end of Niagara Falls near the new train station. Rod's late mother had been Cal's baby sister, his only sibling, and when Maureen Roberts Wakefield contracted leukemia and died four years earlier, her brother's decline was precipitous. It was as if he'd given up and resigned himself to the fact that he wouldn't be far behind her. And when he fell and shattered his hip in his studio apartment six months after his sister's funeral, the search began for a residence where he would receive affordable professional care.

Cal had been a wild child, with a penchant for fast cars and reckless behavior as a youth. When it appeared that the flight path of his life might shift toward an extended stay in Attica, a serendipitous local judge altered its course dramatically. When Cal was arrested and convicted of car theft at twenty, Judge Angelo Montero gave the youthful Roberts an unprecedented choice at sentencing: a year in the Niagara County jail or immediate enrollment in the county police academy.

He opted for the cops and found his calling. Like many wayward youths before him, he discovered that his attraction to a life outside the law was perfectly suited to a career in law enforcement. Throughout history, scores of potential criminals in areas across the country had become police officers, since the skill set necessary to succeed at each was remarkably similar. Cal was a model student at the academy and had been hired as a patrol officer in the Riverton Police Department when he graduated. By the time he'd retired he'd risen to the rank of Chief of Police in Riverton and had hired Rod after he'd been discharged from the Marines, grooming him to become his successor.

Rod owed a lot to his Uncle Cal, which is why he discarded the idea of going to the office on his day off and smiled at his wife across the kitchen. "You're right, it's been awhile. What time are visiting hours?"

Sally looked at the clock on the stove. "By the time we eat, shower and dress, it'll be close to lunch time."

It was 11:15 when Rod backed out of the driveway and headed up the face of the Niagara Escarpment toward Niagara Falls. As they drove through the Deveaux section of the city he admired the stately mansions that indicated a more prosperous time for the city. At the turn of the 20th century Niagara Falls had been a boomtown, bursting with possibilities for the future because of electricity produced at the Schoellkopf Generating Station and the lure of one of the most famous natural attractions in the world. Families of wealth, many of them associated with the factories that soon sprung up and dominated the shore along the upper Niagara River above the falls, had settled in the area because of the abundant supply of electricity provided by the local hydroelectric station.

But times had changed. Once past the campus of the now-abandoned Deveaux School, the landscape was markedly different. There were many theories as to why Niagara Falls, which as late as the 1950s had been a bustling international tourist destination, had fallen on hard times. Most blamed the city's disastrous attempt at urban renewal which began in 1963 and completely reshaped the South End of the city by the Rainbow Bridge. What had once been a thriving and vibrant commercial district was dismantled and reconfigured, and the city had never been the same since.

The signs of blight were everywhere as Rod drove by the new train station on his way to see his uncle. It pained him to see what Niagara Falls had become during the course of his lifetime; the only times he ventured into Niagara Falls these days usually involved a visit to his uncle. Sometimes he drove to The Book Corner, a three-story independent book store on Main Street which had managed to hang on despite the decay all around it. But mostly he stayed in Riverton.

He pulled into the visitors' lot at Scherber Manor and dropped Sally off at the door before he parked as close to the building as he could. The lot was full – a rainy day brought out a robust slate of visitors.

They took the elevator to the seventh floor, where they exited. In front of them was the smiling receptionist, a pleasant woman in her thirties whose ebullient personality had not yet succumbed to the depressing nature of the facility. "May I help you?"

"We're here to see Calvin Roberts," Sally said.

The woman, whose nametag identified her as Tammy, scanned the directory to determine if Cal was involved in any activities or medical procedures. She looked up, beaming. "He's in his room, 720." She handed each of them a visitors' badge, which they clipped to their clothing. "Go on in."

They walked down a narrow hallway to his room. His door was closed. Rod knocked tentatively on the door, not wanting to awaken him if he was asleep. Cal's voice boomed. "Who is it?"

"Rod and Sally, Cal. May we come in?"

"Suit yourself."

Rod swung the door open and ushered Sally inside. The room was small, with a single window overlooking the parking lot below. He could've had a room on the other side of the hallway, overlooking the Niagara River and the international bridge, but the rent was twice as much on that side of the building. Cal hadn't seemed to care about the view or much of anything else when he moved in three years ago, so they'd opted for the more economical, less aesthetic choice.

Cal was in his wheelchair, next to his bed. The broken hip that had precipitated his move to the manor had never fully healed, so if he wasn't in his bed or getting physical therapy, he was in the wheelchair. The room was dark, the curtains drawn. Sally stepped carefully by Cal and opened the curtains. "It's like a cave in here, Cal."

"It's the way I like it," he said gruffly. He shifted slightly to look out the window and snorted. "No wonder you're here. Nothing better to do on a rainy day."

"Oh, Cal," Sally said gently. "It's not like that at all."

110

Sarcasm oozed from his reply. "Really? Bullshit."

Despite his crumbling skeletal system, Cal Roberts' mind was still sharp. Not for the first time, Rod wondered what life must be like for someone who remains totally lucid and engaged in the world around him, yet can't stand on his own two feet for more than a moment without assistance. Cal was still interested in police work and grilled Rod during every visit about any new cases. Lately he'd been following the Corelli case closely.

There was a single chair which Rod offered to Sally. He sat on the edge of the bed next to his uncle and reached down playfully to pinch his ample midsection. "Looks like they're feeding you pretty good."

Cal made a face. "You're shitting me, right? Most of the slop here'll kill you. But if you can't walk it off, the pounds just keep piling on."

"What's for lunch today?" Sally asked.

"Tuna fish sandwich and tomato soup. It's the same fucking lunch every day. You're welcome to it if you're hungry."

Sally shook her head. Cal looked at Rod, whose face was impassive. "So what's new? How's the Corelli case coming along?"

"Did you watch the news last night?" There was a small flat screen television perched on top of his bureau that Rod and Sally had purchased for his last birthday.

"Yeah. Looks like that shrink put another nail in his coffin yesterday. What a piece of shit that Corelli is. A fucking teacher. I can't wait for him to take his first shower in the joint. His asshole will be the size of the Lincoln Tunnel inside a month."

Sally's face reddened, but she didn't say anything. Rod smiled to himself. Same old Cal. "Did you hear about the missing person case?"

Suddenly Cal was all ears, leaning forward. "No. What happened?"

"Missing boater on Lake Ontario, disappeared Wednesday afternoon when a storm blew in. The Coasties and the county LEOs have been searching for him since Thursday morning. No trace so far."

"Anyone I know?" Cal asked.

"I don't think so," Rod replied. "Scott Jamison, from Riverton. A commercial painter. Went out in his boat to check out his new fish finder off Wilson and never came back."

A look of recognition flashed across Cal's face. "Jamison," he repeated slowly. "I know that name from somewhere. How old is he?"

"Sixty-three. Lived in Riverton his whole life."

"Jamison, Jamison," Cal said, trying to remember. "I'm sure I know that name." He turned toward Rod, features alive. "Make yourself useful. Bring me that file box." He indicated a cardboard box on the floor of his closet next to the bureau.

Rod picked up the box and placed it on the bed before removing the lid. Cal spoke again. "Look for the Lorenzo file."

Rod shuffled through the manila file folders until he found one labeled "Lorenzo, Joey." He extracted it and handed it to his uncle. "This the one?"

"Yep." Cal leafed through the documents inside for a moment before holding one up in triumph. "I knew it! I never forget a name."

Now Rod was interested. "You found something?"

Cal nodded vigorously. "Joey Lorenzo. Disappeared on the river, presumed drowned, in 1972. You were just a kid then, but it was pretty big news. I'd been chief for less than a year when it happened."

"I think I remember that. I was ten that summer," Rod said, trying to recall.

Cal nodded. "Biggest case in years in Riverton."

"What was Scott Jamison's connection?" Rod was calculating. Jamison would've been nineteen that summer.

Cal plowed ahead. "There were five of them, five idiots who went tubing at night from Devil's Hole. One of them, Joey Lorenzo, didn't make it. There were all sorts of theories at the time as to what happened, but none of the other kids would talk. Real tragedy. I knew

Joey's father, ran a construction company in town. Joey was his only son."

Rod pressed. "What did Scott Jamison have to do with it?"

Cal held the file up, eyes gleaming. "He was one of the other tubers. One of the survivors."

18

It was still raining Sunday at dawn when Chief Hal Andrews of the Delifin Coast Guard station checked the National Weather Service forecast for the area and discovered that rain was predicted to continue through mid-day on Monday. Reluctantly, he gave the order to suspend the search for Scott Jamison and instructed Ensign Thad Rybicki to inform the Canadian Coast Guard and the Niagara County Sheriff's Department of his decision. Once the rain stopped, the situation would be re-evaluated, but for now he couldn't justify sending a search vessel into the impenetrable wall of gray on the lake.

Rod Wakefield was home, working on his computer when Kevin called from the station house to relay the message from Andrews. After yesterday's visit with Cal, he couldn't wait to find out more about the Joey Lorenzo disappearance and Scott Jamison's connection to it and had mentioned going into the office to check the file on their drive home. Sally fixed him with a cold glare at the suggestion. "You've been doing nothing *but* working lately. You need a break," she said in a tone that discouraged argument.

They'd compromised. Rod dropped by the station house, picked up the file and took it home with him, with Sally's reluctant approval. "I can't wait until Monday. This guy's mother and girlfriend are counting on me to find some answers," he explained defensively.

He spent Saturday evening and most of Sunday familiarizing himself with the file. As Roberts had warned, there wasn't much to it. Just statements from the four surviving boys, some perfunctory follow-up with each of the families and the statements of several friends. Open and shut, according to Cal. A tragic accident, the result of a poor choice: attempting to tube the Niagara River from Devil's Hole to the Riverton sand docks at night.

Cal's theory was Lorenzo lost the grip on his tube and was sucked into a whirlpool and never resurfaced. No foul play or suspicious circumstances involved. "They fucked up by deciding to tube the rapids at night," Cal said the day before. "But no one was at fault. Stupidity, bad luck, sure. One thing, though. Whatever did happen out there on the river that night, those boys have had to live with it for over forty years. Dealing with something like that has to wear you down."

According to documents in the slim file, five boys from Riverton, all either nineteen or twenty and good friends, had decided to float down the Niagara River on the night of Thursday August 24, 1972. What made the trip deadly was the decision of the boys to depart from Devil's Hole State Park, upstream from the international power plants flanking the river and the bridge spanning it, instead of from the Riverton sand docks, the usual departure point for daytime tubers. A consensus was quickly reached among the investigating law enforcement agencies: in spite of a full moon that night and a cloudless, star-strewn sky, attempting to navigate the treacherous rapids, whirlpools and eddies of the Niagara River at night instead of the usually flat water between Riverton and Delifin during the day was the cause of death. The department, after a ten-day investigation, declared Joey Lorenzo a victim of accidental drowning. Case closed.

Wakefield read each of the statements given by the survivors and was struck by the similarity of the phrasing of the events that occurred that night. It seemed to Wakefield as if each of the boys was repeating the words from a script, that their stories were rehearsed. He made a note to mention that to Cal the next time he spoke with him, to see if he'd felt the same way at the time.

According to each of the boys' statements, Joey Lorenzo had been the last of the five to depart from the base of Devil's Hole. No one was surprised when he didn't show up at the Riverside Inn with the rest of them after the ride was completed. Because Lorenzo was the only one of the five who had a job that required him to be up early the next morning, they figured he'd simply gone home to try to get some sleep instead of joining them for a nightcap. Of the other four, three were college students and had left their summer jobs the previous week to prepare to return to school, while Scott Jamison worked sporadically painting houses during the day and had a part-time job delivering pizzas for LaPalermo Pizzeria in Niagara Falls at night. Cal had also interviewed the bartender on duty that night at the Riverside, who confirmed that he'd seen the four tubers come in before last call, but that Joey Lorenzo had not been with them.

On a separate piece of paper, Wakefield wrote down the names of the other people, family members and friends, who'd been interviewed in 1972. He figured the parents of the boys were probably deceased, but some of their friends might still be around. It wouldn't hurt to do a little poking around, see what he could find.

Sally poked her head into his study, wearing pajamas "I'm heading to bed. Don't stay up too late."

"I won't," Rod said. "Just a few more minutes."

He watched his wife disappear down the hallway. He returned his attention to the file. There was a picture of Joey Lorenzo among the witness statements and reports, a head-and-shoulders shot with a note attached saying it was taken by the class photographer for the 1970 Riverton High class yearbook. Joey Lorenzo was handsome, with a dark complexion, dark eyes and curly brown hair. He was smiling broadly in the photo, looking like every other high school senior that'd preceded him – eager to discover what the next phase of his life had to offer, brimming with the type of confidence and optimism only a teenager could muster, the possibilities limitless. As he held the photo gently between his thumb and index finger, Rod wondered if Joey had been smiling at all on the night two years later before he disappeared without a trace.

*****

"Key North?"

Parnell Gomez nodded. "I've heard the term several times since I've been in Delifin. Of course, the weather hasn't been exactly tropical since I've been in town, so I'm having a hard time seeing it."

Kelly Porter pondered the writer's question. It was Monday and she'd just delivered Gomez's lunch when, out of the blue, he asked her if she knew the story behind the origin of Delifin's nickname. Although she'd worked the weekday shift behind the bar at the Delifin Athletic Club for years, she wasn't sure of the answer herself. There were several competing theories, none of which held more credence than the others. From time to time the discussion popped up at the bar, with various characters throughout the years claiming to have been the first person to refer to Delifin as Key North. It was the quintessential barroom argument, a question with a number of possible answers, none which could be proved beyond a reasonable doubt.

"Have you been to Key West?" Kelly asked.

"I have, a few years ago" Gomez replied as he sipped his iced tea. "Nice place to visit, but I wouldn't want to live there. Too crowded and too expensive. And then there's those pesky hurricanes."

116

The bar was fairly crowded for a Monday, primarily because of a group of Canadians who'd motored across the river from Niagara-on-the-Lake to have lunch at the AC. It was Victoria Day, the Canadian holiday that ushered in summer north of the border, and the five men seated in the middle of the bar were enthusiastically embracing their day off from work. Kelly checked to make sure their drinks were topped off – they were a thirsty bunch – before she came around from behind the bar to where Gomez was sitting. "Follow me."

She led him out onto the wraparound porch of the four-story stone building perched on a bluff above the river and pointed toward the juncture of the river and the lake, a half mile to the north. "From here, in late July or early August, the setting sun is perfectly framed by the mouth of the river and disappears into the lake in spectacular fashion. I've seen the sunset in Key West from Mallory Square, and I don't think it's as nice as ours. It's also much less crowded here, since Delifin is the end of the road, just like Key West, but it's a road that very few tourists follow. Most visitors to the area go to Niagara Falls and never venture north. We kind of like it that way."

Gomez admired the view from the porch. "I can see why." Several boats, power and sail, plied the river below, eager to finally enjoy some nice weather after two days of steady rain. "This is a great view."

Kelly continued. "But it's also the ambience here. For years Key West has been a magnet for people who like to think they operate outside the system. It's almost as if they invented the phrase, 'Don't ask, don't tell.' It's the same here. People who live here like the fact that they live under the radar. It's about as diverse and libertarian a place as you'll find anywhere in New York and it's well off the beaten path." She turned at the sound of a couple settling into some chairs at one of the tables on the porch behind them. "I better get back inside."

Gomez stepped around her and returned to his seat at the bar while Kelly took the drink order of the newly arrived couple. The Canadians had risen from their spot at the bar and moved to the shuffleboard table, where an impromptu game was in progress. Peter Malecki, the owner of the Delifin AC, had recently had his vintage table refurbished, and the newly conditioned surface was as fast and tricky as the greens at Augusta. Weight after weight sailed over the end of the board into the channel as the first-time visitors struggled to regulate the speed of their shots.

One of the Canadians touched Kelly on the shoulder as she walked past them on her way back to the bar. "Another round."

She smiled. "Coming right up." She filled their glasses first before she filled the order of the couple on the porch and brought them their drinks along with a couple of menus and her order pad. She stood poised with her pen, prepared to take their orders since they were regulars and already familiar with the menu. Each of the women ordered a small salad to go with their Chardonnay, their usual fare. She walked back inside and went into the kitchen, where Peter was preparing a roast beef sandwich. "Two small salads, one with Italian, one with bleu cheese."

Peter answered without looking. "Pretty busy for a Monday."

"Holiday Monday," Kelly corrected him.

This time he turned. "We have Canadians?"

"Looks like half the Legion from Niagara-on-the-Lake is here," Kelly responded. "That roast beef sandwich you're making is for one of them."

"Make sure you figure in the exchange rate if they pay cash."

Kelly shook her head in wonderment. "Hardly anyone pays cash these days, especially Canadians. You need to get out a little more."

She returned to the bar area. Gomez was at his seat, finishing his cheeseburger while he half-watched the rowdy Canadians futilely attempt to master the subtleties of the shuffleboard table. The scoreboard suspended above the table indicated that Red was leading Blue, 2-1. At their present rate it would take days for these guys to reach 21.

The front door rattled and a UPS driver entered carrying a small cardboard package. He approached Kelly at the bar, a customer service smile on his face. "I have a package for Kelly Porter."

"That's me," she replied. "Do I have to sign anything?"

"Nope. It's all yours. Have a nice day." He smiled, handed her the package, turned and left the bar.

She felt red creep into her cheeks as she looked down at the cardboard box in her hands. It contained the two books written by Gomez

118

that she'd ordered last week; she could tell by the return address on the packaging. At the time she ordered the books she thought it might be interesting to have the books delivered to the bar instead of her home, but today, with Gomez seated at the end of the bar, she felt embarrassed. She hadn't anticipated that.

She smoothly placed the package on a shelf beneath the bar. When she looked up she saw Gomez staring at her with amusement. "Fan mail from some flounder?"

She couldn't help smiling at the reference from her youth. "Uh, no. Just a couple of books I ordered."

"Books, huh. Anyone I know?" Gomez asked pointedly.

She felt her face flush again. "Maybe."

Gomez dropped a ten and a five on the bar, retrieved his bill for his records, stuffing it into his pocket as he stood to leave, still smiling. "You'll have to tell me how they turn out," he said over his shoulder as he ambled toward the door and outside into the brilliant sunshine.

19

By the time Robbie Burnett finished work and returned home on Monday, he was too tired to do anything but grab a beer from the refrigerator and collapse into his favorite chair in front of the television in his small apartment near the river. He hadn't been sleeping well since Scott Jamison disappeared last week. The scenes from last Tuesday night at the rod and gun club kept playing over and over in his mind: a buoyant Jamison, smiling from ear to ear, raising a toast to the crowd after buying a round for the bar, accepting congratulations and thanks from a surprised and grateful crowd.

At the time, he figured his friend's generosity had everything to do with the big check he'd just cashed after finishing the Village Pizza job. But the more he thought about it, the more he wondered if there had been something else going on that night, something darker. Before they'd embarked on their search effort last Friday, Charlie Jaeger had mentioned how the cops had discovered Scott's wallet and cell phone neatly arranged on the seat of his van. He'd been friends with Scott since high school, had been on hundreds of fishing trips with him over the years. Since the advent of the cell phone, he couldn't remember another time they'd gone out on the lake in Scott's boat when he'd left his cell phone behind. Why had he done it this time?

He didn't want to think that Scott's disappearance wasn't random, the result of a storm that had blown in so quickly he'd been unable to get back to shore in time. Or that he'd had a heart attack or a stroke, some sort of medical issue that left him unable to cope with what happened that day on the water. According to Jaeger, the cell phone and the wallet were left in plain sight on the passenger's seat of the van as if he wanted whoever found it to wonder why they'd been left behind. These were the thoughts that came back to him over and over again on these nights when he couldn't sleep, when he lay awake in the dark, wondering what had really happened to his friend.

He felt his cell phone vibrating. He shifted in the chair and pulled his phone from his front pocket. He always shut the ringer on his phone off while he was on a job so that it wouldn't distract him if he received a call. He'd forgotten to turn it back on today when he'd finished working.

There were two messages. One from Charlie Jaeger, telling him the Coast Guard had called off the search. The other was from Wakefield, the Riverton cop who'd been calling him since Friday, wanting him to come down to the station to give a statement.

He glanced at the time on his phone: 7:37. Too late to call tonight. He dropped the phone on the table next to him and picked up the remote, pointing it at the small flat screen. He found *Wheel of Fortune* and slumped into his chair, taking a long swallow of his beer, hoping that Vanna and Pat would distract him from the cascade of troubling thoughts simmering in his head.

*****

Wakefield arrived at the station early Monday morning after his usual stop at Borelli's Bakery for a cup of coffee and a muffin. The bakery opened at six and usually had a steady stream of regulars who stopped by for breakfast and gossip before they started their work week. He'd been hoping to get lucky, maybe run into one of the people who were on the list of names he'd developed over the weekend after poring over the Joey Lorenzo file.

He'd called Kevin Rumsfeld at the station the night before and had him access one of the proprietary law enforcement databases to see if he could track down any of the people who'd been interviewed by Cal Roberts back in 1972. Kevin had been thrilled to be tasked with something other than monitoring the police band and making coffee for the officers who stopped in from time to time from patrol and had texted a list of current addresses for the names on the list Wakefield had compiled. Wakefield had smiled when he woke earlier that morning, checked his phone and saw the time of the text: 4:44 am. The enthusiasm of youth can be a powerful tool when properly harnessed.

Of the eleven names on the list that Wakefield had sent to Kevin, only two were still local: Robbie Burnett, who lived in the village of Riverton, and Andrea Herman, now Andrea Kirkpatrick, former girlfriend of Joey Lorenzo in 1972 when he disappeared, currently living in Niagara Falls.

What caught Wakefield's eye immediately was Burnett, who was also on his list of people to interview regarding Jamison's disappearance. It was the only name common to both lists. A good place to start, he thought.

121

When he reached the station he went into his office and shut the door. There was another note from Kevin on his desk, thanking him for the opportunity to be involved in some real police work. He smiled. Kevin was going to be a good cop if he decided to stick with it.

He slipped the note into his pocket so he could take it home and show it to Sally. Next he dialed Robbie Burnett's number. It went directly to voicemail. He left a brief message, asking Burnett to return the call at his earliest convenience.

He was halfway through Randy DiPietro's weekly report on the Corelli trial when he heard Anne at the door. She rapped lightly on his door before poking her head in. "Good morning, Chief. How was your weekend?"

He motioned toward his guest chair. "Have a seat and I'll tell you all about it."

For the next ten minutes he filled her in on his visit to Cal on Saturday morning and the link between Joey Lorenzo's disappearance and Scott Jamison. When he was finished she nodded her head in approval. "Sounds like you took advantage of the wet weather. What's next?"

"I'd like to get Robbie Burnett to come in for an interview, see what he has to say about Lorenzo and Jamison."

"Want me to call him?"

"I already did. Left him a message an hour ago. What you can do is try to track down where he works. I have a feeling I may have to go to him."

Anne rose to her feet. "I'm on it. How's your coffee?"

"Almost gone."

"I'll make a new pot."

She closed the door as she left. He returned to DiPietro's report. He read a brief summary of the trial activity, skimming through the testimony given on Thursday. He spent more time on DiPietro's summary of Friday's testimony, when DA Charles Moreland spent the entire day questioning the psychologist who'd first interviewed both of the victims last summer following Corelli's arrest. According to her

122

testimony, she'd conducted two follow-up interviews with each of the girls before the trial had started. Prodded by Moreland, she testified that each of the girls, based on their age at the time of the alleged assaults, faced years of intense therapy in their futures.

Wakefield had interviewed each of the girls briefly after Corelli's arrest in the presence of their parents and Dr. Russell and found their accounts of the incidents with Corelli to be both credible and appalling. After the interviews had ended and the doctor and the girls had departed, he drew Moreland aside and asked if he planned to call either of the young victims. The DA shook his head, his face grim. "I hope not. I'm going to do my best to keep them off the stand. If the evidence from Corelli's computers wasn't so substantial, I'd have to consider it. But what Fred Malinowski found is dead solid stuff. Even an unsympathetic jury, which we definitely won't have, would have trouble ignoring it."

Wakefield was relieved by Moreland's assessment. Not only was he worried about the effect testifying in open court might have on each of the victims, but he was also concerned about the effect that one of the victims might have on the jury. He knew what a skillful defense attorney like Max Grossinger could do in a trial like this – turn the tables and put the conduct of the victims on trial. It was one of the main reasons victims of rape often choose to remain silent and never press charges instead of confronting their rapists in court.

His cop instincts told him that one of the victims, Lisette Gaffney, would provoke conflicting emotions among the jurors if she were called to the stand. Although only fifteen – she had been thirteen at the time of Corelli's alleged assault – she looked like she could pass for thirty. Standing five nine, with powerful shoulders, muscular arms and legs and several visible tattoos and piercings, her appearance and attitude, which was often profane and in your face, could do more harm than good on the stand, especially when interrogated by someone as skilled as Grossinger, who Wakefield knew was one of the best in the business at finding weakness and exploiting it for the jury's benefit.

Gaffney was known to local law enforcement, having made several appearances in juvenile court for minor drug offenses, the first of which occurred when she was twelve. Keeping her off the stand would not only protect her from Grossinger, who would no doubt do everything he could to introduce her previous brushes with the law into the record, but it would prevent the jury from developing an image of her as one of those victims who might have, through her own actions, contributed to her fate. Because of the ages of the two victims, they could only be referred to in court documents and testimony as Jane Doe 1 and Jane Doe 2. By keeping her far away from the court and the witness stand, it would be much more difficult for Grossinger to link Gaffney's bad-girl looks and attitude as a contrast to the image of her that Moreland was seeking to project to the jury - that of an innocent, underage victim of a monstrous attack.

Randy, he thought as he finished the report, was doing an excellent job running things at the courthouse. He'd considered returning to Town Hall himself this week to give him a break, but after reading the report and talking to him, he didn't think that was necessary. Friday, when he'd called Randy to tell him he was considering pulling him from the courthouse for a week and returning him to patrol, Randy had objected. "Gimme another week, Chief. At least until the prosecution rests their case. If you want to switch me out after that, then go ahead. Until then, I've got this covered."

The phone on his desk rang. It was Anne. "Coffee's ready."

"I'll be out in a minute." He set the weekly report in his Out box and returned to the Jamison file and the lists of names that had been compiled thus far. With most of his officers on assignment at the Corelli trial, he was the only one available to follow up on information related to the Jamison disappearance. It had been years since he'd last spent any significant time tracking down leads, performing the kind of legwork that was critical to a successful investigation. He was looking forward to getting out of the station house for a change.

He rose to his feet and emerged from his office. Anne was away from her desk, but there was a freshly poured mug of steaming coffee sitting next to her phone. He bent down and sniffed. Black, no sugar. He smiled, grabbed the cup and carried it with him back into his office.

Kelly looked at the clock on the wall and shook her head with frustration. Her shift at the AC ended at five, but Connie Inglis, her replacement as the evening bartender during the week, was late again. Twice last week, three times the week before that. She'd mentioned Connie's chronic tardiness to Peter last Friday, but he'd just nodded and walked back into the kitchen, where he sat down at the table and read the paper and did nothing, his usual MO.

She knew Peter wasn't going to say anything to Connie; he was the one who had hired her. Not for her punctuality, but because she possessed a rare mesh of qualities he found irresistible: a spectacular rack and a below average IQ. Peter firmly believed that the best way to get more customers into his bar was to have a great-looking woman serving drinks to lure them in.

Connie didn't even have to interview for the job. She came into the AC with a group of girls on a night when Peter was sitting at the end of bar, head nodding, an empty glass that had been previously filled a number of times on the bar in front of him. He roused himself enough to notice the tall blonde in the teal tank-top that flashed what looked to him to be a genuine smile when she caught his eye from her position in the middle of the bar. He got to his feet carefully and walked over to her. Emboldened by several glasses of Zaya Gran Reserva, he leaned one elbow on the bar for support and smiled. "Would you like a job?"

She looked at him as if searching for an expiration date. "What kind of job?"

"Tending bar, Monday through Friday nights, five to closing."

Without missing a beat or losing her smile, she leaned forward and dropped her voice. "I'm not going to fuck you."

He swallowed his disappointment and responded weakly. "That won't be an issue."

Her smile widened. It was what she wanted to hear. "When do I start?"

Four years later she had Peter Malecki completely at her mercy. She'd kept her word and hadn't slept with him. His frustration had mounted exponentially as she continued to resist his inept advances until he was virtually subservient to her. Discipline her for being late for work? Not as long as she dangled the prospect of consummation five nights a week.

She finally came in the door at 5:24, apologizing profusely to Kelly as she navigated through the late afternoon crowd and walked behind the bar. She placed her purse next to the cash register and looked up expectantly. Kelly bit her tongue and managed an unconvincing smile before saying in an even tone, "You're late again."

"I know," she said. "I'm so sorry. It won't happen again."

Of course it will, she thought. Instead, she said evenly. "The till's balanced, the fruit is cut. See you tomorrow."

She was out the door before Connie could say another word, heading east on Lockport toward her house on Third Street, the package of books in her hand. Normally she was in no rush to get home, but tonight was different. Her husband Patrick played in a golf league on Monday night after work, which meant she had the house to herself. A perfect night to get a good start on one of Gomez's books.

As soon as she got home she took a knife from the drawer in the kitchen and sliced open the cardboard. The two paperbacks slid out the end, both looking to be modest in size, like most popular modern fiction she saw in bookstores and on tables at Walmart. She tried to decide which one to look at first, then remembered she'd told John Herrington that he could read *Escape From Vagina Ridge*.

She picked up the other book, *Highway 41 Revisited*, and read the blurb on the back, which hinted at a tale of salvation and redemption that occurs for a young man during a memorable summer spent working on a road crew on Highway 41 between Kaladar and Pembroke in eastern Ontario. She had no idea where this place was, so she went to one of the map sites on her phone and looked it up. The highway ran in a north-south direction for one hundred miles through the edge of the Canadian Shield, two thirds of the way between Toronto and Ottawa.

She poured herself a glass of water and took the book with her out to the front porch. It was a mild night, a harbinger of summer on the horizon, perfect weather for her to read in the swinging loveseat on the

126

broad covered porch. She read the short description of the author on the back cover, which didn't tell her any more than she already knew: that *Highway 41 Revisited* was Parnell Gomez's first novel. Soon she was lost in the story. She read until it was too dark to see the pages, then moved inside.

*****

"Everything all set?"

"I talked to the guy at the marina this afternoon. He says we're all set to launch on Wednesday."

"Good. How's Ma?"

"The same. She's looking forward to seeing you and Joanie."

Monday night. Lenny Campbell was sitting on the couch in his house in Delifin, talking with his brother Red, who was flying from Denver to Buffalo tomorrow to kick off the summer boating season. According to the reassurances from Mike Spacone, the mechanic at the boatyard in Wilson where the boat was stored during the winter, the *Scottish Rogue* was spit-polished and seaworthy, ready to launch.

"Any news on Jamison?"

"Not a word," Lenny said. "The Coast Guard called off the search on Sunday."

"I can't believe he allowed himself to get caught out on the lake in a storm," Red said. "He's smarter than that. At least, he used to be. And no sign of the boat?"

"It's camouflage, so it would be hard to see, especially with the rain we had all weekend."

"And they had planes in the air?"

"Helicopters, too, with heat-imaging technology. Didn't find a thing."

"We'll have to take a look when we get there. Have they moved the van yet?"

"Mike, the guy at the marina, said they towed it away on Saturday."

Red Campbell and his wife Joanie lived in the mountains west of Vail, but he flew back several times each summer to western New York to see his mother and brother and to spend time on the *Scottish Rogue*, a 38-foot Sea Ray that, during the boating season, was moored at the marina in Delifin. He owned a thriving electrical contracting business in Colorado, working on high-end second homes for new-money owners in Vail and Aspen. It was a job that allowed him the flexibility to fly east during the summer to spend time on the water, something he enjoyed doing more than anything else. He and Joanie were childless, having married later in life, which made it easier for the couple to pursue their passion for adventure. The more adrenaline produced, the better.

"What are you going to order on the pizza?" There were no good pizza joints in Colorado, at least as far as Red was concerned, so his first priority on landing in Buffalo each journey was devouring a pizza from Buzzy's on Pine Avenue in Niagara Falls that Lenny would pick up on his way to the airport.

Lenny sighed into the phone. He'd only been doing this ever since his brother had moved to Colorado more than thirty years ago. "Anchovies, mushrooms, double pepperoni."

"Good. Don't be late." The phone call ended abruptly.

Just like Red, Lenny thought. He glanced at his watch. Not too late. He punched in another number on his phone.

"Where have you been?" The voice on the other end of the phone was tinged with panic.

"Talking with my brother."

"Did you tell him yet?"

"I was going to, but he hung up on me."

"Did he ask about Scott?"

"Yep."

"And…..?"

128

"He just wanted to know about the search. I filled him in."

"Wouldn't that have been a good time to tell him?"

Now it was Lenny's turn to feel frustrated. "I would've, if he hadn't hung up on me. What did you want me to do? Call him back and say, 'Hey, I forgot to tell you I have a girlfriend. By the way, she's also the girlfriend of Scott Jamison. You know, the guy who's missing.'"

Gillian Hudecki softened her tone. "I don't know. Things have been so crazy lately....." Her voice trailed off.

"I know, I know," Lenny said reassuringly. "Everything's going to be okay."

"How can you say that?" Her voice rose again. "Scott's dead. As soon as the cops find out we're dating – and they will, believe me – than I'm going to be a suspect. You, too."

"Have you heard any more from that cop?"

"Wakefield? No, not since I talked to him last Friday. Some guy named Militello called me from the sheriff's department on Sunday to tell me the Coast Guard and the sheriffs had called off the search. But I haven't heard from Wakefield."

Lenny tried to calm her down. "You need to keep in touch with him. Keep asking how the search is going. You have to make him think you're the grieving girlfriend. Don't give him anything to make him suspicious."

Gillian sounded skeptical. "Are you sure?"

"Positive. You have to act normal, which means anxious and upset."

"I *am* upset."

"Let Wakefield know it," Lenny said. "Call him first thing in the morning, ask him how things are going. Have you reached out to Scott's mother yet?"

"The drunk? I tried, but she wouldn't talk to me. She only wanted to know if Scott had an insurance policy. I guess she figured she'd be the beneficiary." She laughed harshly. "Fat chance. That bitch hasn't talked to him in years."

"Did he have insurance?"

Gillian thought for a moment. "I don't know. We never talked about stuff like that."

"Check his files. See what's there. Maybe we'll get lucky."

"We?"

"Like it or not, baby, we're in this together. All the way to the end."

21

After another sleepless night, Robbie Burnett phoned the Riverton Police Department Tuesday morning as he was preparing to leave for work. Maybe if he talked to Wakefield, put the interview with the chief behind him, he could finally get some sleep. During the week since Scott Jamison had disappeared, he hadn't been able to sleep longer than an hour or so at a time. He kept waking up, tossing and turning for hours before falling back to sleep, only to awaken again. He was exhausted, and it was affecting his work. Even his usual method for avoiding insomnia, smoking a joint before going to bed, wasn't working.

A woman answered the phone. "Riverton Police Department. What can I do for you?"

"My name's Robbie Burnett. Chief Wakefield has been calling me about Scott Jamison. I'd like to set up an interview."

Anne Moretti was all business. "When can you come in?"

"Tonight, after work, around 5:30 if that's okay."

"Let me check with the chief. I'm going to put you on hold for a minute." She was back almost immediately. "Chief Wakefield will be expecting you. Thank you for your cooperation, Mr. Burnett."

"Yeah, okay. See you later."

*****

John Herrington was waiting by the side door of the Delifin AC on Tuesday when Kelly Porter arrived to open up. She was carrying a paperback book which she handed to Herrington before she inserted her key into the lock. "Knock yourself out."

He looked at her quizzically. "What's this?"

"A book. The one you wanted to read written by Parnell Gomez."

"The one about pussy?" He turned it over excitedly to read the reviews on the back. "When did it arrive?"

"Yesterday," said Kelly. "You didn't show up for lunch, or I could've given it to you then." She opened the door and walked inside, Herrington a step behind. She flicked on the lights and surveyed the damage. Not bad, she conceded. Despite Connie's inability to arrive at work on time, she was diligent about cleaning up after she closed the bar. It looked like all she had to do was slice the lemons and limes and check the pantry to make sure they were covered for lunch.

"After two days of rain, I decided to take my boat out for a sail yesterday," Herrington said. "Did I miss anything else?"

"Just a bunch of Canadians from Niagara-on-the-Lake celebrating the holiday. Actually, we were pretty busy for lunch. It dropped off after the Canadians left at around 4:00, then picked up again just before my shift ended."

As Kelly moved behind the bar, Herrington sat in his usual seat, put the book on the bar and began to scan the area. "Where's the paper?"

She looked at him with disdain. "I don't know. I just got here, remember?"

"It's probably in the kitchen," he said helpfully.

"Be my guest. I have work to do."

He found this morning's copy of the *Niagara Gazette* lying unread on the table in the center of the kitchen and returned with it to his barstool. He opened the front section and began to read the account of yesterday's testimony at the Corelli trial while Kelly began to slice fruit. An overhead fan whirred lazily, dispersing the faint aroma of stale beer that hung stubbornly in the air, left over from nearly two hundred years of drinking on the premises.

"Not much on the trial today," he said as he paged through the front section. "I don't see anything about that guy who's missing."

"I'm afraid he's gone," Kelly said without looking up. "What's it been, a week? The water's too cold for anyone to have survived that long."

"You're right. It was 57 yesterday off the front deck of my boat. Not even a Navy Seal could survive a week in that." He dropped the front section and picked up the sports, looking for the weather. "Any idea what it's going to be like this week? The weather, I mean."

"Do I look like Al Roker?" She handed the remote for the television to Herrington. "Check for yourself."

Herrington, who didn't own a television set, took a moment to examine the options of the remote before he was able to turn the set on. "Where's the Weather Channel?"

"619."

He punched in the number and in a moment a man in a rain suit appeared, reporting from what looked like an area undergoing flooding. He watched as an SUV, water above the hubcaps, slowly tried to navigate a washed-out road. The caption crawling under the video indicated the flooding was in South Carolina. "When does the local forecast come on?"

"Local on the eights. Anytime the last digit of the time is an eight."

Herrington looked at the clock on the wall next to the stuffed moose head. "Is that thing accurate?"

Kelly looked up. "Probably not. I think Connie tries to move it ahead a little bit so she can close early if it's slow."

"Peter doesn't care about that?"

"He's usually not here that late. If he is, he's asleep on the bar."

While he waited for the local forecast, he picked up Gomez's book and read the reviews on the back cover. Most of them related to *Highway 41 Revisited*, his previous novel. All of them were cherry-picked to be glowingly positive. "Have you looked at the other one?"

"I started it last night while Pat was playing golf. I'm about halfway finished."

Herrington leaned forward with interest. "How is it?"

Kelly dropped the sliced lemons and limes into a plastic container, sealed the top and set it on a lower shelf beneath the bar. She wiped her hands on a nearby towel and looked up. "Better than I

133

expected," she admitted. "At first I thought it was going to be something to do with Bob Dylan, but it's not that at all. It's pretty good."

"What's it about?"

"A young college student from a Toronto suburb gets a job with a construction company working on a stretch of highway in eastern Ontario. It tells about the adventures he has as the crew moves north along the highway – Highway 41 – during one summer. I know – it sounds boring. But it isn't boring at all. I couldn't put it down."

"Do you remember what suburb the guy was from?"

"Missa something."

"Mississauga?"

"That's it."

Herrington looked at *Escape From Vagina Ridge* with disappointment. "The liner notes for this one aren't what I expected at all. I thought from the title it would be something sexy, something hot. It says here that it's the story of a man who is being held against his will by a group of female amazons at a commune in the Adirondacks and his struggle to regain his freedom."

Kelly feigned sympathy. "Too bad, Romeo. Looks like I ended up with the better book."

"Wanna trade?"

"Not on your life."

*****

"Let me guess. You're going to be late…again."

Wakefield was as contrite as he could be. "I'm sorry, Sally. But it's the only time Burnett can come in. He's one of the last guys to see Jamison alive." Pause. "I'll make it up to you."

"You are absolutely right about that. You're responsible for dinner tonight. I don't care what it is – just have it in your hands when you come home."

He could tell from her tone that she was pissed. "Uh, how about Chinese?"

"I really don't care. Just make sure you bring it with you. And if it's not ready to eat, you're cooking it." She hung up without saying goodbye.

He looked up after returning the phone to the receiver. Anne was standing in the doorway of his office. "In the doghouse?"

He smiled wanly. "Is it that obvious?"

"I think you better do what she said. And try to make the interview as short as possible."

"You know I have no control over that."

"Sure you do. You're the one asking the questions." She spun around and returned to her desk.

Wakefield looked at the notes he'd been working on, wondering if Anne was right, despite the fact that she'd never conducted an interview herself. He knew there was no telling where a questioning session might go or how long it might last. It all depended on how the person answered the questions. Many times their responses opened pathways that Rod hadn't considered. You just go with the flow. You have to be flexible.

What he'd decided to do, after studying the files of both cases, was to concentrate his questions on the Joey Lorenzo case. He figured Burnett was probably preparing to respond to questions about Jamison. Asking about the Lorenzo case would throw him off guard, make him easier to read, his answers less rehearsed. That is, if he chose to answer. He had to consider the possibility that Burnett might not remember what happened more than forty years ago with any sort of clarity. If not, he was back to square one. But if he did remember anything of significance, it might shed some light on the increasingly troubling disappearance of Scott Jamison.

22

There was a minor fender bender on the approach leading to the North Grand Island Bridge that had occurred just before Lenny Campbell arrived. It looked like a Subaru trying to merge onto the bridge had failed to yield to oncoming traffic and plowed into a commercial van, blocking both lanes. As of yet, there were no emergency vehicles on the scene.

Great, fumed Lenny. He was on his way to the airport to pick up Red and Joanie, fresh pizza from Buzzy's on the seat beside him. The aroma was driving him crazy - he hadn't had anything to eat before he left the house and his stomach was rumbling – but he knew he'd be in deep shit with his brother if the pizza wasn't intact when he picked him up at the airport.

He checked the status of Red's flight on his phone while he waited for traffic to begin moving again. He smiled, relieved. The flight was running about twenty minutes behind schedule. If he was lucky, he could still get there in time.

His thoughts shifted to Gillian. He was worried that she was losing it, that she wouldn't be able to hold up under the pressure if the investigation into Scott's disappearance continued much longer. He'd hoped that once the Coast Guard suspended the search things would die down, but Wakefield was continuing to question people who'd been with Jamison at the club a week ago as if this was something other than a tragic accident. He knew it was only a matter of time before the persistent cop discovered his relationship with Gillian Hudecki. Gillian knew it, too.

It had started four months earlier, when Scott was on a fishing trip to the Keys. Gillian had stayed behind to tend to her orthodontic practice while Scott and Robbie Burnett were in Islamorada for a week, fishing the flats and enjoying a respite from the bleak western New York winter.

Lenny had admired Gillian from a distance for nearly a year but had made no move because of her live-in relationship with Jamison. He'd never before met a woman as enthusiastic about firearms and hunting as Gillian was. Not one this attractive. Since they were both members of the Riverton Rod and Gun Club, it was easy for Lenny to observe her without drawing any suspicion.

It happened innocently enough when Gillian had an electrical problem with the furnace at her house while Scott was in Florida. Like his brother, Lenny was an electrician. Gillian knew this from casual conversations at the club and had phoned him after getting his number from Caroline at the bar, asking if he could come over and see what was wrong.

He came over to her house the next night with his tools. He traced the problem to a short in the generator, and was able to replace the wire and get the fan running again in a little over an hour. A grateful Gillian had offered him a drink after he refused the money she tried to give to him. One drink turned into two, and before he knew it Gillian rose from her position on the chair opposite him, walked over and sat next to him on the couch, her thigh touching his. He could barely breathe as she leaned forward, eyes closed, lips slightly parted, and kissed him.

Although he knew this was wrong, especially in the house Gillian shared with Scott, he responded eagerly to her lips on his, returning the kiss and embracing her, his heart pounding. It had been a long time since he'd been with a woman. Gillian was the one he'd fantasized being with, alone in his bed at night, as the woman to end his long dry spell.

She broke the embrace and without a word stood up and extended her hand to him. He grasped her hand and she led him to the bedroom where they fell onto the bed in a frenzy, hands flying over one another as clothes were hastily removed. He was swept up in a mixture of lust and desire that was impossible for him to resist. Even before he'd developed the chronic hip condition that left him with a noticeable limp, when he still considered himself attractive to women, he'd never experienced a deluge of emotions like this.

The next morning, hair still tousled from a tender wake-up session, the two of them sat at Gillian's kitchen table, nursing their morning coffee before Gillian had to leave for the office. He was stunned when she told him she had been eying him, too, but had resisted the urge to act, confused about her feelings for Scott. She hadn't planned for them to sleep together when she called him about her electrical problem, she insisted, but she had no regrets that they had. In fact, she felt alive for the first time in a long time.

That's how he felt, too, as if he'd been in a long period of slumber before awakening to a completely different landscape. They managed two more nights together before Scott returned to Riverton with a healthy tan, spouting the kind of tales that often find their origin in an angling trip to the Keys.

They'd been careful after that, exchanging occasional text messages discreetly and acting as if nothing had happened when the three of them were together at the club. But his desire rose and so did hers, and as Scott became involved with the rehabilitation project at Village Pizza, spending longer days on the job, they were able to rendezvous several times at Lenny's house for a little afternoon delight.

Gillian had told Lenny several times that she was planning to tell Scott about how her feelings for him had changed, but she'd failed to follow through on her promise, always losing her nerve at the last moment. And then Scott disappeared.

Telling Red about Gillian would be tricky. His brother was an old-school guy when it came to relationships with women, especially when it involved the girlfriend of a friend. It was a line not to be crossed under any circumstances. Urged on by an increasingly nervous Gillian, he'd been trying to figure out the best way to tell Red when Scott disappeared. He knew how things would look when it came out that he and Gillian had been carrying on an affair for months. He wanted to postpone telling Red until enough time had passed after Scott's disappearance to make their relationship seem more palatable, to come out after a respectable mourning period for Gillian. But she was pressuring him to tell him now.

He was jolted from his reverie by the traffic beginning to move slowly. Emergency responders had managed to open the left lane and traffic was beginning to crawl around the two vehicles involved in the accident. He eased around the mess, glancing at what had to be the two drivers, two men exchanging insurance information, chatting amiably as if they were old friends.

Once he cleared the toll booths at the bottom of the bridge he hit the accelerator, trying to make up for lost time. It was a little past 7:00. Bill and Joanie's flight was scheduled to arrive at 7:25. He should be right on time.

He was sitting in the cell lot, the aroma of the pizza on the seat next to him still filling the burgundy Coupe de Ville when his phone chirped. "Got my pizza? I'm starving."

He pulled around to the Arrivals area, searching for United Airlines. Joanie Campbell was a flight attendant for United, which meant they were able to fly for free if there were seats available. He spotted his brother standing next to two bags by the curb, staring intently at his cell phone. Lenny pulled up and hopped out to help his brother with the bags.

Red looked up from his phone, his face stern. "About time."

"There was an accident on the bridge," Lenny explained. "Some asshole tried to merge from Buffalo Avenue without slowing down and hit a van. You're lucky I got here this early."

Joanie came over and kissed him on the cheek. "Don't pay any attention to him. He's been grumpy all day. One of his stocks had a bad day. I told him it was only money, but you know your brother."

Do I ever, thought Lenny. "I hope you're hungry. That pizza has been driving me crazy."

"I'm starved," Red said as he opened the door for Joanie to get into the backseat, then picked the pizza up and handed it to her before sliding into the front next to his brother. "Let's go."

Red had two pieces devoured by the time they crossed Genesee Street. He turned to Lenny, mouth working. "How's the boat?"

"Good," Lenny replied. "All set to go tomorrow. Mike promised me it would be in the water, all gassed up by the time we get there."

"Good. I've been looking at the weather. Tomorrow and Thursday look like the best days as far as the weather is concerned. It might rain on the weekend."

"That'd be two holiday weekends in a row. It poured for the Canadians last Saturday and Sunday."

"Any more word on your friend, the one who's missing?" Joanie asked from the backseat.

Lenny kept his voice casual. "Not a word. The Coast Guard called off the search last weekend because of the rain."

"And the water temperature," Red added as Joanie handed him another slice. "No way he's still alive if he's been in the water all this time. I wonder what happened."

139

"Red said you were questioned by the police," Joanie said.

"Yeah. Just routine. I was at the club the night before he disappeared. They're talking to everyone who was there, not just me."

"How sad," Joanie said sympathetically. "Was he married?"

"No, but he lived with his girlfriend. No kids. His mother lives in Riverton, but that's it as far as I know."

"You got anything to drink?" Red asked.

"There's a cooler in the back with some bottled water."

"No beer?"

Some things never changed. "It's in the fridge at home. It'll be ice cold by the time we get there."

Joanie reached into the cooler and handed one of the bottles to her husband, who accepted it reluctantly. "You want one, Lenny?"

"No thanks."

By the time they reached Niagara Falls the pizza was history. Only an empty box, the bottom smeared with grease stains, remained. "We should've gotten two," Red grumbled.

"We're here for a week, honey," Joanie said. "We'll have plenty of time to get more."

Unconvinced, Red looked at his brother. "You got anything to eat at your place?"

"Uh, not much," Lenny replied sheepishly. His brother always knew how to make him feel guilty.

"Maybe we should stop at Ma's." Red suggested. Their mother, still spry at 90, was a widow and lived alone, a half mile down the road from Lenny.

Lenny pointed to the clock on the dash. "By the time we get there she'll be sound asleep."

"How's the pool?" Red asked

"I opened it up ten days ago. Before the rain last weekend, the water temperature was up to 85. I haven't checked it since then."

"Ma still using it?"

"Every day that it doesn't rain."

They cruised through the gathering darkness, down the parkway past the golf course to Delifin. Lenny took the exit and turned right on Lockport Road. His house was about a hundred yards down the road on the right, directly across the street from Jim Castle's Farm Market and a hundred acres of peaches and grapes that stretched out behind the market and Castle's home next door to the shore of Lake Ontario.

Lenny hit the garage door opener, pulled into the garage and closed the door. His brother was out of the car first, stretching, still working off the effects of the long flight and the ride from the airport. Instead of helping his wife out of the car or bringing their luggage inside, he opened the door and went inside the house.

Before the door closed behind Red, Lenny called out. "What about your bags?"

Without turning his brother replied over his shoulder. "You get 'em. I'm thirsty."

23

Originally, the red brick building on North Fourth Street in Riverton was designed as a schoolhouse and was used in that fashion until 1962, when the new Riverton High School campus was built. The new campus consolidated the small schoolhouses in Riverton and Delifin into one district encompassing both communities and left each of the old buildings vacant. In Delifin, the former school building was converted to the village library, while in Riverton, the building was shared by the Village of Riverton Police Department, the mayor's office and the village recreation department, which utilized the tiny gymnasium for basketball and volleyball during the winter months and a small adjoining room for weight lifting.

Because of limited space, the mayor's office and police department shared facilities, including a makeshift conference room adjacent to the mayor's office. It was in that conference room where Rod Wakefield sat late Tuesday afternoon, the Lorenzo and Jamison files on the table in front of him, waiting for the arrival of Robbie Burnett.

He'd spent most of the day making phone calls, trying to track down witnesses that had been interviewed by Cal Roberts after Joey Lorenzo's disappearance in 1972. While going through the Lorenzo file, he'd come across the name of Andrea Herman, the only woman other than the female parents of the boys involved in the tubing expedition to be interviewed. Next to the typed report of her interview, Cal had commented in the margin "evasive, hiding something."

He'd called Cal at Scherber Manor and reached him just after he'd finished his lunch and before he was scheduled for a physical therapy session. He answered the phone in an irritated tone. "What now?"

"Nice to talk to you, too, Cal," Rod said. "I've been going over the Lorenzo file and I have a few questions."

"Make it snappy. I have a swim session in five minutes."

"You made some notes in the margin of your report of your interview with Andrea Herman. Do you recall that name?"

There was a moment of silence at the other end before he responded. "Herman. She was the girlfriend."

"Of whom?"

"Lorenzo. The victim."

"You wrote in the margin of the report that she was evasive. What did you mean by that?"

"Jesus, Rod, you're talking about forty years ago. I can't remember what I did this morning."

"Try."

Another pause as he strove to recall. When he responded his voice was firm, resolute. "She was really nervous, avoiding eye contact. I couldn't get here to look me in the eye."

"Is that it?"

"No. I did a little digging after she left. Turns out Joey Lorenzo wasn't the only guy she'd fucked. She had quite a reputation."

"As what?"

Cal's exasperation was evident. "As the girl at Riverton High who liked to fuck. The bad girl, we used to call 'em back in the day. Guys looking to pop their cherry knew all about her. She was the girl invited to all the parties."

Rod jotted down a note. "Anything else?"

"Not really. As you can see from the report, the boys, the ones who survived, had identical stories. Other than name, rank and serial number, they kept their mouths shut."

"That sounds suspicious," Rod said.

"You're telling me. But I couldn't prove anything. There was no concrete evidence to indicate that Lorenzo's death was anything more than an accidental drowning. I had plenty of suspicions, but no proof. So the medical examiner called it accidental." Pause. "Are we done here? The instructor for my pool therapy has a great set of knockers. I don't want to miss a second of her leaning forward in her bathing suit."

"Yes, we're done," Rod said. "Thanks for your help, Cal." The phone disconnected abruptly without Cal saying goodbye.

After his call with Cal, he'd poked around a little more and confirmed that Andrea Herman was now Andrea Kirkpatrick, divorced and living alone in Niagara Falls. He tried calling her but no one answered. He left a message, asking her to call back.

At 5:00 Anne tapped on his door. "I'm heading home. Need anything before I go?"

"I don't think so."

"What time is Burnett supposed to get here?"

"He said sometime between 5:30 and 6:00."

Anne wagged her finger at the chief. "Don't forget to pick up dinner on the way home."

Rod smiled weakly. "I won't."

"See you tomorrow morning."

Rod brewed a pot of coffee after Anne left, and it was still fairly fresh when Robbie Burnett buzzed to be let into the building at 5:49. Rod opened the door smiling. "Thanks for coming in, Robbie. I promise I won't take up much of your time." He indicated the open conference room door across the room. "We'll talk in here."

Wakefield held the door for Burnett, who walked in warily and took a seat opposite the two file folders on the table. "Would you like some coffee?"

Burnett nodded. "Cream and sugar."

Rod returned with two cups and sat down opposite Burnett, who was dressed in a flannel shirt over a long-sleeved white T-shirt, well-worn jeans and work boots. From previous questioning he knew Burnett was a union ironworker; most likely he'd come straight from his latest job site.

When Wakefield was seated, Burnett spoke. "I'm not sure why I'm here. I already told you everything I know about last Tuesday."

"I know and I appreciate your cooperation. Today I want to ask you a couple of questions about Joey Lorenzo." Wakefield watched Burnett's reaction closely.

Confusion flooded Burnett's tanned face. "Joey Lorenzo? That was forty years ago. What's that got to do with Scott's disappearance?"

Wakefield smiled affably. "That's what I'm trying to find out." He held up the file folder. "I recently discovered that Scott Jamison was one of the four boys that survived the trip down the river when Lorenzo disappeared. You were his friend back then, right?"

"Scott? Yeah. We played baseball together in high school."

"Did you know Joey Lorenzo?"

"I knew who he was, but we didn't hang together. He was Scott's friend, not mine."

Wakefield appeared casual, but he was watching Burnett's reaction intently. "You do remember the incident, though, don't you?"

Burnett nodded, hands clasped in front of him. "Everyone remembers that. At least, everyone who was around at the time."

"Do you know who planned the trip that night?"

No hesitation. "Nope."

"Were you asked to go?"

"On the trip? No way. I didn't know about it until it was on the news."

"So Scott never said anything to you about going along?"

"Not a word."

Wakefield wrote some notes, then looked up, still smiling easily. "Did you know Andrea Herman?"

Burnett reacted immediately to Herman's name, sitting up straight in his chair, his eyes darting down toward the file on the table between them before raising them to meet Wakefield's gaze. He was clearly on the defensive now. "What does Andrea Herman have to do with anything?" His voice was cautious.

"We'll get to that. You didn't answer my question. Did you know Andrea Herman?"

He nodded, choosing his words with care. "I knew who she was. She was a year behind me in school."

"Did you know she was Joey Lorenzo's girlfriend?"

He laughed, a short staccato burst, before he replied. "I don't know if she was his girlfriend, but if you're asking me if I knew she was banging him, I did. But he wasn't the only guy she was screwing." As soon as the words were out of his mouth, he regretted them.

Wakefield leaned forward intently. "How do you know that?"

"Everyone knew she was easy. She had a lot of boyfriends back then."

"Were you one of them?"

He shook his head vigorously. "No way, man. Too many other swizzle sticks in the drink, if you get my drift."

"I think I do. Do you know any other guys she might have been sleeping with?"

Burnett took a sip of coffee but said nothing. Wakefield persisted. "Look, Robbie. If you know anything at all, you need to tell me. Scott Jamison was your friend, and I'm sure you want to do anything you can to help find out what happened to him, right?"

Burnett nodded slowly, considering his answer. Finally, in a tiny voice barely audible, he replied. "Yes."

"Who else was sleeping with Andrea Herman?"

He looked down at the table. In a low voice he said, "Scott."

Bingo. "Do you know when he started seeing her?"

"Not exactly. It was sometime that summer, though."

"1972?"

146

"Yeah. I saw them out together once at the Bloody Bucket, down by the river."

"This is really important, Robbie. Do you know if Scott started seeing Andrea before the tubing trip?"

He looked across the table at Wakefield, his eyes liquid. "I'm not sure. He could've been, I guess. It was a long time ago."

"Can you remember if Scott and Andrea dated after the accident?"

He leaned back in his chair as he tried to recall. After a moment he spoke, his voice trembling. "I think so."

"Did you know at the time if Joey knew that Scott was sleeping with his girlfriend?"

"No," he answered firmly, shaking his head. "I didn't know for sure if he was tapping her before the accident, so I never asked."

"And Scott never brought it up?"

"Never."

Wakefield wrote down a few more notes before he looked back at Burnett. "I think that does it, Robbie. If I need anything else, I'll give you a call." He stood and offered his hand. "Thanks for coming in."

Burnett rose to his feet and accepted Wakefield's proffered hand, shaking it limply. "Have you heard anything else from the Coast Guard about Scott? Are they going to search anymore?"

"I can't tell you that, Robbie. You can call them and ask. I have the number of the station if you want to give them a call."

"That's okay. Charlie Jaeger knows Andrews pretty well from when he was a cop. I'll ask him."

"Thanks, Robbie. You've been a big help."

I'm not so sure about that, Burnett thought. "Then I can go?"

"Yes. And thanks again."

24

When he'd finished reading the paper, Herrington picked up his book from the bar and stood up to leave.

"No lunch today?" Kelly asked, surprised.

"I'm trying to cut back a little." He patted his waistline. "Rachel thinks I've put on a few lately." Rachel Penfield had been his companion for several years now, having outlasted a number of other contenders.

"Tell her I said hi."

"I will," Herrington said as he breezed toward the door humming an unrecognizable tune.

It wasn't noon yet. Kelly went into the kitchen to heat up the soup of the day and check on supplies. Peter still hadn't shown up. She'd checked the small room on the third floor where he often slept when he stayed over, but he hadn't stayed over last night. She hoped he'd show up soon – handling the bar and the kitchen by herself, with any kind of crowd, would ruin her day quickly.

At precisely noon Elmer Hartman walked through the side door and took his preferred seat at the bar. Kelly smiled as she approached him, pen poised over pad. "The usual, Elmer?" Like Parnell Gomez and several other luncheon regulars, the retired railroad worker always ordered the same thing each time he ate here.

He surprised her by shaking his head. "Not today," he said. "I'd like a cheeseburger with a side order of macaroni salad. And a Bud Light."

"Walking on the wild side, are we?" Kelly smiled as she retrieved a beer from the cooler and set it on a coaster in front of him.

"I feel like beef today. So why not?"

"I'll get that going for you right away." As soon as she was in the kitchen, she pulled out her phone and sent a text to Peter Malecki: **where r u?**

Almost immediately her phone chirped: **on my way.**

She put Elmer's burger on the flat top and retrieved the macaroni salad from the kitchen cooler. She heard the side door jingle. In a moment Peter came into the kitchen. "Sorry I'm late. I had to take my mother to the doctor's this morning and it took longer than expected." He washed his hands in the sink and dried them on a nearby towel. "Why do they schedule twice as many patients as they can see?"

She looked at him with an amused look. "Why? M-O-N-E-Y. That's what you get when you have a for-profit healthcare system." She added, "How's your mom doing?"

"Fit as a fiddle. Thanks for asking." Peter nodded toward the door. "Take the bar. I've got this."

It turned out to be a slow afternoon. By 2:30 the luncheon crowd had departed and Kelly was alone. Peter was busy in the kitchen so she grabbed *Highway 41 Revisited* from its spot on a shelf beneath the bar. She'd been disappointed when Parnell Gomez failed to show for lunch. It was only the second time he'd missed lunch at the Delifin AC since he'd discovered the place.

She wanted to ask him some questions about his book. She'd been impressed by the strength of his writing, especially his lyrical descriptions of the rugged Canadian Shield landscape that framed Kings' Highway 41. She hadn't been able to put the book down the night before. Only exhaustion and the arrival of Patrick from golfing kept her from reading past midnight. She was so impressed by the novel that she thought she might want to vacation in the area someday, a fact she'd mentioned to Patrick as they lay together in bed the night before. "Whatever you want, honey," he said as he turned over and fell asleep within minutes, his beery breath raspy as he snored.

*****

The young man who answered Rod Wakefield's phone call to Full Moon, a Chinese restaurant on Main Street in Riverton, sounded swamped. "Can you hold, please?"

"Sure." He was still in his office going over his notes from his interview with Robbie Burnett. "Take your time."

The young man returned in a minute and apologized. "Sorry about that. What can I do for you, tonight?"

149

"I'd like the Szechuan Stir Fry with pork, the family size, to go."

"Anything else?"

"No, that should be it"

"Your number is 52. Should be ready in twenty minutes."

"Thanks." He hung up and returned to the notes from the Burnett interview. He finally had a real lead in Andrea Herman and was impatient to start tracking her down. He tried to curb his enthusiasm as he thought of Sally, however. If he didn't show up soon for dinner she'd be in a fouler mood than when he'd spoken to her earlier in the afternoon. Andrea Herman would have to wait.

It was a beautiful spring evening, in the low seventies, the sun sinking gradually over the river behind him as he walked down Main to the Full Moon. There were several customers waiting for their orders and one couple seated in one of the six booths, attacking shrimp and garlic stir fry adroitly with chopsticks.

He decided to stay outside for a moment and enjoy the evening, breathing in a pungent mix of crabapple blossoms and exhaust from the restaurant's fan. He looked across the street at Stebbins Mobil, which was closed. Rich Stebbins had a great business – he'd been able to translate his first love, cars, into a career that was rewarding both spiritually and economically. The median family income in Riverton was the highest in the county, and he employed the most trusted mechanics below the escarpment. He had more work than he could handle.

One of the customers walked out with his order. Rod moved inside, up to the counter where the young man who'd taken his order was transferring steaming rice from a large pot on the stove to several waiting plates. He turned and saw Wakefield. "Be with you in a second, Chief. You the Szechuan Stir Fry?"

The chief nodded, smiling pleasantly. "That's me. Number 52."

"Be right there." He dropped the ladle, wiped his hands on his apron, and retrieved a plastic bag containing Wakefield's dinner from the shelf next to the stovetop. He knew the price without having to look at the bill. "$11.95."

Rod withdrew a ten and a five from his wallet and handed it across the counter. "Best deal in town." He picked up the bag and turned to leave. "You take care, Ricky."

"Any change?"

"Keep it."

"Thanks, Chief."

He turned right as soon as he walked out the door, then right again down a narrow, one-way alley. He and Sally lived three blocks away in a compact ranch tucked in behind the First Presbyterian Church. The neighborhood had been larger during the 1950s, but when New York State authorized the construction of the hydroelectric pump generating station along the river immediately south from the village, the material excavated in order to construct the facility's underground powerhouse claimed two streets just to the south of them.

He walked by the small, white building housing the Riverton Historical Museum, noting with regret that in all the time he and Sally had lived in Riverton, he'd never been inside its doors. He gave a small amount during the museum fund drive each year, but as far as actually exploring the historical heritage of Riverton, he hadn't yet found the time.

The last light of the day was beginning to ebb as he turned up his driveway. Before going inside, he detoured around the side to look into the backyard. Sally was there, on her knees next to the vegetable garden, carefully clawing away weeds and depositing them in a plastic container. She hadn't heard him approach, so he turned silently and retraced his steps and went in through the front door. He washed his hands and set the table before he opened the back door and called out, "Dinner's on the table!"

Sally looked up, expressionless. Slowly she rose to her feet, removing her gloves to wipe her brow before she tossed the claw into the container with the weeds and carried it to the back corner of the garage. She looked him in the eye and held his gaze. "What time is it?"

"Time to eat," he said cheerfully. "I'm starved."

They ate in silence. Sally knew that inquiring about her husband's day was not always well received, but she usually made small

151

talk about something amusing that had occurred during the day. Not tonight. Once she'd washed up and sat down at the table, she'd been silent, concentrating on eating the still-warm takeout.

Rod felt like he was on eggshells. Usually Sally didn't hold a grudge when it came to his long, irregularly scheduled work days, but tonight there wasn't a hint of a smile on her face as she plowed through the rice and pork like a starving Dickensian child. When she was finished she stood up without a word, deposited her dishes in the sink and went to their bedroom, shutting the door firmly behind her.

Well then. He loaded his plate with another portion and ate alone, thinking that he'd made a mistake leaving the Lorenzo file at the station. He'd thought about bringing it home but had decided against it based on the frosty reception he'd received when he'd called earlier to tell her he'd be working late. He didn't want to push things, so he put the file into his secure desk drawer for the night. If he'd known Sally was going to hold her grudge all day, he could've brought the file home with him, gotten some work done. Now it looked like it'd be the Yankee game.

He did the dishes and placed them in the wooden drying rack next to the sink before he grabbed a beer from the fridge and collapsed into his chair in front of the television. Watching baseball was the ideal companion piece for some theorizing about the Lorenzo case. There were so many slow moments in the game that it afforded Rod plenty of time to speculate about the implications he'd unearthed talking to Burnett today.

If Joey Lorenzo knew that his friend Scott Jamison was sleeping with his girlfriend, it put a whole new spin on his disappearance. Given the age of the tubers and the often fragile infrastructure of adolescent relationships, finding out that one of your best friends is sleeping with your girlfriend behind your back could put you in a delicate state of mind. To Wakefield it meant one thing - the possibility that Lorenzo's death wasn't an accident at all.

25

When the messenger arrived at the red brick municipal building at 9:00 am Wednesday morning, Sal Ducati had already been at his desk in his office for two hours, working on the final details of Riverton's annual Memorial Day celebration. Each year there was a small parade down Main Street and a celebration at Blakeslee Park, where the mayor, the town supervisor and several decorated war veterans placed a wreath by the eternal flame monument that honored the memory of those who had died serving their country.

The parade and ceremony kicked off the bustling summer season in Riverton. In the ten years that he'd been mayor, Ducati and the village council had expanded the number of events and festivals hosted in Riverton exponentially until there was something happening in the village every weekend between Memorial Day and Labor Day. To him, it certainly wasn't rocket science. Luring visitors to the village meant additional cash being distributed among local businesses. And with the explosion in popularity of the free Tuesday and Wednesday concerts offered during the summer at GorgePark, Riverton had become one of the hottest real estate markets in western New York. Thousands of first-time visitors who attended these concerts and events discovered what Rivertonians had known for years: that life below the Niagara Escarpment, adjacent to the Niagara River, was something special.

A light knock on his door interrupted his thoughts. It was a man he'd never seen before holding an official-looking envelope. "Salvatore Ducati?" he asked, striding forward toward the mayor's desk and handing it to him before he could rise to his feet.

The mayor knew what was in the envelope. He'd been dreading this day, hoping against hope that it would never occur. He gazed at the envelope for a moment as the courier spun and left, closing the door on his way out. When the courier was gone, he reached into his drawer for a letter opener and slit open the envelope with trembling hands.

It was a subpoena, issued by Grossinger and Grossinger, signed by Max Grossinger, requesting his appearance to testify at the John Corelli trial. His hand quivered as he read the document. He'd been watching the reports of the trial on the local news each night, and as the prosecution trotted out witness after damaging witness, Ducati knew the likelihood that he'd be summoned to testify for the defense was a near certainty. The document in his hand confirmed his worst fear.

When he'd moved away from the Italian neighborhood on the south side of Niagara Falls where he'd been born and raised and relocated to Riverton thirty years ago, he never dreamed he would be in this position. Even after he sold his Ford dealership and was convinced by the Republican power brokers in Riverton to run for mayor, the thought that he'd be implicated in a political scandal down the road never occurred to him. This was Riverton, after all, where the crime rate was low and the pace was slower.

He'd dodged a bullet five years earlier when the former town attorney in Riverton had been convicted of bribery and conspiracy regarding the land sale and development of the local golf course owned by the Seneca Nation. Investigators from the FBI had failed to find any evidence linking him to the conspiracy, but the process had shaken him. He'd been more deliberate in assessing risk since then, wary of any proposal that came from a source beyond a tight circle of friends and associates.

He placed the subpoena on his desk gingerly and reached for the phone. He dialed the number of Max Grossinger's office that was listed on the document.

After two rings, a woman answered. "Law offices of Grossinger and Grossinger. How may I help you?"

"My name is Sal Ducati. I'm the mayor of Riverton. I'm calling about a subpoena that was delivered to my office this morning."

"What is this in regard to?" She was all crisp efficiency.

"The John Corelli trial."

Her tone shifted immediately to one of gracious deference. "Thank you for getting back to us, Mr. Mayor. What can I do for you today?"

"Well, I've read the subpoena and wondered if anyone in your office wanted to talk to me, give me some ideas about what kind of questions I might face."

"I'm sure Mr. Grossinger would like to speak to you before you testify. Unfortunately, he's tied up all day during the week with the trial. Are you available in the evenings?"

Ducati was cautious. "It depends on whether he wants me to come to his office or not."

"That won't be necessary," she said. "He's in Riverton for the trial every day. He'll come to you, if that suits you."

Ducati was relieved that he wouldn't have to drive to Buffalo. "That's fine. When would he like to meet?"

"Fairly soon, I would imagine. Judging from what we know about the prosecution's witness list, they could wind up their case by the end of the week if nothing unexpected comes to light. If this is a good number for you, I'll speak with Mr. Grossinger and get back to you as soon as I can."

"That would be fine. I'll await your call."

"Thanks, Mayor Ducati. I'll talk with you soon."

The mayor returned the phone to its stand and stared out the window toward the outdoor basketball court behind the building, trying to quell the feelings of uneasiness that were already forming in his mind. Being called as a character witness for a man accused of multiple counts of statutory rape was not a scenario he wanted to be a part of, especially when the accused was a colleague and friend. He wanted the trial to be over as quickly as possible. He'd been hoping that Corelli would accept a plea deal, negating the need for Ducati to testify, but it didn't look like that was going to happen.

*****

"Gillian! Gillian!"

Gillian Hudecki looked up from her desk, shaken from her reverie by the voice coming from her doorway. Therese Short was standing there, looking at her partner with concern. "Is everything okay? You looked like you were in outer space."

If you only knew, she thought grimly. "I was thinking about Scott."

155

"Has there been any news?"

"Nothing," she said despondently. "Not a word."

Therese sat in the guest chair opposite Gillian and reached across the desk to grasp her hands. "Maybe you should take the rest of the week off. I can cover your patients for you."

She squeezed Therese's hands with affection. "Thanks for the offer, but I think I'll keep working. It helps to keep me occupied, keep my mind from thinking about Scott."

Therese wasn't convinced. "Are you seeing anyone?"

Gillian's heart skipped a beat, her breath constricted by the question. She looked at Therese, unable to respond.

Therese broke the awkward silence. "A therapist, I mean. Someone professional."

Gillian was awash with relief. She wasn't referring to Lenny. "No."

"You should. I know a woman in Amherst that I think you'd like. Let me give you her number." She wrote the name and number and a note pad and handed it to Gillian. "Give her a call. It always helps to talk about things." She stood up. "I have to get back to my office. I have a consult at 10:00."

Gillian managed a small smile. "Thanks for caring, Therese. It means a lot to me."

Therese smiled in return. "What are friends for?"

After Therese departed Gillian rose and shut the door to her office. She sat back down and sighed, her agitation returning. She looked at the clock on the wall. She hadn't talked with Lenny since Monday. She missed him desperately, but she knew he was with his brother and his wife, bringing the boat from its winter home in Wilson to its summer berth at the Delifin Marina today. She wanted to call him, but she was afraid he would be mad. He'd told her several times that he wanted to let Red know about his relationship with Gillian first, but the more time passed, the more she wondered when that might happen. She was out on a limb without a net, feeling as alone as she'd ever felt.

156

"All gassed up?"

Red Campbell was talking to Mike Spacone. Lenny and Joanie were already on the *Scottish Rogue*, stowing their gear and preparing to cast off. The gleaming white Sea Ray was in the water, next to the marina gas pump.

"All set." Spacone looked out at Wilson Harbor, which was calm under a cloudless sky. "Looks like a great day for a cruise."

Red shook Mike's hand. "Thanks for getting it ready for us."

"No problem," said Mike. "Have a great trip."

Lenny switched on the ignition to let the engines warm up at idle speed while Red hopped aboard and undid the lines securing them to the dock. Lenny took the first mate's seat and Red slid behind the wheel, preparing to ease them away from the dock. Joanie was still below, storing the drinks and snacks they'd brought.

Red backed out and swung the boat gently around, heading for the jetty and the lake beyond, past the Sunset Grille where the patio was starting to fill with the lunch crowd. It was cool, in the low sixties, with a slight breeze from the south, a good day to make the ten-mile journey from Wilson to Delifin. Red kept his eye on the depth finder as he maneuvered the craft through the tight channel.

Once he was out of the jetty and on the lake he continued at idle speed on a northerly course until he reached the mile buoy, where he swung the boat to the west and gave it a little gas. The sleek craft lurched, and a squeal of protest came from below deck. "Hey! I'm trying to work down here!"

"Hurry up and get your ass up here," Red said to Joanie. "And bring me a water." He turned toward his brother. "You want anything?" Lenny shook his head.

Joanie emerged from below deck with a plastic bottle of water which she handed to her husband. She'd put on a sweatshirt for the ride. He looked at her quizzically. "Are you cold?"

157

"Not yet," she replied as she slid past the two brothers to take a seat in the stern of the boat. "But I will be. It's only May, and the water temperature is in the fifties. I'm not taking any chances."

Red turned to his brother and rolled his eyes but said nothing. There was a lone fisherman drifting off the starboard bow as they cruised past Tuscarora State Park, two lines in the water. Red pointed to the park. "That's where they found his van?"

Lenny nodded. "Yeah."

"With his wallet and cell phone in it?"

"Yep."

Red looked at his brother intently. "Sure sounds like a suicide to me. You said he didn't have a radio on his boat. Why would anyone with any brains go out on the lake without a cell phone?"

Good question, thought Lenny. "Nobody knows," he said.

"That poor man," Joanie said with compassion. She looked at Lenny. "You said he had a girlfriend, didn't you?"

Lenny tried to keep his expression blank. "Yeah."

"She must be out of her mind," Joanie said. "What a terrible thing, to have someone you love lost at sea." She looked out at the dark water and shook her head as she contemplated the area of the search. "It must be horrible for her."

Lenny looked away, toward the shore on his left. More than you know.

26

Rod Wakefield called Anne at the station house Wednesday morning to let her know he'd be a little late because he was going to stop by the library on his way to work to pick up some Riverton High School yearbooks. "I'll be there as soon as I can. Any messages?"

"Nothing urgent."

"Did Randy submit a report from the courthouse?"

"It's on your desk."

"Thanks, Anne. I'll see you in a little while."

He rubbed his neck, trying to work out an annoying kink. He'd spent the night on the couch rather than in the bedroom, opting to give Sally a little extra time to recover from her latest bout of exasperation with his unpredictable work schedule. If he gave her a wide enough berth, he found that her anger would usually subside more quickly.

By the time he finished showering Sally was out of bed, sitting at the kitchen table in her robe, reading the paper. He dressed quickly; although the library was only a five-minute walk from their home, he wanted to be there as soon as it opened.

Sally looked up from the summary of yesterday's Corelli trial testimony as Rod was heading for the door. "I missed you last night," she said simply.

"Me, too," he responded, rubbing his neck. "I'm too old to sleep on that couch."

She took a sip of coffee. "Will you be late tonight?"

"I hope not. I'll call you if something comes up."

She stood up and walked over to her husband. She reached up with both hands to caress his cheeks and gently pull him downward for a kiss. "I hate it when we fight," she whispered softly.

"That makes two of us." He squeezed her hand gently. "I'll see you tonight."

He walked down his driveway and turned left toward the library. It was a cool morning, with a high cloud cover. He was glad he'd worn his long-sleeved shirt today. Summer hadn't arrived quite yet.

Fran Killian, the head librarian at the Riverton Public Library, was standing by the front door, waiting for him to arrive. She was a bright, inquisitive woman in her late fifties, blond with short hair and an irrepressible smile that was on display as he approached. "Good morning, Chief."

He returned her smile. "Morning, Fran. How are the girls?"

"Just fabulous, thanks. Katherine is in New York, working at a bank, and Lisa works at Harry's Pub. She's the hostess." She inserted her key and opened the door, ushering him inside. She dropped her canvas book bag on a shelf behind the front desk and turned to face the chief. "What can I do for you today?"

"I'm looking for some Riverton High School yearbooks, 1970 to 1972."

She smiled. "That's easy. I'll be right back."

The Riverton Public Library building was relatively new, having been built in 1990 when the previous site, an historic three-story white clapboard house on the corner of Fifth and Main, became too small to accommodate the number of books on the shelves and the various programs sponsored by the library. The brick facility, located on a vacant plot of land in the village of Riverton which had previously been the site of the village baseball diamonds, was a striking Federalist design, twice the size of the old building, with a separate wing dedicated to children's programs. Wakefield thought it was one of the finest public libraries he'd seen, especially for a community as small as Riverton.

Fran was back in less than a minute, carrying the three volumes in both hands in front of her. She offered them to Rod. As he took them from her she said, "Normally we don't allow anyone to check these out. But I suppose we can trust the chief of police."

He nodded. "I'll have them back to you as soon as possible. Friday by the latest. I just need to make some copies."

"Working on a cold case?"

160

He smiled. "Something like that."

Fran smiled again. "It was nice to see you. Say hi to Sally for me."

He shifted the books to his right hand, carrying them like a student by his side. "I will. Take care, Fran."

As he walked through the village toward the station house he thumbed through the 1972 book until he came to Andrea Herman's senior picture. Immediately he could see why she had been popular with the boys. She was a raven-haired beauty, with dark eyes and a sensuous mouth featuring the kind of full lips women today sought to attain through plastic surgery. Even though the photos were black-and-white, it was obvious she possessed the sort of look that drove adolescent boys wild.

According to the blurb below her picture, she was a member of the Drama Club. He found the group photo for the club and found her standing at the end of the front row, both hands on hips, in a dark skirt several inches above her knees. She was busty, and the white blouse she was wearing had one too many buttons undone for his taste, at least for a yearbook photo. She looked every bit the good-time girl Robbie Burnett said she was.

Most of the morning crowd was gone from Borelli's Bakery as he walked by. All the service bays at Stebbins Mobil were filled, and an elderly woman walking her dog was sitting on a bench near the village gazebo, taking a break. He tipped his hat to the woman as he passed; she smiled back and nodded.

When the light changed he crossed Main and briskly walked the short block to the station, excited at the prospect of a real lead. He burst through the door and saw Anne at her desk. He was about to tell her about his successful trip to the library when she raised her fingers to her lips and motioned him inside his office. He entered obediently and she followed, closing the door behind her.

He dropped the yearbooks on his desk and looked at Anne. "What's up?"

She slid into his guest chair and leaned forward conspiratorially. "The mayor was served this morning. A subpoena from Grossinger. He's not too pleased."

161

"It's not like it was a complete surprise," Rod said. "He knew it was going to come."

"I think he was expecting Grossinger would have enough character witnesses to be able to get along without him."

He shook his head. "That's Sal – always hoping for a miracle. How's he taking it?"

"He's been holed up in his office with the door closed since the courier left." She looked at the books on his desk. "Find what you were looking for?"

He held up the 1972 yearbook. "I did. I wanted to get a feel for Andrea Herman from her high school days before I started to track her down."

"I think I can help you with that." She handed a folded piece of paper across the table to her boss.

"What's this?" he asked as he took it from her."

"The current address of one Andrea Herman Kirkpatrick. She's living in Niagara Falls, not far from the casino." She laughed at his look of surprise. "I have some friends in the Niagara Falls PD. They were very helpful."

"This is terrific, Anne," he said as he memorized the address. "Good work."

"At your service, Chief." She rose to her feet. "I'll let you get started. Call me if you need anything." She turned and exited the office, closing the door behind her.

He paged through the '72 yearbook but didn't find any additional pictures of Herman. Same with the two earlier years. There was a picture of her with her homeroom class in each, but no candids or club shots anywhere. Apparently she decided to become a thespian when she was a senior and not before.

He checked the reverse phone book to see if she had a phone at her residence. Nothing. Next he tried the three major cell carriers, hoping to get lucky, but none of the people he contacted on the phone fell for his pleas of cooperation. Their responses were identical – no information without a warrant. He tried a Google search of her name and image and came up empty as well. Frustrated, he leaned back in his chair, trying to figure out his next move.

Suddenly it came to him: taxes. He tried the state taxation department in Albany first, but was rebuffed for lack of a warrant. Same at the IRS; despite what he thought were some persuasive statements about inter-agency cooperation, the woman in the North Andover office was adamant. No information would be given out about any taxpayers without a court order, especially over the phone.

He picked up the piece of paper Anne had handed him and looked at the address. After a brief search he found it on Google maps. It was in one of the more rundown sections of the city, between the casino and a number of mostly vacant factory buildings that lined the Niagara River between the North Grand Island Bridge and Niagara Falls. He sighed and looked at his watch. Maybe she'd be home.

On his way out the door he passed by Anne's desk. "I'm going to the Falls to check out that address. Do you want me to bring you back anything for lunch?"

She smiled brightly. "I was hoping you'd ask. Would it be too much out of the way to stop at Viola's?"

"The one on Elmwood, near the City Market?"

"If that one's closer," she said hopefully.

"It is. You want the usual?"

She nodded vigorously. "Large steak and double cheese, extra napkins. Nothing to drink."

He made a note of her order. "I'll call if I'm held up at all. Who knows? Maybe she won't be home and I'll be back in an hour."

"Drive safely."

Andrea Herman Kirkpatrick lived in an area of Niagara Falls that had seen better days. Many of the homes in the neighborhood were neglected and had been for years, a result of a steady exodus of property owners as the factories, which once fueled a vibrant local economy, shuttered their doors. Before the casino was constructed in the old convention center building, blue collar workers, who made up the core of that industrial economy, were left with unenviable workplace options:

163

fast food joints, the outlet mall on the city's east side, or the tourist traps downtown near the Falls.

Many of those displaced workers fled to Vegas, the Carolinas and Phoenix, greener pastures with better weather and boomtown employment. As a result, areas of the city began to deteriorate as absentee landlords failed to maintain their properties adequately. Some places managed to find renters, but with no financial stakes in the homes where they were living, these renters did little to right the blight. Before long the south end of the city of Niagara Falls began to mirror Atlantic City: clean sidewalks and well-lighted streets in the vicinity of the casino, but as soon as you traveled two blocks in any direction, the neighborhoods went downhill fast.

Andrea Kirkpatrick lived in one of those areas just north of Buffalo Avenue in the upper unit of a private home that had been converted into a duplex. There was a rusted bicycle missing its front tire lying in the front yard of the property, within a chain-link fence whose lock was no longer functional. It was the kind of neighborhood used to seeing patrol cars on the street, especially at night.

Wakefield parked his unit in front of the house, got out and locked the doors. Across the street, a young black man in his twenties sat on the front step of a rundown brick ranch, smoking a cigarette, watching Wakefield warily. Rod gave him a wave and the young man stared back impassively, unmoved, determined not to give away a thing to the unfamiliar white cop from Riverton.

27

She came to the door after the third time he'd pressed the buzzer. She parted some curtains and stared cautiously at the uniformed officer standing on the porch. Rod flashed her his best community service smile. "Are you Andrea Kirkpatrick?"

She took in his uniform. "Who wants to know?"

He held his badge up to the window. "Rod Wakefield, Chief of Police in Riverton. I'd like to ask you a few questions."

"About what?" she asked defensively.

"It's about a case I'm working on. May I come in? It'll only take a few minutes of your time."

She hesitated for a moment, considering her options, then unlocked the deadbolt and opened the door. "Follow me. I'm upstairs."

He walked through a small vestibule and up an ornately carved cherry staircase to the second floor. He followed her through an open door into a small room with a threadbare cotton couch, one chair and a small portable television. Most of the floor area was covered with stacks of newspapers and magazines, the top of each stack covered with a fine sheen of dust.

She sat in the chair and pointed toward the couch. "Have a seat. What did you say your name was again?"

"Rod Wakefield, ma'am."

"What can I do for you, Officer Wakefield?"

He pulled out a notepad and a pen. "I'd like to ask you a few questions about Joey Lorenzo."

She shifted in her chair and leaned toward the chief, fixing him with a surprised look. "I haven't heard that name in years. What would you like to know?"

If he looked hard enough, he could envision the girl that had driven the boys wild back in high school. She'd put on weight, especially around the middle, her face was lined with wrinkles and her hair was mostly gray and unkempt instead of dark brown, but she still had the sensuous full lips that had been on display in her yearbook photos. Forty years ago, before the relentless cruelty of life had worn her down, she must've been quite a number.

"How well did you know Joey Lorenzo?"

"Pretty well, I guess. We dated for about a year."

"Do you remember when that was?"

"Oh, geez, it was a long time ago." She looked away, as if the answer was in the distance. "I was a senior at Riverton, I think."

"1972?"

She nodded. "That's the year I graduated, so yeah."

Wakefield jotted that down and looked up. "Were you still seeing him when he disappeared?"

"Yeah."

"Do you remember talking to the police back then after Joey went missing?"

She looked as though she'd bitten into a piece of spoiled fruit. "Yeah. That fuckin' Roberts."

"Cal Roberts?"

"Who else? What a prick. He gave me the creeps. Tried to feel me up in the station, that fuckin' pervert."

Rod tried to steer her back to the subject. "Can you recall if Chief Roberts asked you any questions back then about Scott Jamison?"

Her face softened. "Scotty?" She tried to think back. After a moment she said, "Maybe. I'm not sure. Why?"

"You knew Scott Jamison, too." It was a statement rather than a question.

"Yeah, I knew Scotty. I liked him."

166

"Did the two of you ever date?"

She smiled mysteriously. "I guess you could call it dating."

"Were you and Scott Jamison intimate with one another?"

She ran her hand through her hair and smiled. "You bet your ass we were. We had some heat going on."

Here we go. "Now, Mrs. Kirkpatrick---"

She interrupted. "Call me Andrea. I should've changed my name back when that cocksucker left me, but I had shingles and couldn't think about anything except how much it hurt."

"Andrea. Can you tell me if you were having sex with Scott Jamison at the same time you were intimate with Joey Lorenzo?"

She looked at Wakefield, her eyes suddenly sad. In a low voice she said, "Yes."

"Did Joey know that you were sleeping with Scott at the same time you were sleeping with him?" He watched her eyes closely.

"I don't know," she answered after a moment. "He might have, but I didn't tell him. And I don't think Scott did either." She looked at him expectantly, her eyes bright. "Do you know how Scott is? I haven't seen him in years. He was a nice boy."

"Do you watch much television, Andrea?"

"Not really. I like to watch *Wheel of Fortune* after dinner, but I usually don't stay up much later than that."

It was apparent she hadn't heard the news. "I'm sorry to be the one to break the bad news, but Scott went missing on Lake Ontario last week. There's been no sign of him since."

"Missing?" She looked puzzled. "That's impossible. Scotty was really good with boats, the best. He can't be missing."

"I'm afraid he is, Andrea. The Coast Guard and the sheriff's department searched for him but didn't find anything."

"Poor Scotty....." Her voice trailed away as she recalled her former lover and better days.

Rod leaned forward and patted her hand. "I think that does it, Andrea. Thanks for your cooperation."

He stood to leave, but instead of releasing his hand she gripped it tightly in her own. "But what about Scotty? Is anyone still looking for him?"

"The Coast Guard has called off their search, but a few of his friends are still looking." It was a small lie that might make her feel better.

"You have to keep looking," she insisted, her voice rising. "He knew everything about boats and being on the water. He must be out there somewhere."

He gently extracted his hand from hers and took a step back, toward the door. "I'll see what I can do, Andrea."

"Promise?"

"I promise. Thanks for answering my questions. You've been a big help."

"Help?" Her voice was choked with sadness. "I don't understand. Scotty's lost....."

"Would you like me to call you if I hear anything?"

She brightened. "Would you?"

"Of course," he said reassuringly. "Why don't you give me your number?" He pulled out his pad and pen.

She turned back and shuffled through a pile of papers on the small table next to her chair before unearthing her cell phone from beneath an overdue electric bill. She handed it to him. "Here it is. But I don't remember the number. I wish they'd put it on the phone like they did before cell phones were invented."

He looked the phone over but could find no indication of her number. He wrote his number on his pad, tore off the sheet and handed it to her. "Call my number. Then I'll know what your number is."

Haltingly, she punched in the number Wakefield had handed her. After a moment his phone rang. He punched a number to end the call and saved the number displayed on the screen. "I have it now. If I hear anything about Scott, I'll give you a call. Thanks again - you've been a really big help."

"Don't forget to call me," she pleaded with the urgency of a woman who spent too many hours alone in this depressing walk-up.

"I won't, Andrea. I promise. I'll let myself out."

His mind was percolating with possibilities as he walked down the stairs, through the gate and to his car. It seemed clear now that Joey Lorenzo could've known that Scott Jamison was sleeping with Andrea Herman at the time of Lorenzo's disappearance. Would that have been enough to drive him to commit suicide that night? Or maybe he *had* fled to Canada to avoid the draft, another theory that had been voiced at the time but dismissed for lack of corroboration. Thinking that you've lost your girlfriend to one of your best friends might certainly be incentive enough to push you toward the Canadian shore, especially if you were already considering it.

As he inserted the key into the ignition he looked across the street. The young black man was still there on the stoop, still smoking, watching him as he pulled away from the curb. Wakefield gave him a smile and a wave as he drove away, feeling energized. He finally had a real lead.

28

"So your boyfriend didn't show yesterday."

Kelly Porter gave John Herrington a look of disdain. "You can really be an asshole."

Herrington looked up from the morning paper, smiling. "I can't help what people think. I'm only being honest."

The two of them were alone in the Delifin AC. Kelly had arrived to open up ten minutes earlier and found Herrington waiting for her by the side door. He was wearing shorts and boat shoes, his standard fare, but the chill of the overcast morning had forced him to don a wool sweater.

As she moved between the bar and the kitchen, preparing for the luncheon crowd, he read the morning paper in his usual seat, his first gin and tonic of the day on the bar in front of him. There wasn't much of interest until he reached the obituaries. There his attention was grabbed by a familiar name and face. "Wow."

Kelly stuck her head out of the kitchen. "What?"

He held up the page he'd been reading. "Skip Gunn died yesterday."

"That's awful," she said, walking over to peer at the story over his shoulder. "What happened?"

"It doesn't say. But judging from the write-up, I'd guess it was a heart attack." He shook his head. "I just talked to him at the club last week. He seemed fine."

Skip Gunn was a local legend, one of the finest freshwater sailors in the country, and a former commodore of the Delifin Yacht Club. Gunn had been one of Herrington's advocates when he applied for membership to the club years ago, and although they were not close, they were friendly. With his brother, he'd founded Gunn Design, an architectural and engineering firm that had grown from an initial three-person office in Niagara Falls to an international design firm, with offices throughout North America.

"How old was he?" Kelly asked.

"Seventy-seven."

"That's too young."

"I'll say. He was one of the most active guys I knew, at any age. He still sailed solo to Toronto and back each summer."

There was a noise from the stairwell that led to the upper floors of the four-story stone building. Peter Malecki appeared from around the corner. "Skip Gunn is dead?"

Herrington held up the paper again. "Yesterday. Heart attack."

Peter looked like he'd just fallen out of bed: hair tousled, uncombed, wearing a rumpled T-shirt and jeans that looked like he'd slept in them. "I liked Skip. He was down-to-earth, a nice guy. You'd never know that he was such a big deal." He turned toward Kelly. "Is the soup on yet?"

"I got it out as soon as I opened up," she replied. "Do we have any chili in the freezer? It's a bit cool out today. It might be popular."

"I'll check the freezer in the basement. There might be some there." Peter said.

As Peter descended the stairs to the basement, the side door rattled. In walked Parnell Gomez. Herrington reached across the bar to jab Kelly, but she skipped nimbly out of reach. "Here's your chance," he hissed. "Why don't you ask him for his autograph?"

Kelly gave him a sour look before she walked to the other end of the bar where Gomez had taken a seat. "The usual?" she asked pleasantly.

Gomez nodded. He looked around the bar as his eyes adjusted to the dark interior. He saw Herrington at the opposite end and gave him a slight wave of his hand. Herrington returned the wave. "Glad you could make it. Kelly's been worried about you."

Gomez looked at Kelly, whose face was beginning to flush as she placed a glass of iced tea on a coaster in front of him. "Because I didn't come in yesterday? How nice of you to worry about me."

"Oh, she wasn't worried. She wanted to ask you some questions about your book." Herrington said with a grin. "Did she tell you she's married?"

Kelly's face was full crimson as she struggled to maintain control. "Ignore that asshole. Pardon my French."

"What book is he talking about?"

Her voice was barely audible across the bar. "*Highway 41 Revisited.*"

Gomez nodded, frowning slightly. "My first effort. Not my best."

"I thought it was wonderful."

He looked at her more closely. "You already finished it?"

Kelly nodded. "I couldn't put it down. I read it in two days."

"What did you like about it?" Gomez queried.

She took a deep breath. "The main character, I guess. And the descriptions of the land along the highway, especially that park."

"Bon Echo," Gomez said. "It's a beautiful place, one of the most breathtaking places I've ever seen."

"Why would an American write about a place like that?" she asked. "How did you even find out about it?"

"I grew up in Potsdam, New York, not far from the Canadian border. My parents liked to camp, and we went to Bon Echo Provincial Park for a week when I was twelve. I fell in love with the place as soon as we stopped the car." He smiled, remembering. "The smell of the pines next to the lake was intoxicating. It was the freshest air I'd ever breathed. And there were tons of things to do for kids, all sorts of arts and crafts programs, boats and bikes to rent. When the week was up, I begged my parents to stay longer, but my father only had one week of vacation, so we came home. I made up my mind to come back as soon as I could, but that didn't happen until I'd graduated from college. By then I knew I wanted to be a writer, and that's when I traveled the length of Highway 41 from Kaladar to Pembroke for the first time. The words just seemed to pour out when I sat down at my desk after the trip had ended."

"Have you been back since?" Kelly asked.

"Several times."

Herrington chimed in. "I knew I recognized that name! I've been up there."

Kelly looked at him in amazement. "To that park?"

"No, but I've been to Kaladar. It's a bump in the road you drive through on the way to Tom Martin's cottage."

Now Gomez was interested. "Is his cottage on Mazinaw Lake?"

Herrington shook his head. "No, that doesn't sound right. I think it began with an S. It was an unusual name."

"Skootamatta?"

Herrington's eyes lit up. "That's it! Skootamatta Lake."

"Your friend is very lucky," Gomez said. "It's a beautiful place."

"He used to have a party there every Labor Day weekend when we were in college and a few years after that. Unfortunately, I don't remember much about the scenery except that we were on a lake and there were lots of trees. Oh yeah, and you had to shit in an outhouse."

"That's because you were shitfaced most of the time you were there," Kelly said sarcastically.

Herrington corrected her. "*All* of the time. I've never seen so much beer disappear in four days." He grabbed his drink and walked down to sit next to Gomez. "What about the other book? The one about pussy."

Gomez laughed, a full-throated chuckle. "*Escape From Vagina Ridge*? The title is self-explanatory."

Herrington persisted. "But is it any good? I don't want to waste my time if there isn't any sex."

"Or pictures," Kelly added.

173

"You'll have to be the judge of that," Gomez said smoothly. "You'll just have to read it to find out." He turned to Kelly. "How about putting in my lunch order? I'm really hungry."

"Be right back." She walked into the kitchen.

When she was gone Herrington stuck out his hand. "John Herrington."

Gomez responded with a strong grip. "Parnell Gomez. Pleased to meet you."

"How long are you in town for, Parnell?"

"I've rented a place on Stonewall Street in the village for a couple of months. I should be here until the end of June."

"How do you like it so far?"

Gomez took a sip of his iced tea. "It's beautiful. I'll bet when the weather warms up it really lives up to its nickname."

Herrington looked puzzled. Gomez continued. "Key North. I've heard several people refer to Delifin as Key North since I arrived. When I was in here Monday Kelly explained it to me."

"Key North pretty much sums it up," Herrington said agreeably. "I wished I'd thought of it."

Kelly emerged from the kitchen. "I'm surprised that you don't try to take credit for that," she said in mock amazement.

"I think it was Daffy Franklin who came up with it," Herrington said. "It was a good call, whoever made it." He looked at the clock on the wall, then at Kelly. "I think I have time to eat, as long as Parnell is. Give me a tuna melt with a side of potato salad."

"No soup?"

"Not today." He raised his glass to Gomez. "Here's to a productive stay in Key North."

Gomez clinked his glass lightly against Herrington's. "I'll second that."

174

*****

After dropping off the steak and cheese sandwich Anne had requested, Wakefield spent the rest of the afternoon on the phone, chasing down the remaining survivors of the tubing expedition. He found Ted Stephens living in a suburb of Greensboro, North Carolina. He spoke to his wife Jennifer, who told Wakefield that her husband was on a job site where the cell reception might be iffy. Wakefield asked her to have her husband call him as soon as he could; she promised he would.

He ran into a roadblock with the next name on his list. After graduating from Buffalo State, William Emerson had accepted a teaching position in Valdosta, Georgia, but left that position under suspicious circumstances after two years. He drifted south to Florida where he worked for several years at a canning facility in Tampa, until he was let go following an industrial accident that left him with a head injury, unable to work. Emerson's trail ended in Miami two years ago, at a walk-in clinic in a Cuban neighborhood where he'd been convalescing after a serious automobile accident. After being released from the clinic, he'd simply vanished.

He had more luck with the last remaining participant in the ill-fated trip down the river. Allan O'Rourke was a successful commercial insurance broker who lived in Atlanta and had a summer home in Morehead City, North Carolina. He reached O'Rourke at his office, after convincing O'Rourke's protective executive assistant that it was imperative he speak to her boss immediately.

O'Rourke's voice was clear and confident. "This is Allan O'Rourke. What can I do for you, Chief?"

"I'd like to ask you a few questions about the night Joey Lorenzo disappeared."

Silence at the other end. When O'Rourke spoke again, it was with caution. "Does this have anything to do with Scott's disappearance?"

"So you know about that."

"One of my high school friends texted me last week that Scott was missing."

"Was Scott a member of your group that night in 1972?"

175

"Yes."

"Were the two of you close?"

O'Rourke hesitated before answering. "We were friends. We hung out together. But after college I went to graduate school in Arizona and lost track of him. I haven't seen him in forty years."

"Did you know Andrea Herman?"

"Yeah. She was Joey's girlfriend."

"Did you know that she was also dating Scott back then?"

"No." He sounded genuinely surprised. "But Andrea was always popular with the guys. I guess she could've been dating Scott, but he never mentioned it to me."

Wakefield pressed on. "I spoke with Andrea earlier today. She told me that she and Scott were dating at the same time that she was Joey's girlfriend."

O'Rourke was starting to put the pieces together. "Where are you going with this?"

"I'm trying to find out if Joey Lorenzo knew that Scott Jamison was sleeping with Andrea Herman while she was supposed to be his girlfriend."

"What does that have to do with Scott's disappearance?"

"I'm not sure. I'm just trying to get a sense of everything that happened that night."

"It should be in the report. We all talked to that cop, Roberts, the day after Joey disappeared. He talked to our parents, too."

"But he never asked you about Scott and Andrea? Or Joey and Andrea?"

His response was emphatic. "No. I would've remembered that. Roberts never said anything about Andrea to me. I'm positive."

Wakefield weighed O'Rourke's response before concluding he'd found out all he was going to find today. "Okay. If you remember anything else, please give me a call at my office in Riverton. Your assistant has my number. Thanks for taking the time to speak with me, Mr. O'Rourke."

"My pleasure, Chief. Always glad to help."

29

As soon as O'Rourke finished his call with Wakefield, he dialed Ted Stephens' number. He left a terse voicemail: "Ted, this is Allan O'Rourke. I just talked with a Riverton cop about Joey Lorenzo and Scott Jamison. Call me as soon as you can."

He dropped his phone on his desk and stared without focus out the window. He'd been sure this was behind them – there'd been no contact with the authorities after the boys had given their initial statements to Cal Roberts the morning after the ill-fated trip. The Riverton cop who'd called today had been cagey, fishing for information about Joey and Scott and Andrea Herman, of all people. He'd managed to maintain his composure, but by the end of the call beads of cold sweat had materialized on his forehead and the back of his neck.

The cop hadn't said anything about Mouse. Allan had lost track of him after Mouse lost his job at the canning plant in Tampa. Which was fine - he'd heard that Mouse had really gotten into cocaine after everyone but Scott had moved away from Riverton. The farther he was from Willie Emerson, the better he felt. As far as he knew, Ted hadn't heard from him, either. If he had, he'd never mentioned it.

He hadn't known that Scott had been banging Andrea at the same time she was dating Joey. That put a whole new spin on things. If Joey had found out that Andrea was double dipping, it could explain a lot. Especially the scene that had stayed with him all these years: the sight of Joey Lorenzo willfully removing his lifejacket and tossing it away before slipping off his inner tube and disappearing into the vortex of a whirlpool.

*****

By Friday afternoon District Attorney Charles Moreland had wrapped up the prosecution's case against John Corelli. Thursday and Friday the evidence he presented consisted solely of transcripts of emails that Fred Malinowski had managed to resurrect after Corelli had tried unsuccessfully to scrub them from his hard drives. The conversations between Corelli and his two victims were chilling: deliberate and predatory, it was evident that Corelli had dangled an increase in academic standing in his class to each of the girls to convince them to participate in a number of sexual encounters. One such incident had taken place in the back seat of Corelli's car in a distant corner of the parking lot at the middle school and had been filmed by one of the security cameras used to monitor the area.

During the two weeks of the trial Max Grossinger had seen the chances of any sort of positive outcome for his client slowly evaporate. The only card he still held that seemed worth anything was Lisette Gaffney, one of the two victims. She was a local bad girl, festooned with tattoos and bristling with attitude. If he put her on the stand he felt he could introduce the concept of reasonable doubt where her seduction was concerned. All he had to do was push her buttons and allow her to expose her attitude in the courtroom. If she lost what little composure he'd seen her express during pre-trial interviews, it wasn't a stretch to think that at least one juror might think that she, rather than Corelli, had been the aggressor in the relationship.

But that didn't erase the fact that she was only fifteen. No matter who the aggressor was, despite all the consent in the world, any sexual act involving her and any male would be deemed to be statutory rape. There was no way around that. Even the courtroom wizardry of Max Grossinger would be unable to counter the irrefutable fact that she was a minor, just thirteen when the alleged incidents had occurred.

Moreland had been pushing hard for a plea deal since before the trial had begun, but Grossinger and Corelli had both resisted, each of them in their own way unwilling to comprehend the devastating effect the transcripts and video evidence would have on the jury. Grossinger could see it in the eyes of the jury as the prosecution methodically presented its case. With each new piece of evidence he sensed that they couldn't wait to hand down guilty verdicts, followed by maximum sentences on each of the counts. Grossinger was sure that Corelli's goose was cooked and only some sort of compromise with the district attorney's office could lessen the severity of his punishment.

But Corelli had held fast so far, improbably thinking that the testimony of his friends and associates, like Sal Ducati, would be able to sway the jury in his favor after the defense had rested its case. That Corelli couldn't seem to see the trend of the trial was troubling for Grossinger, further indication that his client was delusional and probably had been for some time.

He mentioned that to his wife as they were waiting for their salads to arrive Friday evening. They were at Hutch's, Grossinger's favorite restaurant in Buffalo, enjoying a Sonoma County Cabernet. "He doesn't see it at all. He doesn't stand a chance, no matter what I do."

"What about his wife? Surely she'd like to see this thing end as quickly as possible." Sheila Grossinger dabbed at her lips using her linen napkin. "Is she still coming to court every day?"

"No. She was a regular the first week, but she missed four days this week."

"There you go," Sheila said. "You said they have two kids, teenagers. I'll bet she's in his ear daily, telling him to end this. She must know the only salvageable thing at this point is her relationship with her kids. I'm sure their marriage was finished the day he was arrested. What's her name again?"

"Liz."

"Leave it to Liz. Encourage her if you get a chance. Tell her how hopeless it is for this to go to the jury."

"I've already told him that. Several times."

"Yes, but you're not the mother of his children. Let her use Catholic guilt – you said they're Catholic, right? – to convince him to take a deal."

"I don't know," he said doubtfully. "He's pretty fucked up. She might not be able to get through to him."

Their salads arrived. When the waiter had retreated she looked across the table and smiled at her husband. "What have you got to lose?"

*****

"Gillian? Who's Gillian?"

Red Campbell, his wife Joanie and brother Lenny were on the *Scottish Rogue*, heading out into Lake Ontario for a sunset cruise Friday evening when Lenny's cell phone rang. Before Lenny could react Red had snatched the phone from the dashboard of the boat and read the Caller ID, turning toward his brother with an expectant look.

Shit. Trying to keep his voice steady, Lenny replied. "Someone from the gun club."

Joanie read the implication immediately. Her voice was brimming with excitement. "A woman? Is she your girlfriend?" Joanie was an inveterate matchmaker and had tried for years to set up some of her friends, other flight attendants, with Lenny, to no avail. As far as Joanie knew, Lenny might still be a virgin. She hadn't seen him with a woman or even heard him mention one other than in friendly terms during the twenty years Red and Joanie had been together.

"She's on my skeet team. We shoot on Tuesday nights."

Joanie persisted. "Why is she calling you on a Friday? Check to see if she left a message."

Red turned toward his brother. "Do I know her?"

"No," Lenny said. "She's from the Southern Tier. She moved here about ten years ago."

"What does she do?" Joanie asked, unwilling to let it go.

He decided to play dumb. "I don't know. I think she's a dentist. One of those who puts braces on kids."

Joanie nodded approvingly. "An orthodontist. How long have you known her?"

"I don't know," Lenny said. "A year, maybe more." He shook his head. "She's just on my team," he finished lamely.

"Maybe you should check to see if she left a message," Joanie suggested again.

Lenny ignored her persistence and instead slipped the phone into the pocket of his shorts. "I'll check later." He rose from his first mate's seat and headed for the cooler in the stern of the boat. "Who needs one?" he asked, opening the lid.

His brother snorted. "I thought you'd never ask."

Lenny grabbed an ice cold bottle of Canadian, slipped it into a coozie and handed it to his brother, who took a long swallow. Lenny looked at Joanie. "How about you?"

"I'll have some water," she said.

He handed her a plastic bottle and returned to his seat, determined to keep the conversation away from Gillian Hudecki. "Let's check out the new monster house going up on the Club Driftwood property before it gets too dark. You guys haven't seen it yet."

Red adjusted their course to head east, past Fort Ontario. As an electrician, anything in the construction realm was something in which he was keenly interested. "How far along are they?"

"The framing is up, and they've fortified the seawall," Lenny said. "Daffy Franklin told me the seawall cost two hundred grand alone."

"Who's doing the electric?" Red asked.

Lenny shook his head. "Don't know. Maybe you should put in a bid. Looks like they have deep pockets."

Red took another sip of beer. "I don't care how deep their pockets are. They can't afford me." He angled the craft toward the shore, eyes on the depth chart. He knew there was a large unmarked rock just beneath the surface to the east of the park, one that had wreaked havoc with many propellers and hulls throughout the years. He wanted to give it a wide berth, so as soon as he spotted it on the screen, he eased the *Scottish Rogue* a safe distance to the north of the rock until he was past it. He could see the seawall reinforced with riprap and huge boulders, and beyond it the framing of the main house as he approached slowly.

It was an enormous structure, even in its rough frame phase. Red whistled and turned to his brother. "Jesus. Looks like a hotel." He appraised it dispassionately. "At least fifteen thousand square feet. Pretty big for a private residence. Who owns it?"

"One of the Michaels brothers. The oldest one, Harry." Lenny said.

"I guess cleaning up hazardous waste still pays pretty well," Red observed, referencing the company that Harry and his brothers owned in Niagara Falls. The four Michaels boys had inherited a general contracting company from their father after he'd retired and transformed it into one of the most lucrative hazardous waste remediation firms in the country.

Red cut the engines and they floated two hundred yards from shore as Joanie snapped several pictures of the lot and structure's

182

framing with her cell phone camera. Lenny felt his phone vibrate in his pocket. He looked up to see if his brother had noticed, but he and Joanie were both staring at the shore. He snuck a quick look at the screen: Gillian Hudecki. He shoved the phone back into his pocket and made himself yet another promise to call her as soon as he was alone.

30

Gillian fumed as the phone rang and rang, finally going to voicemail. She was sure Lenny was dodging her, leaving her to twist in the wind all by herself. She ended the call without leaving a message and dropped her phone on the kitchen table, where she was eating a reheated chicken pot pie for dinner. That bastard, she thought. He was the only one who knew what she was going through, how much pressure she was under.

Her heart leaped when the phone rang a moment later. Thinking it was Lenny phoning her back, she answered without looking at the screen to see who it was. "Hello?" she offered breathlessly.

It wasn't Lenny. It was a female voice she recognized, one that sapped her enthusiasm immediately. "Gillian? Is that you?"

"Yes, Dolores. What do you want?" Impatience oozed from her response.

Scott Jamison's mother got straight to the point. "Have you found it yet?"

At least she was sober this time. "Found what?"

"The insurance policy. The one I asked you about the other day."

Gillian struggled to maintain control. "I've been pretty busy, Dolores. I've had other more important things on my mind."

"Like what?"

Could she be that clueless? "Trying to find out what happened to Scott. And running a business, for starters."

"I'll tell you what happened to Scott," she said with a nasty edge. "He's dead. Which means I have some money coming my way."

"So you say. But so far that insurance policy you're so sure has your name on it is just a figment of your imagination. Besides, Scott's missing, not dead. It takes seven years before a missing person can be declared dead."

Dolores was indignant. "Who told you that?"

"It's common knowledge. At least for anyone who graduated from high school." A direct dig at Dolores, who had dropped out of high school at fifteen to give birth to her only child.

"Maybe I should get an attorney." Her voice trailed off, bravado gone.

"Knock yourself out. And if you do, make sure it's him calling me back. I don't want to hear from you again." She ended the call before Dolores could respond and turned off her phone to dodge the inevitable call back.

*****

It took less than two weeks after her husband's arrest for Liz Corelli to determine that it was necessary for their two teenaged children to spend some time with her sister and brother-in-law in Cedar Rapids. The bullying began immediately, as soon as the video of John Corelli's arrest was shown that night last summer on the three local news outlets. Their Facebook accounts were suspended, but not before a litany of vile accusations, some of the most brutal emotional abuse Liz had ever seen, had been posted. By their so-called friends.

Both Joseph, sixteen, and Maria, fourteen, protested when they were told they'd be moving to Iowa. They had been out of New York only one time previously, six years earlier when the family had driven to Disney World during Easter vacation. Like most of their adolescent peers, their world was myopic, revolving around their friends and their life in Riverton. Iowa? Neither Joseph nor Maria could pick Iowa out on a map of the United States, despite the fact that their father was a teacher. From their perspective, they might as well be headed to China.

A deal had been worked out with the administration of Washington High School, where the Corelli children started attending classes last fall, to register them as Joseph and Maria Simmons. It was a necessary lie that all involved decided would help to shield the children as much as possible from the sort of harassment they'd endured in Riverton. The story for public consumption was that Joseph and Maria were the children of Chandler's fictional brother Kevin and his equally bogus wife Karen, who'd been involved in a serious automobile accident. The story for public consumption was that the two children were staying with their uncle and aunt while their parents recovered from their injuries.

Despite relentless pressure from the various media outlets covering the story, the location of the children had thus far remained a mystery. It helped immensely that Liz Corelli, unlike her husband, had no online presence. She wasn't on Facebook or Twitter; she didn't even trust online commerce or banking. Anyone trying to track down her sister or other family members would have their work cut out for them.

But she missed them terribly. Using a burner cell phone that had been Max Grossinger's suggestion, she called them daily, trying to keep up with their new lives in the heartland. Every call featured a request from one or both of them: when can we come home? It broke Liz's heart to have to fend off these requests, to try to explain that they were better off where they were, at least until the trial ended.

But what then? From the way things looked, her husband would be headed to prison soon and she'd be a single parent. Would she have to leave the area, too, pack up what remained of their lives and start over in some place like Cedar Rapids? She didn't like to think about it, but knew that it was something she had to deal with not too far down the road. Staying in Riverton after the trial ended wasn't much of an option – they all would need a fresh start somewhere far from the whispers and innuendoes that were sure to continue should they decide to stay. And what about trying to sell the house? Who would want to live in a house where such a pervert had resided?

These thoughts and others like them were never far from her mind as the trial proceeded. Now that the prosecution had rested, the end was certainly near. Even Max was starting to condition her to the inevitable outcome: that her husband, the father of their children, was about to be sent away for a long time, labeled for the rest of his life as a child rapist and sex offender. The life they knew, or thought they knew, had ended last June. Nothing would ever be the same again.

*****

Wakefield's line lit up. It was Anne. "Chief, I have Ted Stephens on the line."

He sat up and rummaged for the notes he'd jotted down when he'd spoken with Allan O'Rourke two days earlier. "Put him through."

When they were connected Rod continued. "Thanks for returning my call, Mr. Stephens. Do you have a few minutes?"

Stephens tone was brusque, businesslike. "That's why I'm here, Chief. What can I do for you?"

"I'm investigating the disappearance of Scott Jamison. Are you up to date on the case?"

An hour earlier Stephens had phoned O'Rourke, who'd filled him in on his conversation with Wakefield. "I know that Scott went missing last week. Has there been any progress?"

"I'm afraid not, Mr. Stephens."

"Is anyone still searching the lake?"

"No," Rod said apologetically. "The Coast Guard suspended their search last weekend. A few of his friends have continued to look, but so far they haven't turned up any sign of him or his boat."

"So he's dead." Stephens' tone was flat, dispassionate.

"Officially, he's listed as missing. But it doesn't look good," Rod conceded. "I'd like to ask you a few questions about Joey Lorenzo and the night he disappeared."

O'Rourke had prepared him for this line of questioning, so he tried to sound surprised. "What does Joey have to do with Scott's disappearance?"

"I'm not sure," Rod said. "That's what I hope you can help me with. Were you friends with Scott Jamison in 1972?"

Stephens hedged a bit. "I don't know if you could really say that. I was friends with Mouse, Guinea and OD, but Scott was sort of a hanger-on, if you know what I mean."

"I'm afraid I don't."

"Mouse—"

Wakefield broke in. "Just to be clear, by Mouse you mean William Emerson."

187

"Yeah," Stephens said. "Willie Emerson. He was the only one of us who would've been considered a friend of Scott. Willie had some trouble recruiting people for the ride, as I recall. Scott was probably his fourth or fifth choice."

"Why choose him at all? Why not just go with four people, especially since you were all friends?"

Stephens paused for a moment before responding. "That's a good question. For some reason Mouse, er, Willie, thought we needed five people for the ride. He never said why. He just insisted on it."

"Did you know Andrea Herman?" Wakefield asked.

Another area O'Rourke had mentioned. "I knew who she was. She had a bit of a reputation in high school. There weren't too many girls like that back then, so she stood out. Or her reputation did."

"Were you aware that she was dating Joey Lorenzo at the time he disappeared?"

"Sure," Stephens said. "Joey liked to brag about the way girls were attracted to him. The rest of us just chalked it up to macho Italian bullshit."

"Did you know that Andrea was also sleeping with Scott back then?"

He hadn't known that, but O'Rourke had filled him in when they'd spoken earlier. "I didn't. Like I said, I didn't know Scott that well. He was more of a jock. I wasn't too friendly with the athletes in high school."

"So you don't know if Joey knew that Scott was sleeping with Andrea that night?" Wakefield said.

"No."

"Would you say Joey had a temper?"

"He was pretty emotional, more than the rest of us, I suppose, but I figured it was just because he was Italian."

Wakefield pressed. "If Joey knew that Andrea was also sleeping with Scott, do you think he would've mentioned it to one of the other guys?"

Stephens thought for a moment before answering. "Honestly, I don't know. There was always a lot of bragging about sex back then from all of the guys. I really didn't pay much attention."

"Do you remember the order you entered the river that night?"

O'Rourke had prepped him for this question, reminding him to stick to the story they'd cobbled together at the Riverside Inn that night once they knew Joey was missing. "Willie, Scott, me, Allan and Joey."

"You're sure Joey went last?"

"Positive. The Riverton cop asked us that over and over when he interviewed us the next day. Joey went last."

"Have you heard from Scott since that night?"

Stephens was emphatic. "Not a word. It was the last time I spoke with Scott. I saw him once at the AC the next summer, but we didn't speak."

"The Delifin Athletic Club?"

"Yeah. The AC."

Wakefield was at the end of his short list of questions. "I think that's it for now, Mr. Stephens. Thanks for getting back to me."

"No problem. Say, Chief?"

"Yes?"

"Was Scott married? Did he have a family, any kids?"

"No. He has a girlfriend, but he's never been married as far as we can tell. No kids, either."

"All alone," Stephens said somberly. "What a horrible way to die."

"You're right about that."

189

31

When Joanie finished snapping pictures of the Michaels' mansion, Red swung the boat around and continued to cruise east slowly. He turned to his brother. "Seen Martin lately?"

Lenny shook his head. "No. The last time I saw Herrington, he told me he was traveling a lot again since he got his job back."

"How about his girlfriend?" asked Joanie. "I liked her."

Red nodded. "Me, too. Maya, right?"

"I think that's her name," his brother said. "Haven't seen her since last summer."

They still had about twenty minutes before the sun dropped into the lake. Streaks of teal, magenta and salmon framed the orange globe as it descended slowly. Red continued for a few minutes more until he found what he was looking for. He slowed even more and shifted into neutral as they floated opposite a line of cottages. "No lights on."

They were opposite the cabin by the lake where Tom Martin had lived since his divorce. Curtains were drawn on the floor-to-ceiling windows facing the lake, making it obvious that its inhabitant wasn't around. There was no sign of the kayak he used regularly, either – if Martin was in town the vessel would've been resting on the rack next to the dock.

"Did you know that OD was his landlord?"

Lenny's face was blank as he regarded his brother's question. "Who's OD?"

"Allan O'Rourke. His nickname in high school and college was OD. He made a shitload of money selling commercial insurance and bought a bunch of places: this one, the one in Atlanta where he lives, a beach house in North Carolina and another one in Islamorada, in the Keys. He still has season tickets for the Bills and flies back each fall for the home games."

"Didn't his father have a Chris Craft at the marina in Delifin?" Lenny asked, remembering.

Red nodded. "A thirty-six-footer. OD used to borrow it to take us to Toronto for the weekend. On a calm day, we could make it in forty-five minutes." Red smiled. "Those were the good old days. Single and on the loose in Toronto."

Joanie gave him a sharp jab in the ribs. "You're not single anymore."

Red sighed. "I know. You never let me forget it."

"That's my job."

*****

After his arrest the previous June, John Corelli had spent five months in the Niagara County jail in Lockport before he was able to raise bail money. It had been difficult. As soon as his arrest on statutory rape charges became public knowledge, people he had considered his friends began to back away, suddenly unreachable. Phone calls and emails went unanswered; no one wanted to be associated with a pedophile. Finally, after Liz pleaded with her parents, they'd taken a second mortgage on their home. Liz managed to sell the family's boat, motor and trailer at a deep discount, which finally provided enough cash to trigger his release.

There were severe restrictions attached to his release by the court. Because of the nature of his crime, he was housebound, a monitoring device attached to his ankle to prevent him from leaving his property. He was also forbidden to access the Internet, which meant no computers or smartphones were allowed in the house. The conditions suited Corelli; the few occasions he'd been in the public since his arrest had been unnerving, the level of vitriol he'd encountered fierce and unrelenting. He'd been punched and spit upon several times despite having a police escort whenever he was being transported between the jail and the court. He'd wondered how people knew when he was going to be out in public; he suspected the police leaked the information.

Once he was at home Liz treated him as though he was invisible, a non-entity. She'd interrogated him tearfully as soon as he'd been released from jail, still not wanting to believe him capable of such venal acts. When he finally broke down and confessed that, yes, he'd carried on affairs with two of his students, it was the last straw for her. She told him she would do her best to support him in public for as long as she could, but at home he was on his own. She contacted an attorney and was planning to file for divorce as soon as the jury returned a verdict.

191

She'd begged him to accept a plea deal in order to avoid the spectacle of a trial but he'd refused, convinced that Max Grossinger's experience and skill could convince the jury that he was not guilty even though he'd confessed his guilt to his wife. She'd increased her pressure once the trial began and the prosecution began to lay out its case, including the sordid emails and videos gleaned from his computers, but he refused to budge. He had the best defense attorney in the state, he argued, and despite mountains of evidence to the contrary, he expected to be acquitted of all charges.

She phoned Grossinger after the prosecution had rested its case on Friday and left a message, asking him to call her back. She was watching an inane comedy about two waitresses when her house phone rang a little past nine. Grossinger calling back. "Hello, Mr. Grossinger. Thanks for getting back to me."

"Call me Max. What can I do for you, Liz?"

"How did it go today?"

A measured pause. "I'm not going to lie to you, Liz. It wasn't a good day for the defense. The prosecution rested its case with some powerful testimony. We'll begin to present our witnesses on Tuesday."

"That's why I was calling. Did you talk to John about accepting the deal?"

"I did. Several times. He insists on going forward with our defense," he said, continuing with a gentler tone. "It would be helpful if you were in the courtroom next week. Your absence this week was noticed."

"I know. I just can't do it anymore. I can barely get out of bed in the morning."

"If you're not there, it'll be read by the jury that even *you* think he's guilty."

"What does the jury think?"

Grossinger had been monitoring the jury closely during the week. Rarely had he been able to establish eye contact with any of them, which was a bad sign. He tried to be as diplomatic as possible. "It's hard to say. Each jury is different, and some of them are totally unpredictable.

Anything can happen. Which is why I think you should try to convince your husband to take the deal. Have you talked to him about it?"

"Every day. He's convinced that you're going to get him off somehow, and he won't consider it. Insists he's going to be a free man again." She paused, then continued hopefully. "Is there *any* chance he's right?"

"There's always a chance, but it's not a good idea to get your hopes up. Off the record, barring any last-second miracle, the most realistic assumption is that he's going to be found guilty. That's why you need to do everything you can to get him to accept the deal offered by the prosecution. After this week, it may not be on the table much longer."

"I'll ask him again, but I don't know...." Her voice trailed off.

"Do your best, Liz. Someone needs to get through to him. I haven't been able to. It's going to have to be you."

"I'll try again. Good night."

"Good luck."

*****

On Saturday morning the Riverton Rod and Gun Club held a memorial service for Scott Jamison. Although he hadn't yet been declared officially dead, his friends at the club knew that if he hadn't been found by now he was never going to be found. Charlie Jaeger organized the event, with the help of Robbie Burnett and Caroline Cooke. Charlie had reached out to Gillian to see if she wanted to participate but she begged off. "It's just too soon, Charlie."

There was a decent turnout in spite of having only two days to get the word out. About thirty members and friends were there to celebrate his life and spirit on the kind of morning Scott loved: a flawless blue sky, temperature in the low seventies, with just a hint of breeze from the west.

When it was clear no one else was arriving, Charlie Jaeger, with a few pages of prepared words in his hands, motioned the crowd closer and waited until the murmuring dropped off before he began to speak.

"We're here today to honor Scott Jamison, our brother and friend. I know I'm not alone when I say how much I miss him and how

193

much I will continue to miss him. It's hard to believe that two weeks ago he was with us at the club, being Scott, telling tales and making us laugh. The only good thing I can take away from this tragedy is that, right up until the end, Scott was doing what he loved the most: he was out on the water with his fishing gear, planning for his next adventure. I doubt that any of us, any time we're out on the lake in the days ahead, will fail to think about Scott and what he meant to each of us. We should also think about how fragile life is, how there are no guarantees that tomorrow will find us as well off as we are today. We need to cherish every moment like Scott did and enjoy every day as much as we can."

He motioned to Caroline, who was standing next to a table set up with shot glasses of Scott's signature cocktail, Stoli and grapefruit soda. "Let's drink a toast to our friend and wish him well, wherever he may be. With God's grace and understanding, someday we'll be united with Scott Jamison again. Until that day, remember the joy he brought to all our lives and smile, for the journey isn't over. It's only just begun."

The crowd shuffled toward the table to grab a shot glass. When everyone's hand was filled Charlie spoke again, his voice quavering a bit. "Farewell, friend. May heaven be filled with uncrowded trout streams and plenty of game on the hoof." He downed his drink in a single gulp and placed his glass back on the table. The rest of the group followed. When all the glasses were empty and back on the table the crowd began to disperse, some toward the parking lot, others toward the bar inside the club, lost in thoughts tinged with sadness, struggling to move forward.

32

On Saturday morning the alarm jarred Parnell Gomez out of a sound sleep. It took him a moment to establish his surroundings. He'd been dreaming about being on a cruise ship where everyone was naked but he was fully clothed. No one could speak; he had no idea where the ship was headed and he didn't know anyone else on the ship. He realized he was famished and found one of the cafeteria areas where there was round-the-clock access to food. He was about to fill a bowl with fresh pineapple from a dispenser on the wall when the alarm woke him up.

Groggily, he stumbled into the bathroom and peed, a steady stream of processed iced tea. What an unusual dream, he thought. Was it something he'd eaten the night before? Automatically he started to wash his hands before he remembered he was going to take a shower. He splashed some water on his face instead and turned on the shower, adjusting the temperature until it was where he wanted it to be before stepping inside. The jets of warm water brought him back to life and focused his mind on the reason he'd set his alarm so early on a Saturday: he was going sailing with John Herrington.

Herrington had extended an invitation to both Kelly and Parnell yesterday at the AC to join him for a day on the water. He was pleasantly surprised when Gomez accepted without hesitation but was absolutely dumbfounded when Kelly accepted as well. He tried to remember how many times he'd asked Kelly to go for a sail with him throughout the years. At least a hundred, probably more. She'd always declined, usually citing previous obligations. He wondered how much her acceptance this time had to do with Gomez agreeing to come along.

Because there was a special event this weekend – a fleet of boats from the Royal Canadian Yacht Club in Toronto had sailed across the lake yesterday and were rafted three-deep along the Delifin Yacht Club's transient docking area – he'd told them both to meet him early, at 7:00, so they could get out of the harbor before the hungover sailors woke up. There had been a party at the yacht club for the Torontonians the night before and when the party at the club had ended a significant number of the revelers, not ready to go to bed yet, had trudged up the hill and continued their celebrations until closing time at the AC.

It was a glorious morning, clear blue skies with just a hint of breeze from the west. Gomez, who was a novice sailor, nonetheless realized that there needed to be a minimum level of wind in order to sail and wondered as he strode down Stonewall Street if the morning breeze was adequate. He thought about texting Herrington to see if he was still planning to go, but remembered he didn't have his number. Instead, he'd grabbed a bottle of water and headed for the yacht club.

Kelly and Herrington were waiting for him when he reached the bottom of the hill. They were standing next to the small hut used by the bum boat operator, surveying some of the trash on the grounds from last night's festivities. Herrington raised his hand. "Over here, Parnell!"

Yesterday Herrington had suggested Gomez bring his passport along and had been disappointed when Parnell told him he hadn't brought it with him. "That's too bad. No Canada for us then." Instead he suggested a leisurely sail along the Canadian and American shoreline, well outside the markers set up by the club that defined this morning's race course. "The last thing we want to do is be anywhere near those Canadians," he said. "From what I gathered last night, this group is much more dedicated to drinking than they are to racing."

Kelly was wearing a pale blue sleeveless blouse, crisp white shorts and boating shoes. She carried a canvas bag over her shoulder. "I brought some water and some cheese and crackers, in case we get hungry." She winked at Parnell. "Something tells me Herrington's idea of a balanced meal is a slice of lime in his gin and tonic."

Gomez smiled. He'd noticed the wordplay between Kelly and Herrington at the bar on several occasions, and he admired her ability to respond with zingers off the top of her head when Herrington tried to needle her. She had an active, quick mind and an extremely dry sense of humor.

"You forget I live on my boat," Herrington said. "The galley is well stocked with all the major food groups."

"Gin, rum, tequila..." She counted them off on her left hand, a small smile on her face.

Herrington shrugged his shoulders. "Check it out for yourself when we get on board."

"If there's anything in your refrigerator of nutritional value, I'll bet Rachel bought it." Rachel Penfield was John Herrington's girlfriend. "Come to think of it," Kelly added "why isn't Rachel coming along?"

"She's visiting her daughter at the family cottage in Gravenhurst for the weekend." He turned to Parnell and added in explanation. "A couple hours north of Toronto." The bum boat operator emerged from his hut and looked at the group. "Are we waiting for anyone else?"

"No," Herrington said.

The driver hopped nimbly into the boat. "Then let's go." He took Kelly's bag, set it on the bottom of the boat and reached out to give her a hand down from the dock. Gomez was next, followed by Herrington.

When they were all seated he started the boat, cast off the lines and eased the shuttle vehicle away from the dock. He pointed it toward Herrington's sloop *Soleil* and weaved his way slowly between the sailboats tethered to large orange mooring balls. Although he'd been a member of the club for years, Herrington had rejected any attempt to move his boat to a berth closer to shore. Because he lived on his boat, he preferred the relative quiet of the outer row, away from yacht club parties and late-night music, so when the opportunity to move closer to the shore periodically arose as a result of his club seniority, he always refused.

The bum boat pulled alongside *Soleil*. The driver held fast as Herrington stepped onto the deck first. He extended a hand to Kelly and then Gomez, helping them aboard. With a wave over his shoulder the bum boat driver returned to shore and his shack to resume listening to the program on NPR Herrington's group had interrupted with their arrival.

Herrington stowed Kelly's bag below deck and gave the two first-time visitors a five-minute tour of the boat. "Only two things you need to know: where the refrigerator is and how to use the head." He pointed both of them out before leading the group back up the stairs to the stern.

Gomez glanced around, impressed by the gleaming teak inlays that stretched from stern to bow on each gunwale. "Nice boat," Gomez said, a tinge of awe in his voice.

Kelly was surprised by the immaculate condition below deck, the small dining table and counters free of clutter, everything in its place. Somehow she'd never figured Herrington for a neatnik. Probably

Rachel's influence, she decided. "I must admit it's a lot better organized than I figured it would be," Kelly said.

Herrington smiled. "All it takes is one trip in six-foot seas to teach you how important it is not to leave things out on the table or the counter. Other than my charts, I keep everything stored away until its needed." He looked at his two guests. "Coffee? I brewed a pot before I came ashore. Figured it might come in handy."

Both guests nodded gratefully. "Black," Gomez said.

"Cream and sugar for me," Kelly added.

Herrington went below and returned in a moment with tray containing a pot, three insulated traveling containers, a small jar of cream and a bowl of assorted sweetening packets. "I'll let you doctor it the way you like. The travelers make it less likely to spill once we get underway." He filled one of the containers and handed it to Kelly, who added cream and a single packet of sugar, before pouring Gomez's.

Once his guests were situated he turned the key and fired up the engine. He let it idle for a few minutes, checking his gauges while the engine warmed up. He glanced up at the tell tales on top of his mast. They hung limply; not enough breeze yet to engage them. "Unless the wind picks up a bit, we'll probably stick with the engine," Herrington said.

"Fine with me," Kelly said, sipping her coffee. "It's been awhile since I've been on a boat. The gentler the ride, the better as far as I'm concerned."

Herrington turned to Gomez, who agreed. "I'm a virgin. Nice and easy works for me, too."

Herrington arched his eyebrows. "First time on a sailboat?"

Gomez nodded. "Not many chances to enjoy the yachting life growing up in Potsdam."

When the engines were warm, Herrington grabbed the extendable gaff and walked to the bow, where he unhooked the line and quickly scrambled back to the wheel. Just as the current caught the craft he turned the wheel and pointed the boat downstream toward the lake. He motored slowly past the condos where Rachel lived, offering a running commentary as they chugged along. "Those are two boat ramps in the park, but not many boaters use them since the village upgraded the ramp next to the yacht club. Beyond that is the Coast Guard station."

"Is that where the search for that missing boater was organized?" Gomez asked.

"For the most part," Herrington replied. "The Canadians provided air and sea support, and Niagara County had a crew on the lake as well."

"And they didn't find anything."

Herrington nodded. "Not a thing. They even used heat-sensitive imaging, but came up with zip."

They motored slowly past Fort Ontario and its singular French castle structure, which stood defiantly on the shoreline behind a recently refurbished seawall. Kelly sat back, enjoying her coffee silently as Herrington played tour guide. It was a side of her friend she rarely saw, more deferential than his AC persona, his ego on the back burner.

"When was the fort built?" Gomez asked.

"It was completed in 1679," Herrington said. "It's one of the oldest forts in North America. During the eighteenth century it was occupied by the British and the French before the Americans seized control during the Revolution. Lots of history there – if you get a chance, you should take a tour. It's hard to imagine how soldiers survived the winter without any insulation in that stone building, especially when the wind howled from the north."

They motored slowly past the expansive grass beach that sloped toward the lake on the park's eastern boundary. Several seagulls were lined up along the shoreline, taking advantage of the unoccupied space. Beyond the beach was a wooded area that extended for several hundred yards before a clearing revealed the massive stone structure under construction next to the park.

"What's that?" Gomez asked in amazement. The stone structure was enormous, the size of a hotel.

"That's Harry Michaels' house," Herrington replied. "At least we think it's a house. No one knows for sure what Harry's plans are for the place. Lots of rumors floating around, but no facts. Years ago there used to be a club there called Club Driftwood with live music. Back then the drinking age in New York was only eighteen and Canadians used to flock across the border, especially on the weekends, since the legal drinking age in Ontario at the time was higher. Lots of good times were had there."

"What happened to the club?" Gomez asked.

"It burned down in the late seventies. The owner of the club had no fire insurance, so the property remained vacant except for the stone fireplace, the only thing to survive the blaze, until three years ago when Harry bought the place and built this."

Gomez couldn't take his eyes off the mansion. It reminded him of William Randolph Hearst's estate in California, a sprawling example of ostentatious wealth that bordered on the obscene. Whoever this Michaels guy was, Gomez decided, he must have an extremely tiny penis.

Herrington continued on for several hundred yards more before he began to swing the boat in a slow arc to the left, away from the shoreline. He could see the committee boat from the yacht club a quarter mile beyond their position, setting up buoys marking today's race course. He wanted to be well clear of the area before the race began.

Kelly spoke for the first time. "Have you heard anything from Tom?"

Tom Martin was a mutual friend of Herrington and Kelly who lived in a cabin on the lake another half mile or so to the east. He was an engineer who designed and worked on dams at hydroelectric developments around the world and often was overseas on assignment. During the previous summer he'd been the victim of a nefarious power struggle within the international engineering firm that employed him, one that had temporarily cost him his job, threatening his career, before Herrington and a pair of remarkable women concocted an exotic sting operation that took down his tormentor and returned Martin to his position on the corporate organization chart.

Herrington shook his head. "He's been in Colombia for the past month, working on the Rio Anchicaya. I ran into Shannon the other day at the market in Delifin. She thinks he might be back sometime next month." Shannon Martin was Tom's ex-wife.

"I miss him at the bar," Kelly said wistfully. "Having him around so much last summer was nice."

Herrington had the sloop headed due west now, a half-mile from shore, toward the mouth of the river and the shore of Ontario beyond. "I agree. It's just not the same this year without him."

Gomez listened intently, the morning sun warming the back of his neck as they cruised easily past the fort again and into Canadian waters. He wondered for a moment if he was at peril without his passport – could they nail him for unlawful entry even though they weren't on land?

Herrington seemed to read his mind. "You're okay, Parnell, as long as we don't go ashore in Canada. The OPP generally leave the sailors alone. It's the power boaters they concentrate on."

West of the river they passed the public golf course in Niagara-on-the-Lake, motoring toward the vineyards that filled the fertile bottomland between the Niagara River and Hamilton as Herrington continued his tour guide spiel, pointing out the various wineries and the abandoned munitions site that had been an artillery target range during the second world war.

Gomez took another sip of coffee, listening intently to Herrington's off-the-cuff lecture in the brilliant morning sunshine and thought: this sure beats sleeping in.

33

Sally Wakefield was up when the sun rose on Saturday morning, sipping coffee at the kitchen table, her husband still in bed. She'd stayed up long enough the night before to catch the weather report on the local news, which predicted a hot, mostly sunny Saturday. She had a number of plants she'd started in small pots on the back porch that she wanted to transfer to their garden in the backyard. Because of the crazy weather during the last several years – by now she was a firm believer in climate change – she'd waited until she was sure there wouldn't be a frost. Now, on Saturday morning of Memorial Day weekend, she felt confident that it was time to make the move.

She finished her coffee, rinsed out the cup and placed it in the dish rack next to the sink. In the garage she found her gardening gloves, a small spade and a watering can which she filled with water from the tap next to the garage door. She carried the water and the tools back to the garden and returned for the plants. It took several trips, but finally the plants were laid out in the garden where Sally had diagrammed they would go back in March.

She enjoyed working in the garden, tilling the soil, providing fresh herbs and vegetables for her table as the summer progressed into fall. There was something about eating food you'd grown yourself that had resonated with her since she was a child. Her parents had a garden and she was one of only a few children among her group of friends who ate fresh vegetables at home instead of the canned variety.

She began with her tomato plants. She was planting three different varieties this summer, Roma, cherry tomatoes and Better Boys. Because of the height of the tomato plants, she placed them on the western edge of her garden where the plants, once they were mature, wouldn't steal the sun from the other shorter plants. She dug a hole six inches deep and six inches in diameter for each of the plants and filled it with water before she gently extricated the juvenile plants from their pots and placed them in the ground. She filled in any gaps with a mixture of manure and potting soil before moving on to the next plant.

The sky was cloudless and the sun brilliant as it rose slowly in the eastern sky; perspiration began to form on her forehead by the time she was on her fourth transplant. There was no breeze. If it stayed like this, it would be a scorcher.

Usually gardening was Sally's sanctuary, a place where she could clear her head, her meditation activity. But this morning she couldn't seem to shake worrying thoughts about Rod. When John Corelli had been arrested, she'd been afraid that the case, given its salacious nature and national appeal, would overwhelm him. She'd been relieved when he'd removed himself from that case, handing over the courtroom duty to Randy DiPietro when Scott Jamison went missing.

But now he was consumed by the Jamison case, more so than he'd been with the Corelli arrest. Despite what looked to Sally and most others like a tragic accident, the disappearance of Scott Jamison had taken a much darker, complex turn for her husband. The previous evening, while waiting for the late news, he'd confessed that he was leaning toward an explanation not yet on the radar of the other agencies involved in the case: that Scott Jamison may have taken his own life.

"I know, I know," he said when she responded with a look of disbelief. "It's all based on a feeling I've developed about the Joey Lorenzo disappearance in 1972. If Joey *had* known that Scott was sleeping with his girlfriend back then, it might've been a catastrophic piece of news. Joey's friends all concurred that Joey was an emotional guy. What if the news that his girlfriend was cheating on him pushed him over the emotional brink? What if it drove him to take his own life?"

"That's a bit of a stretch, don't you think?" Sally replied. "You don't even know if Joey knew about Scott and what's-her-name."

"Andrea."

"Andrea. What other evidence is there that Joey would commit suicide?"

"The life jacket. One of the witnesses interviewed by Cal back in '72 said that he saw a life jacket – Joey's life jacket– floating down the river. If it was Joey's, why would he have abandoned it? Each of the boys interviewed by Cal agreed that they'd all worn life jackets. If he'd decided to go to Canada to avoid the draft, he would've kept the life jacket on until he reached the opposite shore. If that were the case, given the current, Joey would've abandoned his life jacket when he came ashore. It wouldn't have been visible to any of the other tubers that night – it would've been too far north for them to see."

"I still don't get it," Sally said, puzzled. "Why would Joey Lorenzo's suicide cause Scott to do the same thing forty years later?"

Rod's eyes were bright, intense, as he leaned forward. "What if Joey did know that Scott was screwing Andrea and decided to end it all in a Romeo-and-Juliet moment? If that was the case, maybe Scott felt guilty all these years. That it was *his* fault that Joey decided to kill himself. Guilt like that, built up over more than forty years, could do some serious damage."

"I don't know," Sally said, shaking her head doubtfully. "Your theory is built on a lot of assumptions that aren't backed up by evidence."

"There is one more thing. Both Cal and I think the boys' version of the night's events sounded too much alike, like they'd been rehearsed. And I got the same impression again this week when I talked to Ted Stephens and Allan O'Rourke. What if they're hiding something? What if one of them *did* see what really happened to Joey Lorenzo? That he deliberately removed his life jacket before he disappeared?"

"That's a lot of what-ifs."

"That's why I have to keep going. The evidence is out there – I can feel it in my gut. If I could only find Willie Emerson...."

"Who's he?"

"The other surviving tuber from that night, the mastermind behind the trip. He's in the wind someplace, dropped off the face of the earth two years ago after being released from an urgent care clinic in Miami. Neither Stephens nor O'Rourke claim to have any idea what happened to him. I believe them."

She'd never seen her husband so consumed by a case. It worried her. He'd always been obsessive about his work, determined as a public servant to give the best he had to everything that crossed his desk. But the Scott Jamison case was something else, a level of focus well beyond anything he'd been involved with since they'd been married.

*****

When Rod woke at 7:30 Sally was out in the garden, digging in the dirt, transplanting her seedlings into the vegetable garden she lovingly tended in the backyard of their Riverton home. He smiled as he walked to the bathroom for his morning constitutional. She should be busy for a couple of hours. Plenty of time to work on the case.

He'd managed to convince Fran Killian to let him keep one of the yearbooks she'd reluctantly let him take from the library a few days earlier, convincing her he would return it safely in a week or so.

After he poured himself a cup of coffee he retreated to the spare bedroom he'd converted to a home office and opened the yearbook on the desk before him. He was trying to find anyone who might've been Willie Emerson's friend, anyone who was still around who might have some idea where he was.

He knew it was a long shot. Given what he knew about Willie's history, there was a strong possibility he might already be dead, another victim of the south Florida drug culture. The last public record he could find had been an article in a weekly newspaper in the Keys, detailing Willie's near-fatal crash on Highway 1. O'Rourke had said he he'd heard that Willie ended up in a walk-in clinic in a downtrodden Cuban neighborhood in Miami. When he was released, he disappeared.

He turned to the page where the senior class pictures were displayed. One by one he went through the names, plugging each of them into a law enforcement search engine, looking for anyone who might have maintained contact with Willie over the years.

It was a difficult task, made more difficult by the number of years that had passed and by Willie's lack of participation in sports or other activities while at Riverton High School, which meant he couldn't winnow the list of Willie's classmates through cross-referencing. He'd started with the A's on Wednesday; he was up to the L's now.

Of the members of the Class of 1970 at Riverton High School he'd researched so far, a surprisingly large percentage of them no longer lived in the area, especially the ones who'd gone on to college. By the time they'd graduated the decline of the local industrial base had begun, and there were many sections in the country where local economies were on the rise, places where their futures were brighter. He found that it was the ones who hadn't attended college who tended to stay in the area. So far none of them that he'd been able to reach had any clue as to the whereabouts of Willie Emerson.

205

He thought about the conversation he'd had with Sally the previous evening. She'd been skeptical of his latest theory, with good reason. The line of investigation he was currently pursuing was based largely on assumption and conjecture and the feeling in his gut that somehow the disappearance of Scott Jamison was linked to the disappearance of Joey Lorenzo forty years earlier. As far as he knew, no other law enforcement agency was continuing to investigate Scott's disappearance. He was all alone.

Why was he doing it? As always, the answer was simple – for the survivors, the ones who'd been left behind, victims by proxy. He felt they deserved to know what had happened to their loved ones. He realized that wasn't always possible, but it was difficult for him to concede that point until he'd exhausted every possible angle, tracked down every lead. He was the final advocate for the survivors, and he couldn't live with himself if he didn't give every case his best effort.

In Scott's case, that person was Gillian. Scott had no siblings; only his mother survived him and they'd been estranged for years. A brief conversation with Dolores Jamison early in the investigation convinced Rod that her only interest in getting to the bottom of her son's disappearance centered on an insurance policy she was convinced contained the name Dolores Jamison as beneficiary. So it was Gillian who motivated him to find the truth.

Her reaction to her missing lover had been a bit off kilter, but he knew that all people responded to tragedy in their own way. Thirty years of experience in law enforcement made it clear to him that there was no textbook response, one that could be declared the norm, when a cataclysmic event disrupted a person's life. Gillian's sense of detachment, her reluctance to engage with the Riverton police any more than a minimal amount, raised no flags with Rod. He felt she was responding the best way she knew how to an event she'd never envisioned would occur. He was willing to cut her some slack as she struggled to come to grips with the loss of her lover. He hoped he could get to the bottom of the mystery, even if the answer at the end of the road wasn't the one she preferred to hear.

34

After months of intermittent pleading from Kelly, Herrington, Daffy Franklin, Grace Dumont and a string of other regular and casual customers, Peter Malecki finally saw the light. They'd been pestering him to schedule live music at the bar to, as Herrington put it, "expand the cultural footprint of the AC." Each of them had cited the success of the final night of the annual Riverstock Festival, held under a tent in the parking lot adjacent to the AC, as evidence that music would be well received. Peter had admitted on more than one occasion that the last night of the festival had been his highest grossing night each year since the festival began.

But when posters advertising the event, scheduled for Sunday evening of the Memorial Day weekend, appeared in the bar and at several locations in Riverton and Delifin earlier in the month, the news was greeted with skeptical caution. Hopes had been raised and dashed before; until the band actually played their first song, some of Peter's more cynical customers refused to believe he could pull it off.

"Are you going to the concert on Sunday?"

Parnell Gomez posed the question to Kelly and Herrington as they lounged on the deck of *Soleil* after their sail on Saturday, waiting to be ferried back to the mainland. There was a flurry of activity in the harbor – the Canadian sailors were awake and on their way toward the lake for their first race. Herrington figured they'd be on the boat for a while.

Kelly nodded. "I told Peter I'd work the temporary bar in the parking lot next to the tent. I'm looking forward to hearing the band. I checked them out on YouTube. I heard they were on one of the late night shows last week."

Jangling Rheinhardt, based in Athens, Ohio, had formed when band principals Artie Colen and Duane Smith met while freshmen at Ohio University. Recently they'd signed a deal with an independent label in Buffalo and were currently in the studio there, recording their label debut after releasing a self-produced CD titled *The Hocking Flood* the year before. Peter's connection to the group was serendipitous – his nephew was employed by the label as a sound engineer and had recommended the band to his uncle.

Kelly continued. "Just two acoustic guitars, but these guys can really shred. Definitely not folk music. More like the Ramones on meth."

"Wonderful," Herrington drawled laconically. "I can hardly wait."

"Don't pay any attention to him," Kelly advised. "His musical sensibilities are lodged in the mid-twentieth century. He hasn't listened to any new music since Elvis died on the crapper."

"Nice image, potty mouth."

Parnell looked at Kelly, hooking a thumb in Herrington's direction. "Is he always this negative?"

Kelly nodded. "Ever since I've known him he's been afflicted with pathological pessimism. PP syndrome."

"I can't help it," Herrington said simply. "I'm a Republican."

*****

Gillian listened in disgust as her call went to voicemail again. She ended the call rather than leave a message as she had on her previous three calls, all made during the last ten minutes. There was no doubt in her mind now – Lenny was avoiding her. Despite leaving him a dozen messages, he hadn't called her since his brother and his wife had arrived from Colorado on Tuesday.

There'd been no word from Rod Wakefield, either. He'd promised to call with any new developments in Scott's case; silence on his end meant that nothing had changed. Scott Jamison was still missing, now presumed by most to be dead.

She felt alone, abandoned by her friends and her new lover to battle a melting pot of emotions that included regret, loss, shame and guilt. She needed to talk to Lenny. She wanted to ask him the big question, the one that had been haunting her for several weeks now: had Scott somehow known that she and Lenny were lovers?

She was certain she had covered her tracks, that if Scott had somehow obtained information that she was cheating on him with one of his friends, it had not come from her. She'd been extremely careful around the rod and gun club, where the atmosphere was known to foster infidelity and an unbridled joy in talking about it. They kept their interactions on their skeet team innocent, two teammates whose bond was limited to their individual competitive spirits. They only met at Lenny's house, never in a public place, and she always parked her car in his garage to avoid detection. If Scott *had* known about the affair, she was confident the news hadn't come from her.

She knew there was talk around the club that there had been no tragic accident, that Scott had taken the boat out to kill himself. To Gillian that seemed ludicrous; the Scott she knew and had loved was too laid back, too non-confrontational to ever consider taking his own life, let alone follow through on the urge. It wasn't in his DNA.

Lenny had been at the club the night before Scott had disappeared and had told her about Scott buying a round for the bar. She admitted it was an unusual move by the historically miserly Jamison, but scoffed when whispers began about it being a farewell gesture to his friends at the club. He was celebrating his big payday after finishing the job at the pizzeria, nothing more. Why couldn't people accept that?

She needed to talk with Lenny, find out if he might've inadvertently let the news of their clandestine relationship slip to one of his friends. She doubted that he had, since he claimed he hadn't even told his brother about the two of them yet, but she wanted to hear it from his own lips, look him in the eye as he responded. She needed the reassurance to calm her jittery nerves.

She picked up her phone and dialed Lenny again. This time she left a message; "Why are you doing this to me? We need to talk. Right away. Call me back as soon as you get this."

She placed the phone on the table next to her and wiped the moistness from the corner of her eye before she rose to her feet and walked over to the small laundry room adjacent to the garage. She placed a load of whites in the washer, added detergent and set the water temperature to hot before turning the machine on. She returned to the kitchen table and stared out the window, seeing nothing, her thoughts a roller coaster of emotions.

*****

Rod had worked his way through the yearbook to the P's when his cell phone rang. It was Anne Moretti. "Anne, Anne, Anne," he chided. "This is Saturday of a holiday weekend. Please don't tell me this is business."

209

"Crime never sleeps, Chief." It was one of her favorite sayings. "I thought you'd like to know what happened at the Riverside Inn last night."

What now, he thought. "Go on."

"This comes from Travis Fickle, who was on patrol in the village. Some of the people from the two news agencies covering the Corelli trial created a little ruckus last night at the patio bar. One of the grips from CNN broke his ankle when he was pushed over the railing by one of the photographers at Fox. According to several witnesses, the cameraman from Fox called the guy from CNN a whiny Commie liberal. The guy from CNN shoved the guy from Fox, he shoved back and the grip went over the railing, landing on the concrete below, breaking his ankle."

"Let me guess," Rod interjected wearily. "Alcohol was involved."

"You didn't make chief by accident. Travis interviewed people from both agencies and it seems there's been a feud of sorts ever since the trial began. They're both staying at the hotel across the street. Working together all day at the courthouse and staying in the same hotel at night must be getting to both sides."

"Any arrests?"

"No," Anne said. "At first the guy from CNN wanted to press charges, but he was talked out of it by one of his female co-workers, the on-air talent." She chuckled. "Travis thought she might've made him an offer to help nurse his wounds over the weekend if he withdrew the charges. If you know what I mean."

"Thank God someone has some common sense. What about the bar? Any complaints from them?"

"Not yet. I think they like the publicity."

"Anything else?"

"That's it."

Rod shifted into his official voice. "Then take the rest of the weekend off. I don't want to hear from you again until Tuesday."

"Whatever you say, Chief."

He went back to the yearbook, shaking his head. He was surprised that there hadn't been an incident between the two agencies before this, given the opposite ends of the political spectrum each of them occupied and the polarizing nature of the trial. Randy DiPietro had done an excellent job of maintaining control at the courthouse so far, which had allowed him the freedom to concentrate on the Jamison case. Randy deserved a little something for his efforts – he'd talk to Sal Ducati next week, see if he couldn't shake a little one-time bonus free from one of the mayor's discretionary accounts.

His phone rang again. It was Austin Lawrence, beat reporter for the local weekly *The Observer* who'd been assigned to cover the Corelli trial. "No comment."

"Good morning to you, too, Chief," Lawrence said pleasantly. "Have you heard about the incident at the Riverside Inn last night?"

Rod kept his voice neutral. "I'm aware of it. No further comment."

"Any charges filed?"

"Not at the present time. Actually, Austin, I don't see this as much of a story."

"You might be alone in that opinion, Chief. Two national news agencies, bitter rivals, in town to cover Riverton's Trial of the Century. After two weeks of riveting testimony emotions spill over, angry words are exchanged, and a man is tossed off a balcony. Sounds like a pretty good story to me. I can already see the headline: Grip Loses Grip."

"Sounds like a candidate for the Pulitzer."

"Last chance, Chief."

"No comment, Austin. Have a nice day."

35

It wasn't until late in the afternoon on Sunday that Liz Corelli's body was discovered. She'd excused herself early on Saturday evening and headed upstairs for bed, claiming a headache. When she didn't emerge in time the next morning to attend Mass at St. Peter's, her husband John thought it strange but not unprecedented, so he didn't investigate, continuing to watch *Meet the Press* and read the Sunday paper.

By mid-afternoon she still hadn't appeared, so John went upstairs to check on her. He found her in bed, on her back, clutching rosary beads to her chest, a half-empty bottle of Jack Daniels on the nightstand next to an empty prescription bottle of Xanax. He reached out to check for a pulse and found her body already cool and stiff.

He backed off in a daze, went back downstairs and dialed 911. "She's dead."

The 911 operator was cool efficiency. "Who's dead, sir?"

"My wife."

"Are you sure?"

He nodded into the phone. "She wasn't breathing, and she feels cold and stiff."

"Where is she located?"

"In the bedroom. Upstairs."

"What's your name, sir? And your address."

He made an effort to speak slowly and clearly. "John Corelli. My wife's name is Liz. We live at 575 Iroquois Street, in Riverton."

"Thanks, Mr. Corelli. I've got a crew on the way. Please stay on the line with me so I can take down some more information."

A police cruiser pulled into the driveway in five minutes, followed a minute later by a second car and an ambulance with two EMT's. The front door was open. When they entered they found Corelli sitting on the couch in the family room watching a golf tournament on television, his cell phone, disconnected from the 911 operator, still firmly gripped in his hand. He turned to the police as they approached and gestured toward the stairwell. "She's upstairs, in her room."

One of the officers stayed with Corelli. "Are you alone in the house, Mr. Corelli?"

"No. My wife is upstairs. That's why I called."

"Other than you and your wife, are there any other persons or pets in the house?"

He looked at the officer blankly, eyes unfocused. "Our dog, Rex, is in the backyard."

"Please keep Rex outside until we finish processing the scene." Corelli nodded, numb.

The other officer and the EMT's pulled on latex gloves and donned booties before they headed up the stairs. They found Liz Corelli as her husband had described, lying on her back in bed. One of the EMT's checked her for vital signs, turned to his partner and shook his head. "She's cold. Probably been dead for hours. Call it in. And contact the medical examiner."

The officer in the room, Karl Krull, had been on the force for two years. It was the first time he'd encountered a dead body on the job and he didn't want to mess anything up. He took a deep breath and scanned the room first before making any moves. He opened his kit, removed some evidence bags and went to work. He bagged the bottle of liquor and the empty pill bottle first. When he picked up the whiskey bottle he saw a small white envelope underneath, the kind of envelope a thank-you note would fit into. Gingerly he reached inside and extracted a single piece of paper, folded once. There was a brief note printed on the paper:

John. This is your fault. Please explain it to the kids.

Officer Krull whistled under his breath as he slipped the note back into the envelope and placed it in one of the evidence bags. Like most of the people in Riverton, he knew about Corelli's trial. This, however, was something else altogether. Something for someone whose pay grade was several levels higher than his own.

He spent the next hour going over the room meticulously, bagging anything he thought might remotely be associated with Liz Corelli's death. He cleaned out the medicine cabinet and, to be on the safe side, emptied the contents of her nightstand. He labeled each item carefully and added it to the inventory before moving on to the next potential piece of evidence.

Thirty minutes after the EMT's had arrived the medical examiner strolled in, having been summoned from a family barbecue, still smelling faintly of molasses and vinegar. Gerard Palmateer was a portly man in his early sixties, about five eight, with a shock of white hair that lent him his nickname: Einstein. Although known for his sense of humor around friends and family, on the job he was deadly serious, never cracking a smile, and he moved around the bed with brusque efficiency as he dictated his observations into a small recorder he held in his left hand. At first glance he thought he was looking at a suicide, but he knew better to assume anything until all the data had been collected and analyzed.

While Dr. Palmateer was examining the body upstairs, the other officer on the scene, Gregory Joy, was interviewing John Corelli. The two of them were seated at the Corelli kitchen table, Officer Joy with his notebook out, John Corelli looking dazed and confused, as if he couldn't believe what was happening, providing emotionless, monosyllabic responses to Joy's questions.

According to John Corelli's account, yesterday morning he'd come up from his makeshift bedroom in the basement where his wife had insisted he sleep after he'd been released on bail when Liz announced she wasn't going to be making sauce today. That was unusual; it was a family tradition in the Corelli house that Liz made sauce on Saturday for Sunday dinner. When probed by Joy, Corelli confessed he couldn't remember the last time Liz didn't make sauce on a Saturday.

Instead, she said she had some errands to run and that she wanted to go to St. Peter's for confession. She said she had some sauce frozen in the freezer that they could use on Sunday; no big deal. Her husband, preoccupied with his own case, dealing with pressure from both Liz and Max Grossinger who were trying to get him to accept a plea deal from the prosecutor's office, barely acknowledged her as she left at 11:00.

She returned a little after six with a pizza and the two of them settled in to watch a movie on TCM, *The Guns of Navarone*. Halfway through the movie Liz excused herself, saying she had a headache, and went upstairs to bed. John watched the rest of the movie and the one that followed, *A Bridge Too Far*. When the second movie ended he went down into the basement and went to sleep.

The next morning he woke at 7:00, his usual time, and came upstairs to make coffee. Liz was a regular attendee at 10:00 Mass at St. Peter's, but she never came downstairs and he didn't hear the shower running upstairs, so he thought she still wasn't feeling well and had decided to sleep in. When 3:00 rolled around and she still hadn't made an appearance, he went upstairs to check on her and found her dead in her bed, her skin cool to his touch, dressed as if she were headed to Mass. He called 911 and waited for someone to arrive.

Rod Wakefield walked into the house just as Officer Joy was finishing his interview with John Corelli. He answered Joy's inquiring glance. "Heard it on the radio. Is Einstein finished yet?"

"No,' Joy said. "He's still upstairs with Krull, sir." He cleared his throat nervously. "Uh, I'm just about finished here, Chief. Would you like to ask him anything before I wrap it up?"

"It's your case, Officer Joy. I'll read it as soon as you write it up."

"Thanks, sir."

Joy was out the door before his boss could reconsider. Rod shifted his attention to Corelli, who was still seated at the kitchen table, absently running the tip of his finger around and around the rim of his coffee cup, looking out the window.

"Mr. Corelli?"

Corelli turned in the direction of the new voice. "Who are you?"

"Rod Wakefield, sir. Chief of Police in Riverton."

He peered at him through hooded eyes. "I remember you now. You're the one that came to my house and arrested me in front of my family last year."

"Yes sir, that was me." He put his hand on one of the chairs. "Mind if I sit with you for a little while?"

Corelli shrugged. "It's a free country."

215

Rod sat down opposite Corelli. "I'm very sorry for your loss, Mr. Corelli. Is anyone else in the house, any family members?"

He shook his head. "Just my wife."

"Where are your children?"

"In Iowa, with relatives."

"Have they been notified of Mrs. Corelli's death?"

Corelli slumped in his chair and began to weep. "Oh my God. How am I going to tell them this? That their mother killed herself?"

Rod's voice was gentle, consoling. "We can send an officer to the house where they're staying, take care of that for you if you'd prefer."

Corelli wiped under his nose with his finger and then deposited it on the sleeve of his shirt. "No. I'll do it. They should hear it from me."

"Is there anyone you can call, someone you can stay with for a few days?"

He pointed to the monitor on his ankle and laughed bitterly. "Whadda *you* think? I'm not allowed to leave the property. Can't even get the damn paper because the mailbox is on the other side of the street."

"We can recalibrate the ankle monitor for any location. Just let us know where you want to go and we'll take you there and make the change."

"My brother Arturo lives in the Falls, on 25th between Pine and Ferry."

"Would you like me to call him for you?" Rod asked.

"No. I'll do it." He reached for his cell phone and began to dial.

Rod got to his feet. "If you're okay here for a few minutes, I'm going to run upstairs for a minute. I'll be right back."

Corelli was already speaking with his brother and didn't respond. Rod slipped on a pair of booties and latex gloves and headed upstairs. Dr.

Palmateer had finished his preliminary examination and was making some notes while they were still fresh in his head. Officer Krull was hovering over the pieces of evidence he'd collected like a jealous mother guarding her young in the nest. "What do we have?"

"I won't be sure till we get her back to the lab and perform an autopsy, but it looks like suicide. Pills and booze," Palmateer said.

"Is she ready to go?"

"I've done all I can do here. She's ready for the morgue."

Rod turned toward Krull. "Find anything?"

"A suicide note, under the whiskey bottle on the nightstand. Addressed to her husband."

"What did it say?"

He recited it from memory. "This is your fault. Please explain it to the kids."

Rod felt a pang of despair as he considered for the first time what this would mean for the Corelli children. Mother dead, father on his way to prison, about to be convicted as a pedophile. He instructed Krull. "Go downstairs, stay with Mr. Corelli until some member of his family arrives. When they do, disable the monitor on his ankle, follow them in your vehicle and plug in the GPS coordinates of his new address once he's safely there. Got it?"

"Crystal clear, Chief."

Rod walked back down the stairs, followed by Krull. Corelli was slumped in a chair, staring into space. "Mr. Corelli, Officer Krull is going to stay with you until your brother gets here. Is that okay?"

Corelli nodded wordlessly. Rod placed a sympathetic hand on his shoulder. "I have to leave now, Mr. Corelli. Will you be alright?"

He looked at the chief with a mixture of sadness and bitterness. "I haven't been alright for a long time."

217

36

Suicide used to be the red-headed stepchild of crime, rarely reported and never discussed except in hushed tones among the most rabid of gossip mongers. Like domestic abuse, it was a subject that rarely broached the surface of public discussion, instead remaining confined almost exclusively to family members directly affected by it.

But since the advent of the Internet and the subsequent explosion of social media platforms, no subject, no matter how private or taboo, remained out of bounds for long. So when Liz Corelli emptied her pill bottle and washed them down with Jack Daniels and slipped into a slumber from which she never arose, all it took was a single curious neighbor, watching the collection of police cars and emergency vehicles enveloping the Corelli property, to start the rumor mill rolling.

Rod Wakefield knew this as well as anyone, which is why he dialed Sal Ducati as soon as he was outside the Corelli home. He wanted to give the mayor a heads-up on the situation before the media caught wind of it and tracked him down, looking for a quote.

The mayor sounded jovial when he picked up the phone. "Rod! To what do I owe the honor?"

Rod could hear muffled noise in the background, a get-together of some sort. "I hope I'm not catching you at a bad time."

"Just having a few cocktails before dinner with Rich Stebbins and his wife. What can I do for you?"

"Uh, I'm afraid I have some bad news, sir. Liz Corelli is dead."

There was silence at the other end of the phone for a moment before the mayor responded, this time in a pained tone barely audible. "What happened?"

"Einstein has just completed his preliminary exam, so nothing is conclusive yet, but evidence at the scene points to suicide."

"How?" he croaked.

"Pills and alcohol. She emptied one of her pill bottles, and there was a half-empty bottle of whiskey on the nightstand next to it. She fell asleep and never woke up."

"Who found her?" Sal asked, concerned that it might have been one of the children.

"Her husband. When she hadn't made an appearance by 3:00 this afternoon, he went upstairs to check on her. He found her in bed."

There was a long pause before the mayor responded. "Thanks for letting me know, Chief. Keep me posted if you find anything else out."

"There's just one more thing, sir," he added hastily, afraid Sal was going to break off the conversation. "John Corelli is going to spend some time at his brother's house in Niagara Falls until we finish investigating. I'm going to make arrangements with the district attorney to re-program the ankle monitor he's wearing to reflect his new address."

"How long will the investigation take?"

"Hard to say. If it turns out to be what it looks like, probably a couple of days. As soon as Einstein completes his autopsy."

"Thanks, Chief." The phone went dead.

Poor Sal, he thought as he got into his car. First the Corelli trial, then Jamison's disappearance and now this. It had been a rough month for the mayor. He was sure that Sal had never envisioned having to oversee this sort of scandal and tragedy when he was first elected ten years earlier. It was Riverton, after all, one of the most idyllic places on the planet, where the most animated public discussion usually involved the decibel levels of the free summer concerts each Tuesday and Wednesday at GorgePark.

Rod glanced at his watch. Time to interrupt another family dinner, he thought, as he dialed the number of District Attorney Charles Moreland.

*****

The tent for the concert at the Delifin Athletic Club was up by 11:00 Sunday morning. Peter called the same brothers he'd used last July for the Riverstock concert; they offered a decent price and, more importantly, had shown up the morning after the event and had the tent down and on its way to its next appointment before the Sunday morning crowd was on their way to church.

Peter had asked Kelly to come in early to help him set up the outside bar and food station. She was in the parking lot at 5:00 when John Herrington, dressed in his newest Hawaiian shirt, crisply pressed white linen shorts and boat shoes, strolled up the hill with a mischievous smile.

Kelly saw him turn the corner as she emerged from the side door of the bar, carrying a case of beer to go into one of the coolers set up behind the table functioning as an outdoor bar. When he reached the table she asked, "What's so funny?"

"Nothing, really. I like watching you work."

Kelly set the case on the table and gave him a look. "Feel free to jump in at any time. There are six more cases in the basement."

Herrington looked around the parking lot. "Where's Peter?"

"In the kitchen, trying to organize the food."

"There's food?" Herrington exclaimed in amazement. "He's going all out."

"Not really," Kelly said as she transferred bottles of Labatt Blue from the case into a cooler. "Just burgers and dogs." She pointed to two grills set up on the opposite side of the lot, to the right of the tent. "I tried to talk him out of the food, telling him it was too much bother for too little gain, but he seems to think since it's Memorial Day weekend, people will want to eat what they would've been cooking anyway at home."

"What if they've already eaten at home before they get here?"

"Another one of my points he ignored." She dropped a bag of ice on the asphalt to separate the cubes before pouring them over the beer and shutting the lid. "I didn't push it too hard, though. I didn't want to ruin his vibe."

"What time does the band get here?" Herrington asked. "The show starts at 7:00, right?"

"They should be here by now." Peter emerged from the side door carrying a cooler that he planned to fill with hot dogs and hamburger patties. He turned toward Kelly. "And when did you ever worry about spoiling my vibe?"

"Are you open inside?" Herrington asked. "I'm getting thirsty watching the two of you work so hard."

"Connie's at the bar." Peter replied.

"Darling Connie," Herrington smiled. "Did you tell her to wear one of those tank tops she fills out so well?"

Kelly glared at Herrington. "You're a pig."

"Really? No need to get personal." Herrington had a pained expression on his face that was completely insincere. He indicated the tent and the parking lot with a sweeping gesture. "I thought the idea was to maximize your take, make a little money. Nothing accelerates the purchase of alcohol like some prime cleavage. Right, Peter?" Peter remained silent, aware that Kelly was watching him closely. Herrington continued. "If you were really smart, you'd have Connie out here and Kelly inside. In this situation, I think you need to go with the younger filly at the outside bar."

Kelly continued to glower at Herrington, who'd backed off a few steps after his last statement, putting some distance between himself and Kelly. "You're an asshole, too."

"Touchy, touchy." Herrington gave her a wide berth as he went inside the bar. He emerged in a few minutes holding a gin and tonic in a plastic cup. "That's better."

A white panel van with Ohio plates pulled up in front of the entrance to the parking lot before Kelly could respond. Three young men piled out, looking bewildered. Peter strode over to them, hand extended. "Jangling Rheinhardt?" he asked. The boys nodded. Peter continued. "You're late."

"We had trouble at the bridge. A traffic jam," one of them replied. "I'm Artie Colen." He indicated the other two with him, who were already unloading the van. "Duane Smith is the tall guy with brown hair. Kirk Clarendon is the other guy, our roadie and merch vendor."

"Nice to meet you," Peter said. "I'm Peter Malecki, the owner. The pretty one is Kelly, one of our bartenders. The guy in the Hawaiian shirt is John Herrington, one of our regulars." Nods all around. "You can leave the van right where it is. Can I get you guys anything?"

"Just some water," Colen said. He was five eight, with wiry black hair in tight curls that spilled over his ears and a full beard. With wire-rimmed glasses, he'd be a dead ringer for a young Jerry Garcia.

"In here," Kelly said, pointing to the cooler containing the water. She reached inside and handed three bottles to Colen, who took one for himself and set the other two on the table He thanked her and said. "I better get to work if we want to have time for a sound check."

"Knock yourself out," Herrington said cheerfully. "I'll observe." He held up his cocktail in salute.

Peter went back inside the bar. Herrington found a plastic chair and plopped himself down in it. He watched as the three young men whisked their equipment out of the van and had it set up in less than an hour. By this time a few early arrivals were in the parking lot, watching with curiosity as Colen and Smith tuned their guitars while Clarendon unfolded a card table and set it up with a variety of band paraphernalia, including T-shirts, stickers and copies of their independently produced debut CD, *The Hocking Flood*.

Suddenly it dawned on Herrington. There was no cashbox, no setup of any kind to handle ticket sales. He turned to Kelly. "There's no charge for the show?"

"If you'd read the poster, which has been in the bar for the last month, you'd know it was a free concert." Typical Herrington.

"I saw the poster," Herrington said. "but I didn't read the fine print. How does Peter pay these guys?"

Sometimes it was like dealing with a child, she thought. Just keep it simple. "He offers them a lump sum against half the alcohol sales. The band gets the higher figure."

"Who keeps track of the alcohol sales?"

She held up a notebook and pen. "I do."

"Peter can't be offering them much."

222

"They're young, just starting out, not from around here. They're doing it for the exposure more than the money." Daffy Franklin walked up to the bar. Kelly was glad to be drawn away from Herrington's queries. "Hey, Daffy. The usual?"

"Yep." She reached into one of the coolers, fished out a Coors Light, and popped the top. "Four bucks."

Daffy stared at her as he reached for his wallet. "When did the price go up?"

"Just for tonight. We gotta pay the band."

Daffy was calculating. "Is it the regular price inside?"

"Nope. You might as well deal with me."

He looked at the stage. "Are they any good? I've never heard of them."

"They're in Buffalo now, recording their label debut at Ani DiFranco's studio in the church. I listened to some clips on YouTube. They have lots of energy for just two guys."

"Energy is one thing. Skill is another," Daffy drawled before taking a long swig of his beer.

"Stick around and find out."

A lifelong bachelor, he scanned the parking lot, interested in what kind of women might be in attendance, encouraged by the two young twentysomethings on stage tuning their guitars. "Should be a young crowd," he offered hopefully.

Kelly smiled. "Compared to you, Daffy, they're all young."

37

After Rod Wakefield's call, Sal went back to his wife and the Stebbins', who were lounging around the circular table on the Ducati's patio in the backyard, laughing at a joke Rich Stebbins had just told. Chi Chi Ducati noticed immediately that something was wrong. "What is it, honey? Who was that on the phone?"

He slumped into the vacant chair and reached for his drink, taking a sip before he responded. "Rod Wakefield. Liz Corelli is dead."

The group was stunned by the news. It took a moment before Chi Chi was able to speak. "What happened?" She was incredulous, not wanting to believe the news her husband had just told her.

Sal continued listlessly. "Looks like suicide. There was an empty pill box and a note. John found her in bed." He lifted the glass and watched how the late afternoon light diffused through the liquid before placing it on the table.

"That poor woman," Mimi Stebbins exclaimed. "Imagine the hell she's been through the last year." She had a sudden thought. "What about the children? They weren't home, were they?"

Sal shook his head. "No, they're staying with Liz's sister out of state." He looked toward the sky as if for guidance. "What else could happen? What else could possibly go wrong?"

Rich Stebbins and his wife exchanged glances: maybe we should go. Rich stood, finishing his beer before placing the empty on the table. "I think we'll head home."

"But we haven't eaten yet," Chi Chi protested.

"That's okay," Mimi replied, looking at her husband before turning back to Chi Chi. "We're not that hungry."

"But what about the steaks?" Chi Chi said plaintively. She wanted the Stebbins' to stay a little longer. For the first time since they'd been married, she didn't want to be alone with Sal.

Mimi drew Chi Chi aside. "Put them in the freezer. Maybe we can reschedule for next weekend," she said in a low voice. "Sal needs you." She gave Chi Chi a firm hug. "Call me this week."

Chi Chi nodded wordlessly as Rich and Mimi, feeling pangs of guilt, walked through the gate next to the garage toward their car. She turned toward her husband, who sat at the table, staring into the distance. "Sal, honey? Have you finished your speech for tomorrow?" He was the main speaker at a small ceremony in Blakeslee Park tomorrow morning, honoring military veterans for their service.

Sal turned toward his wife, his eyes red. "Not yet."

"Why don't we go inside and finish that up? You can try it out on me like you always do."

"Maybe you're right," he said, but didn't move.

Chi Chi offered him a hand up, which he took. She helped him to his feet and walked with him into the house, steadying him as they went. Inside the sliding glass door that led to the backyard, he turned to his wife. "What about the kids? Who's going to take care of them?"

"They'll probably stay in Iowa, with Liz's sister and her husband. That's not our problem." She regretted the statement as soon as it slipped from her lips.

Sal turned toward his wife, addressing her as if she were a child. "Of course it's our problem. I'm the mayor."

She led him to his office and helped him sit down. "Just because you're the mayor doesn't mean you have to solve everyone's problems. For now, let's work on the speech. I'll make a pot of decaf. How's that sound?"

He stared at the screen of his laptop for several moments before he shifted his gaze back to his wife. His voice was full of resignation, all enthusiasm drained. "Whatever you say, dear."

*****

Charles Moreland was momentarily stunned by the news of Liz Corelli's death, but recovered quickly. "Of course we'll allow John Corelli stay with his brother for a few days." He was thinking ahead, wondering if Judge Marquis would suspend the trial. Either way, the shift

225

in attitude toward Corelli likely to occur because of the death of his wife would be a plus for the prosecution. Usually the spouse of a suicide victim would be viewed with sympathy. Not this time.

Wakefield read off Arturo Corelli's address in Niagara Falls. "He should be there until Palmateer finishes his autopsy, probably a couple of days."

"Keep me posted."

"I will. Are you going to call the judge, or should I?"

"I'll do it," Moreland said. "although I'm not looking forward to interrupting His Honor's holiday weekend."

"Do you think he'll postpone the trial?"

"Hard to tell. It could go either way."

"Could be good for the defense," Rod ventured.

"Could be, but I doubt it. In the end the guy had sex with two of his students. And it wouldn't be unreasonable for people to think that, if his wife did commit suicide, his actions drove her to do it."

Knowing the contents of the note Liz had left behind, Rod had been thinking the same thing. "If you do hear anything about a postponement, have someone get in touch with Anne at the municipal offices."

"Will do. Good night, Chief."

"'Night, Counselor."

As soon as he was off the phone with the district attorney he phoned his wife and told her what had happened. She'd been in the backyard, still working on the garden when he got the call from Greg Joy, and he'd left before he had a chance to speak with her.

"That poor woman! And her children – what will happen to them?"

Her children. Not his or theirs. "I don't know," Rod said. "Probably stay in Iowa, if Liz's sister and her husband agree to it."

"Who told the kids?"

"Corelli called them."

"Were you there when he called?"

"No. I was upstairs, talking to Krull and Einstein."

"Lucky you. That couldn't have been an easy call to make."

It never is, Rod thought. "I'll be out for a while. I'm going to drop by the station, see how Kevin is doing. Once the press gets hold of this, the shit will hit the fan like a hurricane. He can probably use another hand."

"Don't worry about me," Sally said. "Just get home as soon as you can. If you're going to be really late, call."

"I will. Love you."

"Me, too."

He drove to the municipal office. Kevin Rumsfeld was alone, his face animated as Rod entered the office. "You know what happened?"

Kevin nodded excitedly. "I heard it when Officer Joy phoned it in. Unbelievable, huh?"

"Any calls from the media yet?"

Kevin shook his head. "Not yet."

"It won't be long. When they start coming in, connect them to my office."

"Sure thing, Chief. How about some coffee?" He held up a cup.

"Decaf?"

"Yes."

"Make it black."

He shut the door to his office and took a deep breath. He was surprised no one had called yet. He knew all the local reporters had police scanners and listened to them religiously, hoping for a scoop, some jump on the competition. The advent of the Internet as a news source had placed a premium on speed over accuracy, a development Rod rued but accepted as an inevitable result of life in the Information Age. He longed for the day when responsible reporters were concerned with getting it right, having their sources verified before printing a story or reporting it on air. He feared those days were lost forever. It was all about the sound bite, the catchy headline. Hardly anyone read what followed, anyway.

Kevin knocked once before poking his head in and placing a steaming cup of coffee on the chief's desk. "Just made a pot," he said proudly. "Maybe I'm psychic."

Despite the long day and disheartening news, Rod managed a smile. "Doesn't mean you're getting a raise."

"Raise?" Kevin arched his eyebrow. "Does that mean you're paying me?"

Rod appreciated the effort to lighten the mood. This kid would make a good cop if he decided to stick with it. "If we're not, I'm going to have to have someone audit Anne's bank account." He smiled again. "Close the door on your way out, Kevin. And thanks."

"Anytime, Chief."

When he got the call about Liz Corelli, he'd managed to grab the 1972 yearbook on his way out the door. He opened it up again to the pictures of the senior class, started his computer and resumed the tedious task of trying to find someone who might know the whereabouts of Willie Emerson while he waited for the phone to ring.

38

Twenty minutes later Kevin buzzed the chief. "It's starting," he exclaimed with youthful enthusiasm. "Austin Lawrence from *The Observer.*"

"Put him through." He waited until the red light went on, then picked up the receiver. "Chief Wakefield."

"Evening, Chief. Austin Lawrence. What can you tell me about Liz Corelli?"

"Congratulations, Austin. You're ahead of the pack. How did you hear about it?"

"The usual way. Over the scanner. Is it true that she committed suicide?"

"No cause of death has been determined so far. Gerard Palmateer will be performing an autopsy in the next few days. We'll know more once the results are in."

Lawrence wasted no time getting to the point. "Was there a note?"

"Because it's an ongoing investigation, I can't comment on that."

"Who discovered the body?"

"Her husband."

"John Corelli?"

"Yes."

"Is there any reason to suspect he was involved with her death?"

"Until I get the coroner's report confirming cause of death, I really can't comment. Sorry, Austin."

"So you can't rule him out?"

"No comment."

They sparred for several more minutes before Lawrence conceded. "Promise to call me when you hear anything?' Lawrence asked.

"You're first on my list. Have a nice night."

A reporter from the *Buffalo News* called next, followed in quick succession by CNN and Fox News. An hour later one of the local network affiliates from Buffalo showed up outside the municipal building with a remote unit to provide film for the eleven o'clock news. The reporter, a young black woman named Naomi Miller, asked Rod a number of questions, looking for something she could use on air but he remained tight-lipped, repeating "no comment" again and again. Kevin Rumsfeld, bursting with excitement, hovered on the periphery, hoping perhaps that someone – anyone – might ask him a question or two. He was ready, having practiced saying "no comment" while looking in the mirror in the rest room, trying to moderate the joy of his smile, not wanting to be perceived as gleeful in the wake of a tragic death.

The calls stopped coming in just before 11:00, and Kevin and Rod watched the late news on the small portable television Anne kept in the mayor's office. Even without a juicy quote from the chief of police, Naomi Miller managed to put together a solid ninety-second piece, using previous footage of John Corelli and a brief clip of Liz observing the trial during the first week.

When the news ended, Rod decided to call it a night. "Thanks again, Kevin. I'm going to head home. You should be okay from here on in."

"No comment," he answered promptly, a twinkle in his eye.

"Exactly."

*****

By the time the band kicked off their opening number at 7:20, there was a decent crowd in attendance. The parking lot was comfortably full, not crowded, with a variety of people from seventeen to seventy, most of them drawn by the novelty of the event rather than the band itself. Business was steady at the outdoor bar, while Peter, at the food station, was making few sales, looking forlorn beside the grill as he waited for hungry customers to materialize. People milled around, drinks

230

in hand, enjoying the evening and the view of the harbor as the sun descended toward the lake.

Parnell Gomez arrived just before the sun disappeared into the lake. He spotted Kelly and walked over. "How's business?"

"Booming," she replied cheerfully. "What can I get you?"

Gomez thought for a moment. "A beer, I guess. What kind do you have?"

"Blue, Blue Light, Coors Light, Bud."

"I'll try a Blue Light."

She reached into one of the coolers and extracted a cold one. She opened it and offered it to him. "Five dollars."

He reached into his wallet and handed her a five. Guiltily, he took out a couple of ones and pressed the extra bills into her hand. "Keep the change."

Kelly smiled broadly. "The staff thanks you. Enjoy the music."

"Are they any good?" he asked, peering at the duo beneath the tent.

"A little too loud for my taste, but both of them can really play the guitar."

Gomez looked puzzled. "How loud can they be? They're playing acoustic guitars."

"Hooked into two big-ass amps. They crank a lot of volume."

Just then both guitars wailed as the duo broke into one of the songs from their new CD, "Show Me Or Blow Me." Gomez couldn't make out the lyrics – the shorter one was singing at the speed of light, the words all running together – but he admired their skill on the guitars as the two exchanged solos in front of a torrid beat.

He walked over to the merchandise table. Kirk beamed as he approached. "Hey."

Gomez hefted one of the T-shirts. Good quality, he thought, not as thin as other shirts he'd seen at concerts. He was a Springsteen man, having seen the Boss seven times. He thought these shirts were better than the ones he'd seen at the last Springsteen gig he'd attended in Saratoga Springs

"Great quality, isn't it?" Kirk enthused.

"Not bad."

"How about a CD? Only ten bucks."

Gomez wasn't interested. "How much are the shirts?"

"Twenty."

"Do you have a large?" Gomez asked.

Kirk smiled brightly. "You bet."

Gomez handed him a twenty in exchange for the shirt. It was a little more than he was used to paying, but he figured the quality was worth it. Especially if Jangling Rheinhardt ever graduated from playing parking lots in a border town – he might end up with a collector's item.

He walked back over to Kelly. She smiled as he approached. "He got you."

"Sometimes I'm an easy mark," Gomez replied with a smile. "The beer must've gone to my head."

"Good thing you're not driving."

From across the lot Herrington spied Gomez and waved. "Here comes trouble," Kelly warned as Herrington weaved his way through the crowd. "Parnell! Glad you could make it!"

Herrington's enthusiasm was unsettling. Gomez wondered how many gin and tonics he'd had already as he replied. "Nice to see you again, John." He looked around the crowd. "Nice turnout," he said lamely.

Herrington didn't seem to pick up on his loss for words, plowing ahead. "Could use a few more women in the crowd. The ratio seems to be a little one-sided." He clapped Gomez on the shoulder. "You should

232

go inside, get a drink from Connie. She's dressed in a fetching summer outfit, and she's very friendly. I think you'd like her." He winked at Kelly, who seethed behind her table but said nothing.

"Uh, maybe later," Gomez responded after a moment.

"Suit yourself." He looked at his cup. "I think I need to visit her myself."

"Go for it," Kelly mouthed savagely under her breath. It was loud enough for Parnell to hear but slipped by Herrington completely as he headed inside, in search of more gin. When he was gone Gomez spoke, raising his voice to be heard above the band. "What was that all about?"

Kelly shrugged. "That's Herrington. He's a self-absorbed chauvinist consumed by sex."

"What's he do for a living?" Gomez asked. "He seems to spend all his time on his boat or at your bar."

"Herrington doesn't work."

A puzzled look crept onto his face. "He doesn't? How can he afford that boat?"

Daffy Franklin interrupted, wanting another beer. He was still alone, still looking for some younger companionship. When he had a fresh beer in his hand and was on his way back toward the tent Kelly continued. "It's a long story. Ask me at the bar someday."

Gomez drifted to the back fence and gazed out toward the mouth of the lake. Darkness was gathering, and the bright green beacon at the Coast Guard station shone brightly in the dusk. Across the river Niagara-on-the-Lake glittered, lights everywhere, as the last boats of the day made their way toward shore. No holiday tomorrow for the Canadians – just another working day for them.

Gomez stayed until the band broke after their second set, promising to be back for a third set in a few minutes. He'd heard enough – they were good but not great, pretty raw for his taste. Maybe the right producer could refine their sound, make it more palatable to his older ears. Or maybe they didn't care to temper their primitive fury. Maybe that's what the kids these days preferred. He'd given up trying to keep up with musical trends at about the same time MTV turned into a reality-show network.

He walked slowly down Main Street past the gazebo overlooking the river, the eight-sided structure empty now in the dark, and the lights of Ontario beyond. He followed the streetlights to Stonewall Street, turned right and headed for the comfort of his rented bed.

39

It was almost 1:00 by the time Rod pulled into his driveway. He'd called to let Sally know he'd be late, so she'd been asleep for several hours by the time he came home. She didn't stir when he slipped into bed beside her.

He lay in the dark for a long time, his brain too wired to rest, wondering what sort of reaction Liz Corelli's death would provoke in the community. The producer from Fox with whom he'd spoken at the station earlier had sounded like a child on Christmas morning as he probed for information about the sudden death of accused child rapist John Corelli's wife. He could almost feel the producer's sense of glee through the phone as he tried to extract as much information as he could about the death of a deeply troubled woman, information he planned to convert into advertising revenue, the kind of revenue that could make a career.

Rod had been disgusted by the media feeding frenzy surrounding the trial from the start and knew that now it would only increase, putting more pressure on his staff and the mayor's office to continue to be the voices of moderation and sensibility. By morning everyone in town would know about Liz's death; it might not make the national news broadcasts until Tuesday, only because of the holiday Monday schedules of the cable networks, but it would be all over the Internet. It was the type of story that would rotate to the top of news food chain, the sort of salacious hook aimed directly at the demographic who gets their news from *Entertainment Tonight*.

The local angle worried him more. He'd have to come up with some sort of statement to let the community know that despite the sudden death of Liz Corelli, the general population was not at risk, that there was no madman on the loose killing local women. He'd have to do that before Gerard Palmateer officially declared her death a suicide, while at the same time not revealing anything about the nature of her death. The wording of his statement would have to be precise, not open to alternative interpretation.

He knew that speculation would begin first thing in the morning, so he tried to put together some words in his head before fatigue finally set in and he fell asleep. Finally, a little after 3:00, he drifted off to sleep, no closer to the answer he was desperately seeking.

*****

Sal Ducati had a restless night as well. After Rich and Mimi Stebbins left he went into his study and closed the door to be alone with his thoughts. What next, he thought. What else could possibly go wrong? He felt as though he'd aged ten years during the past few months as one disaster after another had occurred to alter the public's perception of Riverton.

He tried to work on the speech he was giving in the morning but he couldn't concentrate. Finally, he gave up and decided to use the same speech he'd used last year. After all, the ceremony was sparsely attended and those who did attend, other than local politicians, were mostly older local veterans whose memories had begun to deteriorate years ago. They'd never know the difference.

He located the file on his computer and printed it out. Usually Anne Moretti performed most of the official mayoral tasks requiring use of the computer, but he'd taken a few lessons the year before from Nabil Youssef, who operated a small computer repair business in Riverton next to Hubbard's Ice Cream shop, and now was able to do a few more things without assistance.

He went over the speech several times. It was short, only ten minutes if he didn't ad lib and go off on a tangent. He made one minor change and printed a revised copy. As the sheets of paper were spilling out of the printer, there was a knock on the study door. "Sal? Are you hungry?"

He was. "Just a minute, dear. I'll be right out." When the printer stopped he gathered the pages and checked to see that they were in the proper order before he stapled them together. He rose from his desk, opened the door and found his wife hovering on the other side, an anxious look on her face. He tried a reassuring smile, but wasn't sure that he pulled it off. "I'm famished. What do you have in mind?"

"I have some leftover gnocchi in the freezer that I can thaw in the microwave. And a salad," she added.

"Sounds perfect," Sal said. "How long will it be?"

"Ten, fifteen minutes."

"Come get me when it's ready. I have a few more things to do to prepare for my speech tomorrow. I'll leave the door open."

Chi Chi smiled. "You read my mind." She went into the kitchen and took the gnocchi out of the freezer to thaw. Sal went back into the study.

He sat at his desk, wondering if the new twist in the Corelli case would attract even more national attention to Riverton, perhaps draw MSNBC back to town again. He also pondered his own testimony, scheduled for Tuesday. Maybe, he thought hopefully, the judge would postpone the trial so that John Corelli could properly mourn the death of his wife with his family. At the very least it would buy him a little time, put off a task he'd been dreading for weeks. He wondered if he should call Judge Marquis, suggest that a postponement might be the humane thing to do under the current circumstances.

He could hear his wife moving around the kitchen. He knew the Corelli trial had been especially tough on her. Although Chi Chi hadn't been as close to Liz as Sal was to John, they had moved in the same social circles. They both belonged to the garden club, and because they were the wives of elected officials, often appeared together at public and political events. She would struggle with Liz's death. It was a struggle she didn't deserve.

*****

Arturo Corelli arrived at his brother's house a few minutes before 8:00. He was driving a weathered Dodge van with rust spots over a portion of the rear door that he used for his work as a stone mason. He was shorter and trimmer than his younger brother and wore a Yankees ball cap that covered his mostly bald head. His fingers were bent and misshapen, a result of his trade, but he offered a strong handshake to Karl Krull, who met him at the door. "How's my brother?"

Krull sidestepped the question, inviting Arturo inside. "He's in the kitchen, waiting for you. I'll give you some time alone, but before you go in I need to know your address so we can confirm that we've re-programmed his ankle monitor correctly. I asked John, but he couldn't remember the street number."

Arturo waited until Krull had a pad of paper and pen in his hand. "Niagara Falls, 537 25th Street." He retained a noticeable Italian accent, having been born in Naples before his parents emigrated to the United States when Arturo was two. The rest of the Corelli children had been born in Niagara Falls and there was no trace of the old country in their speech patterns. "Can I see him now?"

"Go right in."

John Corelli was seated at the kitchen table, staring out the window into the backyard. He didn't seem to notice his brother enter the room. On the floor next to his feet was a faded red gym bag with several changes of clothes in it that Officer Krull had helped him select.

Arturo sat next to his brother and placed a hand on his shoulder. "Johnny, it's me. Arturo."

John turned at the sound of his brother's voice. His eyes were vacant, his voice forlorn. "She's gone, Artie. Liz is gone."

"I know, Johnny. I'm here to take you to our house for a few days."

"I had to tell the kids."

Arturo's heart lurched. He hadn't believed the stories about his brother last year when he was arrested, refusing to accept that his baby brother, his own flesh and blood, was what they said he was. Arturo didn't know what a pedophile was; he had to look it up in the dictionary. Even as he believed in the innocence of his brother, he knew his arrest would be a devastating blow to Joseph and Maria. He was relieved when John and Liz decided to send them to Iowa for the duration of the trial, both of them agreeing that Arturo's two-story home in Niagara Falls was too close to home for what was about to come.

"That musta been horrible, Johnny."

"It was, Artie. They started crying and couldn't stop. I had to hang up. I can still hear them crying."

Arturo pointed to the bag on the floor. "Do you have everything you need?"

John looked at Krull, leaning against the door jamb, who nodded. He turned back to his brother. "I guess so."

238

"Would you like to go now? Angela made ravioli. She thought you might be hungry." Arturo stood up.

John Corelli got to his feet slowly. Arturo picked up the bag and with his other arm provided support for his brother as he walked slowly and unsteadily toward the front door. Krull followed them out the door and secured the home. Most of the neighbors had returned to their homes when the ambulance, with Liz Corelli inside, had departed, but there was one woman standing on her front porch across the street from the Corelli house who watched them intently as Arturo helped his brother into the van. She waited until the van, followed by Krull in his patrol vehicle, pulled away before going inside her house.

Arturo had been listening to the radio on his trip to Riverton, but turned down the volume for the ride home. John Corelli sat rigidly in the front passenger seat, staring straight ahead. He was thinking about what a mess he'd made of things, of how he'd destroyed everything he and Liz had created throughout their marriage. Up to this point he'd managed to convince himself that it wasn't his fault that he'd been arrested and charged with such heinous crimes. He'd blamed it on the girls, those saucy little temptresses who flaunted their ripe young bodies whenever they got the chance. How was he supposed to resist when they came to school dressed like that? He'd even blamed his plight on their parents for allowing their children to leave the house looking like teenaged hookers in their push-up bras and short shorts.

But Liz was right, had been right all along. It *was* his fault, just like she'd said in the note she left behind. If he hadn't succumbed to his weakness, hadn't lured two of his students into situations he knew, somewhere in the recesses of his mind, were deviant and depraved and wrong on every level, none of this would've happened. He'd still be teaching, still be on the town council. Most of all, the four of them would still be living together on Iroquois Street, looking forward to another summer vacation, another family road trip to another national park.

He straightened himself in his seat. It was time to face the demon in the room. It would start with a phone call to Max Grossinger.

239

40

It was overcast, raining lightly when Sal Ducati woke Monday morning. He showered and dressed and came into the kitchen. Chi Chi was sitting at the kitchen table with a fresh pot of coffee beside her, the aroma of the French roast Sal preferred filling the room. She indicated a cup on a saucer next to hers. "I figured you'd be ready, especially when you saw the rain. Why does it always have to rain on Memorial Day?"

Sal shrugged his shoulders. "Just my luck, I guess." This was the third consecutive year that it had rained on the morning of the Memorial Day ceremony in the park. Although it was just a gentle sprinkle now, with no wind, he wondered if the threat of yet another soggy parade might result in any of the organizations dropping out. It was a small parade to begin with, usually with less than twenty groups participating.

He sipped the steaming coffee and smiled at his wife. She was doing her best to keep his spirits up, to do whatever she could to help him through this difficult time. He knew if it was possible, she'd volunteer to testify in his place at the trial tomorrow. After his first wife had died fifteen years ago, he didn't think he'd ever marry again. But he and Chi Chi met while she was on the rebound from a disastrous marriage to an Armenian restaurateur and low-level con man. They'd hit it off immediately. She made him laugh again after Sal's first wife had succumbed to breast cancer, and she continued to make him smile on a daily basis. Not many men can say they've experienced true love once, let alone twice, during their lifetime. He knew he was a lucky man.

"It's only drizzling," Sal said as he added another touch of sugar to his cup and stirred it gently with a spoon before taking another sip. "Maybe it will stop by 11:00."

"Maybe not. Don't forget your rain jacket. And don't forget that plastic envelope for your speech – you don't want the rain to blur the type so you can't figure out what it says."

He smiled. "I decided to give the same speech I gave last year. The only people who pay any attention to what I say are the veterans, and they're at the point where they probably forget what they heard five minutes after I've said it."

"Are you saying you have the entire speech memorized?" There was an impish grin on her face.

"Most of it. The important parts, anyway."

She stood up and walked over to the sink. She rinsed her cup and saucer and placed them in the dishrack. "I think I'll take my shower now. Are you hungry? There's some rye bread for toast if you'd like."

"Do we still have any oranges?"

She nodded. "I think there's one or two left in the crisper." She gave her husband one last look before turning and heading for the bathroom.

Sal sipped his coffee as he watched his wife depart. Still looks pretty good, he thought. A man could do worse. A lot worse.

When he'd finished his first cup he poured himself a second and took one of the oranges from the refrigerator. He sat down at the table and peeled the orange, tossing the skin toward the sink like he was attempting a three-pointer from beyond the arc. He inserted his thumb in the end of the orange and gently pried the pieces apart. He plopped one into his mouth. When he bit into it his mouth filled with juice. Probably from Brazil, he thought.

He was looking forward to seeing Rod Wakefield at the ceremony at Blakeslee Park. He wanted to know the latest on the Corelli trial, whether or not Rod had heard anything about a possible postponement. Although he knew it would only be a temporary reprieve, it would give him some time to try to come up with something positive to say about John Corelli, something that wouldn't be construed as naiveté on his part. He'd been having a hard time with the list of questions Max Grossinger's office had supplied to him, trying to come up with answers that would help John yet not reflect darkly on Sal's ability to judge the character of his colleague and friend.

Suddenly he felt guilty. Here he was, worrying about his own image, when John, already in the fight of his life, now had to deal with the ominous implications of his wife's suicide. He thought it would be impossible for anyone, even Max Grossinger, to frame her death in a manner where John Corelli wasn't the villain. He wondered if the veteran attorney wasn't second guessing his decision to take John Corelli on as a client.

Outside the rain continued to fall, ideal for fledgling gardens and thirsty lawns but troublesome for public processions. He checked his watch and waited for his wife to emerge from the bathroom.

*****

Rod Wakefield's cell phone chirped. He reached over quickly to answer it before it disturbed Sally's sleep beside him. It was still dark in their bedroom; the radio/alarm clock on the table next to the bed read 6:03. Filled with trepidation, he spoke quietly into the phone as he slid out of bed. "Rod Wakefield."

A familiar voice chortled on the other end of the line. "No shit, Sherlock."

It was his Uncle Cal, calling from a number unfamiliar to Rod. "Where are you, Cal? I have your phone number programmed into my phone, and this isn't it."

"Phone's on the blink, so I'm using one of the pay phones in the hall. Did I wake you up?"

Trying to keep the irritation out of his voice, he replied evenly. "Yes."

He laughed, a short, explosive burst. "About time you got to work. I've got something for you."

Rod was wary. Because of his lack of mobility and the general lack of intellectual stimulation from most of his fellow residents at Scherber Manor, Cal was regularly trying to engage his nephew on wild goose chases he concocted primarily to keep himself amused. "What is it this time?"

"I've been thinking about that Lorenzo case. You still got the file, right?"

"I do."

"Well, I been thinking." Rod groaned to himself. Cal thinking usually didn't end well for anyone involved. His uncle continued. "I think that boy Lorenzo knew his friend was fucking his girlfriend. I think he knew it before he agreed to go on the ride. Do you have the file handy?"

242

Rod was in his office now. He extracted the thin manila folder from his lower desk drawer. "I've got it here."

"See if you can find which one of those other boys saw the life jacket. Take your time."

It took Rod a minute before he found the interview Call was referencing. "Allan O'Rourke."

"I knew it!" Cal exclaimed triumphantly. "I knew those little bastards were lying!"

Rod wasn't following. "I don't get it. According to the file, O'Rourke was the only one that claimed to see a life jacket, but one was never found. Couldn't he have just made a mistake, maybe saw a log or some other debris floating in the river and thought it was a life jacket?"

"He could've, but I don't think so. I think they lied about the order they went into the river. They all claimed Joey Lorenzo was the last one to leave, so no one saw what happened. Once they realized Joey was gone, the other four got together to concoct a story to keep them out of it as much as possible. I think O'Rourke was tired the next day – I remember he looked like he hadn't slept much – and I think he slipped, just for a moment, when he claimed to see a life jacket. I think O'Rourke, not Lorenzo, was the last person to leave shore that night. If I'm right, everything Lorenzo did would've been seen by the last guy in the group: O'Rourke. What if he *did* see a life jacket in the river? What if he saw Lorenzo take it off?"

Rod considered his uncle's theory, once again amazed at the level of detail he remembered from a case that had occurred more than forty years ago. His body may be failing, but there was nothing wrong with his mind. "So you think he took it off and O'Rourke saw him?"

"Yep."

Rod continued to think out loud. "You think he committed suicide? Over the easiest girl in town?" His voice was edged with doubt. "I don't know…"

"It could be one of two things. Either he offed himself, or he took off the life jacket before he swam to Canada to avoid the draft, trying to muddy his trail by making it look like he'd drowned. The second one doesn't hold water, though. As far as I know, there was never any report of Joey Lorenzo making it to Canada, nothing to indicate he ever made it to the shore, not even after forty years. I think Lorenzo took that life jacket off deliberately and was swallowed up by one of those whirlpools. End of story."

Rod still wasn't convinced. "It's a big stretch to think a twenty-year-old man, with good prospects and his whole life in front of him, would choose to end it all because his girlfriend cheated on him."

"It is pretty thin," Cal conceded. "but it makes sense. He was Italian, after all. You know how emotional those people get."

Those people. Good old bigoted Uncle Cal.

His uncle continued. "I think it's the most likely version of what happened that night."

"More likely than an accidental drowning?"

"Maybe not, if O'Rourke didn't claim to see a life jacket. But he did, and I think when he said he saw a life jacket in the river, it was one of the only true parts of his story. If you believe that part of his story, and I do, then it's probably a suicide."

"It can never be proved, though."

"You're right," Cal said. "But that doesn't mean it isn't the truth."

Rod considered Cal's theory, acknowledging that the scenario he'd laid out was the one that made the most sense if there was a link between Lorenzo's disappearance in 1972 and Jamison's several weeks ago. Making the leap from assumption to fact was a cardinal sin for law enforcement, but it hadn't stopped him from using the uncertainty of the facts surrounding both these disappearances as rationalization for pushing ahead. If he'd simply accepted the premise that Scott Jamison had been the unfortunate victim of a freak weather event that caught him by surprise, he'd never have tried to connect the two cases. But like all law enforcement officials, nothing rankled him more than an unsolved case. It leaves all parties associated with a bitter, uncertain taste in their mouths that often can evolve into unrealistic hopes that someday, somehow the truth will be revealed and there will be closure for the persons involved. In the Jamison case, he'd been willing to go out on a limb, to pursue a theory fashioned from straw rather than concrete, because he felt Gillian Hudecki deserved nothing less.

But life wasn't neat. It was filled with random circumstances and events that often led nowhere, an assortment of journeys down different paths that rarely intersected. Happy endings were rare, but that didn't stop him from pursuing them whenever he could. It was the prime directive of law enforcement: to do one's best to provide answers for the victims left behind.

"So," Cal said. "What do you think?"

"If Joey Lorenzo did commit suicide and Scott Jamison had some idea of why he did it, it puts some interesting things into play."

"Such as?"

"Guilt, for one. Suspecting that one of your friends killed themselves because of something you did would be a heavy burden for most people to bear. Over forty years, it might have worn him down enough so that he might've consider punishing himself."

Cal liked it. "I could see that. But wouldn't something have to push you over the edge to get you to finally act after all these years? Something to tip the scales?"

"Probably," Rod admitted. "But I haven't found anything like that. It's exactly the opposite. According to the people we've talked to so far, he was coming off the biggest payday he'd had in a couple of years. He should've been on top of the world."

Cal couldn't keep the satisfaction from his voice. "Which is why we call 'em mysteries. Looks like you still have some work to do."

41

Lenny waited until Red and Joanie left for breakfast Monday morning before pulling out his cell phone and dialing Gillian's number. He really wanted to send her a text, to avoid speaking with her, but he felt guilty for avoiding her all week. She deserved a call.

Gillian's voice was accusatory. "Where have you been? I've been leaving you messages all week."

"I've been pretty busy with my brother and his wife, visiting a lot of relatives,' Lenny said lamely.

"Have you told them about me yet?"

"Uh, no. Not yet."

"What are you waiting for? Christmas?" No answer. She continued, her agitation rising. "Are you ashamed to tell them about me? Please fill me in. I'm dying to know."

Lenny tried to pacify her. "Of course I'm not ashamed of you. You're the best thing that's ever happened to me."

Gillian wasn't buying it. "Really? Then why not tell your only brother and your mother about how wonderful I am? What's the hold up?"

"I just haven't had time," he said weakly.

"Make time. I'll be down at your house in an hour. Make sure your brother and his wife are there, too."

Lenny tried to head her off one last time. "They might not be back from breakfast in an hour."

"Call them. Tell them to eat fast."

The phone went dead. Lenny placed it on the counter next to the stove. Not the ideal way to start the day, he thought.

*****

The news of Liz Corelli's death was the lead story in Monday's *Niagara Gazette*. Without a confirmed cause of death, the article referred to her as dying under "suspicious" circumstances at home.

Rod could live with that. He was reading the paper at the kitchen table, having been unable to get back to sleep after Cal's pre-dawn call. A fresh pot of coffee was on the counter, steam rising and drifting in the dull morning light. Poor Austin, he thought as he finished the article and moved on to the sports section. *The Observer* doesn't publish until early Friday, with distribution Saturday morning. By that time the story might already be on the back burner, supplanted by the Next Big Thing. He wondered idly how many people read the online version of the weekly.

After reading how the Yankees were unable to hold onto a late inning lead yesterday against the Angels, he put the paper down and thought about what his uncle had said. It all made sense. If O'Rourke had slipped and was actually telling the truth when he mentioned seeing a life jacket in the water that night, then suicide leapfrogged accidental drowning on the short list of possible causes of Joey Lorenzo's death. But without further corroboration from one of the three remaining survivors, nothing would change. All he had was a nice theory, with insufficient evidence to alter the medical examiner's original verdict of accidental drowning. He wished he could find Willie Emerson.

"What time do you have to be at the park for the ceremony?"

Sally had entered the kitchen noiselessly. He'd jumped a little at the sound of her voice. Sheepishly, he responded. "The mayor speaks at 11:00. I suppose I don't have to be there until 10:30."

"Maybe it'll stop raining by then." She sat opposite her husband and reached for the paper. "Anything good this morning?"

"The lead story is Liz Corelli. And the Yankees lost again. Their bullpen just isn't the same without Mariano."

She looked at him over the top of the paper. "Now there's a real tragedy, the Yankees' bullpen. What's a bullpen?"

He started to explain before he caught the amusement in her eyes. She was putting him on. "Nice one. You got me."

"I think you have enough real tragedies to deal with without adding the Yankees to the mix." She looked at him closely. "How did you sleep? I thought I heard the phone really early."

"You did. It was Cal, with a new theory about the Lorenzo drowning."

"He couldn't wait until the sun was up?"

"You know Cal."

"What did he say?"

"He thinks the boys were lying back then, that one of them saw more than he admitted to the night Joey disappeared. He thinks one of them saw Joey take off his life jacket before he went into the river."

She weighed the import of his words before replying. "He's saying it wasn't an accident."

"Right," Rod said. "Cal thinks he did it deliberately."

Sally asked the big question. "Why?"

"He thinks it was over a girl."

"Sounds a little Shakespearean to me." Her voice was filled with doubt. "And quite a reach."

"I know," Rod said. "But I can't stop thinking that the two disappearances, Lorenzo and Jamison, are connected somehow. Cal's theory, if it's true, means there might be a connection. I just have to find it."

"You'll need some energy then. How about some eggs and toast?"

"Sounds good."

Sally scrambled some eggs, adding chopped mushrooms and grated cheddar. Rod ate hungrily – his system, including his diet, had been out of whack for the last two weeks, and he knew he needed to try to eat more meals at home. Missing meals was one of the things about the job that irritated Sally the most, and it was also one of the most correctable.

248

When he was finished he rinsed his plate and silverware and deposited them in the sink. He turned to Sally. "I'll be in the study. Call me in an hour."

She watched as he walked across the family room and closed the door of his office behind him. One of these days, she thought as she filled the sink to do the dishes, we'll be back to normal. The trial will be over, the Jamison case will fade away and Rod will be behind his desk again, working regular hours, complaining about the large amount of time he has to spend on administrative duties. As far as Sally was concerned, those days couldn't come soon enough.

*****

Arturo Corelli's oldest daughter Connie was twenty-nine, living in St. Louis, working as a city planner. He carried his brother's red bag up the stairs of his two-story frame home to Connie's old bedroom, which they had been using as spare storage. Arturo apologized as he dropped John's bag on one of the few unoccupied areas of the floor. "We'll move most of this stuff out of your way tomorrow."

John looked around the room, shoulders slumped. He sat on the edge of the bed. "Don't worry about it. I won't be here that long."

"Angela left you some extra towels in the bathroom, if you want to clean up." No response. "Can I get you anything else?" More silence. "The ravioli should be ready whenever you are. Take your time." Arturo couldn't get out of the room fast enough; he felt that John was on a hair trigger and could go off at any time. He was glad there were no guns in the house.

When he came down the stairs, John ate silently, picking at his plate. He wasn't hungry; after ten minutes at the table, with Angela hovering over him, he rose abruptly and returned to his room without a word, shutting the door behind him. He was tired and wanted to close his eyes to blot out the recurring image of Liz, lying on her back, arms folded across her chest, eyes closed. He wanted to go to sleep, because he wanted her to wake up when he did.

He lay down on top of the bedspread, not bothering to remove his clothes. He slept fitfully, awake most of the night, thinking for a change about the damage he'd caused and not about how he might save himself from going to prison. He deserved to go to prison; he knew that

249

now. Liz was right. He was responsible for her death and he needed to be punished.

When it began to get light he looked out the window and saw the rain darkening the street in front of the house. He waited for what he thought were several hours – he didn't have a watch and there wasn't a clock in the bedroom – before he went downstairs. Angela was in the kitchen. She turned as he shuffled into the room. "Arturo's gone. He's working on a job in Cambria. Are you hungry? Would you like some coffee?"

He sat at the table and looked at her vacantly for several moments before he spoke. "Do you have a phone?"

She nodded. "I have a cell phone, and we still have a landline." She laughed nervously. "We're probably the last people in the city with one."

"Where is it?"

"In the family room, on the table next to Arturo's chair."

Without a word he turned and walked out of the room. He sat in Arturo's chair and pulled Max Grossinger's business card out of his wallet. He dialed the private cell number Max had written on the back of the card. He recognized his attorney's voice. "This is Max."

"This is John."

"John!" His voice was laced with sympathy. "How are you? I've been worried about you."

"She's dead."

Max had read the story in the *Buffalo News* an hour earlier. "I'm so sorry for your loss. Is there anything I can do for you?"

His voice was completely devoid of emotion. "She's dead. I'm at my brother's house."

"Arturo's?"

"Yes."

"Are you okay?"

250

"No. No, I'm not okay."

"Is anyone there with you?"

"Angela."

"May I speak with her?"

"No."

"Well then, what can I do for you?"

"I want to take the deal. I want this to be over."

Max tried to keep his voice calm as he answered. "Are you sure? You have to be sure before I call the district attorney."

"I just want it to end. I killed her. I deserve to go to prison."

This was more than Max had hoped for. He was prepared to start his case tomorrow, but John's change of heart meant that he wouldn't have to make the decision on whether or not to call Lisette Gaffney to the stand. He'd been reading the jury for a week and could see in their eyes that they wanted this to be over. They wouldn't care what his witnesses had to say. They wanted to vote guilty and then go home to their families. Accepting defeat was never easy, but Max Grossinger was a realist. Without a miracle of some sort occurring, he felt certain John would be convicted. At least with a plea deal, they could try to limit the amount of time he'd have to remain behind bars.

"Is this your brother's phone?"

"Yes."

"Let me call the district attorney. I'll call you right back. Don't go anywhere."

"Where would I go?"

42

Max reached Charles Moreland at the Riverton Country Club, where he was sitting in the clubhouse, playing poker as his foursome waited for the rain to let up. He answered the phone warily after reading the Caller ID. "Counselor. What can I do for you?"

"I have some good news. My client would like to accept the plea deal, if it's still on the table."

Moreland sat up straight, dropped his cards on the table, mouthed "I fold" to his opponents. He was elated, yet cautious as rose and walked away from the group for some privacy. "The plea deal as is?"

"We only have a couple of requests, and I don't think they're deal breakers. If possible, he'd like to be housed in a minimum security facility, out of the general population. If it could be somewhere close to western New York, that would be nice."

Moreland was skeptical. "That's it?"

"Yes. He agrees to register as a sex offender once he's released and he agrees to give up his teaching certification."

"I'll need to run this by the judge."

"I thought he was in your foursome."

"Not today," Moreland said. "His daughter drove in from Syracuse for the weekend, but I should be able to reach him at home. Can I call you back?"

"I'll be waiting."

Thirty minutes later Grossinger's phone rang again. It was Moreland. "You have a deal," he said tersely. "He pleads guilty to two charges of endangering the welfare of a minor, but with the stipulation that he register as a sex offender once he's released. He has to admit his guilt in court, and he can never teach again. Seven years, eligible for parole after three and a half."

"I'll call John right away," Grossinger said promptly, before Moreland could change his mind. "How did Judge Marquis react?"

"Relieved, I guess. I imagine he can't wait to get back to conducting traffic court again."

"Can't say I blame him. I'll see you in court tomorrow morning. Thanks again."

Grossinger's next call was to one of his paralegals. She sounded a bit groggy as she answered the phone, not quite awake yet. "Hello?"

"Stephanie, it's Max. I hope I didn't wake you."

The fog lifted from her voice. "No sir, not at all. What can I do for you, Mr. Grossinger?"

"I want you to contact that friend of yours at Channel Two, the one who likes to talk."

"What for?"

"We just made a plea deal for John Corelli. It'll be announced by the judge tomorrow morning. I want you to leak the story to your friend. Insist that you be referred to as a source close to the case. We can't be tied to this."

"Of course not, Mr. Grossinger. I'll get right on it."

"Thanks, Stephanie."

He dialed the number for Arturo Corelli next. A woman's voice answered. "Hello?"

"May I speak to John Corelli, please? It's his attorney, Max Grossinger."

"He's upstairs. I'll get him for you."

Two minutes later Corelli picked up the phone. "Hello."

"John, it's Max. We have a deal. I just got off the phone with the district attorney. There are some minor points that still need to be worked out, but they won't affect the substance of it."

"Do I have to go to court anymore?"

"Just tomorrow," Grossinger said reassuringly. "We'll stand up and the judge will ask you if you understand the terms of the plea deal.

253

You'll say yes, that you understand you're pleading guilty. After that, it'll be over. No more court." He added. "Will you need a ride tomorrow? I can send a car for you if you like."

"Let me ask Angela." The phone clunked as he dropped it on the table. Two minutes later he was back. "She can give me a ride. Will I need a ride home?"

He wondered if John realized he wouldn't be seeing home again for a long time. "No. The district attorney will take care of that. Do you have a clean suit to wear to court?"

"Yes. Artie packed my gray one."

"Perfect. Try to be at the courthouse by 8:30."

"Okay."

The phone went dead. Grossinger stood up and stretched. He had a lot to do before tomorrow morning.

*****

Charles Moreland phoned Rod Wakefield, who was just about to leave for Blakeslee Park and the Memorial Day ceremony. "Did I catch you at a bad time?"

"Just about to head out the door for the ceremony at the park, but I have a few minutes. What's up?"

"I wanted to let you know we've come to an agreement on a plea deal in the John Corelli case. Tomorrow morning he'll switch his plea to guilty, the judge will say a few words, then it will be over."

Rod was stunned. It took him a moment to respond. "What's the deal?" he finally managed.

"Seven years, eligible for parole in three and a half."

"Attica?"

"We're trying for Gowanda. Anyway, I wanted to give you a heads up. If I know Grossinger, he's probably already leaked the news to the press. You might need some extra people at the courthouse tomorrow."

Rod agreed. "I'll get on it right away." Pause. "I can't believe it's over."

"Almost. By tomorrow night, it *will* be over. See you in the morning." Moreland hung up.

Sally was hovering in the next room. "Who was that?"

"Chuck Moreland. Corelli accepted a plea deal. After tomorrow the trial will be over."

"Oh, Rod!" she exclaimed. "That's wonderful news!" She moved toward him and he took her in his arms, hugging her tightly. He knew the last few weeks had been rough on Sally, rougher on her than it had been for him. She'd been waiting for things to return to normal, for the national news crews to pack up their gear and hit the road for the next big story, leaving Riverton to revert once again to its preferred persona as a quiet little village on the banks of the Niagara.

She shifted onto her toes and he lowered his head. Their lips met, clinging for a moment before she gently broke the embrace. "You better go before you're late."

"Right," he said reluctantly, grabbing his hat as he headed for the door. "See you later."

"Don't forget your umbrella."

As soon as Rod parked his car at the park, he looked for Sal Ducati. He found him huddled under the bandstand, out of the rain, going over the notes for his speech. He looked up and saw Rod approaching with an ear-to-ear smile. "You look pretty happy."

"That's because I just heard a great piece of news. John Corelli accepted a plea deal. The trial will be over tomorrow. You won't have to testify."

Sal's knees sagged a bit and Rod moved quickly to his side. But the mayor recovered and looked into Rod's eyes piercingly. "Because of Liz?"

Rod nodded. "I think so. Grossinger and Moreland worked it out this morning. In a few days the village will be back to normal."

"Normal," he echoed. He wondered if that would be the case or if Rod was just trying to make him feel better. The community had been deeply affected by the trial and the publicity it had generated. He doubted that emotions that had been cresting for nearly a year could be turned off so easily. Would things return to normal? He wasn't sure he knew what normal was anymore, but he was relieved that he wouldn't have to appear in court as a character witness for a pedophile, a man he considered to be his friend.

Sal pointed toward his watch. "Time to get started." He peered out at the small crowd, four uniformed veterans, all in their eighties. "We've lost two of our veterans since last year. It's been a tough year in more ways than one," he said as he raised his umbrella and stepped into the rain, notes in hand.

43

There was an unfamiliar car in Lenny's driveway when Red and Joanie returned from breakfast. "Whose car is that?" Joanie asked as they pulled up next to it

Red shook his head. "No idea."

Inside, an attractive brunette was sitting next to Lenny on the couch. She stood up immediately when Red and Joanie entered the room and strode purposefully toward them, hand extended. "I'm Gillian. Gillian Hudecki." Lenny remained seated, unsmiling, looking like a cornered animal.

Joanie caught on first, giving Lenny a big smile before moving forward to shake her hand. "Gillian! From the trap shooting team at the club?"

"That's right," Gillian said. "But that's not all. Lenny and I have been dating, and I wanted to meet his only brother and his wife." She gave Lenny a look. "He kept putting it off, so I finally decided to come over and introduce myself."

Red was trying to remember where he'd heard the name. "Gillian Hudecki," he muttered to himself.

"I'm Joanie," she said, still grasping Gillian's hand. "And this is Red. Honey, say hello to Lenny's friend."

Finally, it came to him. He'd read about the disappearance of Scott Jamison in the papers; according to the reports, Gillian Hudecki was Jamison's live-in girlfriend. He stepped forward cautiously and extended his hand. "Nice to meet you, Gillian."

"Likewise," Gillian beamed. "Lenny talks about you all the time."

"Really," Red said, fixing an inquisitive look on his younger brother. Lenny squirmed in his seat and looked away.

Gillian continued. "Mostly he talks about the boat and visiting you in Colorado. He says you have a beautiful home."

"How did you two meet?" Joanie asked.

"At the club," Gillian said. "We both like to shoot."

"Lenny said you're a dentist," Joanie said.

Gillian gave Lenny a big smile before turning back to Joanie. "An orthodontist, actually. He mentioned me to you?"

Joanie shook her head. "I was snooping. His phone rang while we were on the boat and my husband picked it up and saw your name on Caller ID."

Red stood up. "Would you ladies excuse us for a moment? Lenny said he's been having a problem with his water heater. It should only take a minute. We'll be right back." He glared at his brother, who reluctantly got to his feet. Red followed him down the stairs to the basement.

"Don't worry about us," Joanie said brightly. "We have lots to talk about. Take your time."

When Red and Lenny were in the basement Red turned toward his brother and hissed. "Are you fucking crazy? Isn't that Scott Jamison's girlfriend? Live-in girlfriend?"

"Not anymore," Lenny said feebly, a futile attempt at humor.

Red wasn't smiling. "How long has this been going on?"

"I dunno. About four months, I guess."

"Four months! Jesus fucking Christ." Red shook his head in dismay. "Do the cops know?"

"About us? No."

"Are you sure? You said you talked to the cops."

"I was at the club the night before he disappeared," Lenny explained. "They talked to everyone who was there that night."

Red pressed. "They talked to her, too, right? How do you know she didn't say anything about you to the cops?" He raised his hands in the air in disgust. "You know they're going to find out. What are you going to say then?"

"They won't find out," Lenny said with confidence. "We never went out in public. Every time we met, it was at my house."

"How do you know someone didn't recognize her car when it was sitting in your driveway?"

"Because she parks it in the garage when she comes over."

"Did he know?"

The implication of Red's question was clear. If Scott Jamison knew that his girlfriend was seeing another man, one of his friends at the club, he wouldn't have been pleased. Would he have reacted irrationally, done something that put himself at risk when he was on the lake? It was certainly a line of questioning the police would want to investigate if it came to their attention.

Lenny hesitated before replying. "I don't think so."

"You don't think so? What do you mean, you don't think so?"

Lenny tried to sound confident. "He couldn't have known. We were careful."

Red wasn't buying it. It had been years since Lenny had had any lasting relationship with a woman, at least as far as he knew, which meant the little head was probably doing most of Lenny's thinking - never a good sign when cautious behavior and subterfuge were warranted. It wouldn't take much between the two of them – an affectionate touch, a meaningful glance – to trigger suspicion, especially at the club. A single unguarded moment in public and gossip would materialize like an unwelcome relative during the holidays. It was only a matter of time before their affair became public knowledge.

"Just be careful," Red advised. "She's like a widow – people will talk if she shows interest in another man too soon." He peered at his brother. "What about her? Can she keep her mouth shut, at least for a little while?"

Lenny nodded. "She won't say anything. She's terrified the cops might find out."

"She should be. They'd have a field day with this." He put his arm across his brother's shoulder and gave him a hug. "Let's go back upstairs. I want to get to know this girlfriend of yours."

*****

It continued to rain steadily during the parade, and by the time the truncated procession reached the municipal building and the end of the route Rod had decided to stop by the office, check in with Kevin and have a cup of coffee. He asked Sal to join him but the mayor passed, opting to go home instead and tell Chi Chi the good news about the trial.

Kevin was alone in the office, reclining in his chair, keeping a casual eye on things. He bounded to his feet when he saw Rod. "Hi, Chief. Coffee?"

The aroma of a fresh pot filled the room. "How did you know?"

Kevin shrugged. "Simple. The ceremony started at eleven, so I figured you wouldn't get here until noon. And it's still raining."

Rod poured himself a cup. "Good work, Kevin. Anything going on?"

"Nope. The rain has discouraged mischief of all sorts." He smiled. "Have you checked any social media today?"

Rod took a sip and shook his head. "Why?"

"Mrs. Corelli's death is *the* hot local topic. Hashtag hadenough, hashtag thanksjohn. Stuff like that."

"What's the verdict?"

Kevin leaned in, pleased that someone was interested in his opinion. "Suicide, by a wide margin."

"What came next?"

"The husband."

"Sounds about right." He motioned toward his office. "I'm going to do a little work. Hold my calls."

"You got it, Chief."

He spent the next hour trying to justify Uncle Cal's theory and connect it to Jamison's disappearance. He cleared the top of his desk and placed photos of Joey Lorenzo, Scott Jamison, Andrea Herman and Gillian Hudecki in a rough box, moving them around as he tried to find the elusive combination that tied two mysterious deaths forty years apart to one another.

He placed the ill-fated triangle of Lorenzo, Jamison and Herman together on the table and was holding Gillian's photo in his hand when it hit him. How could he have been so blind? If Joey Lorenzo had killed himself because he found himself the odd man out after Andrea Herman had cheated on him, perhaps Scott Jamison had done the same thing. If Gillian had been sleeping with another man and Scott had found out about it, that might explain the more curious aspects surrounding his disappearance, the farewell round of drinks at the club Tuesday night and the carefully arranged personal belongings, his wallet and cell phone, left behind on the seat of his van. If Cal's theory was correct, add forty years of guilt that Scott must've borne for being the catalyst in Joey's death and suddenly Scott's disappearance doesn't seem so random.

He needed to get Gillian Hudecki back to the station to ask her a few more questions and gauge her reaction. The digital clock on his desk read 2:37 – he wondered what she was doing today. He found her number in the case file and dialed it, but after several rings it went to her voicemail. Rod told her he had a few more questions – could she come in at her earliest convenience?

He ended the call and dialed Sally. She answered on the second ring. "I was wondering what happened to you."

Rod's voice was sheepish. "I was wet and a little cold after the parade, so I stopped at the office for a cup of coffee with Kevin. I started looking at the Jamison file and the time got away from me. Sorry."

"Are you leaving now? It's stopped raining over here."

Rod looked out the window. Puddles dotted the back parking lot, but the rain had stopped. "I'm on my way. See you in twenty minutes."

*****

The four of them were sitting in Lenny's living room. Joanie was telling Gillian about the trip she and Red had taken to Maui last year to do some windsurfing and kiteboarding. "We'd been out on the water all

261

day and were back in Lahaina, at Cheeseburger in Paradise, when Red fell asleep at the table, holding a margarita."

"I wasn't asleep," Red growled defensively. "I was resting my eyes."

Gillian's phone rang in her purse. She reached for it apologetically, explaining. "It might be the office. I have to get this." She looked at her screen: Rod Wakefield. She managed to maintain her composure despite the jolt the chief of police's name had delivered to her system and even forced a smile as she dropped the phone back in her purse and returned her gaze to the group. "It's no one important. I'll call them later."

44

When Kelly Porter arrived for her shift at the AC on Tuesday morning, she found John Herrington waiting by the side door to the parking lot. As she reached for the key and inserted it into the lock she remarked, "You're early today."

Herrington smiled. "It's a big news day. I've been reading about the developments in the Corelli case online."

Kelly opened the door and walked inside, flicking the light switch on the wall. Herrington followed. "When did you start to care so much about the Corelli's?"

Herrington took his usual seat at the end of the bar. He was wearing a white polo shirt, khaki shorts and boat shoes, his normal attire. "It rained all day yesterday. I don't have a TV, so I went online and listened to satellite radio. Liz Corelli's death was all over the online versions of local media. It didn't sound like her death was a coincidence so I started reading more about her husband's case. No wonder she killed herself."

Kelly looked up from behind the bar. "Is it officially a suicide?"

"Not yet, but they didn't arrest the husband, who was the only other person in the house with her when she died, so I have to think it was a suicide.' He looked around the bar. "Where's today's paper?"

Kelly was behind the bar, her hands full with a container of lemons and limes. She nodded toward the kitchen. "Probably in there."

Herrington got up and retrieved the paper from the kitchen table, settling back into his seat. The lead headline, in bold type, was only slightly smaller than the headline it had printed after two planes had crashed in the World Trade Center towers:

It's A Deal

The article, written by veteran *Niagara Gazette* columnist Glenn Donaldson, cited sources close to the investigation confirming that a deal had been reached between District Attorney Charles Moreland and defendant John Corelli. According to Donaldson's account, details of the deal were not yet public but would be revealed in court this morning.

When Herrington finished reading the article he looked up, frowning and shaking his head. "It took his wife's suicide for that piece of shit to stop trying to get away with it. I hope they lock him up for life."

"Not likely," Kelly said. "Why would anyone agree to a deal that would put them behind bars for more time than the maximum allowable for the crimes they're charged with?"

Herrington folded the front section and placed it on the bar. "One can hope." He picked up the second section, looking for the weather. "Sunny through Thursday," he noted with satisfaction. "With a little breeze. Might be some sailing on the horizon."

Kelly expertly sliced the limes and lemons and placed them in a plastic container in the cooler beneath the bar. "Anything in there about Scott Jamison?"

"The guy who disappeared on the lake? No. It's been what, two weeks? By now he's fish food."

"Strange that they never found his boat."

"I agree," Herrington said. "They should've found something by now. A life jacket or something." He smiled brightly. "How's your boyfriend?"

Kelly felt the red creep into her cheeks. After all these years, Herrington's barbs still got to her. "You're an asshole."

"He's not your boyfriend?"

"A huge asshole."

Herrington pretended to pout. "No need to get personal."

"You're the one who made it personal," Kelly stated pointedly. She put her hands on her hips and eyed him steadily. "How about ordering something? This isn't a homeless shelter."

"Gin and tonic. With one of those fresh limes."

While Kelly mixed Herrington's drink she thought about Parnell Gomez. He seemed to enjoy himself Sunday night, despite admitting to her at the outside bar that the music the young duo was playing was not

264

exactly in his wheelhouse. He told her he preferred the British New Wave bands of the Eighties, groups like The Stranglers, Simple Minds and the Psychedelic Furs. "But these guys aren't bad," he added, indicating the stage. "They can really play guitar, both of them."

She wondered how he'd spent the holiday yesterday. Probably writing, she decided. Didn't writers thrive in gloomy, threatening weather? He could've come to the AC – Peter kept the bar open on all holidays except Labor Day and Christmas – but she was off duty, at home with her husband, watching a couple of Hitchcock films.

She placed the drink on a coaster in front of Herrington. "Any lunch today?"

He thought for a moment before responding. "Tuna on wheat."

"Potato salad?"

"Not today." He sipped his drink as Kelly disappeared into the kitchen. No sign of Peter yet. Another late night for him, no doubt. He shifted his gaze to the window overlooking the harbor and the mouth of the lake. Boats bobbed in the river, tethered to their moorings, telltales on their masts indicating the wind was from the northwest. It was a view he never tired of, the main reason he'd never left despite having the means to live anywhere he wanted. Summers in Delifin, winters in the Caribbean. He wouldn't have it any other way.

He watched as one of the HydroJet boats, jammed with customers who'd boarded at Niagara-on-the-Lake, eased away from the dock. When he reached the middle of the river the captain turned and idled slowly southward, adhering to the no-wake ordinance that Delifin had passed several years earlier. As soon as he was beyond the last of the village moorings he increased his speed and swung his customers in a tight circle before continuing south toward the Class VI rapids of the Niagara River, just below Niagara Falls.

Kelly emerged from the kitchen. Herrington indicated the television above the cash register. "Maybe they'll have something about the trial on the noon news."

Kelly found the remote and clicked on the television. The *Today* show was just ending; Herrington, calculating, figured it must be a six-hour show now. He'd barely been able to keep interested when it was

265

only two hours long. How on earth did they find enough stuff every day to keep their audience interested?

After several commercials the local news came on. The noon anchor, a perfectly coiffed blond with the defined musculature of a competitive swimmer, led off with the Corelli trial, switching after a few words of introduction to a live report from the Riverton courthouse.

The reporter on the scene, a young brunette woman in her twenties, spoke from the sidewalk in front of the courthouse. "In a dramatic development today in the John Corelli trial, the prosecution and the defense agreed to a plea deal, ending the nearly year-long case against Corelli, former Riverton town council member and history teacher at Riverton Middle School. Corelli, with attorney Max Grossinger at his side, pled guilty this morning to two reduced counts of endangering the welfare of a minor and was sentenced by Town Justice Harold Marquis to seven years in prison. Corelli, who will be eligible for parole after serving three and a half years, also surrendered his teaching certification and will have to register as a sex offender once he is released from prison."

Herrington snorted. "Endangering the welfare of a minor? Is that what they call statutory rape these days?"

"That's why they call it a plea deal," Kelly explained patiently. "Don't look at the charge. Look at the sentence. Seven years is pretty stiff for a first-time offender, with no prior record."

The station went to commercial. Remote in hand, Kelly looked at Herrington. "Is that enough? I'll leave it on if you want, but I'm going to mute the sound."

"It's enough for me," Herrington said. He held up his empty glass. "How about a refill?"

"Coming right up."

Peter came down the stairs a few minutes later, muttered something about going to the market in town and was out the door before Kelly could respond. Elmer Hartman came in for lunch, followed by a couple in their fifties from Missouri who had come to see Niagara Falls and had wandered north to Delifin, on their way to Fort Ontario. Kelly held down the fort until Peter returned with three bags of groceries,

266

moving swiftly between the kitchen and the bar, doing her best to keep the lunch crowd satisfied.

Herrington was just finishing his third drink after polishing off his sandwich when Parnell Gomez came through the side door from the parking lot. His usual seat was taken by one of the Missourians, so he walked to the other end of the bar and sat on a vacant stool next to Herrington, who greeted him robustly. "You're late. Kelly was starting to worry about you."

Gomez smiled guiltily as Kelly seethed. "I was working and lost track of time."

"The usual?" Kelly asked, pointedly avoiding Herrington's idiotic grin.

"Yes."

She poured him a glass of iced tea from a jug beneath the counter, added a slice of lemon and placed it on the bar in front of him before she went into the kitchen to give Peter his order. When she returned she found Gomez and Herrington discussing the Corelli plea deal. Gomez sat with an amused look on his face as Herrington railed about the relatively minor charges to which Corelli had pled guilty. "I don't even think that's a felony," he said indignantly.

"How long was the sentence?" Gomez asked.

"Seven years," Kelly said. "Plus he has to register as a sex offender when he gets out."

"He was a teacher, wasn't he?" Gomez asked. "And a local politician."

"Not anymore," Herrington said with delight. "At least they got that part right."

"And his wife is dead," Gomez added tentatively.

Herrington nodded vigorously. "Yep. Killed her just as sure as we're sitting here. Destroyed his entire family, all for some underage pussy."

Gomez had read that each of the victims had been thirteen when they'd been assaulted by Corelli. Like Herrington, he was disgusted by

267

the thought of a trusted teacher taking advantage of his students in such a depraved manner. The world had evolved into a strange place since he'd been in school, with darkness too often overshadowing light, especially on the fringes. "I guess the national news guys will be leaving soon."

"They're probably already on their way out of town, headed for the next titillating clusterfuck," Herrington asserted. "Some mother who killed her baby in South Dakota because she was crying too loud, or some nut picking off tourists on the interstate in Florida with an AR-15 because they don't drive like Christians."

Kelly made a sour face. "How about we change the subject? People are eating in here."

Gomez was all for that. "Good idea."

Herrington thought for a moment, mulling the possibilities. He smiled, inspired, and turned toward Gomez. "Have I told you about the time two years ago when I dated the Penthouse Pet of the Year?"

45

For some reason, the day after a holiday was always a busy one at Amherst Orthodontic Associates. Tuesday was no different; Gillian was booked steadily from 9:00 to 5:30, which ordinarily would leave her a little cranky, with no time for administrative duties. But not today – a full schedule today gave her less time to think about the purpose behind Rod Wakefield's telephone call yesterday.

That he'd called her on a holiday was troubling. It meant he was working, following another lead instead of relaxing at home. Or maybe someone had found something of Scott's in the lake and it fell to the chief of police to inform her, although the message he'd left had none of the urgency Gillian associated with some major new development.

She'd spent over two hours at Lenny's house yesterday, getting to know his brother and his wife. She'd liked Joanie immediately; it was clear she had a maternal instinct when it came to her husband's younger brother, and she seemed genuinely delighted that Lenny had found a woman that was interested in him in a romantic way.

Red was a different story. Several times she'd caught him eyeing her in an appraising fashion, as if she were a cut of meat he'd purchased from an unfamiliar butcher. He was cordial but not warm, joining in the conversation sporadically, mostly listening as she and Joanie and Lenny talked about boating, Colorado and their favorite Italian restaurants in Niagara Falls.

But throughout the afternoon the image of the Riverton cop who wanted to speak with her again, not over the phone but in person, at the station, loomed in the back of her mind. What was he after? What had he uncovered? She tried to think back to the times when the three of them, she, Scott and Lenny, had been at the club together during the past few months. Had someone noticed something, some clue indicating that Lenny and she were more than just teammates on a skeet shooting squad?

After her last patient left her office, she checked her docket for Wednesday. No appointments after 4:00 for her tomorrow. She sighed; might as well get it over with. She dialed the number Rod Wakefield had left for her in his message.

A female answered. She sounded like the woman she'd met at the office before, Anne something. "Village of Riverton police station. How may I direct your call?"

"This is Gillian Hudecki, returning Chief Wakefield's call from yesterday. Is he available?"

"He's on another call. May I take a message?"

"Yes," Gillian said. "He wanted me to come into the station to ask me some more questions. I can be there by 5:00 tomorrow, if that's alright."

"Hold please." In a moment she was back. "The Chief will see you at 5:00 tomorrow. Thanks for getting back to us promptly. Do you have any other questions?"

About a million, Gillian thought. Instead she said, "No."

"Then we'll see you tomorrow." The line went dead.

After transcribing a few notes into the appropriate patient files, she gathered her things and headed for the parking lot. She thought about calling Lenny, but resisted the temptation. It was Red and Joanie's last day in town – they were flying back to Denver tomorrow morning and Lenny had told her they planned to spend the entire day on the boat with their mother and one of their cousins. She'd call him tomorrow on her lunch hour to feel him out about her meeting with Wakefield, to see if he had any suggestions. For a moment she wished he could come with her for moral support, but dismissed the idea as soon as it formed. Lenny needed to stay in the shadows, out of sight, especially where Rod Wakefield was concerned.

*****

Both CNN and Fox News did a quick wrap after the trial concluded and the judge excused the jury Tuesday morning. Fifteen minutes after they taped their final clips both crews were on the road, headed toward the next major story, a wildfire currently burning out of control in Yellowstone National Park.

Sal Ducati watched them leave Riverton with mixed emotions. He was glad the trial was over for several reasons, but mostly because the plea deal meant he wouldn't have to testify. To contrast the lurid nature of the alleged crimes, both news agencies had filmed short vignettes about the village that offered different perspectives of Riverton: the musical and cultural offerings at GorgePark, the bustling waterfront, the eclectic assortment of top-flight restaurants in the area. And of course there were sequences shot at Niagara Falls and in Niagara-on-the-Lake, gorgeous overhead shots delivered by the latest in drone technology.

The only unfinished business, the last thread of the unfortunate Corelli saga, was determining the official cause of death for Liz Corelli. By the time Judge Marquis concluded the proceedings, it was common knowledge, thanks to the leaks ordered by and emanating from the office of Max Grossinger, that Liz Corelli had committed suicide, despondent at the situation in which she found herself as the trial progressed. The medical examiner's report, when issued, would confirm that rumor.

As far as the mayor was concerned, he could shift his attention to the upcoming summer tourist season and the variety of festivals scheduled that attracted thousands of visitors to the quaint waterfront village. No more questions, many of which had been painfully personal, from the media concerning his relationship with an alleged pedophile. He was looking forward to a summer without the aura of John Corelli suspended above his neck like the sword of Damocles.

*****

Parnell listened patiently as Herrington told him about his chance encounter with a former Penthouse Pet of the Year in Antigua two Decembers earlier and how they'd had a torrid yet short-lived affair. He noticed that Kelly kept her distance while Herrington told his tale, approaching only to deliver his lunch order; she'd probably heard it all before, more than once.

"Very beautiful, very sexy, but way too needy," Herrington said in conclusion. He winked at Kelly, who studiously ignored him. "It was fun for a couple of weeks, though."

"I might've seen her. I was in college back then," Parnell said. With a rueful glance toward Kelly, he explained further. "I used to buy it for the articles."

Kelly shook her head in dismay. "Not you, too. Somehow I figured a writer would have a higher moral threshold."

271

It was Parnell's turn to snicker. "Hardly. We wallow in low-lying filth. It's our sustenance."

"See!" Herrington exclaimed. "I'm not as bad as you think."

"Yes, you are," Kelly shot back. "There's just more of you out there than I thought there were."

Herrington rose to his feet, dropping a twenty on the bar. "On that note, I bid you adieu. Parnell, do not believe anything this woman tells you about me."

Kelly snatched the bill from the bar before he could change his mind. "Need any change?"

"Keep it. Until tomorrow, my friends." He strode purposefully toward the door and exited without a backward glance.

Parnell waited until Herrington was outside, on his way down the hill toward his boat, before he addressed Kelly. "He's something else."

She wiped the bar and dumped Herrington's empty glass in the sink below. "He's at least that."

"Is that story true?"

"About the Pet of the Year? I think so. He came back with a bunch of pictures, and he's too much of a digital Neanderthal to have PhotoShopped them." She paused, then continued. "Don't ever tell him I said this, but he's a very good-looking guy with a beach bum's lifestyle and the cash to finance it. I can see how a certain class of women would be attracted to that."

"Where did he get his money?"

"He inherited it when his parents died in a plane crash, then got lucky in the stock market. He was in on the initial public offering of Microsoft."

Parnell did the math in his head. "His parents must've died when he was very young."

"He was twenty, a student at Niagara University, when they died. With that kind of cash, he could've dropped out and headed to Europe like a lot of other trust funders, but he stayed and got his degree. After he graduated he sold his parents' house, bought a boat and joined the Delifin Yacht Club. He rents a boat in Miami every fall and spends the winter on various Caribbean islands, then comes back to Delifin, usually in May."

"Sounds pretty nice."

Kelly nodded in agreement. "It's the life most of us would choose around here, if we had the chance."

There was something in her tone that told him she thought differently. "But not you?"

She shook her head. "I've been married since I was eighteen, and my parents have a small farm just outside of the village. I've got too many ties here to adopt the Herrington lifestyle." She smiled. "But he is fun to have around. He's such an easy target."

Parnell took the last bite of his burger, then pushed his plate across the bar toward Kelly, indicating he was finished. She picked up his glass with an inquiring glance. "One more for the road?"

"Not today," he said. "I've got some more work to do when I get home."

"How's the new book?"

He shrugged. "It's always hard to tell until it's finished. Right now it's going pretty smoothly, but there are always bumps in the road along the way. Not getting frustrated when you reach those bumps is the important thing."

Kelly pointed to the sign on the wall above the shuffleboard table advertising the Tuesday night cribbage tournament. "So I can't interest you in coming back later to play a little cards?"

He stood and dropped several bills on the bar. "Not tonight. Do you play?"

"I do," Kelly said. "After my shift ends I go down the street, have dinner at the diner and come back in time for the tournament."

"Maybe some other time," he said as he slipped his wallet back into his pocket.

"I'll hold you to that," she said with a smile as he headed toward the door. She watched as he left the building before she cleared his spot at the bar and looked around to check for thirsty customers.

46

The aroma of meatloaf hit Rod as soon as he walked through the door Tuesday evening. "I'm home," he called as he hung his hat on the rack near the door to the garage.

"I'm in the kitchen," his wife replied. "Hope you're hungry."

"I'm starving," he said as he entered and sat in one of the kitchen chairs. Meatloaf was his favorite dish. "What's the occasion?" he asked with a knowing grin.

She vented the oven door and removed the meatloaf, placing it on a hot pad to cool. Next she removed a pan of roasted potatoes and set them beside the meatloaf. She turned toward her husband with a smile. "I'd say the end of the Corelli trial is worthy of your favorite dinner. Change your clothes. It just needs to cool a few minutes."

He donned a pair of jeans and a long-sleeved T-shirt advertising a marina in Florida and returned to the kitchen. The dining room was set up for an intimate dinner for two, complete with candles and a bottle of red wine. Rod picked up the wine. It was Casillero del Diablo Reserva, a Cabernet Sauvignon from Chile. "Wow," he said approvingly. "You've spared no expense."

"It was on sale at Hubbard's," she said as she removed her apron and placed the meatloaf and potatoes on the table. "Let's eat."

Sally had also put together a green salad with sliced tomatoes and cucumbers and passed it to her husband. "For balance," she explained with a smile.

He poured each of them a glass of wine and raised his. "To my wife, who knows me better than anyone."

Sally raised hers and lightly clicked it against Rod's. "To the end of the trial and the return of my husband."

While they ate Sally peppered him with questions about the plea deal. He answered them as well as he could, not having been in the courtroom today when the judge handed down the final verdict. At the same time, he held back the other good news of the day, what could be a major breakthrough in the Scott Jamison disappearance, until the table was cleared and the dishes were washed and they moved to the family room with two cups of decaf.

"I have some more good news," he said once they were seated.

"More?"

He explained his new theory about the Jamison case, beginning with the early-morning phone call from Cal Roberts yesterday that had opened his eyes. He laid out the love triangle from 1972 and Cal's theory that Joey Lorenzo had, in a melodramatic moment of extreme anguish, drowned himself because he knew his girlfriend was sleeping with Scott Jamison.

"That seems a bit extreme," Sally said, her voice laced with doubt.

"It is," Rod conceded. "But if it's true, then chances are Scott Jamison knew why Joey killed himself and has been carrying that with him for over forty years. I can't imagine how difficult that must've been. Then something happened, something that brought all the memories from that night back. Something that drove him to the edge."

"What?"

"I think it was the same thing that motivated Joey Lorenzo. He found out that his girlfriend was sleeping with another man."

"Who?"

"I don't know," he admitted. "I have an interview scheduled with Scott's girlfriend tomorrow afternoon in my office. If I'm right, I think she's been having an affair with someone and Scott found out, which triggered his memories and feelings of guilt from 1972."

"And those memories led Scott Jamison to kill himself? That's quite a leap without corroboration."

"I know. But it explains the scene he left behind in his van, the wallet and cell phone carefully arranged and easily discovered. That's not a suicide note, but it might as well be. It's the only thing that makes sense. There's no way he would go out on the water, with a storm in the vicinity, without some sort of communication. Everyone I spoke with told me he would never do that. His boat wasn't equipped with a radio – his cell phone was his communication. From all the people we

276

interviewed, Scott Jamison was described as a deliberate, cautious man, someone who rarely took chances. Why would he leave his phone behind, unless he did it deliberately?"

"That *is* the big question," Sally said after a moment. "But your theory is based on the supposition that Joey Lorenzo killed himself in a similar fashion. And there's no way to prove that."

"You're right," Rod admitted. "Not without the last witness, Willie Emerson, the guy who organized the tubing trip. No one knows where he is – he seems to have vanished two years ago."

"Sounds like the longest of longshots to me, even if you found this Emerson."

"It is a bit of a stretch. But it's the only plausible explanation for the cell phone being left behind."

"So what if the girlfriend – Gillian, right? – denies that she's been seeing someone? Wouldn't it be easier for her to lie about that and not open a whole new can of worms? What makes you think she's going to tell you the truth?"

"Cop's instinct. I've interviewed thousands of witnesses over the years. Some of them are very good liars, while some can't help but tell the truth, no matter how it affects them. I think she's one of the honest ones."

Sally remained skeptical. "Based on what? Three previous conversations? If she's so honest, how come she didn't tell you she was seeing someone when you questioned her before?"

"Because I didn't ask her. This time I will and I think she'll tell me the truth."

Sally sipped her coffee. "You seem to have a lot of faith in this woman."

"If I'm right, I think she's already feeling guilty. I think she'll welcome the chance to get it off her chest, to relieve her burden. What she did isn't a crime – she could never be prosecuted for falling in love with another man. It won't change the official declaration that he was lost at sea. She might face some criticism for being unfaithful, but that will eventually blow over."

"What will you do after tomorrow?"

"Me? One way or another, that'll be the end of it. I can't afford to spend any more time on the case. Now that all my officers are released from trial duty, I have to get back to scheduling patrols."

"So Riverton returns to normal once again." It was a statement rather than a question.

Rod smiled. "As normal as we're ever going to be, I guess. I imagine Liz Corelli's funeral will be a big deal."

"When's that scheduled?"

"Saturday morning at St. Paul's."

Sally rose and carried her cup into the kitchen. She rinsed it and placed it on the dish rack before returning to the family room. Rod watched her as she walked, still taken after thirty years of marriage by her lithe grace. She walked toward him and dropped onto his lap, wrapping her arms around his shoulders, nuzzling his ear. "How about showing a little attention to your wife?" she whispered in his ear. "I think she's been neglected lately."

He shifted slightly underneath her, slipping one arm around the small of her back and the other beneath her knees. With a grunt, he stood up, Sally in his arms, and strode toward the bedroom. He placed her gently on the bed and smiled. "You're absolutely right," he said. "Why don't we start here?"

*****

An hour after Sally drifted off to sleep Rod remained awake, his mind refusing to shut down. He knew that whatever happened tomorrow, he'd have to move on from the Scott Jamison mystery. As always, his push to find out the truth behind Jamison's disappearance was driven by a desire to provide the victim left behind – in this case, Gillian Hudecki – with some sort of answer she could live with in the wake of her boyfriend's tragic disappearance.

He disliked the term closure – in far too many cases, the concept was a fallacy. So many mysteries in life remained unsolved, with no verifiable pathway to the truth. Claiming to provide even a hint of closure to the truly desperate seemed to him to be the most cruel and unusual lifeline of hope a law enforcement officer could offer to the survivors of tragic events. They all wanted tragedy to make sense, but it rarely did.

His new suspicions concerning Gillian left him uncertain as to who the victim in this case really was. If his theory was correct and she did admit to having cheated on her live-in lover, what would it prove? Would the act of compelling her to confess her unfaithful behavior make her feel better? He doubted it. Rather than feel relieved, it would likely increase her feelings of guilt. She was already living with the consequences of her actions, whatever they may have been. Forcing her to verbalize her missteps would only compound her sorrow.

But he knew he had to ask the question. It was his job, the quest for truth. Compassion is sometimes trumped by necessity, and he needed to know the answer, for his own sake. Was he being selfish? Of course he was. But he'd have trouble sleeping at night – like he was having now – if he didn't follow the trail to the end. He hoped to be able to minimize the collateral damage, but he knew that often wasn't in the cards.

Beside him, his wife's breathing was like a metronome. He closed his eyes and listened, and slowly his mind let go of the questions and speculations and the excitement of the day and allowed sleep to soothe him like the arrival of an overdue friend.

47

The sun was beginning to inch above the treetops as Rod Wakefield walked to work Wednesday morning. He'd slept fitfully, filled with nervous energy in anticipation of his meeting with Gillian, so he thought a walk through the village might help to distract him from the anxiety he was feeling.

He walked by the cemetery behind the First Presbyterian Church, the oldest graveyard in the area, some of the earliest headstones marking the graves of victims of the British invasion of Riverton during the War of 1812. It was a favorite site of restless local youth, who from time to time liked to vandalize the aging tombstones during clandestine late-night parties. After a particularly destructive binge a couple of years earlier that resulted in several thousand dollars in damages, he adjusted the patrol route of the overnight shift to include multiple stops at the cemetery between dusk and dawn. As Randy DiPietro stated when Wakefield announced the changes to his staff, it lent new meaning to the term graveyard shift.

He continued down Iroquois Street to Fourth, walking briskly. There was a slight following breeze as he walked north on Fourth toward Main, but it didn't prevent him from getting a whiff of this morning's delicacies as he approached Borelli's Bakery. Inspired, he ducked inside and waited patiently in line to buy some scones for his staff, nodding and exchanging pleasantries with some of the regular patrons he recognized. Rich Stebbins was at a table by himself, nursing a cup of coffee. He waved Rod over, but Rod pointed to his watch and shrugged his shoulders; maybe another time.

He could feel the warmth of the scones through the bag as he waited at the light to cross Main. On the other side of the street he saw the mayor in his familiar morning posture, stooped over, peering at the sidewalk, trash bag looped on his belt, on his morning mission to rid Riverton's thoroughfares of litter. Rod smiled; he knew Sal would much prefer his role as executive trash man to that of character witness and was glad he'd been spared that ordeal. He waved but Sal didn't notice him as he bent to pick up a discarded plastic cup and deposited it in his bag.

The light changed and he crossed the street, walking by Doc Brennan's office to the municipal building. Although it was a few minutes before 7:00, Anne Moretti was already at her desk, typing furiously on her computer. She looked up and said, "Good morning, Chief" before she returned to her typing.

He dropped the scones on the table near the coffee pot and took one for himself back to his office. He closed the door and opened the Lorenzo/Jamison file and spread the pictures across his desk. He'd spent much of the night awake, trying to figure out who Gillian's secret lover might be. He'd started with the members of the rod and gun club, but abandoned the effort when he realized she was an orthodontist, with a professional life that Rod knew nothing about. Trying to guess who her mystery lover might be – if she had one - was futile and frustrating, so he gave it up.

Instead he concentrated on developing a series of questions that would help to lower her guard before he finally popped the big question. He decided to start off with some queries about Dolores Jamison and the alleged insurance policy. From their earlier sessions, he knew the two didn't get along, so he hoped introducing Dolores as the focus of his interview would lead Gillian to relax, thinking that Rod wasn't going after her.

His phone buzzed. It was Anne. "Do you want to see the overnight logs?" she asked.

"Anything interesting?"

"Let's see," she said as she scanned the report. "A barking dog on Seventh, a domestic dispute between two males, aged 61 and 67, at the home the two share on Madison, a request for an ambulance, possible heart attack, for a female, aged 73, on Norman Road. The usual."

"Bring it in. I'll look at it. Is the mayor in yet?"

"Not yet. Probably still on patrol."

"Let me know when he arrives."

He wrote down a few questions about Dolores Jamison and reworked them a bit until he was satisfied. Next to his In box was a monthly budget report, waiting to be filled out. He glanced at the calendar on the wall and grimaced. Only three days left in May; the report was due at the end of the month. He sighed and reached for his calculator and a couple of pencils. Because of the added expenses

281

associated with the trial, he knew they were going to be over budget for the month. He just hoped it wouldn't be too bad.

At 9:00 his phone buzzed. "The mayor's in."

"Ask him to come in."

The door opened and the mayor shuffled in. Rod indicated his guest chair. "Take a load off."

Sal sat down gratefully. He saw the stack of papers and the calculator. "Monthly budget report?"

"Yeah. I've been working on it for a couple of hours, trying to get it as low as possible."

"It's going to be high because of the trial."

"I know," Rod said. "I'm not sure how understanding the council will be when they see the numbers."

"Leave them to me," the mayor said. "I'll feed them some BS about how much local sales tax was generated by CNN and Fox." He smiled. "They can be misled as easily as any council we've had since I've been mayor." He looked at the chief carefully. "Anything else on your mind?"

"Not really," Rod said. "I just wanted to let you know that the Scott Jamison case will be winding down this week."

"Anything new?"

Rod shook his head. "Not a thing. A couple of his friends are still searching after work and on weekends, but no one's found anything."

"That case isn't in our jurisdiction, is it?"

"Technically, no. He went missing off Wilson, so it's the county's case. But he was a Riverton resident, so I thought I'd follow up, for the girlfriend's sake."

"How's she doing?"

"She's coming in this afternoon to help me tie up a few loose ends."

The mayor gazed out the window. "Must be hard to lose someone like that. You never really know what happened," he said, alluding to the curious arrangement of wallet and cell phone left behind, a fact Rod had passed along to the mayor.

There was a single knock at the door. Anne poked her head in. Addressing the mayor, she said, "Sir, I have the highway superintendent on the line. He says it's urgent."

Sal Ducati rose to his feet. "Duty calls." He extended his hand; Rod gripped it firmly. "Don't spend too much time on the budget."

"Thanks, Mr. Mayor. I'll try not to." He watched as the mayor walked slowly out of his office, then addressed Anne, standing by the door. "You can leave it open."

He worked through lunch on the budget, doing his best to get it as low as possible. He knew Sal had his back on this, but he also knew the mayor could tap into the Auxiliary General Fund, a new line item that had been placed in the village budget and funded by the Department of Homeland Security after 9/11 because of the village's proximity to two major power generation facilities and the Canadian border.

When he was finally satisfied with the numbers he was surprised to find that it was nearly 4:30. He walked into the reception area. Anne was at her desk, studying her fingernails. "Any scones left?"

"Nope," she said. "They were gone before 8:00. You snooze, you lose."

"But I've been working," he said in mock protest.

She looked at him, smiling. "About time."

"I'm the chief of police. I deserve a little respect around here."

"How little?"

Rod laughed. He could always count on Anne for comic relief. "I'll be in my office. Buzz me when Gillian gets here."

"Ten four."

He called Sally to see what was for dinner and then sat back and waited. At five minutes past five, Anne buzzed him. "Ms. Hudecki is here."

"Send her in."

He stood as she entered the room. She was dressed in a simple white blouse and a gray skirt, with a simple cross around her neck. On her feet were a pair of Nikes. Her expression was neutral, guarded. If she was anxious, she was hiding it well.

Rod indicated the guest chair. "Thanks for coming in. Please have a seat."

When she was seated he continued. "I just have a few questions Shouldn't take more than a few minutes."

"Have there been any new developments?"

Rod shook his head. "I'm sorry, no. I just have a couple of questions about Scott's mother, Dolores."

Rod thought he saw relief flash across her face. She straightened a bit in her chair. "What would you like to know?"

Rod glanced down at the sheet of questions on his desk for a moment before looking up. "Previously, you mentioned that Dolores Jamison contacted you in regards to an insurance policy. Is that correct?"

"Yes."

"Were you ever able to verify the existence of that policy?"

"No," Gillian said. "We have a safety deposit box at the bank. I checked it, but I couldn't find any insurance policy."

"Is there any other place that Scott might've stored it?"

She thought for a moment, then shook her head. "I don't think so. Scott wasn't big on record keeping. His business files were always a mess."

Rod pretended to check something off on the paper in front of him and then looked up again. "Does Scott have any other relatives that you know of? Cousins, aunts, uncles? Anyone who might have a stake in his estate?"

Gillian shook her head emphatically. "He was an only child. So was Dolores."

"What about his father?"

"Scott never mentioned him. According to Dolores, he moved away right after Scott was born."

Nonchalantly, Rod put down his pencil and smiled agreeably across the table. "Just one more question and you'll be on your way."

Gillian smiled back, pleased that the session was almost over. Rod took his time, watching her eyes, as he posed the final question.

"Are you currently seeing someone romantically?"

Her eyes gave her away – they went wide and then down and away from his inquiring gaze. It was the reaction he'd hoped for. When she finally looked up he was waiting patiently for her answer. "Um, I don't know what you mean."

"Are you currently involved in a relationship?"

She squirmed in her seat, looking for a way out. Finally, she responded in a tiny voice. "Why do you want to know that?"

He put on his stern cop voice. "If you are seeing someone, it may have a bearing on Scott's disappearance. It's important that you tell me the truth. I assure you that what you tell me will never leave this room."

Gillian looked down at her shoes for a long moment. "Yes," she said, her voice barely discernible.

Rod leaned forward, bearing in. "How long has this been going on?"

Another lengthy pause. "Four months."

"Did Scott know?"

She shook her head. "I don't think so. We were careful."

"Was it someone he knows? A friend?"

285

She nodded, still looking down. The room was eerily quiet, the two of them lost in very different trains of thought. Finally, Rod spoke again. "Thank you for coming in, Ms. Hudecki. That'll be all."

She looked up at him in disbelief. "That's it? You don't want to know his name?"

At least it's a man, he thought. "If you'd like to tell me, I'll listen, but I don't need to know his name."

She looked at him hopefully. "I can go?"

He stood up, walked over to the door and opened it. "Whenever you'd like. Thanks again for your cooperation. You've been a big help."

She gathered her purse and walked through the door, past Anne at the reception desk, into the parking lot at the rear of the building. Rod watched as she got into the car, backed carefully out of her space and pulled cautiously onto Fourth Street, headed for home.

Anne was staring at him quizzically when he turned around. "So?"

Rod smiled enigmatically, making her wait for it. "She has a boyfriend. She's had one for four months."

"Who?"

"I didn't ask."

Anne was stunned. "You're kidding."

"It's not important." He turned on his heel and headed back into his office. Through the open door he called out, "You can go now. We can't afford to pay any more overtime this month."

EPILOGUE

Parnell sat on the patio, nursing his iced tea, watching a family of four – mother, father, two teen-aged daughters – board the bum boat to be ferried to their sailboat moored in the river. The father handed a canvas bag with green handles to the operator of the bum boat, who placed it on the deck near his feet before he released the lines and glided away from the dock. No one in the boat was smiling.

It was a glorious day: sunny, with only a few cirrus strips high up to mar the azure sky. He'd surprised Kelly by opting to sit on the porch instead of at his usual seat at the bar. "It's such a nice day. A Key North kind of day."

As he ate his lunch he watched a procession of HydroJet boats come and go from the dock across the river in Niagara-on-the-Lake, jammed with tourists clad in bright orange life vests, on their way to a wet and wild ride through the Niagara River rapids. Two jet skis took off from the public boat launch next to the yacht club, headed for the lake, throttles wide open.

He was glad he'd chosen Delifin as the place to write his book. The work was going tremendously – he was ahead of the pace he'd originally estimated it would take to complete the first draft. The lease on his rented duplex on Stonewall Street extended through the month of June; at the rate the work was going, he'd be finished with time to spare. The atmosphere in this small village tucked into the corner of New York, a stone's throw from Canada, was like that of an artists' colony. No one cared what anyone else did; they just got on with their lives and stayed out of each other's way.

He liked the people he'd met at the Delifin AC, especially Kelly and Herrington. He'd encountered some real characters during his stay, people he thought might show up in one form or another in a future novel. In fact, he'd already started a preliminary outline for his next book, one that he planned to set in a village much like Delifin: an end-of-the-road, off-the-beaten-track kind of place filled with eccentric characters leading quiet, extraordinary lives.

A flash of color caught his eye. To the south, barely visible, he made out three people in the river lounging on inner tubes, one of which sported a multi-colored cord attached to what looked like a white

Styrofoam cooler that trailed several feet behind the group. How nice it must be, he thought, to be riding the current in the middle of the river, content to go with the flow, enjoying the beauty of the day, not a care in the world.

65124041R00174